GENIE OF DEATH

Ellen rose from her bed and went downstairs. There was the smell of smoke, an odor that stung her nostrils and burned her eyes. She stood in the archway of the living room and saw her mother standing there, looking at something in the smoke that rose from the hollow stem of the lamp.

A genie!

It trailed up, twisting as it formed, the head, huge, shaped like an enormous egg, with no hair. Its eyes thin and slitted, with nothing in them.

It was wavering above the floor, this genie from her magic lamp, and it was coming to kill her, its slitted eyes pinned on her where she stood. It wanted her. It was reaching for her. But the figure of her mother was suddenly between them, and she shoved at Ellen and told her to run, but her mother had pushed too hard, and she fell instead. But the genie turned then, and his hands found her mother.

She fought. Her hands struck his huge body, and the sound was like the soft thuds of a heartbeat.

The genie was killing her mother and the blood was flowing.

Would Ellen be the next victim . . . ?

A CAVALCADE OF TERROR
FROM RUBY JEAN JENSEN!

SMOKE (2255, $3.95)
Seven-year-old Ellen was sure it was Aladdin's lamp that she had found at the local garage sale. And no power on earth would be able to stop the hideous terror unleashed when she rubbed the magic lamp to make the genie appear!

CHAIN LETTER (2162, $3.95)
Abby and Brian knew that the chain letter they had found was evil. They would send the letter to all their special friends. And they would know who had broken the chain — by who had died!

ANNABELLE (2011, $3.95)
The dolls had lived so long by themselves up in the attic. But now Annabelle had returned to them, and everything would be just like it was before. Only this time they'd never let anyone hurt Annabelle. And anyone who tried would be very, very sorry!

HOME SWEET HOME (1571, $3.50)
Two weeks in the mountains should have been the perfect vacation for a little boy. But Timmy didn't think so. Not when he saw the terror in the other children's eyes. Not when he heard them screaming in the night. Not when Timmy realized there was no escaping the deadly welcome of HOME SWEET HOME!

MAMA (1247, $3.50)
Once upon a time there lived a sweet little dolly — but her one beaded glass eye gleamed with mischief and evil. If Dorrie could have read her dolly's thoughts, she would have run for her life. For Dorrie's dear little dolly only had murder on her mind!

Available wherever paperbacks are sold, or order direct from the Publisher. Send cover price plus 50¢ per copy for mailing and handling to Zebra Books, Dept. 2255, 475 Park Avenue South, New York, N.Y. 10016. Residents of New York, New Jersey and Pennsylvania must include sales tax. DO NOT SEND CASH.

SMOKE

Ruby Jean Jensen

ZEBRA BOOKS
KENSINGTON PUBLISHING CORP.

ZEBRA BOOKS

are published by

Kensington Publishing Corp.
475 Park Avenue South
New York, NY 10016

Copyright © 1988 by Ruby Jean Jensen

All rights reserved. No part of this book may be reproduced in any form or by any means without the prior written consent of the Publisher, excepting brief quotes used in reviews.

First printing: January 1988

Printed in the United States of America

Hong Kong 1835

The child crouched, almond eyes watching the master. His great bulk was still, stretched out on his mat beyond the low table.

The other men, the customers, on mats scattered about the room, were asleep too, satiated, as was her master.

On another mat back against the inner wall the new little girl sobbed. She lay huddled far back, as if she tried to sink into the cracks of the boards. The old woman had brought her in just yesterday and sold her to the master just as Tai Ping had been sold last month.

Tai Ping looked over her shoulder at the doorway, at the curtain that covered it, closing out the light of the outer world.

There was nothing guarding it now, but it was said that the master would change shape and become a large cat, and stalk until death whoever tried to escape through the curtained doorway.

The child turned back. On the table in front of her was a lamp; it sat in the midst of the metal water pipes the master and his customers used for smoking opium. Its flame licked upward into the stale air and moved with the draft.

The child eased out her hand, slowly, until she touched the lamp.

She pulled it toward her across the table and,

holding it, stared at the master. He moved, grunting, his great mounds of flesh shifting. The child sat still, the lamp in her hands.

She waited.

Long after he grew still again she turned and crept forward, letting the flame of the lamp rest beneath the tattered and filthy bottom of the curtain.

For an instant the rags quivered in the heat of the lamp, and then with a great burst, like an expelled breath, the curtain caught fire.

The child rolled back against the wall, covering her face.

She would die, but so would he, the cruel master.

Chapter One

"There's one, there's one," Joey yelled in his mother's ear, his pointing finger going past her head. "Hey, Mom, you passed it. It's down that street. Turn back."

"Yes," agreed Beth, also in the back seat, her twelve-year-old voice sounding calmly mature next to Joey's high-pitched squeal. "There's a sign on the corner pointing that way, Mom."

"All right, all right. Stop yelling in my ear. Joey, sit down."

"Well, *turn,* Mom."

"I can't turn in the middle of the block. I'll have to drive around it, won't I?"

"Yes, she will," Ellen agreed. Sitting quietly in the front passenger seat, Ellen could barely see over the hood without stretching. She probably hadn't seen the garage sale sign either, Blythe thought.

She waited for traffic to clear on the boulevard, the left turn signal beeping.

This searching for garage or yard sales was about to get out of hand, she was deciding. In the beginning she and the kids had gone on bicycles to sales within a few blocks of home, but the bug had gotten all three of the kids, and every Saturday now, as soon as they each were paid their weekly allowance, they insisted on searching the areas beyond their own neighborhood for the "treasure" they were sure they would find. And it was true that in those wealthier neighborhoods, when there was a sale at all, there were good buys on toys. Toys that had seen hardly any wear. They looked completely unused. One had only to speculate that these kids received so many toys that most of them were barely touched before the mothers, looking for more space, cleared it all out of the bedrooms to start in again.

Ellen, who was seven, got two dollars a week. Joey, eight, got three, and Beth, at twelve, now received five. If it hadn't been for the generosity of their father's new wife, the three kids would still be lucky to get a dollar a week, Blythe thought with a touch of resentment. At least she presumed it was the new wife who was sending the extra money.

Well, not exactly new now. Six months, seven? She didn't know for sure when Gavin married again. If it hadn't been for the child support he sent her, she probably wouldn't even know where he lived now.

She made the turn, aware that Joey had sat down in the back seat again.

"Fasten that seat belt, Joey," she said automatically, and in the brief silence she heard it click as he obeyed.

"These are pretty houses," Beth said, almost sighing. "I wish we could live here."

"Fat chance," Blythe said, thinking of the old frame house she had inherited from her parents. It needed a lot of work, but at least it was a roof and walls. Gavin had left her their house in Glendale after the divorce, but she had found it too expensive to keep.

"That way, Mom," Joey said, keeping her informed. "This is going to be a good one."

"I wonder why they're even having one?" Beth wondered aloud. "I mean in this kind of place, where the houses are so big, isn't it kind of out of character?"

"You're right," Blythe said. "Well, maybe it's the kids doing it, the way the kids in our neighborhood do."

A few cars had parked along the street in front of the house with the tables set up in the driveway, and Blythe eased in behind them. She had hardly gotten the car stopped before her three kids were out of the car and hurrying to the piles of stuff on the tables.

She watched them, her three beautiful kids. Two brunettes and one blonde. Her little blonde, Ellen, was like a tender young willow, slender, narrow-faced, pale hair flouncing as she ran. She was proud of all three, but she had an extra-special feeling for Ellen, her baby.

Blythe followed. The tables were piled with dusty articles that looked as if they had come from an attic, and there were other signs around that suggested someone was either moving in or out.

She looked through a few items on the edge of the table, knickknacks that were less than perfect, a chip here, a chip there. She picked them up and put them down, most of them porcelain. None of them looked worth the price of fifty cents or a dollar. Besides, she was only accompanying the kids, letting them spend their allowances as they wished. How different from her own childhood, when there were dime stores to go to, with long toy counters that held quarter items. She could remember spending hours at those counters, trying to choose the best buy for her precious quarter.

Among the women who milled around the tables was one smiling middle-aged woman that Blythe took to be the owner. Or at least the overseer. She was watching the children with a careful smile on her face, and Blythe moved toward them, ready to see that they broke nothing, even though they never had yet. But the owner looked as if she wasn't sure.

Joey's face had a definite look of disappointment,

and Blythe saw why. There were no toys. Beth also was pulling away. There were no clothes that some teenager had grown out of before they had begun to look used. In fact, there was nothing to interest young children. Beth and Joey were looking for her among the people who moved about and moving her way, but Ellen was still at the end of the last table, fascinated by something. The glow of discovery was on her face, a bright contrast to the composed acceptance of Beth's and the outright disappointment of Joey's.

"Mama, look," Ellen said eagerly, coming toward Blythe with something copper or bronze, clutched in both hands.

It was about the size of a large grapefruit, with a long spout curving up and to one side, but its shape was more oval, with a flat bottom and a flat top. There were other apertures and appendages on top, shorter spouts, an opening with a small lid, a delicate chain hanging from the long, curving spout to one of the shorter ones. Blythe felt herself frowning. What was it? Ellen seemed to think she had found a real treasure.

"Look Mama, and it's only two dollars! Can I buy it? Can I?"

The owner was moving closer, the smile on her face more sincere and relaxed. Beth and Joey also were coming close, peering at the thing in Ellen's hands with such puzzlement and curiosity that it struck Blythe as comical. She was ready to laugh and say no, when Joey asked the question.

"What is it?"

Ellen darted a look of disgust at her brother. "It's Aladdin's Lamp, can't you see?"

"Aladdin's Lamp! You're nutty, Ellen, that's no lamp."

"It is too! It is too!" Now she was drawing the curious metal object closer to her breast, protecting it from disbelievers like her brother and sister.

"No, Ellen," Beth said, in her new, mature patience. "It's not a lamp . . ." She glanced up at the owner. "Is it?"

"It is! It is! I knew the minute I saw it that it really is Aladdin's Lamp. It really is! It's magic, and I want it."

Blythe looked at the owner too, waiting for an answer. It wasn't a lamp, there was no place for a wick. But of course it might have been torn off sometime in the past. Or, perhaps lamps didn't have wicks in those days. Maybe Ellen was more right than wrong. Whatever, it was her two dollars, and if it was that important to her . . .

"What is it?" Beth was asking the lady.

"I have no idea," the woman answered. "We're just moving in, and the attic was full of things that we decided to sell. Some if it might be very valuable."

"See," Ellen said desperately, "I told you. It's valuable. It's mine. I found it. Here, Missus, my money." And she handed the two bills to the owner.

With her precious lamp clutched against her chest, Ellen headed down the sidewalk toward the car.

Blythe shook her head, laughing, and put her hands on the shoulders of Beth and Joey. "Okay, kids, let's go."

"It's not Aladdin's Lamp, is it, Mom?" Joey asked, walking on one side of her down the street toward the car, while Beth, on the other side, agreed.

"It doesn't matter," Blythe said. "If she wants to think so."

"Actually, there was no such thing as Aladdin's Lamp, was there? That was just a fantasy, wasn't it, Mom?"

"Of course it was. But there were many old lamps, and that very well might be a lamp."

"Well, I guess it might be all right to let her think so,"

Beth agreed. "But that was a lot of money for such an ugly old thing."

Ellen looked back. "I heard that! It's not ugly! It just needs to be shined, that's all, just like it did when Aladdin had it. Don't you remember? The lamp was dirty, and when he was polishing it, the genie appeared." With her lamp tucked into the crook of one arm, like a baby, she climbed into the front seat of the car and fastened her seat belt.

"So what are you going to do when the genie doesn't appear, Ellen?" Joey asked as he got into the back seat.

Blythe smiled. "What are you going to do when it *does?*"

Beth and Joey began to laugh. "Yeah," Beth said. "What?"

Ellen sat looking straight ahead as if she didn't hear their teasing laughter.

Joey settled down. "Mom, can we go to McDonald's?"

"Do you want to?"

It was a ritual, this question followed by a question and then ending up at McDonald's for hamburgers and fries. It was part of every Saturday morning. Blythe drove on now in search of a street back toward the Los Angeles suburb in which they lived, and the big M of the McDonald's.

After lunch, when at last she was home and was free to put her feet up and read or watch television, she could hear them upstairs, their voices carrying not quite clearly enough to distinguish word from word, only voice from voice. It sounded as though Beth and Joey were arguing with Ellen again about her "Aladdin's Lamp."

Blythe turned on the television.

* * *

"It is, I know it is," Ellen said. "Go away, both of you. This is my room, and this is my lamp."

"Let me see it, Ellen," Beth urged, "just for a minute."

"No."

"Come on, I won't hurt it. I just want to look at it."

"All right, but don't touch it."

"Okay, I won't touch it."

"Promise?"

"Yes, I'll even put my hands behind me. See?"

Beth folded her hands together behind her back and turned so that Ellen could see her hands were locked. Joey stood by waiting, watching.

"All right," Ellen finally said. "I'll set it on my bed, and you can look at it. But you can't touch it."

"Can I look, too?" Joey asked.

"If you don't touch it, you can."

Ellen carefully set it on the bed and stood with her hand on the bedspread next to it, ready to grab should either of them go back on their word. It was hers, and she would have let them touch it if they hadn't made fun of it and doubted that it was Aladdin's Lamp. It was the doubt that was the worst. And the making fun.

She watched them closely, saw Beth's long, dark hair swing forward as she bent. Beside her, his head almost against Beth's, Joey's hair could have blended right in with hers, they were so much alike. Ellen glanced over at the dresser and the old mirror that waved like the surface of a lake. But the reflection was there, showing the contrast of her own blond hair with the dark hair of her brother and sister. She saw her face, wavy, chin looking more rounded than it really was, eyes crooked, one huge, the other drawn out as if an artist's brush had dragged it across the mirror. The two dark heads were bending lower, and she drew her attention back to them, watching closely, ready to give in and let them touch if they were ready to become believers.

"What are all those things on top?" Beth speculated. "Pipes?"

"Stove pipes," Joey said, giggling.

"And the little chain," Beth said. "It's kind of neat, don't you think?"

"What is it for?"

"To hang it up, maybe, on the wall?"

"What's it made of?"

"Brass? Can I lift it, Ellen? To see how heavy it is?" Beth asked.

"No, you can't lift it," Ellen said firmly. They were still disbelievers.

"I just wanted to know if it's made of brass. If it is, it's heavy. And if it's made of bronze, or copper, it's lighter."

"It's not heavy," Ellen offered. "But you still can't lift it. Not until you agree that I really know what it is."

The two dark heads touched foreheads and began to giggle again, then they straightened up and looked at Ellen.

"Okay," Joey said. "Let's see you rub it and bring out the genie."

Ellen stood apart from them and faced the challenge. What if they were right, and no genie would appear? Or . . .

"No."

Joey turned away. "See. She knows it's really not real. She's just pretending."

"I'm not! All right. I'll rub it. You just watch."

She cupped her hands around the oval ends of the small metal box and felt the coolness. The edges, at the seams, were almost black, she saw, and the black was streaked down the sides. She moved her palms to the sides and rubbed her fingers over the metal, feeling tiny lines that had been etched into the metal, but were invisible beneath the grime.

"It really is dirty," she said, rubbing vigorously. "Just like it was when Aladdin had it. I'm going to polish it really good, but perhaps the genie won't come out when you're here. I really doubt that it will. I'll have to be alo—"

She screamed suddenly and jerked her hands away.

She stood back, her hands out, fingers arched clawlike. The palms of her hands were brick-red, the tips of her fingers like fire. She stared horrified at the metal object on the bed.

"What's wrong?" Beth asked.

"It burned," she cried, turning her palms so that she could look at them. "It got hot."

Joey stared from Ellen's face to the lamp, because now he was convinced it was a lamp. "It doesn't have a fire in it, does it?"

"Of course not," Beth said, reaching toward it, then remembering. She looked again at Ellen. "Is it all right if I touch it now?"

Ellen took another step backward. "It will burn you."

"But Ellen, you carried it up here. It wasn't hot then, was it?"

"No," Ellen said thoughtfully.

"Well then . . ." Beth reached out and picked it up gingerly. The metal was cool, as if it had been stored for a long, long time in a dark, cold place. "It's not hot, Ellen."

"It burned my hands."

"Maybe," Joey said, "it was because you rubbed it."

Beth agreed. "Yes. The friction. Look, you uncovered some etchings on the side. Birds and trees. It's pretty. It looks—Oriental." She glanced at Joey. "Of course it would be, wouldn't it? Aladdin was from the Orient, wasn't he? Or was that Ali-baba? Don't you remember? No, I remember now. Aladdin was from Persia. So you see, Ellen, this isn't Aladdin's Lamp after all, because it's Oriental, and Aladdin was Persian. Persia is now Iran," she added, so they wouldn't be confused in their geography.

She put it back down on the bed.

Joey turned away, his interest waning. No genie had appeared. It was just as he had thought.

"I'm going to go see if David can play."

Neither girl answered him. His footsteps thudded on the worn carpet of the hallway as he ran out and down the stairs. Ellen was still staring from her hands to the lamp on the bed.

"What are you going to do with it?" Beth asked.

Ellen took another step backward. She was afraid of it now. If she touched it again, it might be hot again, burning hot, the heat seeming to come out from the interior, from an inner fire. Or it might be cool, the way it was when she carried it. It was magic, she knew, but she was no longer sure it was Aladdin's Lamp.

But she didn't want Beth to know that she was beginning to be sorry she had spent all her money on it.

Beth went to the door and, as she went out, said something about going to the kitchen to bake brownies, but Ellen scarcely heard her. She was staring at the lamp, caught up in the pictures her hands had uncovered on the sides, and she knew for certain that she had found a magic lamp at that garage sale. Not Aladdin's Lamp maybe, but one just like it, for the trees vined around with twisted trunks and delicate leaves just like the pictures in the book that had the story of Aladdin in it. And the birds had long tails, just like those in the book of Aladdin. Beth was wrong. Her lamp was real.

Yet there was something about this lamp that was different. From Aladdin's Lamp had come a powerful, strong genie. What would come from this one if she dared hold her hands on it long enough to see?

Joey and Beth had left her alone upstairs with just her lamp, and she longed to follow them, to play too with friends or on the swing in the backyard where she could see through the fence and watch the people at the convenience store whose parking lot was right at the edge of the fence. She was uncomfortable alone now, now that the lamp was in the room with her.

She didn't want it on her bed.

But she was afraid to touch it again.

It might burn her hands again, or . . .

But Beth had said it wasn't hot. Beth had touched it.

Ellen reached gingerly to its most prominent part, the long spout, or handle, that curved up and out, the one with the thin chain dangling from near its tip to the top. She picked it up by the chain and eased it off the bed.

The chain broke suddenly, and the lamp swung a wide arc down and toward her, and she jumped back, an aborted scream dying in her throat. With the broken chain tight between her fingers, her body arched back out of the way of the swinging lamp, she watched it, waiting for it to slow and hang still at the end of the chain.

With it dangling, she carried it gently to the corner and set it down on the floor. The chain rattled when she dropped it, and then hung still from the tiny ring to which it was attached on top the lamp.

Ellen pushed the closet door back, so that the lamp was hidden behind it.

Chapter Two

The kids were in bed, asleep, and Blythe could relax, at last, totally, for the first time since she had gotten out of bed that morning. What was it about kids that relaxation was impossible as long as you knew they were awake? Even at the ages they were now, she hadn't gotten over the feeling that she needed to be on the alert unless they were in their cribs, so to speak.

Ellen and Joey had gone to bed at nine, but Beth had been allowed to stay up until ten. Then Blythe had waited fifteen minutes before she went up to check on them, to see that they were covered. They were all three asleep. Ellen, with her bright, pale hair flowing out across the pillow, all that was visible of her, was the one who slept in a knot, as if she were protecting her stomach from something. The other two stretched out, arms and legs wide. Blythe didn't know if there was any theory about sleep habits; but in her own mind she had decided that Joey and Beth would get along all right in this world, because they were so open and trusting in their sleep, but Ellen would have a hard time. So, she couldn't help but worry some about Ellen. The one who slept curled in a small knot. Like a little animal in hibernation.

Blythe sat down in her father's old chair and put her feet up on the worn footstool. She had saved the mail and now went through it carefully, looking at the pages of advertising, the junk mail that came in daily. She was one person who didn't mind the junk mail. It was the most mindless activity that she indulged in, this looking through the junk mail. It helped in the relaxation process.

She saved the letter from Gavin until last.

She hadn't even told the kids there was a letter from their daddy because it was addressed by his wife, whatever her name was, just as they all were now. Her penmanship was neat and square. Probably a perfect reflection of the woman herself.

Usually the envelope contained only a check. Once a month since Gavin had married again, six months now, or five, whatever it was, this same type of creamy, heavy envelope came with the same neat handwriting and the same check: fifteen hundred dollars. Before the marriage, the checks from Gavin had been three hundred dollars for each kid, which she knew must take quite a hunk out of his salary. He wasn't a rich man, by any means. He worked for an oil company in Texas, which had been the final breakdown of their own marriage—the last straw you might say—because she had no intention of leaving Los Angeles for some unheard of place in Texas.

But now the checks came from the new wife; and the added money was hers, too, Blythe knew, and she resented every penny of it.

Was she jealous of Mrs. Gavin Pendergast?

She didn't think so, yet she couldn't help feeling resentful that the extra money was coming from her. Indeed she felt like saying, "What gives you the right to give money to my kids?"

There was more, this time, than the check.

The sheet of stationery repeated the request that the three kids be allowed to spend part of the summer at

Gavin's new home in Fort Smith, Arkansas.

Fort Smith, yet. Wasn't that the place where the hanging judge had lived?

The invitation was written in the same handwriting, that neat, square lettering, and was signed, this time, by the name Faye. Just Faye, not Mrs. Gavin Pendergast. Was she trying to be chummy?

Aside from Blythe's own feelings, the kids didn't want to go. When their dad had called, the week school was out for the summer, and asked if they could come, all three of them had pleaded not to be sent away.

Blythe understood, why couldn't Gavin? The children hadn't lived with him since he had taken the job in Texas three years ago. And three years out of the lives of children who were now only seven, eight and twelve, was a long time.

They didn't want to go, and she didn't want them to go.

It might give her more freedom to do something that was fun, but she wasn't sure she knew what would be fun anymore.

She leaned her head back and closed her eyes.

The house was quiet, as quiet as an old house can get. The city had grown around it, other old houses had been knocked down and dragged away, board by board, or piled up by a bulldozer and burned. Empty lots had appeared in the neighborhood, some warehouses, and a convenience store had sprung up just across the back fence; but still it was the best she could afford. The money she could get out of this house would not buy them another one.

Life wasn't easy, money-wise. Her own small job of clerking in a local department store barely kept food on the table. Her pride would go on resenting the money Gavin's wife sent, but her common sense put a firm foot on her pride.

Still, her kids didn't want to go there for the summer, and she didn't know how to handle it because as long as Gavin paid child support, he was entitled to have them visit him.

She hadn't turned on the television, and every sound in the neighborhood seeped through the old walls of the house. A couple of dogs barked, not too close, and a mockingbird in the trees outside trilled a song to the moonlight. Traffic moved sluggishly, and car doors slammed occasionally in the convenience store parking lot behind the house.

But on the stairs a board creaked, a sound outstanding in the busy night, and she opened her eyes.

Someone was coming down the stairs.

She looked at the clock. It was past midnight now. Why would one of the kids be up at this hour? None of them were restless sleepers. Usually, they slept through the night without waking.

She listened, a frown growing on her face. The footsteps became more audible, bare feet on worn carpet.

Ellen appeared in the wide arched doorway between the living room and the foyer. She was carrying her ridiculous buy from the garage sale, the can with the peculiar attachments.

She held it carefully in both hands, straight out in front as if she were making an offering.

She turned, walking oddly, pivoting on her toes to face Blythe, and walked the length of the living room toward her.

Blythe stood up, puzzled, uneasy. What was wrong with Ellen?

She started to speak her name, but paused, waiting. Ellen's eyes were wide open, but there was a still, set look to her face, a lack of consciousness in her eyes, that chilled Blythe.

She knew, then, what was wrong with Ellen.
Sleepwalking.

"Ellen, baby, are you all right?"

For the first time in her life, Blythe was watching a sleepwalker, and it gave her a weird, scared feeling. She waited for Ellen to approach her, but Ellen was not coming toward her after all, she saw. The young girl veered off to the left and went on past toward the door to the dining room, another archway about half the size of the one into the foyer.

She had to stop Ellen, take her back to bed. But what had she read about dealing with somnambulism? Don't wake them?

Blythe put her hand on Ellen's shoulder, and the child stopped.

Without speaking to her again, Blythe gently removed the metal can from her hands and set it on top of the upright piano. Then, turning Ellen, she guided her back the way she had come. The little girl went willingly, with only a touch of a hand guiding her, up the stairs, down the hall to her room and back into bed.

The moment she was in bed, she turned her back and curled into the tight little ball she favored and seemed immediately to be fast asleep. Her eyes were closed again, her long lashes dark against her fair skin.

Blythe put a palm on her forehead, but it was cool. No fever.

She stood there a few moments longer, looking down at the side of Ellen's face, at the huddled body beneath the blanket, the sense of something being very weird, almost frightening, drifting away to an unformed worry.

What was wrong?

Was Ellen's worry that she might be sent to a stranger's house for the summer disturbing her sleep?

Blythe went back downstairs and down the hallway

to the kitchen. It was a dreary hole, had needed paint long ago. Someday, maybe, she'd feel like doing something with it.

But for now there was a fifth of whiskey hidden back on the top shelf that had belonged to her dad. And in the junk drawer, among the pliers, screwdrivers and general odds and ends sometimes needed around a house, was a pack of her own cigarettes. She didn't often smoke anymore, and hardly ever took a drink, but there were times when she felt she needed the relaxation it gave her, that good feeling that she could handle whatever came up.

And tonight she needed it.

She stood on the kitchen stool and poured a shot of whiskey into a glass. She replaced the bottle, pushing it back into its corner.

Climbing down from the stool she took one cigarette, leaving the package in the drawer. She turned on a burner on the stove, stooped and lighted the cigarette. She straightened and took a long drag. A faint light-headedness washed over her. Still, it felt good to be holding a cigarette again. The first sip of whiskey burned her throat, and then the numbness came, and the warmth spreading out from her stomach.

She and Gavin had learned to smoke together when they were teenagers. She had started trying to quit when her children were born and usually took a cigarette only when she and Gavin relaxed with cocktails, when they were alone or out with friends. She no longer considered it a habit.

She went down the hall and to the sofa where she could set her glass on the table. On impulse she drank it all. With her eyes closed she drifted, aware of her mind altering, calming, every muscle in her body easing into a welcome relaxation. The warmth from the unaccustomed drink was like a warm blanket thrown over her.

For a while nothing was going to matter, not the money, not the future. For a while now she could think that in another few days she was going to get with it and do all the things she'd been planning to do. She was going to sign up for night school, and finish her education. Then she was going to get a job that would pay enough money that she could tell Mrs. Whatsername Pendergast to keep her fat checks. They didn't need charity.

She could sell this old house and buy another new one, like the one she and Gavin had bought, which was, like it or not, her own idea and not a very good one. She'd wanted too much too soon, maybe, and in order to pay for it Gavin had been forced to take the job in Texas. But then, the marriage hadn't had much going for it anyway. They'd both been too young. High school love affairs seldom last long. After they'd both grown up, they had discovered they didn't have much in common.

So Gavin had gone and she had stayed.

Why in the hell was she thinking of him so much tonight? She didn't sit around thinking of Gavin. There'd been other lovers since him who were better. More suited to her tastes, at least.

It was the letter, she thought. The check. That was why she'd been thinking of Gavin and his wife.

It really didn't matter to her that he had married again.

She could hardly breathe. The smoke in the room had grown so thick.

She opened her eyes.

The cigarette had burned down and now singed her fingers. She dropped it, then bent and picked it up quickly from the old, dried carpet that would probably burn like dead prairie grass. With her toe, she smudged out the black hole on the carpet, making sure no sparks were left. She put the stub of the cigarette into the ashtray.

Don't forget to empty it later so the kids won't see it, she reminded herself and put her hand to her mouth to stifle a cough. She was trying to set a better example than that.

Why was the room so filled with smoke? One cigarette didn't do that.

She stood up, fear arching through her mind, alerting her. Was the house on fire?

She rushed out into the foyer and found the air clear. When she faced the living room again, she saw the veil of smoke in the doorway, like a curtain, contained in that room.

She pushed back through, blinking in the heavy, acrid smoke, and stood still in the middle of the room, trying to locate its source. There was no fire that she could see. But a black smoke was curling up from the corner of the room, from behind the piano.

No, she saw as she moved nearer, not from the corner behind the piano, but from the piano itself.

No, wrong again.

She stared at the metal thing she had taken from Ellen and set on the back edge of the piano top. The black smoke was trailing silently upward from the curving spout, a full black rope of smoke that was like a snake rising; then, a few inches above the end of the spout, the smoke began to curl, to writhe, to spread, moving out across the ceiling and down the walls, forming walls of its own in the small living room.

Blythe stood staring at it, hardly able to believe what she was seeing.

Throw it out, her mind told her, but she couldn't move.

Heavy, dark smoke poured from the slender pipe of

the metal bowl on the piano, and a sudden realization told her what that container was. A pipe. A Turkish or Chinese water pipe, used a century and a half ago for smoking opium. Had there been a residue of the drug left in the pipe? How had it become lighted?

Why was she feeling that she was watching a supernatural occurrence that had more to do with something in the past history of the pipe than in the present? Why couldn't she move, make her feet walk toward the piano, pick up the metal atrocity that little Ellen had thought was a magic Aladdin's Lamp, take it to the door and throw it into the yard?

As if the smoke that continued to curl from the pipe had already poisoned her, she felt paralyzed. Her skin was cold, and she was beginning to shiver. But it wasn't the cold that was causing her to shiver. It was fear. Unreasonable fear. Or perhaps fear that came from her subconscious, where somehow something was known, a recognition of a mortal danger that continued to rise from the pipe and curl into the room.

Her head turned slightly, and her eyes followed the trail of smoke as it moved across the ceiling and around the wall, watching it thicken and form . . . *form dark shapes that looked . . . looked . . .*

It couldn't be!

It couldn't be alive, this stuff that was filling the room, choking her, holding her, causing her eyes to burn now with terrible pain, to water, to tear . . . to weep the tears of her own death . . .

Oh God, my children.

A figure seemed to be forming in the smoke to her left. Vague, horrible, seeming at first to be small, animal in origin, and then becoming something else. Larger. Spreading, swelling upward. She tried to see it, to make herself move away from it as its vague shape edged nearer to her. It raised a hand that was, after all, a hand . . . human?

She collapsed to her knees, unable to stand, and the dark shape towered over her.

She fell sideways, strangled by her fear, and began to crawl toward the doorway, its bloated, massive shape pale lines in the writhing smoke. Her fingers clawed at the threads of the carpet to pull herself forward to freedom . . . to escape this madness . . . because that was all it was . . . that was all it could be . . . madness . . .

Somebody was standing the archway, she saw, a small figure dressed in a long white gown with blue figures on it. A familiar . . . figure . . .

Ellen!

Her pale oval face was turned toward Blythe, but her eyes seemed to be staring mindlessly.

Run, Ellen, run.

She struggled to reach Ellen, to save her, but it was too late. She could only try to shove her toward safety.

She was forced to turn and fight the figure that had at last materialized from the smoke, which was now, she knew, coming after her child.

Chapter Three

Ellen was trying to run, but her legs were heavy and dragged down as if she were caught in a sticky substance, like a fly in tar. The monster was there, between her and something that was even worse than the monster. It's eyes blazed at her through long, narrow slits. It was rising above her, its arm spread, and coming down to eat her, to devour her into itself so that she would be part of it, so that the essence that was herself would be gone forever, forever...

She tried to scream and couldn't. Her body was sagging with the heavy black smoke that filled her, and her mouth was clogged, her throat choking, so that the only sound she could make was a stifled croak.

She woke abruptly, thrown from the nightmare terror of her dream into a daylight world. She sat up in bed and blinked wild-eyed at her surroundings. Her pink and white striped wallpaper, like candy canes, had replaced the dark, misty world where the monster and the ... the ... She couldn't remember now. What was it that had been there, in the shadows, just a minute ago?

She didn't want to remember, she realized. Let the dream go away. Let her sigh with thankfulness that this world was warm and light and familiar. There was her white dresser against the candy-striped wall, and there was the open window with the pink curtains moving in the breeze. The sun was shining, too, coming in onto the sill of her window, beneath the shade that was drawn almost all the way down. Mama had fixed it that way last night, saying, "So the sun won't wake you up early in the morning. You don't have to get up and go to school now all summer long. You can sleep later."

Where was Joey? And Beth? The house was so quiet. Were they still asleep? She wanted to be with someone. The dark edges of the nightmare were still behind her, just over her shoulder.

She turned swiftly, but behind her was only the head of her white bed and the same bright wallpaper. On the wall above the bed was the group of Walt Disney characters—Donald Duck, Mickey Mouse, Pluto, and others—and over toward the corner was a heavy cardboard cutout of the Cow Jumping Over the Moon. She looked at them each, seeking comfort.

She drew a long breath and turned back, pushing her blanket away and raising her knees so that she could rest her arms and her chin for a while before getting out of bed.

Usually, she had to hurry out of bed before she was half awake, stumble into the bathroom half-blinded with sleep and start getting ready for school. Joey would be yelling at her to hurry up and come on if she wanted to walk with him, and of course she had to, because her mother insisted that he take her to school. Beth went to a different school now that she was almost a teenager. She caught a bus down on the corner. She had also taken her long, dark brown hair out of its braids and was wearing it loose, and it looked so pretty, waved down over her shoulders, so glossy. Beth's hair was prettier than her own, because her own was almost colorless. "You're a blonde," her mama said, to comfort her. "Nothing wrong with being a blonde, honey. Haven't you heard blondes have more fun?"

Ellen pulled her nightgown tightly over her upraised knees, drawing another long breath. An aborted breath. Suddenly she couldn't breathe at all. She stared at her nightgown where it was pulled over her bony knees.

Brown stains spotted it, some of them so big they ran together, making a damp, reddish line where the two stains overlapped.

She straightened her legs and pulled her gown out away from her body and looked sharply down. It had a round yoke that was edged in lace, and beyond that the white with the blue bunnies fabric was gathered into full folds. The stains were all over the front, reaching up onto the lace and onto the yoke. She could see no higher. She folded her hands onto her neck, and it seemed she could feel a crusty, thin substance that didn't belong there.

Her hands felt as if they were still burning, and she jerked them away from her neck and spread them, palm up.

The brown stuff was in the creases of her hands, and in her fingernails, and on the sleeves of her gown.

She stared, hypnotized by it, wondering what it was and how it had gotten all over her. She put her hands to her face to feel if it were there, too, then jerked her hands away, afraid the bad stuff on her hands would get on her face.

If she moved over just a little she'd be able to see herself in the mirror of her dresser, but she was afraid to. *What had happened to her while she slept?*

The door to her room began to open, and Ellen stared at it in horror. She watched the knob turn, ever so silently and slowly, and heard the latch release. Then there was an inch crack, another inch, three . . . She almost screamed, just before she saw Beth's shoulder and brown hair.

Beth's eyes were not on her, but on something on the floor. She was looking behind her, then straight down, then on across the carpet to Ellen's bed. Then, widening, her eyes jerked up and stared in wild silence at Ellen. Swiftly, the strange stare covered Ellen, going from her hair down the length of her gown.

Ellen watched her expressions, from puzzlement to a growing horror that matched her own.

"Ellen!" Beth cried in a harsh accusing whisper, staring at her, at the stains on her gown. Then she was pulling back with a hurried whisper. "Wait here. Don't move!"

She was gone, leaving the door open a few inches.

Ellen thought of her while she was gone, obeying her and not moving, but trying to imagine where she had gone and what was wrong. Was Beth looking for something, for the source of the ugly stains?

The minutes stretched, it seemed, into a long, aching time. Still, Ellen did not move. And she hardly breathed. Dread crowded into her throat, making it dry and raspy as she sucked breath in through her mouth.

Suddenly Beth was back again, her face white, her chin jerking, her teeth clicking together faintly as if she were cold, *cold*.

Then came the settled look, the distant, grown-up look that Beth had started getting sometime in the past year.

Ellen could remember her as a noisy, kind of bossy older sister, grabbing things away from her, making her do things she didn't want to do and not letting her do things she wanted to do; and then she became almost a teenager, and she began to change. Suddenly it was like Beth was living in a world that did not include Ellen anymore.

Without a word now, Beth came to the bed and began to pull Ellen's nightgown off over her head. That left Ellen sitting in her panties, and she saw in sudden, leaping terror that the brown stain had even soaked through to them.

Ellen's throat made a squeaky, involuntary sound as she picked her nylon panties away from her body, using a finger and a thumb. She could feel a cool, sticky spot on her bare skin beneath the material.

Beth grasped her hand and jerked it back, making her own sound, an order, a demand. *"Shhhhush!"* And then, still holding Ellen's wrist, she pulled her toward the door. "Come on," she whispered, "you have to clean up. Hurry."

Ellen ran at her side to catch up, with Beth jerking her this way and that across the carpet to the door. Ellen saw that she was trying to avoid something that was on the carpet, and when she looked down, she saw the same stains, spotted from the door to the bed as if . . . as if they were footprints in sand. Only these weren't really footprints, they were just blobs of dark stains. Just blobs. Not real footprints.

"What's that?" Ellen cried. "Where's Mama? Has Mama gone to work?"

"Shhh." Beth jerked her, angrily it seemed, in a desperate hurry. She opened the door and looked out, up and down the hall, and then she pulled Ellen into the hall and toward the bathroom.

At that moment Joey stepped out of his room, his eyes opening wide the way they always did when he first woke up, as if they were glazed and he was having trouble seeing. He was still in his pajamas. Ellen looked for stains on him, but there were none. His pajamas were wrinkled, but clean. He blinked a couple of times, then suddenly he was wide awake.

"What's wrong?" he asked. "What's Ellen got on her?"

They stood still, Beth's hand gripping Ellen's wrist so tightly it was beginning to hurt. They stood in silence. Ellen didn't know what to say, and Beth said nothing.

Joey demanded, "What's she got all over her? Why is she dressed like that? Did she vomit? Where's Mama?"

Ellen stared at him, aware of the pain in her wrist, of time passing as if they were all part of a picture that was just painted in the hall, just cardboard characters like the characters on her bedroom wall. Time was passing, and they were standing still in a silent house, while outside life was moving on, the birds singing and the sun rising in the sky. Kids were playing on the sidewalks and in their yards just as if things were right and normal everywhere. Then she heard her sister speak, softly, calmly, as if this happened every day.

"I think it's blood."

Joey blinked several times, and his face changed, looking scared, and pained, and other things that Ellen didn't understand. She saw him looking at the nightgown Beth held in her free hand and saw him looking, too, at the dark blobs on the floor. Ellen looked also and saw the blobs were not only in her bedroom, but out here on the pale beige carpet of the hall, going toward the stairs, going down, getting darker and darker the farther away they were, the farther down the steps. She could not see beyond the curve in the stairs. But through the railing that made the empty edge of the hall safer, she could see the foyer below, and there the stains were again spotted toward the living room. The prints of a wild jungle animal sunk in mud, or of a camel who had left nothing behind him in the desert sand but his footsteps.

Joey's blue eyes suddenly screwed up, narrowing, as if he were going to cry. He reached up and flipped the dark hair off his forehead as if it bothered him, hanging down like it always did, almost to his eyebrows, even right after he had wet it and combed it back.

"Blood," he whispered harshly, a sound that touched Ellen's ears as forcefully as a shout.

Like an animal tracking he began to follow the blobs on the carpet, bent slightly forward, going faster and faster, down the stairs, around the curve.

Beth followed him, pulling Ellen along with a yank, crying, "Joey—Joe! Wait! Don't! Joe, we don't know—"

She said no more. They were running down, Ellen stumbling, trying to keep up without falling. She stubbed her toe on the step third from the top and it hurt, but she only gasped and let Beth pull her on, down the steps, following Joey.

He had disappeared by the time they reached the bottom of the stairway; but the trail of dark blobs led them across the foyer and into the darkened living room, and Joey was standing there, in the far corner, his back to them, staring at something on the floor.

The draperies were drawn over the wide windows at the front. A light at the end of the sofa was still burning, but it gave out a dim, sickly, yellowish glow that made only a pool of light on the table and on the arm of the sofa. The corners were in darkness. Especially the corner behind the piano, where Joey stood.

Beth saw her mother's high-heeled sandals on the floor. One was lying back near the archway into the foyer. Her blouse was there, too, a crumpled white thing like a big silk handkerchief.

Ellen tried to reach down to pick it up, to hold it to her face and smell the sweet perfume of her mother, but Beth gave her a vicious jerk away from it. Ellen began to whimper, her throat swelling with a terrible hurting.

In the dark and shadowed corner, a dim figure moved, beginning to pull out of the brown wallpaper, and Ellen tried to scream, to warn them. But they weren't aware of her, or of the monster.

"She's dead!" Joey screamed, and as though released from an invisible hand, Ellen began screaming, too. *Couldn't they see the monster?*

Didn't they know he was hiding in the corner and was coming out to kill them, too?

A memory struggled to surface, like a dream almost recalled, but it turned and lay like heavy lead just beneath her consciousness, as dark and as dangerous as the monster in the corner.

"It's there, it's there," Ellen screamed, pointing at the corner behind the piano. "Don't let it out! Don't!"

Neither Beth nor Joey noticed. They were staring at the thing on the floor between the piano bench and sofa.

Beth took a couple of steps nearer to it, and her hand, clamped so tightly around Ellen's wrist, pulled her along. Ellen saw, from an unwanted glance downward, that the dark stains were all over here, and lying in the midst of them was the paper-white, sprawled body of their mother. She was lying sideways, almost on her stomach, one leg drawn up over something red and ropy that was spilled beneath her. She was lying on it as if it were a pillow.

Ellen began to try to tell them, whimpering in her throat, "The—the—the monst—" A vague skulking of movements in the darkness of her memory moved nearer to the surface. Monsters . . . in the night . . . she had seen . . . but they, Beth and Joey, weren't listening to her.

She looked at the corner again, and it was empty, the dark brown and tan geometric figures in the wallpaper no longer dimmed by the half-formed body of the monster. It was gone. Or maybe—*it had only moved*.

Joey began to run, as if he were running away, forever, to the ends of the earth. He ran out of the living room and down the hall, and Ellen was being dragged along behind Beth, following him.

Beth was crying softly in a hushed voice as if she were afraid of being heard by someone other than Joey. "Where are you going? What are you going to do?"

But Joey didn't answer. He was making dark footprints of his own from the soaked carpet of blood in the living room all along the hall to the kitchen.

Just as Beth and Ellen pushed through the kitchen door, Joey was taking the phone down off the hook. Ellen saw that his hands were smeared with blood, and he had gotten blood all over the phone. This blood was wet and red, and Ellen knew he had touched their mother or the carpet she lay on. Or maybe he had tried to see what kind of pillow was beneath her. Maybe he had tried to pull it out so that she could be more comfortable.

Beth snatched the phone away from him and hung it up.

"What are you doing!" she hissed. "Do you know what you're doing?"

Tears gathered in Joey's eyes and began running down his cheeks. He put his fingers up to wipe it away, and his cheek turned pink with teared blood. His white lips trembled. "I'm calling the police."

"We've got to clean her up first!"

Beth was still hissing, her voice spewing out, sounding like she was furious with Joey.

"Don't you see, we've got to clean her up first?" She gave Ellen's arm a shake, and Ellen knew Beth meant her and not their mother.

"The monster," Ellen cried, "It's still here. We've got to leave. We've got to hide in our rooms." Urgency and fear changed her voice, making her sound like a stranger to her own ears. "Please! *It will kill us, too.*"

But they weren't listening. Beth began dragging her back toward the living room, and Ellen struggled, her own tears coming in desperate terror. *The monster, the monster . . .*

"No. No. No."

"Shhh!"

Yes, be quiet, or the monster will know you're coming near again. And this time . . . this time . . .

Ellen forced herself to silence and allowed herself to be pulled on up the stairway and into the bathroom. Beth released her, then hooked her fingers under the elastic of Ellen's panties and yanked them down, and Ellen stood naked and exposed.

She started to object, but no words escaped her tight throat. She saw then it didn't matter. No one was looking at her. Beth had grabbed a washcloth from the drawer of washcloths and was running hot water over it. She handed it dripping to Joey.

"Go wash up the footprints in her bedroom. Hurry. Then take these clothes downstairs and get rid of them." As she gave him orders she was taking another washcloth from the drawer. She slopped it in a pool of water that was running into and through the basin and then rolled it around a block of soap.

Joey's chin was shaking so hard his words sounded shattered. "Wh-wh-where'll I p-put them?"

"I don't know. Just go on, Joey!"

"I can't. I'm scared. What if he's still there?"

"What if who's still there?" Beth was not looking at Joey. She began scrubbing Ellen roughly, all over her face and down her neck onto her chest and stomach.

"The m-man who k-killed her."

"It wasn't a *man,* Joey," she said through her teeth. "Can't you see that?" She scrubbed Ellen hard, the movement of the cloth against her skin the only sound in the whole house, it seemed, with a scrape, scrape, scrape that was raspy and loud.

Joey stood there awhile longer, visibly shaking,

watching Beth scrub Ellen's body, but not really seeing. Then he turned away and Ellen could see him down on his knees scrubbing the spots on the carpet, working from one to the next and finally going into her bedroom out of sight.

When Beth shoved Ellen ahead of her into the bedroom, still naked, Joey was on his knees right beside the bed, and the stains on the floor had turned to a line of pale damp spots in the short shag of the pink carpet.

At the chest of drawers, Beth turned her back on Ellen and threw out a pair of panties, a blouse and a pair of shorts. Ellen began to dress.

Joey stood up and looked at Beth for approval. Her eyes traced the wet spots on the floor, and she nodded. Then she shrugged.

"It's okay, I guess. We have to call now."

Joey went to the top of the stairs and stopped, looking back at Beth. She too had stopped, halfway between Ellen's bedroom and the stairway. Ellen looked down. The blood stains were there, on the steps, forgotten.

Beth shrugged again. Joey looked tired now, exhausted, his face sagging in a way that made him look like a little boy that had turned in one hour to an old man. His shoulders sagged. And finally, he sat down on the top step and leaned his head against the baluster of the stairway.

"I'll make the call," Beth said. "I'll use the upstairs phone."

Ellen watched her go toward the end of the hall, toward the closed door of their mother's room where the upstairs phone was, and she wanted to scream at her not to go in there. *It* might be there, behind that dark, closed door.

She wanted to tell Beth it was not she who had killed their mother, it was the *thing,* the monster, but her throat only worked soundlessly as she watched her sister go toward that room.

A woman answered the phone, and Beth did not understand exactly what she had said. She could hear, and yet the noises in her head, the sounds of a river rushing, of a thousand hearts beating, drowned out the exact words. "The po-police," Beth said. "We—our mother has been killed. We need help."

The voice asked her for her name and address, and it took another long while for Beth to remember. Her name? Her name? Beth Pendergast. Address. At first she told her old address, the place she had lived before her parents were divorced, and didn't notice what she had done until the woman on the phone repeated it. She remembered then, this address was the one. This not that.

"What happened to your mother?" the voice asked, after the address was corrected.

"She—she was killed. Murdered."

"Who did it?"

"I don't know." This time her voice was firm. *Ellen.* But she'd never tell, never. Why would Ellen murder their mother? Ellen was—something was wrong with Ellen's mind. She was—she was *crazy.* Insane. What was the other word, when a person went mad and murdered without reason? Psychotic? Psycho.

She talked of monsters, when everyone knew monsters were not real.

Ellen had to be protected.

She would never tell what Ellen had done. She would tell the police that a strange man had come in the back door, that perhaps their mother had inadvertently let the man in. Perhaps he had come pretending to sell something. Or maybe he had wanted to use the phone, the way it happened sometimes. Anything, she would tell anything to protect Ellen.

But she couldn't help, when she left her mother's bedroom and went back out into the hall, when she saw Ellen standing there with her young face so sweet and so scared, she couldn't help feeling scared, too.

Scared of Ellen.

The three children were huddled together on the cracked cement patio at the back of the house when the first patrol car arrived. They stood as if they were going to have their pictures taken, the tall girl in the back and the smaller girl and the boy, who was about half a head taller than the younger girl and a full head shorter than the older, standing slightly between them, his left shoulder behind the right shoulder of the little girl. His hands were hanging at his sides. One hand of the tall girl was resting on his shoulder. Their faces were reminiscent of the photographs of the nineteenth century, as if they were carved in stone.

Rick Powell had a hunch they had been standing there for a long time, that perhaps the teenaged girl had told the younger two what to do and what to say.

But then, as he approached with his partner at his side, he almost changed his mind. It could be a state of shock.

The report had been of a death. Were the kids alone? How do you talk to kids about death? He wished he'd been farther away when the call came through so that a more experienced officer could have come here instead. He glanced at his partner, an older man with a few more years of experience, but he didn't look as if he were willing to take over.

Rick said, "You kids alone here?"

The older girl and the boy nodded. The boy pointed toward the kitchen door. "Our mo-mother," he said.

Rick hesitated, then decided to go ahead and have it over with. In this part of town, where no houses were left but the old run-down kind, an occasional death was not unusual.

He went through the kitchen, Jameson at his heels. The white telephone on the wall had streaks of blood or something that looked like smeared blood. He glanced over his shoulder at Jameson and saw his eyes taking it all in.

"You might as well go on back to the car and call homicide," he said, the instant he looked through the archway into the living room. The floral pattern of the rug was splotched with blood, from one end of the eighteen foot living room to the bay windows at the other. He had never seen so much blood. The woman lay at the far end of the room, her face down. He was glad of that. He didn't think he could stand to look at her face.

He went back out to breathe the fresher air on the porch and to try to decide about the children.

"Come along," he said. "You might as well get into the car."

The first stop would be the police station, and then it would become somebody else's responsibility. Like wooden dolls, they moved ahead of him to the car and climbed into the back seat, the tall girl pushing the smaller girl ahead of her and pulling the boy in last.

Then they sat staring ahead, that same stony look on their faces.

Ellen's first impression of the police station was of

noisiness. Telephones seemed to be ringing everywhere, all the time. The air, too, was cold, and her skin was like ice. But she had been cold all morning, ever since she remembered—and knew—that her mama was dead. Killed by the monster that could change forms.

But Beth had told her to keep her mouth shut. "Don't talk," she had said while they were waiting for the police. "Don't tell about any monster, Ellen. No one is going to believe you."

Beth thought she had killed their mother, because of the stains on her hands and gown, because no one else was in the house, and the doors and windows were locked. *But I didn't, I didn't.*

She listened to the questions and answers. Beth gave the answers, while she and Joey sat at her side.

No, they didn't have any close relatives except their father, Beth said, and gave his address and told them where they could find his phone number.

And no, their mother had not had company last night before they went to bed, but she might have had afterward. Someone must have come to the door and wanted to use the phone, or something. Their mother might have opened the back door to her killer.

"The front door was bolted from the inside," a policeman said, and Beth answered quickly.

"Yes. But the back wasn't. It just had the button lock set. Anybody going out of the house could have set the lock behind him. It was someone off the streets." She drew a long breath.

Ellen gave her a long, dark stare. Beth was lying. The back door had been bolted, too. No man had come in from outside. They had stood together, the three of them, while Beth unbolted the door. Then they had gone out to wait for the police.

*   *   *

They were given breakfast to eat, but Ellen could not swallow. She saw that Beth was watching her a lot, and she tried to eat; but she knew if she took another bite she would be sick right there on the long table in the bare room.

They were left sitting on hard chairs where men and women came and went, some of them asking questions and some of them just looking as they walked by. Some wore uniforms, and some did not.

Ellen watched them all closely. They appeared to be real people, but were they? Somewhere deep in her mind was a vague memory of the monster that had been in the room with her mother last night, and it had been—had edges that were human.

Now, staring at all the strange people, she could see that one of them was different. He was disguised as a police officer, and he sat on a chair behind a desk far back in the corner; but he kept looking at her, especially her, through slitted eyes that hid the black pupils, not Beth or Joey, as if he knew that she had seen him last night, before he was human, while he still was disguised as part animal.

She hadn't realized she was making a sound of any kind until Beth said in her ear, "Shhh, Ellen. Don't cry. And"—she dropped her voice to a whisper that only Ellen could hear—"if anyone asks you any questions, be sure, be *sure* you do not say anything about monsters. Just tell them you don't know anything at all. *Don't say anything.* Do you hear?"

"Beth," Ellen cried in a whisper, grabbing her arm with tight fingers. "Beth, that—that man over there, in the corner, Beth, *he's the monster. He has followed us.*"

"Who?" Beth was frowning and trying to get her arm free from Ellen's grasp. "What are you talking about, Ellen?"

"That man," she hissed in her sister's ear, clutching her for dear life. *"That's him—his face—see his eyes,*

Beth, that's him—the monster—"

"Shhh! Don't be silly, Ellen. He's just a policeman. He's Chinese, or Korean or some other Oriental. You've seen Chinese before, lots of times."

For a moment Beth had gotten between Ellen and the monster who was disguised as a policeman, and when Ellen's vision was once again unobstructed, he was gone.

But she knew.

The monster was following her.

Chapter Four

From the time of the first phone call asking for Gavin to contact a certain number in California, Faye had felt uneasy. The call had come in the evening about six o'clock, which meant it had been made at four from Los Angeles. Nothing was told to her. The caller had a calm, professional voice that gave nothing away.

Faye had immediately placed a call to Gavin's apartment in Dallas, where he lived during the week so that he would be close to his work. He was not at home, so she called his office.

He was working a bit late, he told her when he answered the phone, so that he could get off at noon tomorrow and come home. "Is something wrong? Nothing's wrong, is there, Faye? Tell me you're okay, just lonesome for me."

"I'm always lonesome for you when you're away," she said, "but that isn't the reason I'm calling at this hour." They talked together every night at eight and made plans for the day when Gavin would be working nearer to home, so they wouldn't be separated at night. When she told him about the California call he was as puzzled as she, which was obvious by the silence on the line.

"Gavin?" she had prompted, wondering what the number might mean to him. After all, there was a lot of his past life she knew nothing about. They had met in Dallas three years ago, while his divorce was in progress. All he had told her was the marriage had been wrong from the start. They were a couple of high school kids who thought they knew what they wanted. The only good thing that had come out of the marriage was the kids; but he'd had to leave, because of work, and he didn't know how that was going to turn out. His wife, of course, would keep the kids. She was a good mother, so there was no reason she shouldn't keep them. The main reason for the divorce was she didn't want to move away from her folks. Both of them were in ill health. She was an only child, and her home was in Los Angeles.

Faye and Gavin had gone on from there. He had flown back to see the kids several times a year, but when he was with her he rarely talked of the past.

"Gavin?"

"It must have something to do with the kids," he said. "But that number is an unfamiliar one. I'll call and see what it is, and let you know soon afterward. You'll be at home, won't you?"

"Of course."

His return call came within minutes, and the information was hurried and brief. His wife had been murdered, and the kids were being taken care of at the police station until he could arrive. He would go on, as soon as he could get a flight out, without coming home first. He'd call from California.

Now, spending what seemed an endless time without Gavin while he was taking care of the problems caused by the murder of his wife, Faye couldn't get rid of the dark cloud that hung over her. Not even the brightness, the gentle atmosphere of the new nursery helped.

46

She sat in the yellow rocker in the room that would be waiting for her baby, folded her hands across her rounding abdomen, tried to feel with her hands the fluttery movements she could feel in her body and searched within herself for that incredible and wonderful happiness she had known two weeks ago.

Even though Gavin had decided it was easier to live during the week in Dallas, near his work, than to commute daily back and forth, she hadn't felt alone. In the beginning of their marriage, she had stayed part of the time in Dallas in the apartment, but with her pregnancy, she had settled down in the big old house in Fort Smith, the house of her grandfather, and had started redecorating the nursery. Occasionally, Gavin flew home during the week, on Wednesday night, so that the week passed quickly, and he was with her again for the weekend.

But now, though he'd been gone only a couple of weeks, she felt very much alone.

Search though she did, the happiness had disappeared. She felt a natural horror at the murder, but it was brought closer to home, of course, because it involved people she felt she knew even though she had never met them. And of course it deeply involved Gavin, her husband.

His first family had seemed distant, and almost unreal, even though she had expected that the children would be spending some of their vacation with them. And now circumstances, horrible circumstances, had dictated a different future.

She tried not to dread the coming changes, but she did. She was developing a deep-seated worry that was giving her nightmares.

"It's not the children, it's just me," she murmured aloud, looking at the colorful wallpaper that was, so far, without hangings. "It's my pregnancy. It just makes coping harder. I should have known it couldn't have been all perfect."

Her friends had warned her. "You won't like it," they had said. "You might think it will be the greatest time of your life since you want it so much; but you'll be sick, and you'll feel like an elephant later on. You'll get constipated. You'll have aches and pains, and you won't be able to rest or sleep well. You'll look at the world differently. You'll get emotional. You'll hate it."

"No," she had told them laughing. "I don't believe it."

She remembered the luncheon in which that conversation took place. At Janie's house, after the baby shower, she had sat with old friends at the white wicker table on the back porch, looking out over that wonderful tangle of woodland left wild that she had looked upon periodically since she was a child. They were all old friends, school chums, playmates, tennis partners. Only for a few years while she was busy with school and getting her small chain of gift shops started, had she not occasionally sat on that back porch with those girls. Grown now to women they had looked out at the heavy limbs of the sycamore and oak trees and the tangle of vines that the gardener left undisturbed. Once they had played there, getting grubby in the dirt beneath the vines. It was similar at her own house, inherited partially from her grandfather and purchased from her sister and brother.

She had looked at her own backyard and thought what a beautiful place for her child to play, just as she had played.

She had never, not once, considered the fact that three strange children would play there.

They were only photographs to her.

A smiling little girl, aged seven in the picture, with long, blond hair and light-colored eyes, not quite blue, and surprisingly dark, thick lashes, her face always smiling, was Faye's favorite. Maybe because she could imagine her own child looking like that. And also because she resembled Faye's own first grade picture, except Faye's hair had been even blonder than Ellen's, and her eyes had been a definite blue.

The little boy had a solemn face and looked older than his eight years. Dark and handsome like his dad, he was what some of Faye's friends called a heartbreaker.

The older girl, Beth, a pre-teen of twelve, had the same dark brown eyes of brother and father, and long, wavy dark brown hair. She had a pretty face, small nose, full lips, rounded chin. She resembled the woman in the large, family photograph, the mother.

Ellen's features were even and sweet, still too childish for genetic quirks to show up. In the pictures, she didn't resemble any of the others, neither brother nor sister, nor mother or father.

Three kids who had sent their school pictures to their dad.

And now they were coming here to live. To play in her backyard.

She had planned for them to come a few weeks during summer vacation , but she had never expected this.

But, of course, who had?

Getting up with a sigh, Faye pulled her robe closer around her body. She was bulging in front now, her five-month pregnancy beginning to show. Her reflection in the mirror brought a smile to her face. So far, she liked the way her figure was looking.

She went downstairs and out onto the brick stoop at the front of the house. No paper. At least not in sight. She walked down the curving brick walk, through the tall trees that forested the long front yard and kept it shady, and found the fat roll of newspaper on the top of a shrub. At least it's on top, she thought peevishly, and then thought in contrition, what's wrong with me? Can't I smile anymore at the peculiar places the paperboy leaves the paper? Those amusing, creative places? As though the boy worked at finding new places with which to surprise her, a kind of I-spy game in which the object was not a thimble, but a daily paper.

She unrolled the paper as she went up the walk, a coil of dread increasing with each word that became visible. The murder had appeared for a while on the front page because of her family's importance in the area. As soon as the relationship became known, there were pictures, stories, speculations picked up from the Los Angeles papers, and then embellished upon, adding each day that the murdered woman was the mother of the stepchildren of the locally prominent former Miss Faye Dover Featherston, of the Dover and Featherston family that had settled the community and helped create the town several generations ago. There were also calls from the local newspaper people asking questions, questions . . . none of which she could answer. It took several days to convince them she had never met the children, didn't know the mother, had no suspicions, speculations, even thoughts. Of course that wasn't entirely true. Of course she had thoughts, but not about the murder. That was far away from her own world and, she made it clear, was not to be brought any nearer. The children lived two thousand miles away and were not to be disturbed when, or if, they arrived at her house. By that time she was furious, and because of her family's earlier importance in the town, and old family money having remained in the area, now being controlled mainly be herself, the owner of the local paper hushed the story. Still, each time she unrolled the paper, it was with dread.

She went through the long central hall and out onto the terrace at the back of the house where she leaned over a table. She spread the paper and searched it hastily for that unwanted headline. When she didn't find it, she sat down, went back to the front page, and began to read.

"Hey, anybody home?"

Faye looked up. Nordene Summers, her neighbor on the west, was coming along the walk from the side gate. She was wearing a Sunday brunch coat, a short-sleeved, floral cotton, and carrying a plate of cinnamon rolls that literally oozed melted butter and brown sugar. The smell of the rolls came to Faye in a wave, mingling with the fragrance of honeysuckle and wisteria. Nordene had lived next door all her life, remaining there after her marriage fifteen years earlier, bringing up her children, Katy and Dwayne, who were ten and eight, in the same house where she had been brought up. Nordene and Faye were all that was left of the old families in the immediate area. The rest of the old homes had been sold and, in some cases, torn down so that more modern houses could be built. Down over the hill to the north, a shopping mall had taken over the residential section. It was within walking distance, if a person didn't mind walking a mile, just as the single grocery store that had originally been there had once been a nice bike ride away.

Nordene had never been one of Faye's friends. She was older by at least fifteen years, but she had become a friendly and welcome next door presence.

"Good morning, Nordene. What on earth are you planning to do, fatten me? As if I weren't fat already." Faye folded the newspaper and pushed it to one side to make room for the plate of rolls.

Nordene's face crinkled with her smile. Even her

nose developed a couple of wrinkles across the top when she grinned. Faye had grown used to it and saw it as cute, even pretty, though Gavin said she was a funny-looking little duck.

"I hope you haven't had breakfast, Faye. My bunch took off for a day of fishing, Sam and the kids. I packed them a lunch and told them to go on, but be sure not to fall out of the boat and into the river. I told Sam to be sure those kids wear their life jackets. Of course they raised a fuss. Life jackets can get hot and bulky, and the kids hate to wear them. But I insisted. Now whether or not they obey is another thing."

She sat down and began to pull apart one of the cinnamon rolls, taking off a strip that had a sugary, moist, spicy interior.

"So I said to myself, Nordene, since you're all alone and lonely, take your rolls over and see if Faye has eaten. There was a chance your husband might be home by now, but I guess he isn't."

Nordene cast an inquisitive eye up at Faye as she stuck a curled leaf of the roll into her mouth.

Faye smiled and remained standing, preparing to go after coffee. Ordinarily she would have laughed with affection and humor at Nordene's excuse for coming to see if Gavin and the kids had shown up yet, but today a smile was all she could muster. Nordene's decision to bring the rolls over had without a doubt been based more on finding out about Gavin than on being lonely. Her life was filled with people, as were the lives of most of those who had remained in their hometown, and especially in the same house in which they had lived as children. Southern families tended not to roam the country as much as their more adventuresome northern cousins, it seemed to Faye. Perhaps, she thought, it had a lot to do with atmosphere. Since she had come home, much of her former anxiety had dissipated . . .

until the phone call from California.

"No, he isn't home yet," Faye said. "I'll bring out a pot of coffee."

"Don't go to any trouble, Faye."

"No trouble at all. Certainly not the trouble those rolls cost you."

Nordene giggled, reminding Faye of a very young girl, letting her see for a second the girl Nordene used to be. Young, flirty, vivacious.

"Not me," Nordene said. "Don't tell my family, but I had Julie make these yesterday. Sam and Dwayne and Katy don't know that, but I don't mind if you do. They were ready to set to rise this morning and bake."

"I forget sometimes that Julie is still working for you. It seems she would have retired years ago."

"I stay dreading that she will want to. She's a lot older than Mom, well, six or seven years. But instead of getting fat and lazy, like me and Mom, she just got reedy. Wouldn't it be great to be reedy? Well, you're not fat, you're sort of the—uh—willowy type."

Faye laughed. "Not reedy, not yet, right? And not very willowy recently."

"That will pass. Julie still comes in twice a week, more if I need her, and I don't know what I'd do without her, bless her soul. I'm afraid when she's gone I won't be able to find daily help with as much dedication to the work. Julie keeps my house as if it were her own, bless her."

"Plus she's a fabulous cook."

"Oh, yes. She makes the world's best hushpuppies. Not at all greasy. Crisp. Ummm."

Faye had been standing and waiting for a hole in the conversation so she could run to the kitchen and bring out the coffee, but now had to interject an "Excuse me."

In the kitchen she drew hot water from the tap and

put it on the electric stove while she mixed instant coffee in a ceramic pot. There wasn't time to brew the coffee properly. At Nordene's house, Faye knew, a pot of perked coffee was kept hot and waiting all the time. Rich and dark and delicious. She added another spoonful of coffee to the pot to try to make it look more like the kind of coffee Nordene was used to.

She got matching cups and saucers and put them on a tray. She added a small cream pitcher and sugar bowl and a couple of napkins. When she carried the tray out, Nordene was looking through the paper. She sat back, looked up and put the paper aside almost guiltily.

"Oh my," she said. "That certainly didn't take you very long."

"At my house coffee making is not an art. I hope you don't mind."

"I didn't come to criticize your cooking, my dear girl. Oh, this looks fine. Had you read the paper yet?"

"Only the headlines."

Nordene bent her head over her cup and sipped. Her hair was medium brown, short and neatly waved. The hand that held the cup was pudgy but well groomed with nails manicured in pink polish and a diamond ring on her third finger that was within the bounds of safety, but which caught the filtered light that came through the treetops splintering it into rainbows. She was carefully not looking at Faye, and her voice was so controlled that Faye knew it covered a private turmoil.

"I hope you won't think I'm stepping out of bounds, my dear. But I've lived next door to you, and your mother while she lived, all your life, except for those years you were gone, and I do feel concern for you. Everything was going so well, and you were so happy. And you are in that stage of pregnancy where—well, you could still miscarry if you are subjected to—well, too much stress."

She cleared her throat with a soft sound deep in it. She sat back and daintily held a cinnamon roll between her thumb and third finger. "You know the story has been in our paper, too, and everyone else's around here, but of course we couldn't speak of it to you. That wouldn't have been kind. However, Sam said if I'm worried, I should say something. He's been following the story, too. That is . . . not with any thought that it might affect us. But Sam feels you should be warned. And he said as I'm a friend of the family—"

"Warned?"

"Well, there is a rumor that the children will be coming here to live, because it seems of course your Gavin is their father—"

Faye's own uneasiness about having Gavin's children enter her life on a permanent basis surfaced now in anger at Nordene, her husband Sam and all the other people who were probably gossiping behind her back. Nordene was the first to even mention the subject to her, other than the reporters from the newspapers. Under no circumstances was she going to discuss her doubts and dreads with anyone other than Gavin, and perhaps, in consideration of his feelings, not even with him. Nordene had overstepped the bounds of Southern propriety.

Faye said, "I can't see where that would affect you. I'm sure the children are well behaved. I'll see to it that they don't bother any of the neighbors."

Nordene closed a warm hand over Faye's and squeezed. "My dear! I wasn't thinking of myself, nor was Sam. We're concerned about you."

"But why? If they can adjust to the changes in their lives and accept me, I'm sure I can accept them."

"I'm sure you can. That isn't the problem. Haven't you been reading the stories about that murder? What must have really happened in that house? Didn't Gavin tell you?"

Faye stared into Nordene's brown eyes.

"Faye, there was no one there but the children. Even they said that. There was a witness who said no one entered or left the house during the time of the murder. She was parked nearby, a worker from somewhere, having her lunch, or something. A midnight snack. Resting."

Nordene sipped her coffee, and Faye waited, sensing Nordene had paused only for effect. She could feel her skin tightening, turning cold, and her defenses sharpening. Nordene looked up over her coffee cup rim.

"Who could have killed her but the children?"

Chapter Five

"That's preposterous!" Faye cried. "They're only seven, eight and twelve years old. Blythe was their mother! Children don't—" She paused, biting her lower lip.

"Don't they?" Nordene said softly. "What about that thirteen-year-old who shot his mother a couple of years ago, in our own neighborhood, so to speak?"

"But he had mental problems."

"Yes, so? And as for their ages, what about that two-year-old who battered the younger baby to death with a hammer, calling him a bad boy? That happened in Florida, not long ago, remember?"

Faye drew her sweater closer around her. "Those are horror stories, Nordene. These children are Gavin's children. Those children—well, we don't know them, don't know their backgrounds or anything."

"You don't know Gavin's children either, Faye. I wouldn't be saying these things, Faye, you know that, if I weren't concerned about you. You'll be staying with those kids of his for seven days a week if you take them into your home, while he'll be here only for the weekends. And you don't know what you're letting yourself in for."

Nordene reached out again and patted Faye on the arm, then she sat back. She had fulfilled her purpose in coming over, and now her facial expression changed and became smooth and almost blank. "I really think you should be on your guard. You'll be needing help, too, and I'm sure Julie either knows someone, or will help you out herself one day a week."

Faye looked into the tangle of large trees and undergrowth at the rear of the two-acre grounds that surrounded the house and at the narrow brick walk that wound toward it. Nordene's voice droned on, but Faye wasn't listening anymore. She wanted to get up and walk, be alone in her own yard. She couldn't be angry now at Nordene, even though the woman had added a new dimension to the problems Faye already faced.

She felt tired suddenly, as though she hadn't slept well in all these past nights.

"I hope," Nordene was saying, evidently seeing Faye's mental absence, "that I haven't upset you, dear. I would never, ever have said a word about this if I hadn't been concerned about you. I do think you should think very carefully before you bring those children into your home. Of course, perhaps someone else is taking them?"

"No, they're Gavin's. They're coming here," Faye said, feeling exhausted now. "They have no one else. Can you imagine your children in that situation, Nordene?"

Nordene said nothing. Faye could see her horror. It hadn't been a fully conceived thought, only a slip of the tongue. But Faye didn't feel like apologizing.

"How are Dwayne and Katy these days, Nordene?" she asked, her voice offering its apology in its tone. "I haven't seen them to speak to for weeks. Dwayne was riding his bike by the other day, but although I waved at him, he didn't see me. I was planting petunias in the flower beds on the front corner."

It was a question that served a purpose. Nordene would lose herself in talking about Katy and Dwayne and would then happily go home.

Faye sat quietly through several stories, listening more for the phone to ring than to Nordene's voice. Gavin had been calling her every night, but each night he said they might be able to leave the next day and he would call before they left. However, the days kept passing. The authorities continued to need them, for one thing or another. The hearing, further questioning. The funeral. Also, she supposed, realizing she had never given it thought before, there would be the necessity of disposing or storing Blythe's personal property so the house could be put on the market or otherwise secured for the children. Gavin had said nothing about any of that.

The phone didn't ring, and finally Nordene said her goodbyes and left.

Faye sat longer at the table. The sun had moved, and cool shade fell now where sunlight had warmed. Faye began to feel chilled.

She heard the gate click shut on the far side of the backyard as Nordene went through into her own spacious backyard. It too had a stand of tall trees, and the fence between was overgrown with vines and backed by shrubs, so that it was a perfect green wall between the two houses.

Faye got up and walked down the winding brick walk into the rear of the yard. It ended at a gazebo that had been built in a clearing of the trees. She went in and sat down on the bench, but stayed only a few minutes. She was too far away from the house to hear the phone if it rang, and she could think of little else.

She went back to the terrace and began to read the paper. There was no mention of the murder, she saw, even in the back pages. The relief was like air being let out of a balloon. The tension within her body dissolved.

In the middle of the afternoon the phone call came.

Gavin, sounding tired and faraway, asked, "How're you feeling?"

"Okay, and you?"

"Ready to come home. At last. Can you pick us up tomorrow?"

"Oh Gavin, yes! This has seemed such a long time without you. I'm so glad you're finally free. What time will you be in?"

"About four o'clock."

"I'll be waiting. I love you."

"I love you, too, Faye."

"The uh—children will be coming with you?" She immediately bit her lower lip, wondering why she had asked that. Of course they would. Where else would they go?

"Yes. They're looking forward to it, as much as they can look forward to anything right now. See you, Babe. Love you."

Gavin had put off until the last minute this duty that he most dreaded, going back into the house where Blythe had been murdered. He drove the rented car into the backyard and sat there, the front tires in the edge of the small amount of lawn that had been salvaged from the surrounding weeds and shrubs, though that too was brown, starved for water. The back patio of the house was only a few steps away. He could see the cracks in the old slab of cement. The back door of the screened porch had a sagging board off the right side of the frame, needing a good, solid nail to put it back in place.

It had been five years or more since he had visited

this house. At that time it was fairly well put together and not so much in need of paint. The lawn had been well cared for by Blythe's father. Then, there had been another house across the back fence, instead of a Seven-Eleven store.

After their separation almost four years ago, and then after Blythe had sold the house the two of them had been buying together and moved back here, he hadn't been to her home. He had moved to Texas and finally to Arkansas, at least partly, when he married Faye. Now it seemed that this part of his past was only a dream, faraway, receding daily. A not very pleasant dream. To be brought back into it now was nightmarish, and especially for this reason: Blythe murdered?

The kids had stayed in the motel. When he had told them he would have to go to their home and get their clothes they had looked at him with those wide, silent eyes that told him nothing. He knew the horror they must be living with. At least he thought he knew. Maybe he didn't. That they could even act half normal struck him as being incredible in their ability to cope. Their silence, their staying close to one another, seemed only natural at this point, though it was so unlike the active, talkative kids he had known. They had looked so tall and so thin. Their sweet young faces so mature. And their recognition of him had been a shock. They had been standing in a kind of huddle in the police station room, and they hadn't moved one step toward him. He had hugged and kissed each of them without getting a response. He had the sick feeling that he had become a stranger to them in this past year of absence.

He got out of the car and opened the trunk to get the suitcases he would need. At the last minute he had bought only three, deciding that he would take that many clothes and nothing more. They had a few things, purchased for them by a police matron. And when they got to Fort Smith, Faye could help them get new clothes. Or, he could. Perhaps he shouldn't saddle Faye with that responsibility. After all, he didn't really know how she was going to feel about having them around all the time, from now on. He couldn't ask her to take over such a responsibility.

He sat down on the step and stared at the ground. This feeling of sickness inside, of a great hollow place, had started the minute he had heard that his former wife had been killed, and had grown steadily wider ever since.

Maybe when he got back home and got settled— maybe when things worked out—when the baby was born—when time had passed—maybe . . .

He drew a long breath and stood up, pulling one suitcase up under his arm, carrying in his hands the other two. He crossed the screened porch. At the kitchen door he set one suitcase down and took the key out of his pocket.

The smell of the house hit him like an invisible pocket of gas when he stepped into the kitchen. It almost sent him back outside.

He stayed solid on the threshold, holding his breath as long as he was able, expelling it slowly. He began to breathe the stale, stinking air shallowly, trying not to be physically sick.

What in the living hell was that odor? Blood, death, rotting food that had been left on the table? And something else . . . a strong, sickeningly sweetish smell that he seemed to remember from somewhere. He tried to place it and couldn't. Smoke? Not tobacco—but something . . .

There was more to be done, and he had to work fast. He had forgotten about the appliances, the food, the cleaning up that had to be done.

He put the suitcases down in the middle of the floor and opened the door and windows of the kitchen, letting in smoggy air that was far better than the trapped air of death in the house.

He cleaned out the refrigerator, dumping the food into a box and feeling slightly shocked at the small amount that had to be dumped. Obviously Blythe hadn't shopped far ahead.

From the cabinet he took down boxes of cereal, Post Toasties and Raisin Bran, and boxes of Earth Grains macaroni and cheese. He remembered now that the kids had loved macaroni and cheese. He could remember Blythe saying, "I might as well not ever cook anything but macaroni and cheese and hot dogs. These kids won't eat anything else."

The echo of her voice filled the air around him, as if she had spoken again, and he became suddenly aware of the dark doorway behind him that led into the front of the house. It took a lot of self-control to keep from whirling around to see if she stood there, staring at him.

He had to get out of there. Now.

He unplugged the appliances, the refrigerator and toaster and microwave, and wiped his hands on a paper towel. The house could be attended to later, in a few months. Then, maybe, it would be easier to enter.

He picked up the suitcases and went through the dark hall to the stairs, carefully avoiding the arched doorway into the front room where they said her body had been found. But he couldn't help seeing the dark blotches on the stairs, the bloody tracks left by Ellen. They had been smeared to indistinct edges which, he guessed, was caused by Joey trying to wash them away. It had looked like an attempt at a cover-up, and puzzled the detectives. Joey had only said Beth told him to, and Beth had no explanation. They were scared kids, that was all, Gavin told the police. He resented any suggestion otherwise. What did they have to cover up?

The smell was not so strong in the upstairs. He stood in the dim hall and looked at the four doors, hoping he didn't accidentally go into Blythe's room. He couldn't bear that—seeing her personal belongings scattered about the way they used to be in the room he shared with her.

What was he going to do with all her things? Maybe he could hire someone to pack it away, to save it for the kids. He could think about it later.

He went to the open door on his right and found a small room with a narrow single bed. On the wall were posters that had to belong to Joey: muscle men and space ships, skeletons and robots. He didn't know who they were or what they indicated, but he supposed they were important fictional characters.

He opened the chest of drawers and found folded jeans and tee shirts, socks and shorts, pajamas. Some of it was neat, and some in a mess, indicating the handiwork of at least two people, one of them Joey, no doubt. He smiled mentally and stuffed the suitcase. There were toys in the corner, and he stood a moment looking at the pile, recognizing in plastic some of the figures on the wall. Although it stretched the suitcase beyond its intended limit, he added a few of the figures. Then, he pulled the pillowcase off the pillow, and filled it, too. Shipping it home might be a problem, and there was a chance Joey would not want to see these things again. Might they now have negative connotations? Well, he'd have to take that chance.

Across the hall he found Ellen's room, and from her toys he chose one old doll, the one that looked most handled.

The other two doors were shut, and he hesitated,

then decided that Beth's room would probably be next to Ellen's.

He opened the door slowly.

Another narrow, single bed. Unmade. A young girl's clothes were scattered about. A blouse hanging on a doorknob, a pair of jeans over the small vanity bench. Beth's room. Quickly he filled the last suitcase until it bulged. He zipped it shut and fastened the belt. There were clothes left hanging in the closet here just as there were in the other two rooms, and personal items that would have to stay, at least for the time being.

He wanted out of the house. Now that he was not busy, he was aware of the strange silence within the walls and of the odor drifting up from downstairs.

He would have to make two trips, but first, he was going to take it all to the foot of the stairs.

He carried down one heavy suitcase and the pillowcase of toys and left them in the lower hall, carefully avoiding even a glance toward the shadowy archway. When he went back upstairs, he decided to bring a few more of the girls' things and filled another pillowcase. Struggling under the load, he took the final two suitcases and the partly filled pillowcase down the stairs and out to the car.

He stood on the porch then and watched the traffic in and around the store across the fence. The reality of the daily world, of people putting gas in their cars, going in and out of the store, a kid eating a candy bar as he got on his bicycle, was suddenly one of the most refreshing sights he had seen. The shrubs and trees between the fence and patio put up just enough of a veil for him to be unnoticed by any of them.

He remembered what the police had said about the nignt of the murder.

The store had closed a few minutes past eleven, and the clerk had gotten in her car, which was parked against the fence, and had sat there a long time eating a sandwich and drinking a Seven-Up. She had been looking at the house because it was in her line of view. She could see a faint light through the kitchen windows, just as she always did. But no one had come to the back door, either from the inside or the outside, while she sat there, and she had not driven away from the parking lot until after midnight. She had been listening to music, she said, after she ate. And just sitting. No one had come to the house. She could see the walk to the front door, too, from the street light on the corner beyond.

The murder had occurred around midnight, the pathologist had determined, and the house had been quiet.

Blythe had been alone in the house with her three children.

Ellen said very little. She couldn't remember.

Neither Beth nor Joey said much of anything. "Joey's hands shook and his chin jerked when he was questioned," the police had said, "the boy's nerves couldn't take it." They hadn't questioned him much.

Gavin found himself frowning intently at the garish rear of the convenience store and hardly seeing it. He turned away and forced himself to reenter the house, to go boldly across the kitchen, his footsteps loud and hollow-sounding, to go on into the narrow, dim hall and to the luggage he had left at the foot of the stairs.

He got a suitcase in each hand, and when he straightened and turned, he was facing the dark living room. The time would come when he would have to go in there, unless he were to turn it all over to a real estate company to sell it as it was, furniture and all.

He could see the old floral rug on the living room floor and the dark blotches and streaks of blood. The draperies were tightly drawn over the bay windows at the front, creating a near-dark twilight in the room. That smell—that smoky, sweetish smell—was stronger here than at any place in the house.

... and Ellen had whispered to him finally and said there had been a lot of dark smoke, and the monster had come out of that, too ... she could remember seeing the monster ...

What had the child seen?

Maybe the answer was in there, in that darkened living room with the blood-soaked rug. Maybe he should go in and look.

He stood on the strip of bare floor that separated the hall carpet from the rug on the living room floor and looked in. The room was small for a living room. Old-fashioned. Most of the furniture there had belonged to Blythe's parents.

Across the room was a television, and on each side were chairs with footstools. At the left end of the room he could see a sofa. The light there had been on according to the police. It was off now. To his immediate left, against the inner wall, stood the old upright piano. He could see only the end of it. The walls? The walls were papered, a vining flower on geometric frames, once gold and green, it had turned to varying shades of brown.

Gavin stepped back and went toward the open door at the back of the house, his hollow footsteps resounding through the old frame house. He put his load down, stood looking thoughtfully at his feet, then he took a hammer and nails from the drawer where his father-in-law had kept tools for the house, went back upstairs to the bedrooms and pulled a blanket off a bed.

He took it downstairs, brought a chair from the dining room and, using it as a ladder, nailed the blanket over the arched door.

He returned the tools to the kitchen drawer, put the luggage into the car, then returned just long enough to securely lock the door.

Ellen huddled in a lounge at the side of the swimming pool, the sun spilling warm and unobstructed on her body. Even so, she held her legs tight in her arms and lay just enough on her side to be able to have a full view of the area beyond the pool. There, the shrubs grew, and she had seen one of the shrubs move just a bit. She stared so hard at it that the shrub and the wall behind it began to blur.

Beth and Joey were in the pool. Someone had left a big ball and a lifesaver in the pool, and Joey was throwing the ball to another little boy who was also playing in the pool. Their dad had tried to get Ellen to go in to the motel room before he left to go get their clothes, but she hadn't wanted to. There were shadows in the pool that might be the beginnings of the monster.

But it was really hiding in the shrub, she decided when she saw the shrub move.

It slipped around so silently, forever just at the edge of her vision.

Sometimes, she realized, she was just afraid it was there.

Somebody dived into the pool near her, and water splashed out onto her bare arms and legs. She stared at the droplets, seeing the reflections of colors, of green and blue and the red of Beth's new bathing suit as she climbed out of the pool. The colors shimmered and faded as the drops disappeared.

She wished her daddy hadn't gone back to the house.

Beth's legs, getting so tanned, flashed in front of her as she ran by, and Ellen looked up in surprise. Their daddy was coming along the walk by the side of the motel, and Beth had gone to meet him. It was the first time Beth had run to meet their father, and Ellen followed her. Immediately she saw he had something familiar in his hand. Her old rag doll, Susan. She started to reach for it and to touch his hand to be sure he was here, safely back from the house. But then she stopped, eavesdropping on Beth as she talked to him.

"Daddy, did you finish there? Did you—get everything?"

"No. Just what I thought would tide you over until you can go shopping with Faye. She'll help you get whatever you need. I only brought one suitcase for each of you and a few toys."

"Are you ready to leave here now?"

"Yes. Our plane leaves tomorrow morning just before lunch."

"I don't want to go there, Daddy."

"Why not?"

"Daddy..." Beth looked at the ground, standing close to him, her hands on his wrist. "Daddy, do we have to go live with her? Couldn't we live with you in Dallas? At your apartment? I promise I would do the cleaning. I can even do laundry. Mama taught me. I did the laundry when she was working."

"I know, I don't doubt you can; but sometimes I'm sent to other places, Beth, and I don't get back to the apartment for several days. I'm away from it more than I'm there. You'll like Faye when you get to know her."

"But... how about Aunt Jane's? Could I go there? I wouldn't be any trouble."

"Beth, Aunt Jane is in her eighties. She's been alone for years, and she probably likes it that way now."

"Then she needs me, Dad. She needs someone to stay with her."

"She has her daughter right next door, and her grandchildren and even a great-grandchild now.

Besides, Beth, you haven't even seen her since you were five or six years old. My home is with Faye, and that's where you belong."

"But . . . I'm *afraid,* Daddy."

"Of what?" he asked, beginning to sound impatient and tired. He had wrinkles at the corners of his eyes, Ellen saw, and the edges of his hair, above his ears, were turning white.

Beth turned and saw Ellen, and she pressed her lips together and said nothing more. The look in Beth's eyes was for a moment hostile and distant, and Ellen felt a cold wind brush her heart.

Their dad handed the doll to Ellen and put his hand on the back of Beth's neck and shook her slightly as if she were a little dog. "Hey," he said. "You'll love it in Fort Smith. Your stepmother is a great person, you know she is, or I wouldn't have married her. She lives in a big house on a hill with lots of room, and there are plenty of kids in the neighborhood to play with. There are a couple right next door named Katy and Dwayne that are about Ellen and Joey's age. And I'll be there every weekend, to be with you. You'll like her, Faye, when you meet her."

But Ellen knew it wasn't the stepmother Beth was afraid of. And knowing this, she felt abandoned by everyone. She reached out to touch Beth's hand, but Beth drew away and went back to the pool.

Beth swam with her eyes closed, her head under water, back and forth across the pool. Once her hand brushed somebody's legs, and she swerved aside and kept swimming. When she could hold her breath no longer, when her lungs felt a screaming need for air, she put her face out of the water and gasped, filling her lungs with air. Replenished, she swam again with her head under water.

She was torn by her feelings. On the one hand she couldn't stand to have Ellen near her, when she remembered what she had done. But then she'd think—it couldn't have been Ellen. Ellen was too little to do that. Besides, Ellen loved their mother just like she did, like Joey did. There was no way Ellen could have killed her.

And yet, she'd had the blood all over her.

She didn't want to live with Ellen anymore because she was afraid, part of the time, when she was around her. When Ellen came up so quietly behind her, she was startled. And another thing... what if Ellen did the same thing to their stepmother she had done to their mother?

But, on the other hand, she felt responsible for Ellen. She wanted to protect her. She didn't want the police to know what she had done. To have Ellen taken away and put in jail would be terrible. She couldn't live with it.

She came up for air again and opened her eyes. Water blurred her vision so that the lines of the motel were wavy, and the chair Ellen sat in seemed crooked. Ellen herself, in a lounge chair playing with her doll, examining its face and straightening its wilted old bonnet and dress, was like someone reflected in a crooked mirror. But...

Beth gasped.

A figure towered above Ellen, bending low over her. She saw a grossly fat, naked body like a cloud behind Ellen's chair, with huge rolls of fat hanging from his face to his thighs. Yet he had no legs, only a tapering, thinning strand of flesh, like melted wax. But his face seemed the most horrible, the slick, hairless head, the great hanging jowls, the eyes that were mere slits in the flesh, hiding the black pupils that stared at the little girl . . .

Beth started to scream, to warn Ellen.

Ellen looked up, straight at her, unaware of the gross, hideous danger that was, in some way, going to destroy her.

Behind Beth, as if they were unaware of the monstrous, naked man who wore only, Beth saw now, a kind of thin diaper beneath his hanging flesh, the other swimmers played and splashed. The beach ball bounced over the surface of the water past Beth, and Joey raced after it.

Beth brushed her hand across her eyes to clear the water away, and her vision cleared. She stared, astonished. There was no one hovering behind Ellen.

Chapter Six

Faye waited in the passageway that led into the airport terminal and watched the people surge out intermittently from each plane landing. When at last she spotted Gavin among the crowd coming toward her, the eagerness she had felt turned inexplicably to anxiety.

They would not be alone.

For the first time since they had met and fallen in love they would not be free to do just as they wished, to make love without restraint, to relax and talk openly. Seeing him made her yearn for the warmth and passion of his large, smooth body, his marvelous weight heavy on her, his strength capable of destroying her, yet his touch so gentle. She needed him to take her home and hold her, for hours and hours.

But the children were there, following him.

The crowd thinned and passed by her, and she waited.

The tall young Beth was taller than she had expected. Her long, dark hair was pulled back into a ponytail, and her dark eyes looked at Faye without smiling, with only the faintest recognition.

The young boy in the pictures was at Beth's elbow, and like his sister, he was not quite what Faye had expected. His solemn face was thinner than in the school picture, which was several months old now. His skin was tanned, as if he'd been sunbathing lately, or spending long hours in the swimming pool.

The little girl came behind them. Her eyes were darting back and forth as if they were searching the crowd for someone other than Faye. The eyes came to Faye and lingered briefly, then gazed on past her, apprehension obvious in her every nervous turn. The smile that was captured in every picture that Faye had ever seen of her was missing.

She carried a small suitcase in one hand. And under her free arm, clutched tightly in the crook of her arm, was a limp, large, ugly rag doll. A creature that had gone through countless nights of being hugged and slept on, no doubt, who had suffered through tears and heard laughter. But had never been put aside for a new doll.

The three children walked together a few feet away from Gavin, as though they didn't know him very well.

Faye moved forward, then stopped. Gavin's eyes, haunted, tortured, said in silence that he had not told her everything.

Ellen felt as if she had just awakened, and that everything was all right. As if the night and the nightmares were gone. They had come a long way today, high and fast, and she had looked for the monster in every face, in every hiding place in the body of the plane that she could see from her seat, and it was not there. She had hoped that it would stay behind, hidden in the shrubs at the motel pool, or perhaps gone back into the house where it had killed Mama.

She couldn't allow herself to feel homesick. It was as though she had stepped through an invisible wall into another world. She adjusted the doll under her arm, got a tighter grip on the small suitcase she carried and followed the others out of the airport terminal and to the waiting car.

It was a big white car with a red plush interior. Big enough for all five of them to sit in. She sat in the middle in the back seat and found it difficult to see out past Beth and Joey, but it didn't matter. She looked at the back of Faye's head, and her dad's, and sometimes she saw their profiles as they talked to each other.

They stopped on the way home at a restaurant to eat, and Ellen found herself hungry. She looked around at the dark panel and the bright wallpaper, and all the people who sat beneath the muted lights, and began to be sleepy.

It was almost dark when they left the restaurant. Lights had come on along the curving streets and in the houses. They drove up a hill where it seemed there were more trees than houses, and finally the car turned into one of the forests of trees and slowly moved along a long driveway to stop beneath a roof that was attached to a huge, dark house. The lights of the car revealed a red brick wall with vines climbing on it. Beth's elbow jabbed into her side.

"Wake up, Ellen," she said.

"I'm awake." Ellen realized she had let her head fall to one side to rest on Beth's shoulder. But she had only been trying to see through the darkness behind the house.

When she got out of the car, she saw there were some other houses, but not close. Through the trees she could see their lights.

They went into a hall and stood together waiting, she, Beth and Joey. Their stepmother, Faye, smiled at them, as if she didn't know anything to say either.

Ellen looked over her shoulder, but the shadows in the corners of the hall were empty.

"We might as well get them to bed," Gavin said. "I know they're all tired."

They followed the grown-ups upstairs and down another long hall almost to its end. Three doors, two on one side, and one other door across the hall, stood open, and Faye turned on lights in each of the rooms. Then she smiled at them again in the hall.

She was beautiful in the pale light of the hall. The embroidered Hawaiian muu-muu she wore was a deep purple with glistening white, and it made her skin look pretty and pale.

"I've fixed up these three rooms for you, but if you'd rather share one big room, that can easily be arranged."

Beth and Joey shook their heads.

"No thank you," Beth said in that dignified voice that she used around teachers and sales women. Ellen recognized it as being slightly strained and ill at ease.

Joey sounded more like himself when he said, "I don't want to share a room with them."

"Then maybe you'll like this one," Faye said, touching his shoulder lightly, guiding him toward the room across the hall. "It was my brother's room, and some of his model airplanes are still there, as well as some other boy things. I know he would like for you to have it all for your own if you want it."

Joey had a pleased look on his face when he passed over the threshold.

Ellen peeked into his room to see a comfortable, double bed against the wall, with desks, shelves and bookcases lining two other walls, leaving an opening only for the window, while beneath it there was also a desk. It was a small room, not much larger than the one he'd had back home, and it was so filled with model airplanes, metal cars on shelves and books, that it looked lived-in already. Ellen could see that Joey liked it.

Ellen waited, standing in the hall beside Beth.

In a few minutes Faye was back with them again, and their dad was coming up the hall carrying a load of suitcases. The deep emptiness of the long hallway seemed to push away from him as he drew nearer, and Ellen felt more at ease.

He had been almost like a stranger, like someone they hadn't seen for a very long time. But his presence helped to make her feel warm and safe. She knew he would take care of them.

"This room," Faye said, looking at Beth, "belonged to my sister, Janet. It's also what we call the blue room. And this, Ellen, was my room. If you don't like these rooms, we can find others."

Gavin said, "But not tonight, please girls. They'll be fine, won't they? Aren't you going to thank Faye for all the trouble she's gone to?"

They mumbled thanks, embarrassed, ill at ease in this strange house with this strange lady who was married to their father.

Ellen put her doll to bed first, and then, after her bath in the bathroom a few doors down the hall, found that the sheets were smooth and sweet-smelling and the bed soft and comfortable. With her head resting on a softness like a cloud—like the clouds she had seen out of the window of the plane—Ellen fell asleep.

Faye rested with her head on Gavin's chest. She could hear the beating of his heart, slow and steady now that he was relaxed. The sheet over them was cool, the breeze coming in the open windows soft and fragrant. She lay with one arm across him, and her leg drawn up and resting on his thighs. His skin was warm against hers, with the closeness of their bodies, and feeling even closer in their nudity.

His arm, curled around her with his large hand clasping her shoulder lightly, gave her a sense of security that she was reluctant to leave, even though she had to get up and take a shower.

They hadn't talked yet, they had made love. She felt that he needed to talk. She waited.

The moment she had most dreaded was over. The meeting with the children had been awkward, but no more awkward for her than for them. She thought of them in their rooms, settled now, grouped at the end of the central hall. They seemed satisfied with the rooms she had given them, yet how could one tell? They were so quiet. They had talked hardly at all even during their hour of dinner in the restaurant. She hadn't heard a sound from them since she and Gavin had closed the bedroom door.

She hadn't thought of them at all for a while, but now she could almost palpably feel their presence in the house.

"I hated to do this to you," Gavin said softly, as if he could read her thoughts. "Having the kids come for the summer was all I thought would ever happen, and really, I doubted Blythe would let them come for more than a couple of weeks. If I were settled here in my own business instead of being gone all week, I wouldn't feel like I was dumping such a job on you. If you want me to settle them in Dallas, I'll see what I can do."

"Of course not. They're yours and that makes them mine. We'll get acquainted and it'll work out."

She longed to offer him financial assistance again to start his own office closer to home. But she knew he would refuse. He was an independent soul, and she understood how he felt, she thought, even though at times she wished he'd forget his determination to do it all on his own. He had known when he married her that she had inherited quite a lot of money from her grandparents, and for a while before he finally relented, she had been afraid that he would let it scare him off. So she didn't offer now to help him out financially. He knew it was available whenever he changed his mind.

She admired his independence and could only guess at how he had felt about bringing his children to her. But she would love him just as much if he weren't so proud and stubborn.

"We'll have a good summer," she said, reassuring herself as much as him. "It won't be so lonely during the week now that they're here."

His hand tightened on her shoulder. "Don't expect too much, okay? They've changed a lot since their mother and I got our divorce. They don't seem like the kids I used to know so well, and it's no wonder. What they've been through would change anybody."

"Gavin, do the police have any suspects?"

"No, not that I know of. I . . ." He paused, and then added with an emphasis, "No."

Faye stared at the ceiling. The light from the private, adjoining bathroom was on, the door half closed, leaving the bedroom deeply shadowed. But the ceiling had a broad streak of light across it, and the slowly revolving ceiling fan cast a long shadow. Faye watched it flicker, flicker as the fan moved. The sound the fan made was soft and comforting, a familiar steady, low-pitched whir. She had begun to think Gavin had gone to sleep when he spoke again.

"They were alone. The kids were upstairs in bed. She

was downstairs in the living room. The witness said no one entered or left. The windows and front door were locked, and Joey said the back door was locked, too. The witness saw no prowler, or anyone."

"Couldn't the killer have entered earlier? Before the witness went to her car? And left afterward, after she was gone? Just how reliable a witness was she?"

"Very reliable, the police seem to think." His voice was low. "Also, Beth's and Joey's stories differed. She said the back door was open, but he said it was bolted."

She whispered, "Gavin, that isn't possible. She was murdered, stabbed to death by someone."

He stared upward at the fan, too, and when she turned her head slightly she could faintly see the frown of worry and concentration on his face.

"No," he said, "the autopsy found no fatal stab wound."

"But the paper said . . . she'd been slashed."

"Yes. But the cause of death was not a stab to the heart or any other part of the body. She'd been disemboweled and died of shock."

"Oh my God."

"There was also heart damage. They thought she probably lost consciousness almost immediately."

"Small blessing."

"You might as well know, Faye. My own children were the only suspects. But although it seems like I don't know them very well anymore, I know them better than that. They didn't do it."

He cupped her hand between his palms and turned so that he could see into her eyes. She hoped he didn't notice the coldness of her hands. She wanted desperately to believe his children had not murdered their mother, but there was an anxiety rising, about to break surface and become an open fear, to express itself in a thought she hadn't wanted to acknowledge. If they were there, and the house was locked, and there had been no visitors, then they had to know more about it than they had told. She hadn't wanted to think it, but there it was.

"But it's in the past, Faye," he said, a yearning, a pleading in his voice that caused her heart to constrict painfully. "I want the kids to forget and be happy. I feel so much better having them here, and I hope it won't be a burden on you. Whatever happened to their mother happened far away from here, and I'm determined it won't affect our lives."

She held him and kissed him, and he relaxed. But she held him in silence, staring into the shadowed corners of the room. She heard his breathing lengthen and deepen, and when he was fully asleep she withdrew from him and went to take her shower.

She had left the hall light on, and a soft glow fell from their bedroom door to the top of the stairs and back into the hall where the children's bedrooms were. Before she went to bed she opened the bedroom door and looked out, but the house was as silent as it usually was. With the door left open she went back to bed.

Although the bed was king-sized, and there was plenty of room for her to lie comfortably without touching Gavin, she eased closer. She needed the warmth of his skin against hers. He was covered with the sheet blanket pulled up to his chest, his bare arms lying free on the white blanket.

Beyond the bed the front double windows were open, and a breeze billowed the thin curtains into the room, then died away, letting them fall back again. The air was fresh and cool. She could smell the river, it seemed, which wound through the valley a good walk away.

Faye closed her eyes.

A faintly harsh, acrid smell made her nose burn.

She wrinkled her nose and turned her head, trying to escape it. Then she realized what it was, and she came out of her half-doze and sat up, alert.

Smoke.

She turned her head toward the window, trying to locate its source. It didn't smell like a leaf fire, or even a trash fire. Burning trash outdoors was not allowed within the city limits, but occasionally, on the outskirts, the rule was broken.

She got out of bed and went toward the open bedroom door.

The smell of the smoke was even more concentrated in the hall, but the smoke detectors that were scattered strategically through the house had not been activated.

She hurried downstairs and knew before she was halfway down the stairs that the source of the smoke was not there. The air was fresh and clear again. So it was somewhere, she thought as she looked up the stairway, on the second floor, or maybe even in the attic.

She climbed the stairs and stood where the halls came together in a large area above the stairway. The smoke was gone, as mysteriously as it had come, it had gone.

So, she decided, it must have come in from outdoors.

Vastly relieved, she started back toward her bedroom.

There was a sound behind her, a mere whisper in the silence.

Faye turned.

Ellen was standing in the opening to the rear hall, staring straight ahead. Faye started to speak to her, and then felt a curling of chills move up her spine and across both shoulders. She stared at the child.

Ellen looked as if she had been hypnotized. She stood with her arms limp at her sides, with her chin high and still. Her steady, unblinking gaze was aimed somewhere past Faye, past any certain point in the house.

As Faye watched, she began to move again, going slowly forward.

Faye knew then. Ellen was asleep. She had no idea where she was or what she was doing.

Chapter Seven

Faye approached Ellen quietly. As if Ellen sensed that someone was near, she stopped. She seemed hardly to be breathing.

Faye put her hands gently on the child's shoulders and turned her back the way she had come. Ellen began to walk forward, with Faye's hands guiding her back toward her bedroom.

She got into bed willingly and immediately huddled into a little knot on her side, her palms together and tucked under her cheek. Her eyes closed and she drew a long sigh.

She was asleep.

Faye pulled the blanket up over her shoulders. Light from the muted hallway bulbs barely penetrated the room, but Faye didn't turn on the bedside lamp.

When she went back to the doorway, in preparation to leave it seemed she could smell the smoke again. She stood still, looking back over her shoulder into the small, heavily shadowed bedroom.

It was almost as if Ellen herself had been smoking here, some stinking, poisonous weed. But of course that was ridiculous.

*   *   *

Nordene said to Sam, her husband, "You know they came today, don't you, Sam?"

They were in the den, both of them leaning back in comfortable recliners, watching the Carson show. Sam muted the television and yawned. He never got through the show, had no idea how they ended it. About halfway through he always gave it up and went to bed.

"Those kids," Nordene said. "Right next door now."

"What time did they get here?"

"Well, I don't know. I haven't seen them. But Faye was supposed to pick them up at the airport late this afternoon, five or six, probably, the way planes are nowdays."

"So Dwayne and Katy haven't met them yet."

"No, and Sam, I don't know if they should."

"Of course they should. For the first time they've got playmates next door. It will help keep them occupied."

"Sam, those kids may be murderers."

"Nonsense."

"You don't know they're not."

"And you don't know they are. Let's give them the benefit of doubt and leave them alone. It will be good for Dwayne to have a buddy in the neighborhood, and Katy, too."

"I don't feel good about it. I worry about Faye, too, being alone all week with them. Who knows what might happen?"

"I hope you don't talk like this with anyone else."

"No, of course not."

"Well, forget it. They're three kids who've come here to live, and our kids are lucky enough to have playmates next door for the first time in their lives. It'll be good for them."

He returned the sound to the television in the midst of laughter and a joke he had missed.

"Wonder what was so funny?" he asked Nordene, but she only grunted.

Joey had never seen such intense green. It was everywhere. The trees were deep, rich green, and grass grew where the vines didn't. Even the shadowy places beneath the trees and bushes were green. It was almost like the air itself was green. But it wasn't. He had gone out to stand in the street the first thing and looked up, and the sky was a bright blue.

As far as he knew, he was the first one up this morning. But he couldn't stay in bed. As soon as his window got light, sleep was gone. He had dressed and found his way out of the big house. He had gone downstairs and found double doors right there at the front. But he hadn't known how to unlock them. So he had followed the hallway back into the house, where he eventually came to a kitchen. That door had a lock he could handle.

Once he had gotten outside he had begun to run.

It was great, this freedom he felt.

It was as if he had been born again. That heavy, old dragged-down feeling was gone. The fear was gone, and the dread, and he didn't want to remember it anymore. He didn't want to remember how much he missed his mother either, and the sadness of her memory returned to him. They were safe here, he and his sisters.

The front of the yard was long and wide, and it was filled with tall trees, almost like a forest. The only difference was the trees weren't that close, and the ground beneath them was grassy; and sometimes, in places, there were shrubs that were blooming, and flowers. The driveway was long and straight down the left side of the yard, against a wall of green that was, he found on examination, a wall with vines growing on it. On the other side of the wall he could see the upper story of a big house that was made of white brick, not red like this one. There were trees in that yard, too, but not as many as here.

In the backyard he found buildings. One of them was a long garage that had two cars in it and, to his utter delight, an old buggy. But he didn't touch it, he only walked around it, his eyes bugging in wonder.

Another of the buildings was two-story, like the house, only smaller. It had small rooms off a hall that had no floor. The rooms had fronts that were gates, rather than walls, and it seemed to him he could smell the horses that used to live there. Harnesses still hung on the walls, and there was a wagon, its tongue propped up on a piece of a tree, a short log. A stump.

It was fantastic. He only wished he had someone to share it with.

There was a hole in the green of the back fence, he saw, when he reluctantly left the barn. He carefully closed the small door through which he had entered. He'd have to ask *her* if he could go into the barn, and he wanted to show it all to Ellen. She'd like it, too. He wished she'd wake up and come on outside.

He went to the hole in the green and saw there was a narrow gate leading through into the neighbor's backyard. The gate was made of wrought iron, and he clutched the bars and put his face through.

He half-screamed and jerked back.

Another face was on the other side, and it jerked back, too.

Then they looked at each other.

Joey saw a young face, with freckles on the tipped-up nose and reddish-blond hair falling down on the forehead. All in all it seemed to belong to someone about his own age and sex.

"Hi," it said. "My name is Dwayne."

"I'm Joey."

"You can come over to my house if you want to."

But at that moment a woman's voice called, "Dwayne? It's breakfast time."

Dwayne looked over his shoulder, but his hands held on to the bars just below Joey's. Into the path behind him came a short, plump woman with a nose like Dwayne's. She put her hands on Dwayne's shoulders and looked over his head at Joey.

"Hello," she said. "You must be Faye's stepson."

"Yes."

"His name is Joey," Dwayne said. "Can he come and eat breakfast with me?"

"I expect he has to eat at his own house, Dwayne." She smiled at Joey as if in apology for not adding her invitation to her son's. "Come along now."

"Can we play later?" Dwayne asked, relinquishing his hold on the iron bars of the gate, looking back at Joey wistfully.

"Later we have to go shopping," the mother said, drawing him away. Then she said, "Maybe sometime. Goodbye, Joey."

"Bye, Joey." Dwayne waved. "I'll see you later."

"Okay."

Joey stood with his face pressed between the bars of the gate, watching the pair go along a path to the open terrace at the back of the house. He watched until they disappeared from his view.

With them, oddly, went his feeling of freedom and joyousness.

He released his hold on the gate, followed the path through the grass and found himself at the rear of his stepmother's house, by a terrace similar to the one next door. He sat down on the steps to wait for someone else to get up and come downstairs.

Ellen lay in the center of her bed and listened to the strange sounds in this strange place. Back home the freeway had roared like a great river, especially early in the morning and again in the evening when the workers used it to go to work, or go home. But here it was quiet except for birds singing in the trees.

She could see a tree through her open window. Its green limbs were covered in leaves and made a wall just feet from the window.

She didn't feel like moving yet. Her doll still lay with its head on the other pillow, and she put her hand on its body and felt the comfort of having it so close once again. During all the weeks they had lived in the motel she'd been without her doll.

Something was in her mind, but so far back she couldn't reach it well enough to remember. It was a dream . . . that much she knew. It was like she had stood on an opening in the earth, had teetered there, had almost fallen in. But it hadn't been the earth that was reaching for her, it was something else.

Why was she trying to remember it? She didn't want to know.

She got out of bed and found her clothes. They had unpacked when they reached their rooms, she and Beth and Joey, and the lady had helped each of them some, telling them where the clothes went.

Ellen pulled open the drawer of the chest and took out clean panties and a pair of jeans. She found a blouse on a hanger in the closet.

The bed, she remembered, just as she was ready to leave the room. She mustn't forget to make her bed.

She spread it up smoothly, working hard to get the

lumps out from beneath the bedspread. Then with her doll under her arm she went out into the hall.

Joey's room was empty she saw without even going to his doorway. The door stood wide open, and his bed, made but looking very sloppy, was in full view.

She went on to the next room. The door was almost shut, and she put her hand against it and eased it open.

Beth screamed, then, cried out, "Good God, don't do that, Ellen!"

Ellen stopped on the threshold, looking at her sister. Beth sat on the side of her unmade bed, putting on her sandals.

"Don't do what?"

"Don't startle me like that. You scared me half to death."

"All I did was push your door open."

"Well, don't push my door open anymore. You know that when a door is shut you have to knock. Mom taught you to always knock on a door, didn't she? You know she did. So after this, *knock*. Just because she's dead now doesn't mean you can forget all she taught you, for gosh sakes."

"Don't say that!" Ellen cried, bursting into tears. "Don't call her that!"

"What?"

"Dead! Don't say that anymore."

Beth stood up, her own face crumpling, yet her eyes remaining dry. She looked for a moment as if she might come to Ellen and comfort her, but she didn't move. Her voice, when she spoke, was compassionate.

"But she is, Ellen. She is."

"But you didn't have to say it. I can't stand to hear you say that anymore." Ellen was weeping wildly, and her body trembled as if a violent storm had surrounded her.

Through the funeral, through all the days before and

after the funeral, she had not cried. Even when they were taken at last to see their mother, and then found that they could not see her after all for the casket was permanently locked, and they would never see her again, she had not cried. But now it came out. The new house, the feeling of safety was gone. She realized it had been gone since she woke this morning, or perhaps since her dream last night—whatever it was—whenever it was. She screamed her emotions at Beth, her sister, and saw Beth respond, her face turning pale, and then red. And then the words came out. The true words. The true feelings.

"If you don't want to face the fact that she's dead, Ellen," Beth screamed, "then you shouldn't have done what you did to her!"

"I didn't do anything!"

"You did, you killed her!"

Ellen covered her ears and screamed, but the accusation was there, in the open, explaining why Beth drew away from her in small ways now.

. . . killed her . . . killed her . . .

Their dad stood in the doorway, large, nearly filling it. He reached for Ellen and held her against him until her cries subsided. Over her head he watched Beth, her face bleak and tearful. He could see the sorrow in her face, but she had said too much. She couldn't just say she was sorry and it would be gone.

"Beth, Ellen, listen to me," Gavin said. "Ellen, no one really believes you killed your mother. Beth, why don't you apologize to your sister for saying that?"

Beth looked in misery up at her father. "I can't, Daddy. Ellen . . . she had blood all over her that morning after Mama was killed. She had been downstairs, in the living room. I saw the blood, and the tracks; and I went down to see what caused it, and I found Mama." She was weeping.

This was the first she had told him on Ellen. She had skirted the questions from the police, never really admitting anything. But the tension had been building up in her to its present intolerable force. She had gotten so she couldn't bear to have Ellen near her. She was afraid of her, more and more. And yet, she hurt for her. Hurt so badly inside that her sleep was increasingly disturbed. Nightmares, like pieces of jigsaw puzzles, lingered in her memory when she woke from sleeping. Horrible bits that she could not put together.

And now, here in this strange place, a strange world with a woman who was their stepmother, she could bear it no longer. She hadn't wanted to come here. Now she knew, she had not wanted to live with Ellen anymore, even though it tore her heart out to think of leaving her.

"Daddy," Beth murmured, "Ellen was all—I mean—there was no one else. Mama... didn't do it to herself."

"I *didn't*," Ellen wailed, her face against her father's shirt, her arms around his waist. Her muffled voice sounded choked. "I didn't, I didn't. It was the monster... the monster..."

Gavin said, "Beth listen to me carefully. It happened in the night. After all of you were asleep, right?"

Beth nodded, her tear-filled eyes watching him desperately, as if he had all the answers, if he would only release them.

"None of you know who she might have let into the house that night. They could have let themselves out of the house again, the—the back way."

Beth was already shaking her head. "It was bolted, Daddy, just like the front door. I unbolted it myself."

Ellen wept, "The monster. It was the monster."

Beth saw that Faye had come to stand in the hall behind her father. But she was only standing there, saying nothing.

"Beth," Gavin said. "It could not have been Ellen. You see, Beth, Blythe was raped."

Raped.

Beth gasped. She gaped at them all, Gavin, Faye, and Ellen hugged against Gavin.

"But . . . how did he get out of the house?" she cried.

Gavin shook his head. "Maybe he was still there, Beth, and managed to slip out unseen sometime later."

Beth sat down on her bed, leaning forward, her head bowed. "I'm sorry, Ellen. I'm sorry. I'm sorry."

Faye stepped forward. "Have neither of you been hearing Ellen?"

Gavin faced her, but Beth didn't lift her head.

"She's been saying that she saw who did it, I believe. Would you like to talk about it, Ellen?"

Ellen stepped away from her father and looked with gratitude at Faye. She was the first to encourage her, to offer to believe her. But now that someone was listening she realized she had no words, no description.

"It . . ." she said, mentally drawing away from that night and the vague, smoky, horrible images that whirled in her memory. She began shaking her head, mentally willing herself away from it, unable to grasp anything clearly. "It . . . came out of the . . . the edges of the room. It was all full of smog and smoke and I couldn't see it very well. I—I don't remember anymore. It was—"

Gavin asked, "Did you see a man, Ellen?"

"I don't know. It changes. Sometimes, sometimes it's a man. It was a man in the police station. It followed me."

Beth looked up. "Oh, Daddy, she saw an Oriental, a Chinese or Vietnamese, and she got scared. That was all. In the police station, that first morning when we were taken there. He was just a police officer."

"Ellen, sweetheart, you've seen Chinese before. They

don't frighten you."

"But this one was—different. Don't you see?" She was on the verge of wailing again.

Beth and Gavin were staring at her, and her stepmother stood in the background not able to help her after all.

"It was a monster," she cried. "I know it was! I saw it! It can disguise itself, and it was the man in the police station."

"Look," Faye said, her voice artificially bright. "Why don't we all go downstairs and make plans for the Fourth of July weekend? It starts tomorrow, and Gav—your dad—doesn't have to go back to work until Monday morning, so there's no reason we can't do a lot of special things."

They had yielded to her lead, and the day progressed toward the weekend, but through all that first day she was aware of that look in Gavin's eyes that still indicated there was more than he had told.

She saw the effort he was making to be cheerful and to try to help the children forget. She saw also the touches of tenderness that Beth gave Ellen at intervals, though Beth, like her father, tended to stare off into the distance in deep thought when she was left alone.

Why hadn't he told her, Faye wondered, that his wife had been raped?

Immediately she realized how her thoughts had formed the words. His *wife*. Was that the way they both felt? That Blythe, not Faye, was his real wife?

She dressed for bed, her thoughts at last her own, the house quiet, the children—hopefully—asleep in their beds. Today they had driven around the countryside, showing the kids their new terrain. They had bought too many fireworks, and too much junk food. They had started preparations for the picnics they planned for the weekend. And her thoughts had been held in abeyance, with a strange new hurt that was beginning in the middle of her being.

She had thought there were no secrets between herself and Gavin, that he would hold nothing of consequence back from her. But for some reason he had held back the part of his wife's—*ex-wife's*—rape. And she had a strong feeling he was still holding back.

She thought she was alone in the bathroom, but suddenly his hands were on her shoulders. He kissed her on the back of her neck, and she hunched her shoulders as the tiny, wriggling chills went down over her body. Little snake thrills, she had called them when she was a child and young teenager, when her daddy had kissed her on the back of the neck.

"What were you thinking about?" Gavin asked, wrapping his arms warmly around her and resting his chin gently on the top of her head. "You were so far away."

"No, not far away," she said.

"You were great with the kids today. Thanks."

"It required no real effort. I like them."

"You know, I never realized before how little I know them. I like them, too. It's as if I am just now getting acquainted with them."

"You've been separated for quite a few years," Faye offered.

"Not only that, but when they were little, I was working during the day and going to night school trying to get my degree. I just wasn't with them very much. I don't suppose I changed more than half a dozen diapers in all. And on the weekends I had to study. Most of the time I went to the library where I could have a table to myself and relative silence." He paused. "I guess I wasn't a very good husband, either."

So was it a form of guilt? Faye wondered. But whatever it was, it had drawn him away from her. Though they stood together, they were in some way apart. She had a deep sorrowful dread that it would never be the same between them again.

"Gavin," she surprised herself by saying, "Gavin, why hadn't you told me Blythe was raped?"

His arms dropped away from her. In the mirror she saw his reflection turn. He was going to leave the room without answering her. But at the door he stopped, his head down, one hand on the doorjamb.

"It wasn't a normal rape," he finally said, in a voice low and halting. "It was more a sexual mutilation. The police told me there was no semen, but there was a lot of damage internally. It was, they said, for lack of other comparisons, like a small girl who has been raped by a huge man. Yet, there was no semen."

Faye whispered, "Then it *was* an intruder."

He didn't hear her.

"It's been bothering me. It's like there's something I should know but can't quite grasp. The feeling came over me when I went back to that house to get the kids' things. *Something*. But I don't know what."

The room was dark and smoky and her eyes burned. The smoke seemed to infiltrate her nose, her lungs, her brain. The edges of the room were buried in the haze, the shadows. In the midst of the room was a rough table, and on it a light. The light flickered, and at first Beth thought it was a candle; but then she saw it was a metal base lamp, with the flame growing out of the top. Was it Ellen's Aladdin's Lamp? No, it wasn't that. It was another lamp.

The table was low, no more than a couple of feet off the floor, and through the smoke she could see bodies lying on pads around the table. The body across the table was grossly heavy and seemed in the darkness to be naked. If there was a loin cloth it was hidden in the huge rolls of fat that enclosed the body. The head was smooth as if it had been shaved, and the flickering flame of the lamp reflected off the tight yellow skin, as if a twin flame danced there. The man's slitted eyes were staring at her across the table . . . no, not her, but someone else.

She turned slowly, to see, her movements and her vision minimized by the heaviness of the smoke.

It was a small girl, she saw, being forced through the dirty curtains that hung over the doorway. Her mouth was drawn back into a silent cry, and the terror in her eyes revealed the depths of a hell entered. In the room was silence. yet the heavy man on the pad across the table was laughing. She could sense his laughter, see it shake his body. The old woman who had pushed the child into the room was nearly hidden in the rags that covered her. The wrinkles of her face showed eyes still black as night, and slanted like the man's.

She held out her hand, and someone at the end of the table put coins into it. She turned and was gone through the curtains. They swayed in the smoke and fell still.

Why didn't the small girl run?

She stood as if nothing about her was alive except her terror.

The huge man on the pad put up an arm that had more girth than the child's body and reached for her.

When he drew her toward him Beth saw the child's face in the light of the lamp.

Ellen.

Beth woke suddenly, her body lurching in fear.

She blinked in the deep shadows of her room, trying to remember where she was. There were white curtains at the windows, priscilla curtains, and the cool breeze that blew in ruffled them and they swung, ghostlike, at the bottom of the window, in, out, in . . .

She remembered. This was her stepmother's house.

But there was something wrong with the air she was breathing, as if the freshness of the outdoors stopped halfway over her bed and was met there by a wall of . . . *smoke?*

She slipped out of bed and stood undecided at the side of it. It was the memory of the strange dream. The smoke was not real.

Was it?

She opened the door to the hall, but the air there seemed undisturbed, not filled by the smoke she had dreaded would be there. If there were a fire in the house, wouldn't there be alarms screaming?

The dream . . . that was all.

There were lights along the hall at intervals, dim lights just bright enough to show a person the way. The sounds of the night were left somewhere beyond the walls. The silence was undisturbed even by the creak of a settling house, as if the house, built a hundred years ago, had settled all it could.

The silence was unnerving.

Joey's door was open, but she didn't go into his room. It was Ellen she felt worried about. Because of the dream, she reminded herself, and it had been her dream, not Ellen's. Ellen was all right. But still, she had to see, to make sure.

The dream, horrible in its sense of a terrible danger, had seemed so real. As if it existed in some form a long time ago and still existed on some plane because nothing is ever lost, neither experience nor emotion, of human or animal. Everything is imprinted, somewhere, to remain in existence forever.

The dream had told her those things.

As if the curtain that had opened over the doorway also opened over a part of her mind she had never reached before.

Ellen's door was closed.

Beth paused. She had yelled at Ellen this morning for not knocking, but she couldn't knock and wake her little sister if she was sleeping. She only wanted to check and make sure she was safe, that was all.

She opened the door softly, a crack, another small space. The room beyond at first seemed dark, but then she saw a faint glow in the room.

A strange glow, red, dim, as if it were coming from an artificial light, a lantern covered by red paper. Or, as if a small flame were glowing in the midst of a smoke-filled room.

Beth shoved the door open, the wall of smoke choking her. The bed glowed, lighted by an invisible flame, and in the rolling shadows beyond the bed was a faintly outlined figure that had the shape of a huge, naked man.

He was looking down at the sleeping Ellen.

Chapter Eight

Faye heard the strangling, choking scream the instant it started. She had been lying awake for hours staring at the ceiling fan, watching its shadows rotate lazily as it spun on low. The cry sounded as if it were coming from a nightmare one of the children was having. It was not a full-throated scream of a waking person.

Faye slid out of bed instantly and ran, leaving the master bedroom door half open behind her. She ran around the banisters of the stairwell and into the hall of the rear wing. There was no one in the hallway.

Before she reached the rooms of the children the cry stopped and was replaced by voices. She passed Beth's room, saw the door was open and the room dark. The voices were in Ellen's room.

She stopped on the threshold.

In the shadows of the room she saw Beth standing halfway between door and bed, with Ellen sitting up in bed.

Faye turned on the ceiling light.

Both girls turned and stared at her in silence.

Faye looked from one to the other. Though both had pale, startled faces, they seemed to be all right.

"I heard someone screaming," she said.

Ellen pointed at Beth. "It was her. She scared me."

Beth tried to explain. "I—I guess I was still dreaming. I thought I saw . . . I thought I smelled . . . but Ellen just sat up and everything went away."

"Were you walking in your sleep?" Faye asked, remembering last night and Ellen's somnambulism. She hadn't told anyone, not even Gavin. She hadn't wanted to add to his worries. It would take time, she felt, for the children to start living a normal life again. There would be nightmares, and yes, even somnambulism.

It seemed to be one of the ways in which they were expressing their feelings.

"No," Beth said. "I don't think so. I've never walked in my sleep. None of us do. I was wide awake; I'm sure I was. I had a horrible dream of being . . . in a bad place a long time ago. In another century, maybe in the eighteen hundreds, or even the seventeen hundreds. There was a little girl in it, and just at the end, when I woke up, I saw the girl was Ellen." Beth shuddered visibly. "There was a huge man. He was going to do something bad to Ellen. But I woke up. And then . . . I smelled smoke, so I got up and came to see if Ellen was all right. And her room was—"

Beth turned, hugging her body with her arms, as if she couldn't stand the memory. "But then Ellen sat up, and everything went away. It was back to normal. And you came and turned on the light."

Faye found herself uneasy, cold, fleshless fingers touching her spine. Fear rising, unwilled. Smoke? But the air was clear. Yet it reminded her of last night, when the smell of smoke woke her. She reached out a comforting hand to Beth, and the girl did not flinch away as she half expected.

"Someone must be burning trash in the neighborhood," she said. "I was awakened last night by the smell of smoke. But I could find no trace of it, no source, and within moments the smell was gone. That's the way a trash fire can be, a nuisance one minute and gone the next. It probably entered your room through the window and caused you to have the nightmare. Then, you probably weren't quite awake, and the nightmare continued."

"It was so real," Beth said, her eyes examining the room in detail as if somewhere here were the remnants of her dream.

Ellen sat in the middle of her bed, her hair tangled as if she'd spent a restless few hours, the ugly old rag doll clutched in her arms, its bonnet gone. Her eyes seemed enormous and darker than usual, as she looked from Faye to Beth, from Beth to Faye.

Faye went to the bed and gently eased the child down upon her pillows. She pulled the light blanket up around her shoulders, covering the doll, too.

"Do you think you can go back to sleep?"

Ellen nodded and closed her eyes.

Faye turned out the light, left the door open, and with her hand on Beth's back, guided her gently back toward her own bedroom.

When she left her a moment later, Beth had climbed into bed and was staring upward at the ceiling. Faye left her door open, too.

The man in her dream . . . that parody of a man. Where had she seen him before? Beth wondered, frowning with the strain of trying to remember. He was too huge, too gross to ever be a real person, yet she had a feeling she had seen him.

The pool!

Back at the motel. When she had raised her head out of the water, with water streaming down over her eyes, she had seen him behind Ellen's chair. He wasn't real.

He had disappeared when her vision cleared, but it was the same man, the same excess of man, the same grossly distorted caricature of a man.

Why did she keep seeing him?

Why was she beginning to feel like Ellen was in some kind of terrible danger from him? As if he were real.

But that was silly. Even in her darkened room, now that she was fully awake, she could realize how silly her fears were. The man was only a figment of her imagination. She had dreamed him up. Somehow.

Yet he seemed so real that even the thoughts of him sent a cold dread through her heart.

He was after Ellen.

He was going to take Ellen, somehow, sometime.

No, silly. Turn over, go back to sleep, or get up and read a book. Don't think such dumb things, Beth, she told herself.

Faye did all she could to make the weekend enjoyable, to keep the kids occupied. At times she felt she was on the edge of hysteria trying to keep a holiday spirit.

On Saturday morning, the day of the Fourth, they drove up over the Boston Mountains to Beaver Lake and the small cabin they had bought to spend their honeymoon in. Even then Gavin had mentioned that he would like to bring his kids here sometime, and she had agreed it would be a great place for kids to play.

The cabin was situated on a hillside low over a hollow that was filled with lake water. The water eased gently up to the sloping shores amidst the many flat-topped bluffs that stuck out of the hillside. There were shallow places and deep places, fit for wading, for swimming or for fishing. The more densely populated areas were over the hill, or around the next hill. The road that led to their cabin ended in a cul-de-sac farther up the hill, and their driveway down to the carport, which was attached to one side of the three-room cabin, was no more than a trail.

The feeling she had when she came here was different from any other.

Here, standing on the deck at the back of the cabin, she saw only the trees, the hills across the hollow, the lake below and beyond the mouth of the hollow where it widened into the huge water playground of so many people.

But on the deck, standing alone, surrounded by hills, she was part of nature. Calmed. Relaxed. She looked down at the lone fisherman in his boat below and knew how he felt. It wasn't so much the fish he was there to catch—very often he threw them back into the water—it was the solitude, the sense of change only in the geological sense. The peace. The tranquility.

Within her the baby stirred lazily and then lay still, as if he or she knew the gentleness of the day.

And then, out front, a firecracker popped. Birds in the trees flew in a swarm, alarmed. The fisherman in his boat, so far away she could not see whether he was young or old, or even if he were man or woman for that matter, turned his head and looked up at the cabin. He stared, as if he hadn't realized it was there.

Faye murmured, "Sorry, mister, but today is the Fourth of July, and the kids must have their fun, too."

She went out into the front yard and watched Gavin and the three kids with their fireworks. Joey was excited, his voice loud.

"When it's dark, we can light these others, huh, Dad? These sparklers will really be something in the dark, huh, Dad?"

The girls stood by as Joey threw a popper to the ground. Beth hunched into her shoulders and covered her ears.

"I want to go swimming! Why can't we go swimming?"

"Just a few more minutes," Gavin promised. "Let Joey set off a few more."

Faye went back into the cabin, thinking of the fisherman, smiling, visualizing his horror when the noisy bunch invaded his hollow to swim. But there were other hollows, other hidden coves. Hundreds of them. Maybe he could find one where he would be alone.

She yearned for a moment to find one for herself, but she threw the feeling off and went to make the beds.

The kitchen, dining area and living room were all one large room on the left side of the house, with doors opening out to the front, out to the carport along the side and out to the deck at the back. There were only two bedrooms, with a small bath between. In one room was a double bed, hers and Gavin's room. But the back bedroom had been outfitted with bunk beds, enough to sleep four. Making them up with sheets was no picnic. It required, she decided, a contortionist.

She was panting from the exertion when she climbed down the last ladder.

"Whose idea was this?" she asked the room in general. "Buying bunk beds? Not mine, surely."

But it was the only way to make use of the limited space.

She went to the kitchen and tested the water. The heater had been lighted as soon as they came into the cabin, and the water was now hot enough she could wash off the table and cabinet tops. In the cabinet they had left a minimum of stoneware plates and cups. The glasses were plastic. She felt she almost understood how some of the settlers had lived, except of course she had hot water at the faucet and a stove that was fueled by the small propane tank below the deck. There was even a stack of wood under the deck, in case they needed to use the fireplace.

She made sandwiches to go with the salads they had brought from a deli back at a shopping center. There was a redwood picnic table, with benches, on the back deck, and she was carrying food out to it when Beth came into the house.

"Can I help you?" Beth asked.

"Thanks, yes. There are plates and flatware on the cabinet. Would you bring those please? And whatever else in the fridge that you want to eat."

Beth worked quietly, going back and forth between deck and kitchen. She brought out a package of cold hot dogs, Faye noticed.

"You can heat them in the microwave, if you want, Beth."

"No, I like them cold." Then, as if she remembered she was not the only person present, she looked at Faye. "Would you like me to heat some for you?"

"No thanks. Since I've been pregnant, hot dogs, among some other things, don't agree with me." She patted her belly. "I guess my little guy just doesn't like hot dogs."

"You're *pregnant?*"

Faye met Beth's astonished gaze.

"Yes. Why?"

Beth shrugged, her cheeks reddening. She looked away. "I just didn't know."

Faye said, "You mean you thought I was just naturally this fat?"

Beth glanced up, met Faye's eyes, and they both laughed.

Still smiling broadly, Beth said, "I just thought you liked to wear muu-muus."

"No, shapeless dresses were not ever my favorite

style, but right now they seem to fit better. I'm not quite to the stage where I want to start wearing maternity pants with an overblouse."

Beth's gaze went briefly to Faye's stomach.

"Uh... when... I mean, it's not any of my business, but, I was just wondering..."

"October twenty-fifth. And of course it's your business. After all, it's another brother or sister we've got here."

"That's right, it is, isn't it? I like babies."

"Good. I'm glad you do."

"Maybe I can babysit sometime."

"That would be helpful, I'm sure. I don't have any experience with babies, much, but I know from seeing friends, and my sister, that sometimes a mother needs time to herself."

"You have a sister?"

"Yes, and a brother. But my brother is a major in the Army, and is stationed in Germany, and my sister lives in Little Rock. I expect you'll be meeting her soon, but Dan hardly ever gets home. I haven't seen him in two years."

"Where are your mother and dad?"

"I lost them when I was young. I was the youngest of my family, and both my parents were killed in a plane crash. My grandfather took us in, Danny, Janet and me. He lived until he was in his nineties, and he left the house to all of us; but I bought Dan and Janet's part, so I could bring up my own children there. I loved it. It was a haven, you see, after my parents were gone. Grandpa lived alone. Grandma had been dead for several years."

"That's kind of like me," Beth said, her head down as she carefully but absently placed the flatware precisely at the sides of the plates.

"Yes, kind of like you."

"Except my dad is still alive."

"Yes, thank God. We need him, don't we?"

"I guess so. Yes," she added emphatically.

There were footsteps and voices in the house as Gavin, Ellen and Joey came through onto the deck. Joey slid in on the bench, but Beth grabbed him by the back of his collar.

"Hey, no way. You think you don't have to wash just because we're up here on the lake? Go wash."

"Oh nuts, Beth, my hands aren't dirty."

He went back through the door looking at the palms of his hands, grumbling. Gavin laughed and made an exaggerated turn.

"I guess I'd better go, too, and so had you, puddin' pie," he said to Ellen, his hand collaring the back of her neck.

They returned, the edges of their hair damp around their faces. Joey's hair was combed back, waving slightly. It dried in the air, breaking loose into soft curls that fell again across his forehead.

"Ellen," Faye offered, "Would you like me to braid your hair before you go swimming?"

Ellen shoved a potato chip into her mouth and talked around it. "How long would it take?"

"A very few minutes. I braid hair fast."

"Okay."

"Good. It won't get into your eyes when you come up out of the water if it's braided."

Faye made another sandwich, smearing an extra spoonful of sandwich spread, adding an extra slice of cheese. Her appetite was growing faster than her stomach. The hunger gnawed at her even after she had eaten a full meal. What was she going to look like after the baby was born?

When the meal was finished Ellen wriggled restlessly in front of Faye as her hair was braided. Gavin and

Joey went down the steps from the deck and looked at fishing gear that had been stored in the area beneath the deck. They were waiting around for Ellen. Faye wrapped a rubber band tightly around the end of Ellen's single, thick braid while the girl edged farther and farther away in her eagerness to follow her brother and dad.

Beth sat on the bench across the table watching Ellen get her hair braided. She had changed to her bathing suit, a one piece blue with ruffles around the hip line. Ellen's suit was a plain little thing that did not disguise in any way her shapeless body. Beneath it, her legs looked long. But they were warmly tanned, and under her bathing suit, at the buttocks, a thin strip of white flesh showed.

"There!" Faye said, laughing. "Go. It didn't take so long, did it?"

Ellen ran without answering, down the steps and around the path.

Beth stood up, hesitating.

"Would you mind braiding my hair, too?"

"Why of course we'll braid your hair if you'd like. Do you want a single French braid like Ellen's?"

"Yes."

Beth sat on her heels in front of Faye. Her hair was thicker and heavier than Ellen's, and much darker.

"You have lovely hair," Faye said. "So rich in texture. It's a feminine version of Gavin's."

"Thank you."

"Ellen's hair is more like mine. You must have had some blond grandparents."

"I don't know. I guess so. My one grandma had gray hair, I remember. It was prematurely gray, Mama said, and Mama's hair had some gray in it even though she was only thirty-two."

"Thirty-two? Gavin's age."

109

"Yes, they graduated from high school together. They were high school sweethearts."

"I see."

Faye braided the dark, rich hair in silence, the former life of her husband intruding upon her mind as she pictured him a teenager in love. She could see him and the young Blythe—hadn't she looked a lot like Beth?—holding hands as they walked from classroom to classroom, or out across the grass of the campus.

She finished the braiding.

"Are you going down to swim?" Beth asked as she got to her feet.

"No, but I'll walk down with you if I can make it down the path. Then I'll go on around the beach and back up the path from there."

Gavin and the other children were out of sight along the path that wound down through the trees, a crooked path, laid out in a slanting pattern on a steep hillside, the only way to walk down without sliding right into the water below.

Faye moved carefully, but found the path safer than she had remembered.

"It seemed awfully steep at first," she told Beth, following behind her. "Gavin took a pick and shovel and scooped it out a little better. The people who had owned the cabin had done a fairly good job of mapping it out, though."

They reached the shoreline. Gavin had brought along a web folding lounge chair and was already in it. His wet hair indicated he had taken a swim first. The two kids were playing and splashing in the water.

Faye stood on the shore, the water lapping her toes, and watched Beth join her brother and sister.

This was the first time, Faye realized, she had seen Ellen without the rag doll.

Did that mean she had a reduced need for the

security it gave her?

Faye leaned down and kissed Gavin.

His hand grabbed her and held on. "Want me to unfold the other chair for you?"

"No, thanks, I'm going to walk around the beach. I won't be coming back this way."

"Okay. Be careful. Don't slip." He pulled her closer and kissed her again, then released her wrist.

She walked on, just at the edge of the water, sometimes over a flat bluff that stuck out into the water, sometimes being forced to go around a boulder and up onto the hillside. Trees grew thickly near the point of the hill, and beyond, the lake widened.

The lone fisherman had left, she noted, looking back up the narrow arm of the lake. And out in the wide middle, the ski boats made it dangerous for the little guys.

The shoreline widened and began a gentle slope to more beachlike proportions. Trees fell back, leaving only tall waving grass and green cedar trees spaced apart as if someone had landscaped the area.

There was another lake-filled hollow on the other side of the point, and beyond that a large level piece of land that had a recreation area, filled now with people, cars, and boats being launched into the lake to add to the congestion of the waterways.

The noise reached her here: the roar of the ski boats as they passed the point she stood on, the resulting rush of water onto the shore in waves that swept all vegetation away. Just as the waves from one boat died back to ripples, another boat would pass along the central channel of the lake, and the waves would begin again.

She could hear the shouting of children, their voices thin on the air.

Turning away from it all, she began to walk toward

the rise of the hill. She found the path at the treeline, and the noises from the recreation area were absorbed by the foliage.

By the time she reached the cabin she was tired.

She lay down on the cool comforter that covered the bed. It was going to be all right, she assured herself.

Nordene had been wrong about the kids.

They hadn't had anything to do with the murder of their mother.

That was all behind, two thousand miles away.

The weekend was going to be a success, and even though Gavin would be leaving Monday morning for work in Dallas, and would not be home again until Friday, the week would be a success, too. She was determined that it would be. Plans were made to take the children shopping for new clothes, to take them to the nearest park and show them where they would be swimming and playing ball.

Also, she planned to call Nordene and talk to her, for after all, there was no reason to keep Joey and Ellen from enjoying the company of Dwayne and Katy. At least to meet them, to see if they were compatible. And kids generally were, weren't they?

She sighed and slept, feeling as if a great load had been lifted from her mind.

It was going to be all right.

. . . all right . . .

Yet as she fell asleep she began to sob, involuntarily.

She jerked awake, the anxiety she had tried to push away working again at her mind.

Chapter Nine

"Hello, Nordene, this is Faye. How are you?"

"Fine, Faye. Did you have a good weekend?"

"Great. We went up to the lake, spent one night and two days. The kids loved it there. They swam and fished and did their fireworks bit. When we got home last night everyone just fell into bed. I was still asleep this morning when Gavin left. That is, he woke me, of course, when he kissed me goodbye, but I hadn't realized he was up."

"Oh. So he's gone. The children stayed with you?"

"Nordene, I've called to ask you to come over and bring Katy and Dwayne. I feel the kids should get acquainted, and I do need to talk to you."

Nordene hesitated, far too long.

"Nordene, Ellen and Joey would love Dwayne and Katy. They need playmates, and your kids are such great leaders, I'm sure they're just what Ellen and Joey need." She felt shoddy, using flattery. But she sincerely felt the children would be good for one another.

Nordene sighed. "Sam agrees the kids should meet. When shall we come over?"

"Now. We can have coffee. I even have some rolls on hand, but I'll admit I bought them at the bakery in the supermarket last night on the way home."

Nordene giggled. "Are they gooey?"

113

"They're gooey."

"I'll be right over."

Faye began a pot of coffee, putting in enough for four cups, just in case. At the table the kids were eating breakfast, silent this morning, as if the weekend at the lake had drained them of energy.

"Would you like company?"

"Who?" Beth asked.

"The kids next door. They might be too young for you to enjoy, Beth, but Joey and Ellen should get along fine with them. Dwayne is Joey's age, and Katy is ten."

"I met him," Joey said, lifting himself to sit straight. He had been slumping over the table and allowed to get by with it. "He lives on the other side of the gate, doesn't he?"

"Yes, he does."

"When did you meet him?" Beth asked.

"The other day. The first day we were here. But his mother called him and he had to go."

"Well, maybe today you can get better acquainted."

Faye put the coffee pot onto the stove to perk. It started almost immediately, a soft, blip, blip, the aroma filling the room. On a platter she arranged an assortment of rolls, choosing the ones with the most frosting and filling.

"I'm sorry, Beth," she said. "There aren't any girls your age who live close, but you'll be meeting some at the park. Also, there are the activities at church that you'll be getting into."

Beth shrugged. "It doesn't matter."

Faye carried the coffee and the platter of rolls onto the terrace and put them on the glass-topped table.

"Joey, would you like to go down the driveway and get the morning paper?"

Beth said, "I'll do it."

"If you'd rather."

Faye sat down to wait for Nordene. Joey stood by the table looking at the platter of rolls. He'd eaten only half his cereal, but Faye yielded to the look of hunger in his eyes.

"Take what you like, Joey."

"Thank you." He chose a doughnut.

"Can I have one, too?" Ellen asked.

She was carrying her doll under her arm again.

"Of course."

Ellen took an iced roll and sat down on the edge of the terrace, her feet hanging off. She began murmuring to her doll, offering it a bite of the roll.

Faye waited restlessly. She had to admit something to herself that she hadn't wanted to. The children made her nervous. Only when she was alone, or in bed at night with Gavin, did that feeling leave her of having to be on her toes, alert to something she couldn't quite define.

Was she viewing them as guests?

They were permanent; they were family, she reminded herself. They were going to be here tomorrow, and tomorrow after that, for years. She couldn't go around on edge, wondering what to do next, what to say, how to entertain. Kids were kids; they would entertain themselves. She had only to be sure they were fed and clothed and . . . wasn't that what mothers did?

It would have been much easier to be broken into motherhood gradually. The way she had thought she would be.

She had felt uncomfortable thinking about asking the children if they had made their beds and straightened up their rooms, if they had put their soiled clothes into their hampers, and on and on. So she hadn't asked.

Give it a week, she told herself. Maybe those habits were already ingrained into them.

She was going to have to get someone to come in a

couple of times a week to do the laundry and cleaning, rather than just once a week. How did the women who couldn't afford extra help handle all that?

She longed to be free to get into her car and drive down to her one remaining gift shop and see how things were going. There was so much pleasure in going into the shop where the colors were so varied and so brilliant, where lights reflected off glass figurines, making rainbows everywhere.

Later, she told herself. The kids can go, too. Why not? They could have lunch downtown somewhere.

Nordene and her two children were coming along the path. Ellen and Joey stood up and waited. Katy, still carrying what Nordene called her baby fat, had her own doll tucked under a plump arm. She held it out immediately to show Ellen.

Faye heard her say, "I got it for the Fourth of July. I get dolls for my birthday and for all the holidays."

"All of them?" Ellen asked.

"Hey," Dwayne said to Joey, "Can we go play in your barn?"

Joey looked questioningly at Faye. She nodded and started to tell him they could play anywhere within the fenced grounds, but Nordene's voice came first.

"Be careful! Old barns can be dangerous places."

"Let's go to the barn, too," Katy was saying to Ellen, already leading her away.

"Well," Faye said as she watched the children go along the path toward the rear of the grounds and the barn that once had housed her grandfather's horses and buggies, "Introductions were not necessary, it seemed. They don't even know each other's names, do they?"

"They will," Nordene said, helping herself to a stuffed doughnut. "Kids are born rude. Within minutes they'll have asked each other not only names, but birthdays and everything else that is relevant to them."

Faye smiled. "How simple and easy."

"Sure." Nordene sat back and took a large bite. "Don't you just hate calories? I was told at a diet place I went to, to see if I wanted to join or not, that I shouldn't eat more than a thousand calories a day. And a doughnut like this, I guess, has about six hundred. Well, what kind of reasoning is that? That just leaves me four hundred more. And I've already had a piece of toast and an egg. Where does that leave me for the rest of the day?"

"Foodless?"

"Or fat. Well, fatter. I'd like to get my hands on the guy that discovered calories. Long ago, they said either you were fat or you weren't, that food had nothing to do with it. Did you know they said that?"

"No, I didn't. I suppose a century ago they were too busy preparing the food to worry about what was in it."

"I can remember my grandmother saying either you're fat or you're not. She didn't worry about it. Well"—Nordene sat back and sipped coffee from the cup Faye had poured for her—"You're looking good. How're you feeling?"

"Great."

"Sam insisted that the kids be allowed to play together, but I still have my reservations, Faye, I'll tell you. They're certainly good looking kids, though, aren't they? But isn't there a third one?"

"Yes. Beth is twelve. She's gone out looking for the paper."

"Do they seem to be accepting the change?"

"As far as I can tell, they are. How does one really know? They're good kids, Nordene, and easy to have around. I'm sure we'll get used to one another eventually."

"You said you wanted to talk to me?"

"I do . . ." Faye smoothed the material of her dress over her stomach. It was against her principles even to bring up the subject, yet since Nordene had been so outspoken about the children's possible guilt, she felt she had to. "The children had nothing to do with their mother's death, Nordene, that's what I want to tell you. To assure you, so that you won't feel . . . afraid of them."

"How do you know?"

"She was raped."

"Raped!"

"Yes." Something Gavin had said came clearly to her mind, as if his words were being spoken again: *. . . there was no semen . . . there was no instrument found . . .* The police must have looked for an instrument, must have had reason to look for one. Which meant . . . it wasn't necessarily a man they suspected . . . so therefore . . .

Her mind refused to finish the thought.

Nordene said, leaning toward her, voice low, "There was nothing in the paper about that!"

"I know. But of course our newspaper would not have carried the whole story."

"Then someone did break into the house?"

No.

"Evidently," Faye answered, realizing with a coldness seeping into her being that she was covering for the children. It was just as well that Nordene, the people Nordene had talked with and Faye's own relatives think that after all an intruder had broken in.

Faye stared past Nordene's head, seeing the trees, the patches of sky above where the hill sloped away toward town. She drew herself back with effort. Later, later she would try to piece together these feelings that nothing was right after all.

Beth came around the corner of the house and onto the terrace. She had the thick newspaper in her hand and was looking at Nordene with a faint, uneasy smile. Faye was struck by how pretty she looked. For the first time she noticed a faint dimple in her chin.

"This is Beth," Faye said. "Beth, this is Nordene, our neighbor on the west. She's the mother of Katy and Dwayne."

"Hello, Beth."

"Hello." Beth laid the newspaper on the table. "I saw a bicycle," she said. "Is it okay if I ride it?"

"Of course. That's probably my old bike."

"Thanks."

She went back around the corner of the house and toward the garden shed where the bike was sitting in its rack beneath the overhang of the roof.

"So many of them," Nordene mused, looking after her. "What a change in your life, Faye. Suddenly the mother of three big kids. But at least Beth is big enough, old enough that she can help with the younger ones."

"Oh, definitely. In fact, it's almost as if she's their mother, the way she looks after them."

"I've read and heard of many cases like that—the mother dies, and the oldest girl takes her place. It was that way with my great grandmother. Her own mother died when she was only five. Her father—she called him Papa—married again, of course, immediately I guess, the way they did back in the eighteen hundreds, those men. Of course he had three babies younger than Granny-great, so I guess that was his only avenue. He wasn't rich enough to hire proper help. Anyway, that mother, the stepmother, the one Granny always said was like the only mother she'd ever had, died when Granny was twelve. By that time there were four more babies. So Granny grew up mothering seven children younger than herself. Her father didn't marry again. Had all the family he could handle, I guess. In those days there was strictness, but no abuse. Granny would have been horrified at the very whisper of that sort of thing. Men had more control."

"Maybe they had to work too hard to think of anything else."

"No idle hands or idle minds to get into mischief? At least Granny's life was better after she married. Grandpa-great, her husband, came from a wealthier class of people. I wonder where the kids are?"

"In the barn. They'll be all right. Nothing but mice has lived in that barn for years."

Ellen clutched her doll and followed the other girl. Joey and Dwayne were somewhere else in the barn, only their voices, high-pitched, excited, with Dwayne doing most of the talking, but Joey's voice there, too, assured Ellen she was not alone with the strange little girl, who was three years older, but not a lot taller.

"Let's build a playhouse," the girl was saying as she set her beautiful new doll on an old wooden box about the size of an orange crate. As if she noticed there was a lot of dust on the box, she picked up the doll again, dusted its skirt and white satin panties and extended it to Ellen.

"Here, hold her. Her name is Christina. You can call her that, if you want to. Hold her very carefully."

Ellen took the doll. It even smelled new. Her own old doll had its own special smell, though, which was even better.

"Did you put perfume on your doll?" Ellen asked.

"No, she's carrying a little perfumed handkerchief, see in her hand?"

It was, Ellen saw, tied to her wrist by means of a little

gold thread.

"Now then. I'll clean the box. It will be our table."

Katy wiped the top with her hand and the dust fogged. She moved back, her nose wrinkled. When she wiped her hand on the side of her cotton shorts she left a dusty streak.

"I'd better get a broom. Look around, Ellen, and see if you can find something that would be a nice broom. I could go home and get my own little broom. And my dish sets, and all of that."

She turned, the palms of her hands pressed together, and surveyed the interior of the barn. It was a shed room, all along one side. The door opened out at the far end, and small dusty windows spotted the walls, set high, too high for them to see out. Katy's face was round and eager, round blue eyes gleaming, even in the shadowy light. She had short, reddish hair, which had been curled into ringlets, and freckles. She was a young Nordene, plump, round and looking for something to do.

"I know," she cried. "To save time we'll go to your house and get some of your dishes and a table cloth. We can even get the broom. If you don't have a little broom, we'll get the big one. I can handle a big broom. Come on." She grabbed Ellen's elbow.

Ellen let her jerk, but she didn't move. "Faye might not want us to."

Katy stopped, staring round-eyed at Ellen. "You call her *Faye?*"

"Yes," Ellen answered defensively. "She told me to."

"But she's your *mother.*"

"No," Ellen answered quickly and firmly, drawing back from Katy. The hand fell away from her elbow. With both dolls in her arms Ellen returned Katy's stare. "My mother's . . ." She couldn't say it. She knew it was true, but she couldn't say the word.

121

"Well, she's your *stepmother*," Katy said. "Which is almost the same as being your mother, that's what Mama said. So you should call her . . ." Katy crinkled her eyes thoughtfully at the rafters of the sloping ceiling. "Let's see—"

"Faye. She said to call her Faye."

"You could call her Mom, or Mum, if you didn't want to call her Mother. Or Mama, like I do. How does it *feel* to have a stepmother?"

"I don't know," Ellen answered. "I hadn't thought about it before."

The boys dropped through a hole in the ceiling, legs coming first. The first pair of feet pawed the air, feeling for support, and finally found the ladder that was built against the wall. Dwayne appeared, and then Joey.

"Hey," said Dwayne. "It's really neat up there. There's still some hay. And at the end of the barn are some doors, shut; but we could see through the cracks, and you can see way over the trees. Almost."

"You can see through 'em," Joey agreed. "You can see the tops of hills and the roofs of houses."

"We're going to look the rest of the barn over. But you girls had better stay here, because there might be dangers."

"Oh, bosh, what dangers?" Katy challenged. "You've got trash in your hair, Dwayne. You'd better clean it out."

He felt upward, and picked out a couple pieces of straw.

Ellen became aware that a face was looking at them from the distant corner of the barn. It was surrounded by shadows, nearly invisible within its dark corner.

It was on a ledge that surrounded the barn, the top of a post that ended at the ledge.

She felt its eyes staring at her.

The eyes were slitted and tilted upward at the

corners, as black as death, glittering in the darkness there in the corner.

The monster . . . the monster had followed her after all . . .

Somehow it had found her, though she came through the clouds high in the sky.

She began to back away, trying to put space between her and it, trying to escape the eyes that were clinging to her as if they were connected to her by an invisible string.

She opened her arms, put her hands out to ward it off.

Both dolls fell to the floor.

Katy looked down at her beautiful new doll on the dirty old floor and started to scold Ellen for dropping it, but she stared instead, her mouth an open O. The voices of the boys gradually ceased as they turned to look at Ellen.

She was trying to scream, but her voice was a mere whisper of harshness like someone in the throes of a nightmare.

The monster . . . the—

Joey and Dwayne both turned, their eyes following her stare. Dwayne glanced back.

"What's wrong with her?" he asked. "It's only a cat."

The cat leaped suddenly, a large yellow ball in the air. Snarling, it whirled and ran out the open door.

Ellen could go no farther. She had backed into the rough corner of the barn, the choked sound gradually dying away to silence. The other three stood in a small semi-circle around her, staring at her.

There was a sound at the door, a footstep on brittle hay.

Beth stepped through and stopped, blinking in the lack of light.

"What's wrong?" she asked. "Is something wrong?"

"The *monster*," Ellen cried hoarsely. "The—"

"It was only a cat," Dwayne said in disgust. "I don't know why she's calling it a monster. It was sitting on a post in the corner, and it just jumped down and ran out the door. Hasn't she ever seen a cat before?"

Beth came along the length of the shed and took Ellen's hand. "Come on out into the fresh air, Ellen."

Katy picked up both dolls, looking critically at her own for signs of dirt. She shook it. "Here's her doll," she said, offering the limp rag doll to Beth.

"Thank you."

They stopped in a spot of sunlight beyond the door. "Why don't you play out here?" Beth asked. "Where it's not so dark? And you've got cobwebs in your hair, Joey."

"But it's neat in there."

"Yes, and there are mice, and where there are mice there are going to be stray cats."

"It wasn't a real cat," Ellen said faintly, clutching her sister's hand. "It was the monster. It was in disguise. It just make itself look like a cat. But it was really the monster that killed Mama."

Katy stepped nearer and peered into her face. "Your mother was killed by a monster?"

"No, she wasn't," Beth said. "Not a real monster. Come on, Ellen. She can't play anymore today, Katy."

"Oh damn," Katy said, stamping her foot, frowning. "We were just getting ready to build our playhouse."

"Maybe tomorrow," Beth answered, pulling Ellen toward the house.

She hadn't seen a cat, Beth was thinking. She couldn't get it out of her mind. The voices of the kids, sounding so excited, had attracted her, and she had wondered what they were doing. She parked the bike against the wall of the barn, just at the side of the door, and for a minute or so she had stood there, listening to them. Feeling glad that Ellen and Joey had found friends and were having fun.

And then Ellen had begun to make that horrible noise.

Beth hadn't seen a cat.

It must not have run out the door, the way they said, after all. Because she was right there, all the time.

But she wasn't going to tell Ellen that.

Ellen had grown quiet again and was just sitting around with her doll, picking at it as if it had bits of lint all over its face and body.

Beth was glad when their stepmother asked them if they'd like to go out for lunch.

"We'll eat wherever you prefer, and then, if you'd like, I'll show you my store."

"You have a store?" Joey asked.

"Yes. It's my last one. It was my first one, too, and then I started more, in other areas, and then sold them."

"Why'd you sell them?"

"Because I married your daddy, and wanted to be at home more."

"But he's gone."

"Yes, I know." She laughed a little.

Beth asked, "What kind of store is it?"

"A gift shop, with a few antiques. My other stores were mostly antiques, and it was very interesting work. I learned quite a lot about buying antiques, but it's almost impossible now to find anything that hasn't already been found."

"You mean it's all been discovered?"

"It seems that way. The quaint little auction back in the hills just doesn't exist anymore. Certainly not where you find old treasures that have been left in someone's attic. Too many people are aware of what's valuable and what's old."

Beth leaned over Ellen. "Go up and get changed, Ellen, and Faye will take us out to lunch. Want to?"

Ellen nodded.

With her doll under her arm she went into the house.

Faye's eyes followed her. "Perhaps what Ellen needs is a pet of her own. Has she ever had a kitten?"

"No."

"If she had a kitten she might get over her fear of cats," Faye said.

"She said it was the monster," Joey offered.

"That's silly, Joey," Beth said, wishing he'd forget about it. "You better go clean up, too. Both of you look like you've been rolling in hay."

Joey brushed at his clothes. "I'm not dirty. I only climbed the ladder up and then down again. And swung on the board up in the barn roof."

"Well, go wash anyway. You have to wash before you can eat."

He started into the house and stopped as if he had come up against an invisible wall.

Ellen was screaming, a shrill cry filled with terror.

Chapter Ten

Beth was running instantly, it seemed to Faye, going past Joey and into the kitchen. She could hear her sandals on the tile of the kitchen floor and the squeak of the door between the kitchen and the hallway.

Faye followed, bumping against Joey as she passed him. She felt awkward running, heavier than was normal for her. But the scream kept rising, with faint gasps punctuating it.

As she crossed the kitchen it became even more shrill and soul-tearing as the child, no longer sounding even human, let out her terror in her cries.

When she entered the large foyer at the front of the house, she saw that Beth had stopped in the middle of the room and was staring at something beyond Ellen.

The room was furnished only slightly, a large mahogany glass-fronted display cabinet on the left wall, a few feet this side of the dark oak, double front doors that were rarely used. And across the broad space was a settee and matching chairs, with small, marble-topped tables.

Ellen was at the foot of the stairs, standing on the bottom step, one hand on the banister. The doll was twisted beneath her arm and hand as she clutched it. She seemed to know that she was no longer alone, even though her back was toward Faye. The scream began to die down and finally fade to silence.

Faye spotted the animal that both Beth and Ellen were staring at.

It was sitting on the back of the settee, a large yellow cat that seemed almost to be a ball of fur, its body hunched, as if it were ready to spring.

But what caught Faye's attention most, and held it, was the cat's stare. Its slitted, evil-looking eyes were pinned on Ellen. It seemed unaware that anyone else had come into the room.

She heard her own voice denying her feelings. "It's only a cat. It's probably the same stray cat you saw in the barn."

How did it get into the house?

She walked past Beth and unlocked the front doors. She opened them both back. A wide streak of sunshine flooded into the house.

"Come on, scat, get out of the house!"

She circled around between the cat and the girls and clapped her hands.

It leaped, a huge body uncoiling, and dashed for the open doors.

When it disappeared beyond the doors, she drew a deep breath of relief and shut and locked the doors again. When she turned, Beth had gone to Ellen and was holding her.

Faye went to them and put her hands on a shoulder of each of the girls.

"It's nothing to be afraid of, Ellen. As fat as it was, I'd say it probably belongs to one of the neighbors. In fact—" She licked her lower lip. The coldness of Ellen's skin came through her blouse. The child was trembling as if she had a chill. "In fact," she carefully lied, "I've seen that cat around many times. It belongs down the street. I've even seen it there on their doorstep. It was probably as scared of you as you were of it."

"Do—do you think so?" Ellen asked.

"Yes, I'm sure of it. Now, why don't you go up with her, Beth, and as soon as you're ready, we'll spend a fun day. We won't come home until we're too tired to go anywhere else. And I'll lock up the house carefully so that kitty cat won't get in anymore."

They went up the broad staircase together, Beth holding Ellen's hand. Faye could hear Beth talking to her in low, soothing tones.

Faye went through the house, checking the four outside doors. They were all locked, except, of course, the door from the kitchen. None of the downstairs windows were unlocked either, except the ones in the breakfast room. But the screens were tight. Nothing had entered.

The screen on the kitchen door should have prevented the cat from entering.

The only explanation was that somehow, before Nordene and the kids left, someone had inadvertently allowed the cat to enter when he or she went into the kitchen.

She stood gazing toward the barn.

Something was wrong.

If anyone at all had gone into the house, she hadn't noticed it. But with kids around, one of them . . .

Ellen.

Ellen had gone in. The only one of them who had. In some way the cat had gone with her.

As if it were following her.

Faye tried to shake off the feeling of horror that Ellen's scream had settled upon her. She got her purse off the table by the back door and went out onto the terrace. Joey was still standing there, his face pale.

"It's all right," she said. "Why don't you come with me? We'll get the car out and be ready to go."

He trotted along beside her. Faye opened the garage

door where the station wagon was parked and left it up. Joey climbed into the back seat.

It felt kind of good, she realized, to have him there. It was comforting in a way she had never known before.

She backed the car out and turned it around and waited within view of the terrace as the girls came down.

The screen door of the kitchen slammed.

"Do you want the door locked?" Beth called. Ellen came across the lawn to the driveway.

Faye put her head out the window. "No. It's all right. Nothing ever happens around here."

At least it hadn't—in all the years she had lived in this house there had never been a burglary. Farther downtown was a whole different story.

Faye had said good night to the children and gone to her room, so tired that her bed looked like heaven, when the phone rang. It was Gavin, she knew. They had agreed on the hour past bedtime for the children, so they could talk without interruptions.

Faye leaned back on the lounge at the foot of the bed and exchanged endearments with Gavin.

"How's it going?"

"Fine, Gavin. We spent the day playing around, I'm afraid. We ate lunch at Burger King, then went to the park where they swam for a couple of hours."

There was no point in telling him about Ellen's nervousness, she had decided ahead of time. Certainly not over the telephone. It would only worry him during the night, and there was nothing he could do about it.

"I knew you were out galavanting around," he said, and she giggled, reminding herself of Nordene. "I tried to call you this afternoon."

"Why?" She felt a touch of alarm. They had agreed

on calls at ten P.M., his idea.

"I have to be out of town for several days. My flight leaves at midnight. They're sending me to Alaska and back into the wilds. We have to check on some problems on an oil pipeline there. I've never been that far away from a town before, when I've gone to Alaska, but my supervisor tells me I might not get to a telephone for several days, maybe a week or more. I'll call you as soon as I find one. Do you think you will be all right?"

"I—yes, of course." She always had this lonely, deserted feeling when he was sent away somewhere, even though it was usually only for a couple of days. But that was another of the things she would not tell him. He had to do what his job called for.

"If—" he said. "if you need me during that time just send someone after me, okay? If our plane can make it in there, so can someone else's."

"Yes, don't worry, Gavin. You don't know how long you'll be gone?"

"I hope to be back by the weekend but"—he wasn't committing himself—"we stay until the problem is solved."

They talked longer, about things at home. She told him about Nordene and her two kids coming over, even though she hadn't told him that Nordene in the beginning had not wanted Katy and Dwayne to associate with Ellen and Joey.

"They played well together," she said. "I think they're going to be friends." No mention of the cat, except "I was thinking it's about time we get a pet, Gavin. It seems odd to be here at home again with no pets around. When I was growing up there was always a cat and a dog, and when they grew old and died, others were brought in. They died while I was gone, and we've lived here for four months now without anything. Do you know if any of the children are afraid of animals?"

"Ummm . . . no, I don't know, I'm ashamed to say. I hadn't even thought about it. But I don't know why they should be."

"We'll wait and let you help us decide."

"You don't have to do that. Go to the Humane Society shelter and get one. Those homeless creatures need homes."

"Yes, that's a good idea. I'm sure they have kittens."

"Pups too, but an old dog needs a home also."

They exchanged newspaper stories of which Dallas seemed never to run out. And then came the mundane.

"I have a girl coming tomorrow to do the laundry," Faye said. "I called the cleaning service today and they gave me a name. She lives down in old town, and her name is Rhoda Shelly. She'll come twice a week if she works out."

"Remember, Faye, Beth is old enough to help do laundry and anything else. Ellen and Joey should be able to keep their own rooms and help with other things, too."

"I'll take them swimming again. They seemed to enjoy that."

"When are you going to stop treating them like guests, Faye?" Gavin asked gently, as if he were afraid of hurting her feelings.

She felt stunned. "Am I doing that?"

"I think so."

There was a pause.

"I'd better go, Babe," Gavin said. "I've got to pick up some things at the office."

Faye looked at her wristwatch and realized they had been talking for almost an hour. She gave him a kiss over the phone, told him again that she loved him and then told him good night. She never told him goodbye when he was taking a trip.

She hung up the phone and went to stand in front of her dressing table. She removed her watch and the ring she had worn on her right hand today. Her wedding set was left on, day and night. She removed her earrings, and the thin, gold necklace, and put it all into her jewelry case, closing the lid. Her eyes felt heavy with tiredness. The house was quiet.

To make sure the kids were settled, she went to the door and looked out into the hall. The silence here was more pronounced than in her bedroom where she could hear more of the night creatures: the katydids, the jarflies with their constant summer buzz, beginning now to drift away for the night. They slept, too, it seemed, for the hour of three A.M. would be silent. That quietness would last for about two hours, and then the noises would begin again .

No one was moving in the hall, and she decided against going to each bedroom.

The phone rang again, and she returned to her bedroom, closing the door behind her. She felt a jangling sense of unease at the sound of the phone. A call this late was unusual. But could it be that Gavin had forgotten something?

Her sister's voice, yawning, came lazily into her ear.

"Hi," Janet said. "You've been gabbing for a couple of hours. Or does that teenager of yours already have the phones tied up?"

Faye's spirits lifted, the uneasiness sliding away into relief. Nothing was wrong, no one had died, Gavin hadn't forgotten anything.

"I have not been gabbing for two hours," Faye said, "and my so-called teenager is not, yet, and won't be for almost a year. Why are you calling at this late hour?"

"Because I couldn't get you earlier. And I tried all day, too."

"Well, I admit we've been out and around. What's happening?"

"Nothing."

"Nothing at all?"

"That's why I'm calling you. I'm bored."

"Well, thanks a lot."

They giggled together briefly, then Janet yawned again. Faye could almost see her. Janet was three years older than herself, twenty-eight now, and she was also taller and heavier. Her face was more round than Faye's, with dimples in her cheeks. Her hair was darker and worn shorter. They really didn't resemble each other at all. No one would have said, "You're sisters, I can tell by the resemblance." The way she'd heard people say about other sisters.

"I was just thinking about us," Faye said. "And other sisters. How they so seldom look like sisters. Had you noticed that?"

"No, but I'm glad you brought that to my attention. What a revelation!"

They laughed again.

"But seriously, Faye, how's it going? You and your readymade family?"

"Fine."

"Get that hearty sound out of your voice and tell me the truth. This is Janet, remember? And even if we don't look like sisters, we are, and I'm concerned about you. I'd drive up and see for myself, but I really need to keep at my job. If I took a day off now, I think my boss would fire me. He's all up in the air about something. Probably had a fight with his wife."

"I am telling the truth. The kids are good. I like them."

"I hope it works out, but I sense a strain in your voice, Faye. I think there's something you're not telling me."

"No. Of course I can't give you a blow by blow—"
"Blow by blow?"
"Poor choice of words."
They began laughing again.
"At least it hasn't come to that, huh?"
Faye said, "Of course not. You know it won't. I'm no fighter."
"Maybe that's why I'm kind of worried about you, Punkins. You've always been such a gentle kid, that if you did come up against two or three strong wills, what would you do?"
"Uh . . ."
"That's what I thought. And especially since Gavin isn't there to help you during the week. Is he coming home mid-week the way he does sometimes?"
Faye said carefully, "I'm sure he will if he feels it's necessary." What Janet didn't know about his trip to Alaska wouldn't hurt either of them. "How are Rob and Lanny?"
"Good. They're both asleep. Lanny has a better daycare than he did before. I got him into the church daycare. Since they were good enough to take him, I think we'll go more often. We're even thinking of joining and really getting into it. It's time we prepare a background for Lanny, something solid. And I kind of like what the church is doing for the community. Are you taking your kids—what are their names again?"
"Beth, Joey and Ellen, in that order, from oldest to youngest."
"Oops. I said Lanny was asleep, but I hear him crying. Got to go, Faye. Call me."
Faye hung up, feeling relief steal over her again. Anytime she had to talk about her stepchildren to neighbors, friends or relatives, she could feel herself tighten. She was becoming defensive. But why was it that not one had expressed anything but concern? Was

it because of what had happened to their mother? She felt it was, because the negative attitudes had not started until then.

She went to bed, determined to sleep well, to forget everything.

Maybe Gavin was right, and she was treating the kids too much like guests.

Maybe she should stop trying so hard to see that they were kept busy and entertained.

She hadn't finished the nursery; her sewing machine was still set up. Right in the middle of the room. Fabrics were on chairs and still in packages. Come to think of it, she hadn't even been in the nursery since Gavin's children had arrived.

Well, she had more or less promised they would go back to the park and the swimming pool tomorrow, but after that she'd try settling into a more homelike routine. Maybe they would be more at ease, too, because, come to think of it, they acted as if they were guests. A bit uncomfortable, a bit too polite.

And Ellen . . . showing signs of a deep terror that lived with her, covered by her shyness at being in a strange place.

Faye turned over, realizing that she was staring at the fan again as if she were prepared to stay awake all night.

She shut her eyes and concentrated on the movements in her belly.

Sleep, baby, sleep.
Papa has gone a'hunting . . .

Ellen listened to the night sounds. They were so different here. At home the sound of the freeway had lingered into the night, punctuated by sirens and horns. Sometimes the mockingbird sang in the tree in the yard, and she heard a similar bird here, but mostly in the daytime, not at night. Here the night seemed darker, with all the trees that surrounded the house shutting out the street lights. Sometimes she heard a siren, but it sounded far away. Downtown, Beth had said, as if they lived a long way from downtown.

She hadn't been asleep. Her door was shut, and her room was dark; but she lay facing the window, seeing the pale rectangle. It was only slightly less dark outside the window than in her room.

In her arms she clutched her doll, its head pressed tightly beneath her chin.

At first she had left her light on, but she felt uneasy, as if *it* could see her better that way.

So she stared at her window and wondered what would happen if it—the big cat or whatever it had turned into now—found her window and leaped to the sill. Would she see it? Before it got to her?

She heard sounds, a buzzing outside in the trees. Not crickets, but something else. And coming now from somewhere far away she heard a sound that made her skin tighten, that made her want to run to her mama for protection.

It was the cat again, screaming out in the night, yowling an evil, dreadful sound, letting her know it had not gone away.

She sat up, fear stiffening her back. The meowing was coming nearer, growing louder, coming across the hills in front of the house, with all the trees covering whatever it really was, coming now into the yard and toward the house.

It was coming to stand beneath her window, as if to mock her, to let her know it had many forms, and it knew where she was. Silence now. A terrible silence, broken by scratchings on the wall outside as it climbed toward her window.

It knew she knew it had killed her mother, and it was playing with her, a cat and mouse game; and when it tired of the game it would pounce—!

She ran out of her room, her doll in one arm. She threw her door open and left it, and then stopped in the middle of the hall.

The yowling had stopped, but its echo came with each frantic beat of her heart.

She stared at the closed doors along the hall. Beth's door was closed and so was Joey's. Why had they closed their doors?

Turning, she faced the length of the hall toward the big room above the heading of the stairs. Faye's room was there, at the front of the house. The pale light in the hall ceiling made deep shadows at every turn, behind every piece of furniture, even around the heavy frames of the pictures of scenes and people that hung on the walls.

Tentatively she went forward, her bare feet silent on the carpeted hall floor. She passed closed doors and came into the room off the stair landing. Her stepmother's door was around the railing of the stairwell and at the end. She had seen her go in and out there.

Ellen looked down over the banister. The large entrance hall was dark. She stared into that well of darkness, and she could see movement there, darker darks within the lightless corners beneath, things that moved and watched her.

She stepped back from the banister and slid along the wall, her back to it.

When she came to the door to her stepmother's room, she put her hand up to knock, a small fist made. Then she uncurled her fingers and dropped them to the knob.

She hesitated.

No, you can't do that.
Don't ever enter a room without knocking.
Please...
The yowling came again, rising softly from somewhere outside the house and curling over Ellen's skin like furry fingers clawed with knives.

She pressed hard against the wall and turned the knob on the door.

Faye's room was not totally dark. A light had been left on in the adjoining bath and shone out softly through the crack the slightly open door made, stretching across the carpet toward her as if showing her the way.

Ellen slipped into the room and eased the door shut behind her.

Then she went to the corner and sat down, her knees drawn up, her doll cradled between her chest and her knees.

She put her head down on her arms.

The terrible meowing drifted away, and the night grew quiet.

Faye woke and stretched, feeling out with her arm for Gavin, then chiding herself for always doing that when she woke up. It was as if she always expected him to be there, within reach, like a child expecting candy.

She squirmed, feeling achey. Something had woke her—but what? The hour was early, she could tell by the lack of sunlight in her east window. The trees kept it out, except for a streak now and then, but early in the morning there was always a spot of sunlight on the floor, as if signaling time for her to rise.

She felt a vibration in the house, a movement somewhere. Then she realized what it was.

Someone was running.

She sat up, reaching for her robe.

The sound became definite footsteps, thudding along the hall, around the banister toward her room. Simultaneously there was a knock and a voice.

"Faye," Beth called. "Faye!"

The door opened, and Beth's face, pale and terrified, looked into the room.

"I can't find Ellen!"

Faye's feet were on the floor, and she stood up, still tying her robe as she rushed toward Beth.

A movement in the corner, back behind the end of a chest of drawers, caught her eye.

Ellen was uncurling from the ball she had made of herself, standing up, blinking sleep from her eyes.

Beth and Faye stared at her.

Ellen stood with her back against the meeting walls of the corner returning their stares.

Beth broke free from her trance and went toward Ellen.

"What are you doing here?"

Ellen looked from one face to the other. "I heard something," she murmured. "It scared me. So I just came here, that's all."

"Oh, Ellen!" Beth scolded. "Why didn't you come to me?"

"Your door was shut."

"You shouldn't bother Faye—"

Faye stepped forward. "No, it's all right. Ellen, I didn't even know you were here. Why didn't you wake me?"

She started to reach out to Ellen, but Beth was leading her away, her hands on Ellen's shoulders. Faye saw a set and angry look around Beth's mouth, a whiteness edging the pink lips like a thin line of ice.

Faye stepped back, out of their way, puzzled. Beth's anger might have been brought on by fear, she decided.

Fear and relief when she discovered that Ellen was all right after all.

"Beth," Faye said, "it's all right, really. I want all of you to know that if you feel frightened in the night you can come to me."

"Thank you," Beth said. "We'll be all right."

Faye watched them go down the hall. Joey evidently had not awakened, and she was glad he hadn't. What should she do, she wondered, just leave them alone to work it out as they wished?

After a few minutes she backed away and went to get dressed. Down to breakfast, she decided, where she would prepare something out of the ordinary. Muffins, maybe. Poached eggs. Maybe even waffles, even though she didn't often approve of sugary things so early in the day. This morning called for an exception to the rules.

She was still playing hostess, but for the time, how else could she handle it?

The house was built in 1882, the plaque on the brick post at the corner of the porch said. Rhoda Shelly looked at it and looked at the house. It was tall and wide, with a lot of windows and porches. There was even a porchless roof under which cars could park and let out the riders, to keep them out of the rain, she guessed.

What a lot of windows! What a lot of washing that would amount to. Who kept them so sparkling? Not her, that was for sure. Thank the Lord she wasn't no window washer. Clothes were bad enough.

Out behind the big brick house was a bunch of other smaller buildings, and one of them was the wash house.

The lady had shown her around, shown her where the clothes were that had to be washed and told her to just fold them and leave them on the table in the wash house, at least until they got back this afternoon. They were going swimming. When they got back she would tell her where the clothes went.

The lady sure looked young to have such big kids. Another one on the way, too, the way she looked. Slim little girl with a tummy that pushed out the front of the smocklike dress that she wore. She must like kids, because otherwise she probably wouldn't be having them. People here on Honky Hill had money enough to have abortions whenever they wanted one.

The wash house was over toward the northwest corner of the big house, a low, one story brick building with one door in the corner closest to the kitchen door of the house, and one small window at each end. There were no curtains on the windows, but still the light that came in was so slight that Rhoda had to pull the cord on the electric bulb that dangled from the center of the ceiling. Even the light didn't seem to get rid of the patches of dark in the corners, like leftover pieces of night.

She stood in the middle of the room and looked around. The boss gal hadn't come into the building. She had just stood at the door and told Rhoda she'd find the washer and dryer there, and the soaps and all, and she could leave the clothes on the table until they got back this afternoon.

Rhoda could see why she hadn't come in. It was not a pleasant place. Though the outside air was warm, inside the wash house was like being inside an igloo. Rhoda could smell the dampness oozing up from between the bricks in the floor.

It was an uneven floor, and she suspected it hadn't been redone since it was built back in 1882. Moss grew in small patches here and there, and against the wall she saw some small toadstools sticking out, like tiny gray umbrellas. She'd bet the big house didn't look like this.

The table in the middle was long and narrow, covered with a floral oil cloth. Somebody had washed it off recently. Rhoda tested it for dust by swiping a finger down the middle, and found none. She grunted approval. At least she wouldn't have to wash it before she started her work.

Against the wall on the north side was a line of white washers and dryers, two of each. At the other end she saw a washing machine with a wringer, and beside it two zinc tubs. Still there, the old stuff. At one corner of the rear wall were some engine-looking parts, taking up a good piece of the corner. She stared at it for some time before she figured it out. A generator. Delco. For the days when electricity had not been piped in. It had probably throbbed day and night providing lights for the big house, and it was still there, unused, gathering dust.

The hampers were sitting just inside the door. She had carried out a couple of them herself, but most of them were already here, brought out by the lady and her kids, Rhoda guessed. Fine, it wouldn't hurt them to do a little work. By the time she was six years old she was helping her mama with the laundry.

She dumped the clothes out onto the long table and began sorting them: the whites, the darks, the cottons, the underwear. Within minutes the washing machines were going, and then the dryers. She was busy moving clothes around, from the table to the washer, to the dryer, back to the table for folding.

Her arms began to feel chilled, and as soon as she could take a break, she went out into the yard and walked around.

It was a big yard, with a stand of trees in front reaching all the way to the street like a forest. The area beneath was planted with azaleas and rhododendrons, but their blooms had withered now and hung dead and faded. Sometimes there were ferns, green and reaching, like green spiders.

She walked over to the driveway. It was paved with brick, too, from the street to the roof that hung out over it, but there the brick ended. Cement began and widened, going back to a long garage that looked as if it would hold at least five cars. She opened a small door and looked in. One of the stalls had an old car that was probably an antique. She knew cars pretty well and judged this one to be from the thirties. A Packard. It was black and long. Not quite a limo.

Around a path and down through more trees was a barn. In it, she saw when she looked through the door that was standing partway open, was a buggy.

These richies hung onto things, she thought to herself as she backed away. They had 'em and kept 'em. Lucky bitches.

In her own family they hadn't even been able to afford a good family picture to hand down.

She walked around behind the barn and came to a high fence. Beyond it she saw the backyard of another large house that had, as this one did, an acre to spare in the backyard, say nothing of the front.

She turned and almost stumbled over the cat.

It ran, a large yellow tube of fur, and stopped again about ten feet away. It sat down, hunkered as if to spring, and glared at her. She liked cats, had three of her own. She put her hand out, smiling.

"Here, kitty, kitty."

Its yellow eyes, peculiarly slanted in its head, continued to glare at her. Puzzled, slightly wounded in her feelings, she slowly drew back her hand. No cat was unfriendly unless it had been mistreated by someone.

Yet this cat didn't look as if it were neglected. It got plenty of food from somewhere. But it was big, bigger than any cat she had ever seen.

She met the glare of its eyes, beginning to feel uneasy. Was it really a cat? Perhaps a feral cat, or a bobcat? Something wild and dangerous?

No, not bobcat. She could see its long tail reaching out into the fallen leaves behind it.

Its teeth were suddenly bared, and the sound that came was like a deep growl from a nightmare.

Rhoda backed away, half afraid it would spring.

"Kitty, kitty," she tried again, timidly.

The cat didn't move.

Rhoda kept backing, putting more and more distance between her and it, until suddenly it was only a part of the winter's leaves that hadn't been raked and removed. She stared, trying to find it, and decided that somehow it had slipped away, right while she was watching it.

She turned, looking behind her. Nothing but trees, leaves, ferns, reaching green fronds like spider legs.

She hurried back to the wash house and pulled shut the door.

Her hands shook as she pulled clothes out of the dryer. She felt itching cold with the dampness in the building, the chilly air and the odd fear that still crawled over her.

That was no cat.

It was something else. She didn't know what.

Nervousness was increasing. She desperately needed a joint. She looked around, unconsciously looking to see who was watching her. No one, of course. Mama watched her a lot, but Mama was not here, nor was any of her big family. Her mama threatened to throw her out if she ever got into drugs again, so she had to be careful, even with her pot smoking. There was nowhere she could go, with her two babies, that she knew of. Her mama took care of them while she worked, but only on the condition that she behave herself. Nineteen and the mother of two, she had no husband—never had one—and not even a steady boyfriend anymore. No decent job, either. Where else could she go? She felt like crying, it was all so hopeless. Welfare didn't pay enough to rent a house, and besides, her mama didn't approve of welfare for able-bodied people, or people over sixteen.

She opened her purse. In the bottom, tied up in a handkerchief, carefully hidden from her mama, was the only medicine she had for her nervousness or boredom. She pulled it out and laid it open on the table. Precious dried pot leaves.

She crumbled the leaves in her fingers and scooped them into a cigarette paper. She rolled it carefully, not spilling a bit, and licked the paper closed.

Looking over her shoulder guiltily, as if Mama were there, she struck a match under the wood table and lighted the reefer.

She drew the smoke in deeply and held it, feeling the relaxation steal over her, like a big, fluffy blanket unrolling from the inside. She smiled at the ceiling, hoisted her rear up and sat on the table, legs swinging.

She smoked, puffing, sucking, holding, getting every morsel of smoke, keeping it going and letting little of it drift away.

And yet the smoke seemed to have filled the tight room suddenly. The bulb above was a mere pinpoint of light in the smoke-filled room. The dark gray smoke writhed around her head, and she found herself trying to fight it away with her hands. It only stirred more, like clouds rolling in a stormy sky.

Puzzled, wondering, she slid off the table, realizing it was not her marijuana cigarette that had made so much smoke. The building must be on fire!

She began peering through the smoke for signs of a

flame and saw none. She tried to find the door.

Running her hands over the wall, she sought the crack that would be the door, and when she found it, she ran her hands downward in search of the knob. The smoke was burning her eyes, filling her lungs with something stronger, darker, deadlier than pot smoke.

She found the knob and twisted it. The door was stuck. Or locked from the outside? She had seen a bar on the door, one that could be fitted down into a metal holder, barring the door from the outside. Why?

She twisted the knob back and forth, panic building. Then it gave abruptly, and she almost fell over the threshold. She took a gulp of fresh air, and her head cleared.

Fire!

She had to try to put it out. If the lady came home and found her wash house on fire she'd . . . call the police, and Rhoda didn't want no dealings with the police!

She turned back, searching. The smoke was thinner now near the door, but Rhoda looked into the nucleus of it and saw it writhing and rolling, an angry cloud that was forming—*forming into figures . . . hard to see . . . to piece together*—

Rhoda reached instinctively for her handbag and held it with both hands against her chest as she stared at the figure that was forming in the smoke as if it were giving birth . . . or as if the smoke were spewing it upward and creating a solid being from—from what?

She began to try to scream. The eyes looked at her, saw her, and the outlines of the face and body became solid, trailing at the bottom into smoke, hidden by smoke, made of . . .

She turned and ran, sensing that it was behind her.

She stumbled to her car, got in and turned the switch. The car sputtered, caught. The engine roared as she backed out of the driveway toward the street.

But something was in the back seat. She couldn't look, she just knew it was there. Her foot pressed the accelerator to the floor, and the old car jerked and jogged, cutting across the street into a vacant lot that was filled with trees, and then it died.

Rhoda opened the car door and fell out, but she wasn't able to rise. It had come with her, as insubstantial as the smoke, as strange and dangerous as the wild creature that looked like a cat, as deadly as a human killer.

She tried to crawl away in the crisp leaves of last winter's freeze.

The leaves rustled underneath her as she moved her body in her feeble attempt to escape.

She turned to fight it, at last, her underbody exposed, and saw above her the materialization of something she didn't understand. It looked real, this huge yellow-skinned body, the huge head hairless, the eyes slitted, skin drawn tight over them, revealing only a burning blackness between the lids.

What did it want of her?

It, not he, for it was not human; it was only in human form. Huge, gross, human form.

And then she knew.

Chapter Eleven

"What's that?" Joey cried, pointing past her shoulder as Faye guided the car toward the driveway.

"It's police cars," Beth said. "Something's happened."

Joey asked, "Can we go see? Please?"

Beth answered for Faye, "No, Joey, weird! Why do you want to see? It's probably a car wreck."

Joey sat back, but his head turned, keeping his eyes on the blue flashing lights of the police cars that were parked at the side of the street half a block down the hill.

Ellen had looked in silence, and then drawn back into her corner, watching the blue lights warily.

"They're like Christmas lights," Joey observed. "The police car lights are like Christmas lights."

"Not to me they're not," Beth said.

Faye parked the car in the garage. It had been a long day, and she was glad it was coming to an end.

"I guess Rhoda finished the laundry and left," she said, realizing belatedly that the small red car that the young woman had been driving was no longer in the driveway. "I told her to wait, but she must have decided we were away too long."

Car doors opened; kids got out. Joey hurried out beneath the garage door before Faye closed it.

Stop treating them like guests.

"Wait, Joey," she called after him. "You have clothes to carry up to your room."

He stopped, looked back at her, his face puckered slightly in disappointment. "Can't I do it later? I just want to see the police cars."

Faye half expected Beth to say something, to run an interference of sorts, but she didn't.

Faye said, "All right, ten minutes. But don't go out of the yard. Don't go into the street."

"I won't," Joey shouted, and went running away, his feet smacking the uneven brick of the narrow drive that led from the house to the street.

Before he was halfway to the street he cut off across the front yard, going beneath the tall oak and sycamore trees. He reached the ditch between the yard and the street and jumped across it, but stopped with his feet carefully off the pavement of the street.

The cars were only a few yards away now. He could see the men walking through the trees on the other side of the street, and when he stretched to his tiptoes, he could see the top of a small red car there.

It was the car that had been in the driveway earlier. The one that belonged to the girl who had come to wash their clothes.

It didn't look as if she'd had a wreck. But why had she driven down into the woods?

A siren wailed nearer, and the nose of an ambulance with the letters *ecnalubma* across the front came up over the hill, speeding toward the scene. Its siren cut away and wailed down. Joey stepped back, going across the ditch to the yard. The white automobile passed him and stopped near the police cars.

Joey could hear their voices but few of their words. He watched the activity with growing unease.

It was like...

An ambulance had come for her, too, while he and his sisters sat in the back of the police car.

He saw two men carry a stretcher up out of the woods, and on it was a roll of something, like a sleeping bag all rolled up with the sleeper still in it.

Just like...

They put it into the open double doors at the back of the ambulance, and then shut and locked the doors. The two men got into the ambulance, and it started and drove away, going on down the street, its siren off.

Just like when they took... Mama...

Something stung and burned his cheeks, and he reached up and found them wet. Now his eyes blurred. He hadn't known he was crying.

Remembering and crying.

The uniforms of the policemen blurred. Tones of brown, they grew larger and larger through his tears. He blinked, swallowed and used the backs of his hands to clear his eyes.

One of the men was less than ten feet away from him, coming closer, looking at him, reminding Joey of the policeman who had come to help his mother.

"Hello, son, what's your name?" he asked, stopping on the edge of the street, across the ditch from Joey.

Joey looked past him, and saw another cop standing by one of the cars. Two more were getting into a car that had the lights off now and were just sitting there with the door open. One of them picked up the radio mike and began talking into it.

"Joey," he said. "Joey Pendergast."

The policeman nodded toward the brick house set back an acre deep in the trees. "That your home?"

"Yes, sir."

"Why don't you just run on back now? Someone will

be there to talk to you and your folks sometime soon."

"What happened?" Joey asked. "Did she have a wreck?"

"Did you know her?"

"I think it was Rhoda's car."

"Rhoda? You knew her?"

"She came to—" Joey looked over his shoulder at the house in the trees. It wasn't really his house, so he couldn't call it "our house" as he had started to. And it was hard to say "Faye's house" because it didn't seem right to call his stepmother "Faye," even though she had said it was all right if they did. His mama had always told him to call older people by their last names, or some other title. Mostly, he didn't call them anything.

"To what, Joey?"

"She came to do our washing," he managed. "This morning. She was here when we left to go to the park. We ate out at the picnic grounds. We took some sandwiches there. And then we went swimming, me and Beth and Ellen. *She* just sat on a chair and watched us."

"She?"

Another car, with men in it, came slowly by and parked by the other cars, but this one was just a regular blue Buick. Joey watched it.

"Yes, sir," he said, coming back to the officer in the street. "My stepmother. Faye."

"Why were you crying, Joey?"

He started to deny it.

His mouth worked soundlessly. He had wanted to give a flat no, and then he had wanted to tell the policeman about his mother; but he couldn't. It was a bad dream that hadn't really happened. His mother was well and living in California. She was working all the time. She was waiting. They had come here for the summer, that was all.

"Me and my sisters," he finally said, "are visiting my stepmother. We only just came."

"Today?"

"No, last week."

"Joey!"

The call came from halfway across the yard. Joey turned and saw Beth. She was standing beneath the limbs of a smaller tree in amongst the tall forest trees, and she had changed her clothes and was now wearing jeans and a striped red and blue pullover, a new one that Faye had bought her when they went shopping. Beth liked to wear new clothes. Her dark hair was pulled back in the braid that Faye had made on the back of her head and down her shoulders.

"Faye said maybe you should come in now," Beth called.

Joey told the policeman apologetically, "I got to go."

"Fine, you tell your stepmother that some of us will probably be in to talk to her pretty soon."

"Okay."

Joey ran, sadness and fear replaced with excitement as he hurried toward his sister. He had things to tell them.

Beth turned and ran ahead of him, so that he didn't catch up with her until they had gone around the house and up onto the terrace. Their stepmother was sitting at the glass-topped table sorting through the mail, separating it into piles. Most of it looked like junk.

"It's a car wreck," he said excitedly.

Ellen, sitting with her doll, looked up, squinting through the light of the lowering sun. Faye looked up, too. He had their attention.

"It was the lady who came to do our laundry."

Faye said, in a surprised voice, *"Rhoda?"*

Joey nodded, and started to tell more, even though he realized now that he had very little to tell. The ambulance had come and got her . . . but . . .

Faye was standing now, looking toward the wash house. "I was wondering where she was."

Joey followed her as she went down the steps from the terrace and walked the nearly invisible path through the leaves and grass to the door of the wash house. Beth and Ellen came, too.

Faye opened the door and pushed it back, going in, wrinkling her nose. Joey smelled the smoke, a heavy, dark smell, strong and burning as he breathed it. But behind him, through the open door, the fresh air surged, and the leftover smell of smoke was pushed away. He followed the others into the room.

It was shadowy and cool, as if it were air conditioned. The brick floor was uneven. Some of the bricks looked loose, though they felt solid when he stepped on them. A long table in the middle of the room was covered with clothes, some of them in a pile, the rest folded.

Faye was looking around, sniffing the air. "Where on earth is that smell coming from? I don't understand it. That's the second or third time lately I've smelled that. At first I thought it might be coming in from someone's trash fire, which, I might add, is illegal in the city limits."

"I don't know," Beth was saying, walking around the table, looking at all the things against the walls, the washers and dryers.

Joey spotted the machinery against the rear corner, deep in shadows even with the ceiling light on. It had pulleys and knobs and screws and bolts. "Hey," he said. "What's this?"

"That's the old generator," Faye said absently as she looked into unlikely places for the source of the fire. She opened the washing machine and then the dryer. Both were empty. She checked the clothes hampers. They were empty, too.

"What's that?" Joey asked.

"A generator that creates electricity," Faye said, still looking for something that might explain the source of the smoke. She tried to open the small window at the end, but it seemed to be permanently set into the wood frame. "It was used to light the house and provide power for the washing machines, and things like that. It's old, Joey."

"Does it still work?"

"Probably not."

Faye began to fold clothes. Some of them she shook out and put on hangers. Beth was moving piles of the folded things, separating them into groups.

"Can I put these back in the hampers so they'll be easier to carry?" Beth asked.

"Good idea," Faye said.

"Here then, Ellen and Joey, take your things upstairs."

"Awww," Joey complained. "I want to look at the generator before it gets too dark to see."

"No, you'll get greasy. Come on, take your clothes up."

He picked up his hamper, his arms around it. It was made of wicker and wasn't very large or heavy. Behind him came Ellen.

He opened the doors for her, let her pass through and then followed her into the kitchen, across its tiled floor, through the next door into the narrower rear hall, and along its tiled floor. Then there were double doors, where the wide carpeted hall of the front part of the house started. He left one of the doors open. Ellen went ahead of him now, silent, into the big entrance hall that was like a living room, and then around the newel post and up the stairs.

It was like the house had swallowed them. All around was the silence of the house, but Ellen was looking around in jerky little movements, her eyes bugged as if she were scared.

"It's all right, Ellen," he said soothingly. "There's nothing to be afraid of here." Even his voice, to his own ears, was muffled by the walls and the floors, and it seemed, as they drew near their own rooms at the back of the rear hall, that he could smell that awful smoke again, or whatever it was.

Faye had just finished carrying the last of the clothes upstairs when she came down to find the police car in the driveway, pulled back near the terrace. Two uniformed men had come to the edge of the terrace and were talking to Beth.

Beth turned toward Faye and took a couple of steps backward, as if to escape. "They want to know about Rhoda," she said.

"Has she had an accident?" Faye asked. "My stepson seemed to think so."

"Joey Pendergast? Are you Mrs. Pendergast?"

"Yes, and this is Beth. The little girl by the table is Ellen. We've been gone today. Rhoda Shelly came this morning to handle the laundry. She left before we got home, and she hadn't finished the work. She left no note to say why she wasn't waiting for us, as she had said she would. I'm sorry if she's had an accident. Is she hurt?"

"She's dead."

"Dead?" Faye's voice was a shocked whisper. She

cast a quick glance toward the street, as if she could see through the house to the scene of the accident. "There?" she said. "But how could she get up enough speed . . . ? Or was it a collision?"

"It wasn't a car wreck, Ma'am."

There were footsteps in the grass, a faint series of footfalls on the brick path beyond. Faye looked over her shoulder. Nordene and her two children were within hearing distance and must have heard part of what the policeman said. Nordene was staring at him with her lips parted.

Dwayne and Katy were unaffected, if they had heard. "Can you play?" Katy was asking Ellen, and Ellen stood up, ready to follow Katy.

Nordene came close to Faye and asked in a hushed voice, "What happened?"

Faye explained to the policemen who Nordene was, while behind Nordene, Katy was leading Ellen away.

Nordene glanced frantically over her shoulder. "Do you think it will be all right if they play?" Then called out, without waiting for an answer, "Don't go far, Katy. Don't go to the barn!"

Faye watched the kids run, their voices coming back, joyous, untouched by the tragedy down the road. She was glad to hear that even Ellen's voice was among them, that silent, inwardly hurt little Ellen, so fearful of every shadow. Let her play, escape for a while from those monsters in her mind.

"There's nothing the children can tell you anyway," Faye explained to the officers. "They were with me all day, and they don't know any more than I do."

"What on earth is wrong?" Nordene asked.

One of the officers said, "A young woman by the name of Rhoda Shelly was murdered near here this afternoon. Her car was driven into the edge of the timber in a vacant lot across the street and down the hill; the car door was open. She was found in the winter leaves about thirty feet on down the hillside from the car. It seems she spent most of the day here."

"Here?"

"She was doing the laundry," Faye explained.

"Oh." Nordene looked worried and more . . . afraid, Faye decided, as she saw Nordene's eyes dart toward the wash house, and on past it, then around to other buildings and shrubs that would hide a killer.

For the first time, feeling Nordene's fear contagious, Faye's skin grew cold. Goosebumps rose on her arms, a tingle of warning went down her spine. The back door of the house had been open all day. The murderer could be hiding anywhere.

"I was at home all day long," Nordene said. "I live just next door. I didn't hear a thing. God! And someone was being killed, and I didn't know it. Oh God, how horrible!"

"Did you see any cars here other than Mrs. Pendergast's or Rhoda's?"

"From my house, as you can see, you can't see anything. The trees in the summer fill in the space. In the winter, I can see the upper story of Faye's house, but the vines on the fence are evergreen. How was she killed?"

"We can't give out that kind of information yet. In fact, we won't know how she died until the report from the medical examiner comes in."

The air was turning cool, Faye decided, trying not to look as if she were hugging her arms. She folded them across her diaphragm and clasped cool palms to her upper arms to ward off the chilling effect of the air. But the coldness remained.

Nordene was looking around for the kids. "Do you think they're safe?"

They had gone to the wash house. The pull of the

generator, Faye thought in wry amusement. Their voices sounded as if they were in a cave. She could hear all four of them, Ellen's voice occasionally punctuating the others, just enough to let Faye know she was there, and safe.

"Since the dead woman was last here, so far as anyone knows, we'll need to search the premises, with your permission," the policeman said. "We'll try not to disturb you."

Faye nodded. They moved away but remained at the side of the car, one of them talking on the radio transmitter.

"Would you and the kids like to come over to my house for the night, Faye?" Nordene shuddered and hugged her arms against her. "You can't stay here. Alone. Come home with us."

"Nordene, that's very nice of you, but I'm sure we'll be all right. This has nothing to do with us, not really."

"We've never had a murder in this neighborhood before."

"It was probably someone she knew. An old boyfriend, maybe. Someone who followed her up here."

"Well, maybe. God knows there's plenty of crime down where she came from, if she came from downtown."

"She did."

"Drugs, maybe. There's a lot of drug trafficking downtown, they say. Drugs and murder seem to be related." Nordene was frowning, staring off toward the wash house. "You said the kids were with you all day?"

A brief flash of anger rankled over Faye's skin, like goosebumps raised by frigid air. "Nordene," she said firmly, "you still don't have that ridiculous idea that Gavin's kids are involved in anyone's death, do you? *Not in the murder of this girl!*"

"No, no, no," Nordene protested hastily. "No, not really. It's just all . . . so weird. So . . . coincidental?"

"Yes, maybe that. And very tragic. Rhoda was so young. She didn't look much more than sixteen, though she was old enough to have two small children."

Nordene was still staring off, not listening, eyes troubled. Her thoughts, Faye sensed, were just as troubled. Faye's own thoughts were fragmented and distressed. There was a sense of being invaded, somehow, by something she couldn't control. And the horror of knowing that a young, healthy woman she had talked to only this morning now lay dead, at the hands of an unknown killer, added a sense of unreality.

Faye urged Nordene toward the terrace, to sit down for a cup of coffee. Neither of them, she was sure, would feel like having their most favorite gooey snack.

Nordene forced herself to sit still for a polite length of time. The kids had been pestering her all day to let them come over and play with Joey and Ellen, but she hadn't felt like sending them alone. Was it a form of intuition? She shuddered again, chills rippling over her body. She didn't mind them playing with the Pendergast kids as long as she was within hearing distance, but she still felt uneasy, though Sam scoffed at her. But the kids had been with Faye. Of course Ellen and Joey and Beth had nothing to do with the killings. She had stopped thinking they did. It was just . . . she felt uneasy. Something she'd have to get over, for Katy and Dwayne loved the Pendergast kids, and Sam thought it was great. Let them play.

Nordene sipped coffee and listened more to the voices of the kids than to Faye. Her conversation with Faye was the most trivial of small talk: the weather, the crowd at the swimming pool this afternoon, just a few words that struggled to bring back a semblance of normality.

The police car left, but a couple of others came. Some of the men who came to Faye and asked permission to search the premises were in casual clothes.

Nordene stood beside Faye after she had shown them into the house.

"Detectives, right?" Nordene said. She looked toward her own house remembering suddenly that she had left her door open. "It's time for me to round up my kids and take them home."

"If you want to leave them for an hour, Nordene, I'm sure they'll be all right. With all the police in the neighborhood, they should."

"No, they'll get in the way. Why don't you send Ellen and Joey home with me? The kids would love to have them." Nordene bit her tongue. Why had she said that?

"I'm sure they'd love it," Faye said. "But can we take a raincheck on that? I think I should keep them close for a while."

"Sure." Nordene patted Faye's arm and found it even icier than her own cold hand. "If I were you, I think I'd call Gavin to come home."

Faye started to speak, hesitated, then said, "I might eventually. But we'll try it this way first."

They didn't want to go home. Faye went with Nordene to roust the kids from the wash house and found them sitting in the middle of the long laundry table playing some kind of game that involved slapping their hands down on the oil cloth of the table.

"Come kids, let's go home," Nordene said.

They complained. Katy got off the table whining. Sometimes Nordene felt like slapping her when she whined like that, even though she remembered she had been a whiner in her own childhood. She could almost remember her own mother threatening to slap her, too.

"Come on!"

Eventually they were separated, Nordene's kids from Faye's—she was beginning to think of them as Faye's kids, probably because it was simpler that way.

She waved goodbye and herded her two ahead of her along the path, past the hedges and shrubs and to the vine-covered fence and the wrought iron gate.

"What're all those men doing, Mama?" Dwayne asked.

"They're searching Faye's place for a suspect, and you'd better get into your own house and stay there."

"A suspect of what?"

"Stop asking so many questions," Nordene said impatiently, wishing she hadn't gone uninvited to Faye's house to start with. If she had called first, she would have found out about the murder, and she wouldn't have taken her children right into the middle of it. Dwayne was saying something about a car wreck that Joey had told him about, but she didn't answer.

She got them into the house and settled in front of the television, then she went through the house carefully, cautiously, making sure the killer hadn't sought a hiding place in her house. Then she went back out and to the gate, where she could see through and watch, more or less, the search. A police car at the front of her own yard aimed a search light along the hedges. It inched on, the light searching.

The activity lessened. A car left, another arrived. Shadows were deepening in the yards, beneath the trees. Nordene looked around her own backyard, seeing all the hiding places among the flowering bushes that had been planted around the small open area of her back lawn, the darkness they created in the edge of the trees and the distance to the street lights.

She began to feel as if eyes were watching her.

There was something in the juniper at the corner of the house. She had seen it move slightly, near the bottom. A swish of a green branch.

She stared, fear cold on her back, tight around her chest.

Why hadn't she stayed in the house with the kids, where it was safe? It was time to cook dinner anyway. It was going to be a microwave dinner tonight, as most of them were lately. A couple of vegetables, and baked potatoes . . .

The face in the shrub became visible, like the outlines of a face hidden in a puzzle. The slitted eyes, the pointed ears. It was staring . . . no, *glaring* at her, and her chills deepened.

She could see it clearly now, its furry head outlined, its lips drawing back in a silent snarl.

She felt startled, and stepped backward.

At her movement it leaped.

She half-screamed and threw her arms up to protect her face.

But the large cat leaped past her and ran in long lopes toward the back of the yard.

She stared after it, remembering what the kids had told her about Ellen being scared of a cat.

"She called it a monster, Mommy," Dwayne had said, his voice both excited and disgusted. "She thought it was a monster!"

Nordene could see why. It was the largest cat she had ever seen. Wild and long-bodied, it seemed rather to be a relative of a mere cat, some off-breed.

Tomorrow, she promised, she would call the animal control officer and have him come pick it up.

She saw her husband's car come into the driveway, and she hurried to the kitchen to prepare dinner. Fortunately, in these days of the microwave, she thought as she tried to look like she'd been busy for hours, that was a simple job. Open a few cans, slice some cold roast, dab on a couple of spoonfuls of gravy, put it in the microwave and it came out ready to eat, each plate prepared for serving.

"What's going on down the road?" Sam asked as he came into the kitchen, as if she should know every neighborhood detail. "Looks like an accident of some kind."

Katy and Dwayne came running in from the den to throw themselves onto their daddy. He laughed and caught them up into his arms, one on each side. Nordene paused to look at them. It gave her such a warm family feeling to see him with the kids. To see him at all, so far as that went.

He was a throwback to his Irish ancestors, so much that he might not have had the half-Indian mother which he did indeed have. He was tall and square-shouldered, a big, bony man with crisp, curly red hair, brown eyes and a great face with dabs of freckles still sprinkled down his nose and across his forehead.

Dwayne looked so much like him it almost broke her heart to see them together. It made her want to cry with her joy of having two of them, father and son, and they were all hers. Thank God.

He set his children aside and went into the bathroom off the kitchen to wash up. He left the door open, and the kids crowded in with him. His voice raised over theirs.

"Looked like it might be a car wreck. I saw a wrecker pulling an old red car out of the trees, but from our driveway I couldn't see that there was much damage."

Dwayne and Katy were talking at once, trying to tell him different versions. The only unjumbled part that came through, even to Nordene's ears, was "The police are over at Ellen's and Joey's house..."

They sat down at the table in the dining alcove. Bay windows looked out over the lawn at the back of the house. The kitchen lights reflected in the glass, so that Nordene could only see the outlines of trees beyond, and they were fading as the day darkened.

"It wasn't a car wreck," Nordene said. "It was m-u-r-d-e-r." She spelled it out, over the children's heads, she thought.

But Katy said, "I know what that spells. It spells mur-der."

Nordene looked into Sam's eyes. "They'll probably have nightmares," she said.

But Katy was eating as usual, and so was Dwayne, as if the word really meant nothing to them. She knew how to spell it, but the actual meaning escaped her. Nordene mouthed silently to Sam, "She doesn't know what it means."

Katy said, "That means that somebody was killed by somebody else." She looked up. "And do you know what, Daddy? It was their laundress. Ellen's and Joey's."

Dwayne added, "And Beth's and Faye's."

"Of course, dummy," Katy said with an acid glance at him. "Everybody knows that it's really Faye's house, and the laundress is Faye's, and Beth lives there, too. But the person who was murdered had been doing Ellen's and Joey's clothes. She didn't even finish getting them done before she ran away. And do you know what?" Her voice lowered to a harsh whisper, and she leaned across the table toward her dad. "Do you know *what?*"

"No, what?"

"It wasn't a real person who murdered her. It was the *monster.*"

She sat back, a smug, but half-frightened look on her face.

Dwayne kept eating, clearly having heard this story before.

Nordene cried, "Where did you get an idea like that?"

"Ellen told me."

"Me, too," Dwayne said.

Nordene fastened her gaze on Sam. Now maybe he would listen to her. "What do you think of *that?*" she demanded.

He glanced away from her and asked Katy in a serious voice, "Why does Ellen think that, Katy?"

"Because it was a monster that killed her mother, and it followed her here. It's going to kill her, too, if she isn't careful."

"Katy!" Nordene cried. "What a terrible thing to say. Now, I don't want you talking about it any longer. If you've finished eating, go wash your hands and face and watch television. Both of you. Now. I'd like to have a few minutes to see Daddy alone, without you sitting there telling wild stories. Go on."

They went out, and Nordene could hear them fighting over who was going to wash first. Water ran and splashed, but finally it was turned off, and the kids came back through the kitchen and went toward the den.

"Come on, Daddy," Katy said.

"I'll be there pretty soon."

It was a family ritual. After dinner he went into the den with Katy and Dwayne where he read his paper while they watched an hour of cartoons. After that, they were sent to bed, and he then caught the news at ten o'clock. After cleaning up the kitchen, Nordene spent her evening in the den, too. Ordinarily. But already she had plans for a change. She wanted to get back outside and see what she could without going all the way down to the scene of the murder. Curiosity was eating at her.

But there was something else, too.

"You see," she said to Sam as soon as she was sure the kids were out of hearing. "See what it's doing to Katy and Dwayne? Monsters indeed. Two-footed monsters."

"Don't be so hard on the kid, Nor," Sam said. "This little Ellen is only trying to understand in her own mind what happened to her mother. And having a murder right here in this neighborhood, happening to someone she knew, again . . . well, she has to explain it somehow. And she's scared. She thinks they're going to come after her next. The poor kid probably lives in terror."

"I'm not arguing that. I'm just saying it's not good for our kids."

"They don't seem to be very adversely affected by it."

"Maybe not yet."

"Katy and Dwayne are probably good for Ellen. I wonder why Joey isn't as disturbed about this as Ellen is?"

"No idea. Except he's a boy."

"What does that mean?"

"Boys seem to take things at face value more than girls."

She really didn't know what she meant. She knew she had lost. Sam would never agree that small children can be bad influences. Some of them had poor backgrounds, sure, he'd admit that. But he didn't think any of them were born bad. To think that one of those children, or all of them, could have murdered their mother was ridiculous. Now, Nordene had to agree they probably didn't. Especially now. They certainly didn't have anything to do with this murder.

"But isn't it a coincidence, Sam?" she mused, staring at the kitchen reflections in the window glass, but not seeing it as such.

"The murder?"

"Yes. Someone close to the children. Well, not close in a family sense, but close in proximity. What do you make of that?"

"As you said, coincidence." He got up from the table and put his hand affectionately on her shoulder. "Coming in soon?"

"It'll be a while. I've got some things I want to do, first." Curiosity drew her. With Sam home she felt safe.

She took her sweater off the clothes tree, as soon as Sam was out of the room, and put it over her shoulders. She opened the French doors and left them open, sliding shut the screen. For a few minutes she stood on the patio looking around.

Through the trees at the back she could see twinkles of lights from down over the hill, some of them moving, as cars drove downtown or out of town. House lights shining steadily on the hill across the valley and below, nearly hidden by leaves this time of year, were flecks of neons, like fireflies, or stars in a far-off sky, blinking, blinking.

She looked toward Faye's house, but there was nothing but darkness in the house itself, so far as she could see. The upper story would be visible in the wintertime, and sometimes she could see lights on in bedrooms there; but now the only lights were the yard lights, coming on at dusk, one in the back, one in the long driveway. Out front the street lights were pale yet, not fully in power.

She went around the house and down the driveway toward the street. The concrete sounded loud beneath the wood heels of her sandals, so she moved onto the edge of the front lawn. She went on, steps muffled, toward the street.

More cars than usual were driving by, it seemed.

Slowly. Like the cars of sightseers. They wouldn't see much, she was sure, if that was what they were doing. Of course, she might not have noticed before how many cars used this street this time of day. She was usually in the house, tidying up the kitchen, getting ready to go into the den with her family.

By the time she reached the street it was empty. Houses down the block behind were closed and silent, lights coming on here and there. A neighbor's dog barked at her a couple of times, then sat down, a dark shadow at the corner of the neighboring yard on the west.

She pulled her sweater around her and looked eastward, past Faye's front yard. The only sign of a house there was the mail box at the end of the driveway.

Nordene left her own yard and walked down the edge of the road to stand by Faye's mailbox. From here she could see that at least two cars were still at the murder site. Their lights were on, shining into a dark forest of trees in the undeveloped acreage, but she could see nothing else. Voices reached her on waves of air, like a radio station fading in and out.

After a few minutes she turned and went back toward her own yard.

The dog in the yard beyond began to growl suddenly. He was only a dark blotch now in the rapidly falling night. The street light failed to reach him, but Nordene saw him leap up to stand a moment staring at something; then with a final deep-throated growl he ran across his own yard and out of sight toward the house hidden among the trees.

Nordene hesitated, a coldness caused by more than the evening temperatures bringing out a rash of goosebumps.

The dog had been facing into her yard, but it surely

was not she that alarmed him. He had only barked at her. And, so far as familiarity went, he knew her well enough. She often went over to see his owners, an elderly couple who had lived there for years. She'd been going to see them since she was a teenager, and she knew the dog's name was Russell—strange name for a dog—and he was getting really old. He must be at least fourteen years old now.

But maybe he was losing his eyesight, and she, coming back down the road, had looked like a stranger.

Still she hesitated, looking around. The night seemed more quiet than usual. The sounds of traffic had drifted away. The deep silence of the forest down over the hill seemed to spill its soundlessness into the populated areas of the hill street. The lights of her own house seemed faraway, set back in its own deep yard of trees.

The street light at the corner of the yard hardly penetrated the darkness between her and her own house.

She had gone only a few steps along her own driveway, walking this time on the hard surface as if her own footsteps were company to be comforted by, when she saw the eyes.

Like small twin lights they hovered in the darkness of the shrubs, reflecting the street light behind her.

The cat again, she decided with a lurch of fear.

And now there was more than one. In the darkness to her right there were others, glowing eyes in the dark.

This, then, was what Russell had been growling at.

She wished he would return and walk at her side down the driveway the way he occasionally did. But though she called for him, once, twice, he didn't come.

And the eyes didn't move.

They seemed to be everywhere now, in the black

spaces beneath the shrubs at the edge of the driveway. In the yard beneath the trees.

She hurried, faster, faster. But she could hear them now, low growls that sounded more feral, wilder and less real than a mere animal growl.

Growls built not of fear, but of aggression.

She began to run.

Chapter Twelve

Ellen stood in Beth's doorway, dressed in her pajamas, her hair still damp from its shampoo. In her arms, clasped tightly to her chest, was the old rag doll, even though Faye had bought her a beautiful new doll. There were tears in Ellen's eyes.

"Can I sleep with you, Beth?" Her voice was a whisper, barely audible.

Beth was sitting in her bed, both pillows behind her back. She had found a bunch of mystery books for young people down in the big library on the first floor and had brought up a stack of them. They were on her bedside table, beneath the glow of the light. She had just opened one and was ready to read.

"Why aren't you in bed asleep, Ellen?"

"I was scared."

Still the whisper. The pleading in her eyes, the tears that hadn't broken loose and run down her tight cheeks, glistening there, made Beth's heart ache. She was sorry she had accused Ellen of such a terrible thing as killing their mother.

Had she ever really believed that?

Beth softened though she didn't like to share her bed. Ellen looked so young standing there, so little and thin.

Ellen whispered, "You told me not to go to Faye's

172

room anymore. You told me to come to you. You did."

"Yes, I did." Beth moved over and patted the empty side of the bed. "All right, you can sleep here. But go get your own pillow."

Ellen turned obediently away, hesitated in the edge of the faint light of the hall, looked both up and down, then walking quickly, went out of sight.

Beth kept watching the empty hallway beyond the open door, the slight annoyance she had felt at the interruption changing to worry.

Was Ellen going to be worse now? Now that this new thing had happened?

A deep and fervent wish, a kind of hopeless prayer, surged up from deep inside. *Oh, Mama, why did you have to die?*

Ellen paused at the open door to her room. She had left the light on, but still she was afraid to go back in there.

Her bed was mussed, the cover thrown back, just the way she had left it. She could see it from the doorway.

And the window was shut, as she had left that, too. She had stood on a chair and struggled with shutting it, because she had heard the scratching on the wall again.

But she had to go back in and get her pillow.

The window stared at her, and she could feel the eyes beyond it. They were in the trees outside, the cats that were not cats, but part of the monster itself . . . part of something that was in her mind, back where she couldn't reach it all. When she tried to reach it, she felt as if a great wall had been built down the center of her thoughts, so that she couldn't go beyond and find it, and remember exactly what she had seen . . . that night . . .

It could see her, but she couldn't see it. Not really.

She could see it only as something familiar, like the cat.

Cats.

There were more than one now.

She slipped across the threshold silently and stood on the blue carpet of her room. The icy chill of fear enveloped her. The light at the side of her bed seemed thin and weak now, unable to light the corners of the room.

And there was that other thing—that faint smell of smoke.

It was in her room, just as it had been in the living room that night. And just as it had been in the wash house, where the washer lady had been before she ran away and was killed.

She eased toward the bed, her glances darting from corner to corner across the room. When she reached the bed, she grabbed up the nearest pillow and ran.

In the hall she aborted a scream by throwing her hands to her mouth. Both the pillow and the doll dropped to the floor.

Someone was standing in the hall.

A shadow blocked her way to Beth's room.

But then it spoke.

"Ellen, what's wrong? Where are you going with your pillow?"

It was Joey's voice, and now she saw that it was really Joey, not another part of the monster.

She bent and picked up the pillow and the doll. She remembered the pretty new doll and wished she had brought it with her, too, but it was back in her room, sitting in the chair in the corner.

"I'm going to sleep in Beth's room," she said, seeing now Joey's face, shadowed, screwed up like it was when he had just awakened.

Joey yawned and went on across the hall. "I forgot to go to the bathroom," he said, just before he shut the bathroom door behind him.

Ellen stood looking on down the hall where it widened into the stairwell room. She could see the railing that went around the stairwell and the edge of the door that might be her stepmother's.

She wished she could go there.

She felt safer with Faye than with Beth, as though Beth, too, in some way, drew to herself whatever it was that had killed their mother, and the lady who had died today.

Faye went through the house again, making sure every window, every door on the first floor was locked. For the first time in her life, special care was being taken. She remembered her grandfather used to lock the outside doors at night, but windows were often left open because he liked fresh air.

The police had been all over the place, searching, she supposed, for the killer himself. They had been in the barn and other buildings in the backyard, and they had looked through every room in the house.

Not quite satisfied with their search, she had gone through it herself.

And now again she was going through it, turning on lights in each room, seeing the rooms too heavily furnished with their original furniture, too dark and old. She had made tentative plans to change some of the wallpaper, at least, and in some cases to get rid of some of the more uncomfrotable pieces of furniture and replace it with modern. Tonight, she wished she had, it all seemed so bleak, so likely to hide behind its massive pieces the body of the killer.

The music room, behind closed double doors at the

front of the house, was a silent reminder of the days when the house had vibrated with the noises made by herself, Janet and Dan. Dan, older than she by six years, had played the drums. Their grandfather had gone around looking pained and finally had taken to his private rooms on the second floor with all doors shut between. Still, he had never outwardly complained about the noise. They'd had quite a band then: she on the piano and Janet blowing various other instruments. Blowing was the only thing to call what Janet had done to the trumpet and the clarinet. She could get out a tune, but with a lot of squawking. Janet, like herself and Dan, had taken lessons since she was a child, but with Janet, who jumped from violin to trumpet to others, proficiency never arrived. Still, they'd had fun.

She touched the piano, ran her fingers softly over the keys, but made no sound, leaving them cold and silent.

There was an old organ in an alcove of the wall, centered, as though in its day it had been something grand to be displayed. The only person who had ever played it had died when she was too young to know her. Grandmother Mary Jane.

The drums were covered with a gray-white sheet of cloth. It hung to the floor all around, lying in folds like the bottom of a stage curtain.

Faye stared at it, imagining beneath that cover the crouched body of the killer. She could almost see him, see the sheet move, just slightly, as if someone were breathing against it, or brushing it with a shoulder.

Nonsense.

Whoever killed that poor girl followed her here. Probably one of her rejected lovers. Or someone who simply had followed her. One of the policemen had said something about rape. Not to her, but within hearing. All she had heard was the word, so outstanding, it seemed. For some reason no one would ever know, probably, why Rhoda had tried to leave. She had driven away and was stopped less than a block from the house. She drove her car into the edge of the woods, then got out and ran. She was caught.

Those facts had been gathered and put together, overheard in bits and pieces and in some cases told to her.

Still, she stared at the covering of the drums, a coldness starting between her shoulder blades and going up the back of her neck.

You can't stand here all night, she told herself. Get it over, pull it off.

She stooped and picked up one folded corner of the large, unbleached, heavy square of sheeting. With a hard pull, it came toward her, reluctantly. It was even heavier than it looked.

The drum at the back was revealed, and the stool Dan had used. Another hard pull and the sheet lay crumpled at her feet, drums uncovered entirely.

Nobody there.

Faye drew a long breath. Of course the searchers would have looked under the sheet.

She left it folded on the floor, the drums uncovered.

The heavy, velvet draperies were open, and the windows reflected the lights from inside. She saw her image in the glass, cut into small sections from the many panes. She went from one to the next around the room, pulling cords, closing heavy, dusty draperies. Shutting out the night, and the eyes it might hold.

There was so much work to do on the house. These faded draperies should be taken down and replaced with something light and bright. The draperies could be boxed and put away in the attic, with all the other things that nearly filled that vast space.

The attic! Had anyone searched there?

177

She went upstairs, turning out all lights on the lower floor. The attic door was in, of all places, one wall of a large linen and utility closet. But the door was bolted on the outside.

She stood looking at the bolt, so securely in place, and imagining the steep, dark, narrow stairs on the other side. She didn't want to go up those steps. And obviously no one was hiding up there. They couldn't have bolted the outside of the door.

She went out into the hall. Dim light lost its strength at the end of the hall, fading to deep shadows. But there was a window, opening out onto a sloping roof. She had to check the window to see if it was locked.

Her footsteps were muffled on the carpet; she was aware of the silence, and she did not find it comforting. It was almost as if the silence itself had taken on an entity of its own and was listening, listening and watching as she moved about in the large house. She kept wanting to look over her shoulder, that coldness in her back a perpetual reminder that she was unprotected. That the children in her care were her responsibility alone, while their father was gone.

The window was locked. She looked out over the dark slope of the roof and into the backyard. The light had been left on in the yard below, but its pool seemed no larger than a wading pool, bright water glistening on the mown grass, its edges fading swiftly to blackness beneath the trees.

But something was there, in the edges of the darkness, close enough to the light to catch the rays in its eyes.

It seemed to be staring directly up at her.

The cat.

She wondered who was feeding it. Why was it hanging around here so much?

The memory of it being in her own house, sitting on

top of the settee in the entrance hall, spread the cold chills from her back to her arms.

She frowned, only half seeing her reflection in the glass as she pulled the draperies slowly shut. She'd had a feeling then about the cat, something elusive and frightening. Something about Ellen seeming to draw the cat, though she was terrified of it.

Faye wondered at the pity she did not feel in this case. Usually, a dog or cat alone, obviously lost or strayed, aroused her sympathies. So much so that she felt crushed by it at times. She helped whenever she could and called on the Humane Society to help when she couldn't. But with this animal it was different. As if it posed a danger in its presence.

Then she saw that it was not alone.

Like dim lights glowing brighter as they grew nearer, suddenly there were other red, slanted eyes in the darkness of the yard, just outside the rim of the yard light. They seemed to be everywhere. She closed her own eyes tightly and opened them again, to see if she had only imagined those glowing twin orbs in the darkness.

But they were still there. Then, as if blinking out, one by one, the darkness closed in on them. She stared, trying to find them again.

Finally closing the drapery completely, she went back down the hall wondering if it had been her imagination after all.

She went into the hall where the children's bedrooms were and found Ellen's door open. She crossed the threshold and stopped.

The bed cover had been thrown back. The light was on. But Ellen was not in her room.

This was rather late for the child to be up. Was she ill?

Faye went back out into the hall and tapped on the

bathroom door. It moved with her touch, and she saw that no light was on. She pushed the door open with her fingertips and turned on the overhead light. The bathroom was empty.

She stood in the middle of the small room looking around. It was as neat as if three children had not used it at all.

The panic began building. Where was Ellen?

But of course . . . Ellen had left her room last night and slept on the floor in Faye's room. Beth had told her to come to her if she needed anyone in the night. Praying that Ellen had listened to her sister, Faye hurried across the room to Beth's closed bedroom door.

She knocked lightly, once, then opened the door.

Beth's bedside light was on, and she was sitting up in bed, pillows at her back, a book in her hands. She stared rather wild-eyed at Faye, and Faye realized she had scared her.

"I'm sorry," she said in a low voice, "But Ellen isn't in her room and—"

She saw Ellen then, on the other side of Beth, huddled, looking so small, only her bright hair visible.

"She's here," Beth said. "She's asleep."

Faye nodded. There was plenty of room, so far as that went. The bed was a double, as all of them were in the bedrooms in this wing.

"Are you comfortable?" Faye asked.

Beth nodded. Faye murmured good night and backed out, pulling the door shut.

Joey's door was standing part-way open; but he had wanted a nightlight, and a small seven watt bulb had been plugged into a wall socket. Its light was surprisingly sufficient, casting a low gleam over the floor, throwing deep shadows above it.

Even from the doorway she could hear him

breathing. Deep, steady.

He was less worried than the girls, Faye realized. It was as if he had been able to move away from the past, and the death of his mother, with more ease. Maybe it was just a cover-up, but Faye didn't think so. He was too open and spontaneous to be concealing any deep, noxious feelings.

He's sweet. I like him.

Faye felt the smile on her lips, a gentle tug that broke the stiffness. She realized she had been holding her mouth in a tense clamp for hours.

She went back into the large opening of the stairwell room and around the banister toward her own bedroom. The door to the nursery was closed. She paused and went in, turning on the overhead light at the door.

Here was a different world. The yellow and white wallpaper cheered her immediately. She sat in the rocking chair in the middle of the room and looked at the stacks of material still to be sewn into curtains and quilts and bed ruffles. Boxes were stacked in the corner, waiting to be unpacked. A plastic bag of stuffed toys lay on the floor in another corner, waiting to be put up onto the white shelves.

Tomorrow I will get back to work in here, she promised herself. Beth, Ellen and Joey can begin to make themselves at home. Tomorrow I will stop treating them like guests.

After almost going to sleep in the chair, long minutes later, she got up, turned out the light and went to her own room. She fell into bed exhausted. The baby moved once, as if turning over and finding a comfortable position.

Then they both slept.

* * *

Beth closed her book and laid it on the bedside table. She looked at the sleeping face of her sister. Ellen had turned onto her back and thrown up her hands so they framed her face, palms up. The palms looked red, and Beth remembered how she had burned them on that thing she had bought at the garage sale. The thing she had called her Aladdin's Lamp. She had rubbed it and rubbed, trying to bring forth a genie; and then she had screamed, and her palms were bright red. She said it had burned.

But Beth had touched it herself, and the metal was cool.

Ellen had always had a wild imagination.

Yet something bothered Beth, something about . . .

She put out a forefinger and gently touched Ellen's palm. Before she could test it for fever, Ellen's hand closed convulsively, fingers tightening into a fist. She sighed and turned over again, facing the wall, body rolled into a fist of its own.

Beth turned out the light and slid down into bed.

She liked the room dark. She couldn't sleep with a nightlight the way Joey could. He'd never needed a nightlight at home. It was only since they had moved here that he wanted a nightlight, and Faye had given him one, a little plug-in thing that looked like a lantern.

The house was so big and so strange.

Beth closed her eyes.

She could hear Ellen breathing.

Faintly.

Just loudly enough to disturb her.

Beth turned over, putting her back to Ellen.

The pillow muffled her ear on one side, and she covered the other with her hand. A long sigh split the division between her daytime brain and her nighttime, as she thought of it, and she could feel the softer rhythms of the nighttime come on.

She drew a long, deep breath and made an effort to sleep. There was silence now in her head, except for the rush of her own blood, of sounds in her own body. She couldn't ever remember sleeping with anyone before, except for the few weeks in the motel after Mama was killed and Daddy had come to be with them. Then she'd had to sleep with Ellen, but it hadn't seemed so—so—*uneasy*.

Light filtered through her closed eyelids.

Light.

Her eyes flew open.

A pale light outlined the white paint of the bedroom door and the chest of drawers that stood between it and the wall.

She sat up, whirling.

Where was the light coming from?

A tiny flame flickered in the air, suspended between the edge of the bed and the wall beyond. Like a candle flame, it burned, turning this way and that, as if a draft of air disturbed it. Like a bright fiery tongue in the dark room, it hung, without a body.

... coming from nothing ...

With her heart exploding in terror, threatening to burst from her body, Beth crawled backward out of the bed. She felt for the lamp on the table and nearly knocked it off in her panic. She pushed the button, and the bulb burst into full light, dispensing all shadows in the room.

The flame disappeared instantly.

Beth stared at the spot where it had been until the floral wallpaper beyond blurred into a smear of colors with no form. She closed her eyes, opened them, and looked, all around.

There was no flame.

But there had been.

It had not been a dream.

After several minutes of kneeling on the floor at the side of the bed, she got into it again. But now she was afraid to turn out the light.

She lay down with its glare full on her face, and after a long, wondering time her mind simply quit trying to make sense of what she had seen.

She fell asleep, tired, comforted by the light that fell undiluted on her face.

Nordene hadn't told Sam about the wildcats. By the time she had run into the house, she was beginning to feel silly. Scared of cats? Mere cats? They were more to be pitied than feared.

Still, tomorrow she would call the control officer to see if he could catch them.

She slept in the comfort of her husband's arms. Slept and woke and found herself alone on her side of the king-sized bed. But she could hear his light snore, a comforting sound if ever there was one.

She slept again, after having looked at the clock. Its numerals glowed green in the dark room, stating 12:47.

It seemed only minutes later that she woke again, cold fear crawling over her body.

The cats were fighting, she realized, after listening to the wild and alien noise for a few moments. It was the most awful yowling she had ever heard, distant, and yet close, so that it was impossible to tell just how far away they were.

She should get up and go downstairs and out onto the patio and yell at them, scare them off. But she stayed where she was, wondering how Sam could sleep through it.

Finally she got up and closed the bedroom windows, and the yowling stopped. But sleep was gone for Nordene. Now the clock read 3:17, and she stared at it as it pulsed along, going from one set of numbers to the next.

Daylight came, like twilight in the evening, filled with grayness.

Nordene got up wearily and put on a robe. She went downstairs and sat in the kitchen wishing she had a cigarette to go with her coffee. But she had quit smoking two years ago, after a terrible struggle with it. She had also gained fifteen pounds afterward, but she was determined never to smoke again, pounds or no pounds. One of her older sisters had died with lung cancer, and it had scared the shit out of her. A horrible way to die, that, and not worth the cigarettes. Of course she had known of people who had never smoked, and still got the nasty disease. But those were cases where something else was to blame. A poor immune system, maybe.

She wanted the newspaper but was reluctant to go outside.

She kept sitting, drinking one cup of coffee after the other, waiting for Sam.

He came downstairs with only minutes to spare, as always. He kissed her, grabbed a cup of coffee to take with him. "I'll eat with the boys," he said, as he always did. There was a doughnut shop where he and his co-workers gathered for half an hour each morning.

When he was gone, the house was deadly quiet again, but at least she felt less uneasy about going outside.

The newspaper was in the middle of the front yard. The boy must have given it a mighty throw this morning, to land it so precisely behind the azalea bush. It took her several minutes to find it.

She kept looking over her shoulder for the big cat, expecting it to leap out unexpectedly from wherever it was. But the yard was no different from any other morning. There was dew on the grass, so heavy her house slippers were wet.

When she got back to the kitchen, she left them sitting on the patio outside, in a spot of sunshine, and went barefoot into the kitchen. The carpet tickled the soles of her feet, and she drew them up and sat on them.

The children came down one at a time. Dwayne looked into the kitchen and then disappeared, and Nordene heard the chattering of chipmunks on T.V. soon afterward.

Katy came to the kitchen and stayed, and in silence Nordene poured her a glass of milk and a dish of cereal.

They were silent people in the morning, Nordene thought with amusement. Sam was the only one who talked before ten o'clock.

At nine Nordene went upstairs and showered and dressed. When she came back down to the kitchen she was ready to make the phone call. Both kids were on the floor in front of the television, but she left them alone. She wasn't worried that what they saw in cartoons would hurt them. The only thing she screened was the sex shows. They weren't allowed to watch late night movies.

"Hello," she said to the voice that answered the phone. "I'd like the animal control officer to trap some cats that are terrorizing the neighborhood."

The unconcerned voice on the other end asked her name and address, and Nordene gave it.

"These are not ordinary cats," Nordene said. "I think they are feral cats, and possibly mixed with wildcats. That is, bobcats, or some other large breed."

The voice said calmly, "They've probably just wandered in from the woods, looking for an easy source of food. They'll leave again."

"They haven't left. They were all around my house last night. The sounds they made were horrible. All the yowling and fighting."

"Mating season, possibly," the voice said in infuriating calmness. "They have probably left by now. They're actually quite harmless."

"They haven't left. I'm afraid to go outside. And I'd rather not have them in my yard, so please send someone up to trap them."

She hung up the phone and turned to see Dwayne helping himself to a cinnamon roll.

He stuffed part of it into his mouth and said, "They can't catch those cats. They're not real cats. They're monsters that change what they look like."

Nordene frowned after him as he went back into the TV room. The influence of the other kids, again. Fortunately, it didn't seem to have an adverse effect on Dwayne.

She walked out onto the patio. The sun would not shine here all day long. It was on the north side of the house and shaded by trees on both the east and west. But the summer air was warm, and there was no reason for the coldness she felt as she peered toward the shrubbery that made green, lumpy outlines around the edges of the mowed lawn beyond the patio.

Monsters, indeed. She'd take a mere monster over a horde of wildcats anytime.

She sat down to wait for the animal control officer.

Chapter Thirteen

Not until dawn did Beth finally fall asleep. She was still propped up on her two thick pillows, drooping sideways in her sleep, her head hanging on her shoulder.

Ellen woke, got up and looked at her sister. So uncomfortable. Like pictures of old people sleeping in their chairs. Only instead of Beth's book being on her lap, it was on the night stand.

Ellen went quietly out of the room and closed the door. She had to go into her own room to get her clothes, and the sense of release from fear that she had felt in Beth's room was closing in on her again.

She didn't like the room her stepmother had given her.

She stood on the threshold and looked in. It was shadowy and dark, the blind pulled, the sun streaks against the outside of the blind showing inside like light slashes.

. . . knife slashes across white flesh . . . blood flowing . . .

She backed away, quivering, looking in desperation down the hall toward the front where Faye's bedroom was.

A door opened in the hallway, and she gave a silent burp of a scream, the only kind she could manage, it seemed. Those sudden flings of fear in a voice that wouldn't speak.

The door widened, inward, and Ellen stared, forgetting where she was.

Joey came into sight, rumpled, hair mussed. He blinked at her.

She almost ran to him, jerky fast movements that closed the space between them. "Joey," she said, in vast relief.

He didn't seem to notice her agitation.

"Hi, Ellen. I got to go to the bathroom. Did Faye call us yet?"

"Faye never calls us. We can get up when we want to."

"Oh."

He started across the hall toward the bathroom, but Ellen grabbed his arm.

"Joey, will you help me get my clothes?"

"Where are they?"

"In my room."

He blinked again and put one fist up to rub sleep from his eyes. "Are they too high or something?"

"No, I'm afraid to go in there by myself."

He gazed at her as if trying to figure it all out. "In your own room?"

"Yes."

"But—didn't you just come out?"

"No. I slept with Beth last night."

"Oh."

As if that explained it satisfactorily, Joey went with Ellen into the room, leading the way. He stood in the middle of the room, at the foot of the bed, while Ellen hurriedly picked out her things from a dresser drawer.

Out in the hallway again, Ellen stood with her folded clothes in her arms.

"You go ahead," she said. "I'll wait."

Joey went in, leaving the door part-way open. "You can come in if you're afraid, Ellen."

"It's okay. I'll wait. Just don't shut the door."

"I won't."

The hall was so quiet, she could almost hear the subtle roar of its silences. There was no sound from Beth's room, nor from any other part of the big house. Water ran in the bathroom as Joey washed his face and hands. He flushed the toilet. There was a brushing sound as he dried his hands and face, and the comb clicked on the counter top as he laid it down. He came out again, dressed, hair combed, face still damp at the edges.

"Okay, you can go in now. I'll wait."

In the bathroom she felt safer. The room was small, and there was a lot of tile. It gave it a close and cozy feel that she liked, as if nothing could reach her here.

They started downstairs the front way, then Joey said, "Hey, Ellen, do you know there's another stairway?"

"No."

"It's here. Come on, I'll show you."

There was a hall leading to the right, past the mezzanine of the big open area of the front. It went down a ways in darkness then Joey opened another door that led into another narrow hall.

"I found it," he said. "When I was following those policemen around yesterday evening. Look."

They turned another corner and there was a landing, small and square, and from it dropped a second set of stairs.

"They called it the service stairs. See, it goes right down to the hall where we first came in. By the side door. Under the *porte-co-chere*."

"The what?"

"*Porte-co-chere*. That's what they call it. That's the

roof over the driveway, so people can get out of their cars without getting in the rain. The way we came in the first time."

"Oh."

She followed him down the stairway. At the narrow, dark bottom he opened another door, and they stepped out into the side entrance. The door was closed and bolted, the stained glass window in the door letting in streaks of light that were red and green and yellow.

"Okay," Joey said, as if that were well accomplished, "Race you to the kitchen!"

He took off before he finished speaking, giving himself the lead by at least a yard, but Ellen took after him as hard as she could run. They pounded down the side entrance hall and into the hall that ran through the length of the house. The kitchen door was open. Joey slowed, and Ellen almost ran into him.

They entered the kitchen at a walk and saw Faye was already there. Ellen wondered briefly if she might be mad at them for running in her house, but she was smiling.

"Good morning," Faye said. "Are you ready for breakfast?"

"Yes, ma'am." Joey slid into a place at the table.

Ellen sat down beside him.

"Today is going to be different," Faye said, as she brought them hot cereal from the stove. She ladled oatmeal into the cereal bowls that were already at the places set. "Today, we're going to stay at home. I have some work to do up in the nursery. Do you think you can find something to keep you busy?

Joey and Ellen exchanged glances.

Faye went back to the stove and brought a plate of biscuits.

"You can play, watch the Walt Disney channel on television, or read or whatever you do when you're at home. Because that's what we're going to practice today. Being at home."

She poured milk in their glasses and in her own. Beth's place was sitting untouched on the other side of the table, cereal bowl in the plate, flatware and napkin at the sides, milk glass empty.

"Because," Faye said as she sat down with them, "this is your home now."

They stared at their plates. Ellen felt a huge knot form in her throat. *No,* she wanted to cry aloud. *No, home is the old house on the corner, across the fence from the convenience store. Home is with Mama.*

Joey said, in a small voice that cracked slightly, "Yes, ma'am."

Ellen swallowed, once again. She lifted her glass and took a drink of milk, and it helped dislodge the knot, that terrible ball of pain in her throat. It moved down into the middle of her chest and stayed there, as if it had become part of her heart.

She asked, "When is Daddy coming back?"

"I don't know," Faye admitted. "He had to go to Alaska, and he's so far back that he doesn't even have access to a telephone for a few days. But it won't be long, I'm sure. It never has been before."

They ate. Faye put butter in the biscuits and jam on the plates. Ellen could feel her stepmother's blue eyes watching, watching, but it wasn't a critical watch the way some teachers did, even though it reminded Ellen of being in a classroom with a teacher.

Finally, Faye touched Ellen's shoulder. "Maybe you would like to come up to the nursery with me? I'm going to be sewing curtains. You can see the room where your baby sister or brother is going to be staying."

"Baby *brother?*"

"Yes." She smiled, her narrow face going all pretty

and soft. "In a few more months. After school starts, and you're used to living here. We hope."

Ellen looked at Joey, but he was as surprised as she. Could Faye's baby be her—their—baby brother? Or sister?

She'd have to ask Beth about it later. Beth would know.

Beth woke and lay still, only her eyes moving, taking in this room that she had thought was so pretty when she first saw it. It had been some other girl's room—what was it Faye had said? Hers, or her sister Janet's. There was a dressing table with triple mirrors so that you could see the sides of your hair. The table had blue and white lace ruffles hanging down around it in tiers. White lace curtains that matched were at the window, with blue satin draperies on each side. The bedspread matched the draperies. The carpet was thick and soft, a darker blue. The wallpaper was a white background with rosebuds in pink, and little blue flowers scattered between.

It was pretty, it was homey, it was . . . *scary.*

The flame had danced in the air over there, between the bed and the wall. Her light now looked sickly yellow in the brightness brought into the room by the day. She snapped it off.

Ellen . . . where was Ellen?

Beth got up and crossed the hall to Ellen's room. She was gone, of course. She wouldn't have gone back into her own room. The bed had not been made.

She looked into Joey's room, and he was gone, too.

They were together, she told herself, as they always were. They played together. She had never been able to play much with either of them because the things they wanted to do were so childish. Little cars and trucks and sand piles. Dolls and trains and transformers.

She hurriedly cleaned up for the day, then made all three beds. Joey had half-assed made his, but the sheets beneath the spread were so wrinkled the bedspread had lumps all over it. Also, it was crooked, one corner hanging to the floor, the other halfway up, exposing the lower edge of the mattress.

She hadn't imagined the flame, but she didn't know what it was. It was as if this part of the house were haunted by something.

She was glad to leave it, to go downstairs to the kitchen where she wouldn't be alone. Ellen was at the table with Joey and Faye, eating the way she ate now, slowly, picky, tiny bites as if she had no appetite but knew she must eat to avoid drawing attention to herself.

Nordene sat on the patio and watched the pickup truck with the cages in the bed. A man came from it, taking his time, looking around at the yard.

"You the lady with the cats?" he asked when he reached the edge of the patio.

"Yes." Nordene stood up and approached him, halting a couple of yards away. "I haven't seen any signs of them this morning, but I know they're there. I can feel it."

He kept looking around, his head turning this way and that. "Got a lot of hiding places here. Lots of bushes and shrubbery. Houses not very close together up in this area, and some empty woodland across the road and down that way. All I can do is set out a trap."

"What kind of trap?" Nordene asked, thinking of the dog next door, and the domestic cats that wandered around occasionally.

"Oh, just a cage, a wire cage, with bait inside. Don't

worry, it won't catch your dog. He'd have to be pretty small to get in there, and if he did it wouldn't hurt him."

"I don't have a dog, or a cat either. Our old cat had to be put to sleep last year. It developed cancer. We had one operation on it, and a tumor was removed; but it came back again. There was nothing else we could do."

"Yes, too bad. Happens to animals just like to people, that cancer. We're not too different, you know, animals and people. The people who claim animals were put here on earth just to feed and entertain the people are settin' themselves up so high and mighty that when they fall they're going to bust themselves wide open. These animals are our cousins, and you better believe it. The Bible says '. . . and I give to you the fruit of the trees and the grain of the fields, and it shall be meat for you.' Nowhere does it say the animals were made for man to eat, not the cow nor the lamb. The animals will teach us compassion, that's what. Those animals mourn for each other just like humans, you better believe. You take a calf away from a cow and it bawls for days, both of them cry and bawl. You take one dog away from another it's been raised with, and it mourns; and what's more, it never forgets."

"Ummm," Nordene said, folding her arms across her chest and relaxing one knee so that her weight fell on the other leg.

"Yes, you better believe," the man said. "What's more, you take a dog or cat or any other animal away from some person who has taken care of it and loved it, and it will mourn for that person. And when it sees that person again, even after years, it remembers. Now, you sure can't say that for a lot of people. Me, now, when I trap an animal, I try to put it where it will be happy. It's got just as much right to be happy as any of us. I'll take these wildcats of yours and put them back out into the wild, down into the Ouachita Mountains, even though

I have to do it on my own time, and on my own money. I don't get paid for these extra trips and things, simply because I don't go ahead and kill the animal, I just move it. They can call it putting the animal to sleep, or whatever else fancy word they can come up with, but it's plain killin'; that's what it is."

"Ummm," Nordene said, and changed legs, letting her weight fall on the rested one.

"And what's more . . . well, hi there, young fellow." The man's whiskered face brightened. All the droopy sadness that had been in and around his eyes was gone, briefly. "How're you this bright morning?"

"Okay. Are you the man who's going to trap the cat?"

"I'm going to try. Do you want to watch me?"

Dwayne jumped off the patio. "Yes. But I'll tell you something."

They went walking toward the pickup together. "What?" the man asked, looking down at Dwayne.

"You'll never do it. You'll never get it. Do you know why?"

"Why?"

"Because it's not a real cat, it's a monster."

They had reached the pickup, and the man was pulling a wire cage out of its bed. Nordene turned away with a sigh.

Katy had come out onto the patio, and was looking toward the pickup, but instead of running to join Dwayne, as she usually did, she followed Nordene back into the house.

"Can I go over to Ellen's?"

"Oh, good Lord, so early?"

"It's not early! It's eleven o'clock. Please, Mama, please?"

Nordene began to clean up the kitchen, wishing she had maid service every day of the week instead of just two.

"Please, Mama, please."

Katy could whine so irritatingly sometimes. "Oh, shut up, Katy."

"Mama, please!"

"All right, all right!"

Katy ran toward the door, and Nordene followed her, yelling instructions.

"Don't you stay one minute after the clock strikes twelve, do you hear? You come home before lunch! And if they're going somewhere, you come straight back! And Katy!" She screamed, seeing her daughter running along the path to the gate, sometimes already out of sight behind the bushes that spotted the side yard. "Be careful of that wildcat!"

Katy was gone, the gate left swinging open.

If she had heard one word, she hadn't acted like it.

This had all the earmarks of the beginning of a very bad time. Having kids right next door. Katy would be pestering to play with Ellen from now on.

Nordene started to go back into the house, then changed her mind and sat down on the patio.

A few minutes later the pickup started and backed out of sight, and Dwayne came around the corner of the house.

"Mama—"

"Go on," Nordene said. "What the heck? But be back by noon."

"Okay!"

Dwayne ran joyously, but at least he had answered her.

She felt oddly depressed, sitting there alone, staring into the green foliage at the back of the yard. Everyone was gone. She had a dirty kitchen to clean. She hated house cleaning. Shopping might be fun, but she couldn't go without the kids.

Unless she called Faye and asked if they could just stay the whole day there with Ellen and Joey . . . ! Well, why not? Didn't she deserve a day all of her own? Even when a babysitter was available, such as the cleaning woman, the kids wanted to go shopping with her. Sam thought it was foolish and unmotherly to want to be without the kids sometimes. But he was a more patient person than she. Besides, he wasn't with them as much as she was.

Not that she didn't love her babes, she did. She appreciated them.

But, today, if Faye would let them stay at her house, Nordene was going to have a day to do just what she wanted to do. She might even go out and park by the river for a while.

She made the call, and a strange voice answered. At first she thought she had gotten a wrong number, and then she remembered the oldest girl, Beth. It must be her voice. Sometimes Nordene forgot there was a third child, too young to be a teenager, but too old to play with Katy and Dwayne.

"Beth, let me speak to Faye please, if she's available."

A moment of silence came in which Nordene wondered why Beth was answering the phone in the first place.

"Hello?"

"Faye? Were you in an awkward spot?"

"I was for a moment. Had my hands wet, that's all."

"Are you going to be home today?"

"As far as I know, why?"

"I just wanted a favor. Could you keep my kids until about three this afternoon? I don't think they'd be any trouble. They'll probably just play around outside with Gavin's two."

"Sure. That's fine. Three?"

"Yes, please. I'm going to sneak off and go shopping. Alone."

"Happy hunting."

Nordene drew a long sigh of relief when she hung up the phone. Here she was, all alone, with several hours to do just as she wished.

She went upstairs and dressed, choosing her clothing and accessories carefully, dressing as if she were going to church. Why not, she asked herself. She could wear her prettiest new dress if she wanted to.

She changed the contents of her straw bag to the leather one that matched her shoes, took another look at her hair and makeup and went out and down the stairs. She checked the front door again to be sure it was still bolted. She had secured the house last night before she went to bed, and the only door that had been opened this morning was the French door out of the kitchen onto the patio. Even Sam had gone out that way, rather than through the passage into the attached garage. Although their house had been built back around 1900, a three-car garage had been added after World War Two, according to the history on the place. The old, narrow detached garage was still there, over toward the west fence, vines growing over it. It was used now as a garden shed.

She started to close and lock the doors in the kitchen, then decided against it. If Katy and Dwayne came home before three, for some reason, they would need to get in.

She stood on the patio outside the doors and stared into the shrubbery.

The murder in the vicinity just yesterday was like a bad dream that had no connection with her life. The killer was someone the laundress had known, of course. He had followed her, chased her, killed her.

And then he had gone back wherever he came from. So it would be all right to leave the patio doors unlocked.

She wished she had given the kids a key to the side door.

She shrugged and adjusted the shoulder strap of her bag and started toward the back door to the garage.

Crash!

She stopped, heart rising into her throat, and looked back at the house.

What on earth?

The silence that followed the sound of the fall was pregnant with meanings. Images, broken, puzzling, flashed through her mind. Something had fallen in her house, a large mirror off the wall, crashing, shattering to bits of glass on a hardwood floor. Nordene frowned, unaware that she was frowning.

There were hardwood floors in the house, all right, everywhere, but they were covered with carpets and rugs, or linoleum. Her mother used to varnish and polish those wood floors, but not she. Too much work.

There were mirrors in the house, too, not only in the bedrooms, but in the halls and in the dining room and living room. There was a large one over the one sofa that was against the wall in the living room. And there was one hanging over the buffet in the dining room.

She went back through the French doors and laid her shoulder bag and her thin, white gloves, on the catch-all table just inside the door. With the frown pinched between her eyebrows, she tapped across the rug of the kitchen and through the door to the dining room.

The mirror was still on the wall, reflecting the windows across the room and the rose lace panels that covered them. Deeper red draperies on each side of the wide windows seemed to tremble, stirred by air, a draft, from somewhere else in the house.

Mirror okay.

She went out into the hall and from there into the living room. There were two mirrors, twins, one over the sofa against the wall, the other at the end of the room over a narrow table. She had forgotten it. The room was neat and cool, hardly ever used. The fireplace was closed for the summer. In the fall they would decorate it for Thanksgiving, and again for Christmas, and would have small parties there. But otherwise the family used the room off the kitchen, the TV room, or family room.

She went out into the entrance hall. Mirrors still hung where they belonged.

Just to be sure it wasn't a window instead—late thought, and not a very comfortable one—she went into the library-den across the hall and peeked in. No, no windows broken out.

She went back to the entrance hall. The front door was half glass, covered by a sheer curtain, but that was intact too.

She went to the foot of the stairs and looked up, her hand on the knob of the newel post.

She didn't want to go up there, inexplicably. Just the thought of climbing those stairs stirred the hair at the back of her neck. Was she afraid of her own house? Of course not . . . and yet . . . she sensed the presence of something, up there, somewhere.

She could hear her own breathing, a breathless, uneven rasp. An unusual nervousness had overcome her.

Things were different here, she thought viciously, angrily, ever since those kids had moved in next door. Things had been *happening,* and she defied Faye and Sam to deny it.

But she was not going to be intimidated in her own house.

She climbed the stairs, her footsteps clumping on the carpet of the steps. When she reached the top, she stomped into the bedrooms one by one, the frown a deep line between her eyebrows, threatening to become permanent, her lips pursed.

When she reached the end of the hall, she smelled smoke. She stopped, sniffing the air. It was faint, but definite.

She walked back down the hall, slowly, sniffing it out, trying to define its boundaries. She turned. It was strongest at the end of the hall, right beside the door of the room they used for storage.

She opened the door gingerly, peering in, wondering if the crashing sound had been something falling here. The room was half-filled with furniture that was too good to throw away, and boxes of stuff of which she had forgotten if she had known what was in them in the beginning. Part of it had been put away by her mother, and others before her, years ago.

It was a large room, in which the attic stairway dropped, a room that caught the overflow from the attic.

A nearly forgotten room.

It was shadowed and dark, the windows covered by blinds that were drawn. The thought of a fire in the house sent a touch of panic into her stomach.

She stepped into the room, pulling the door shut behind her. The light, when she turned it on, seemed little brighter than a seven-watt nightlight. Her own fault. She could remember, back in her conservative days, putting a forty-watt bulb in the ceiling fixture.

But there was no fire, thank God.

Feeling weak suddenly, she sat down on a chair that was covered by an old blanket. The furniture bulked around her, with stacks of boxes making humps and aisles. It was here, she remembered, she had hidden her cigarettes when she was trying to stop smoking. In the bottom drawer of the chest over there.

She stared at it, feeling a need that might be based on a recent battle with stopping smoking. One cigarette, that was all she needed. Just one more.

She'd had a trying time lately. First, there was the worry about having Gavin's kids next door, because she had known it would be impossible to keep Katy and Dwayne away from them. Now, even though she no longer believed they killed their mother, she still felt they had something to do with it, somehow, or they knew something. And that little Ellen was so—weird. With her . . . fears?

And then came the murder, right on her doorstep, you might say.

And the cats.

Surrounded by wildcats.

She deserved a cigarette. Just one.

Tiptoeing to the chest as if she weren't alone in the house, she eased the drawer out. It stuck halfway, and she had to wrench on it. It nearly came apart in her hands, but she pushed the ends of the wood back together, the teeth of one into the teeth of the other, and persuaded the drawer to move unevenly.

It was filled, it seemed, with strange articles: bits and pieces of junk, small boxes, old costume jewelry. The cigarettes were gone. Who had been into the drawer? Katy? Dwayne? Had they been playing in this room without her knowledge?

She began to empty the drawer. Had those nosy kids found her cigarettes? Damn. If she ever caught them smoking, she'd—

Her hand touched the crumpled package, and she jerked it out. It was half full, and the small, cheap lighter was still there, tucked into the cellophane.

She sat down on a footstool nearby, pulled out one

mashed crooked cigarette and snapped the wheel of the lighter. What a great feeling, to get that little wheel under her thumb again. The flame shot upward, as lively as ever. She eyed it, seeing it alive, bright, fluttering. She put the cigarette into her mouth and sucked the flame into the end of it.

The smoke threatened to choke her. She coughed, coughed again. She fanned at the smoke that filled the air around her. It thickened, swirling.

It had been so long since she smoked that she had forgotten how burning the smoke could be.

She spent a few minutes coughing, her eyes closed, watering tears from irritation oozing out onto her cheeks.

Messing up her makeup.

The smoke was so thick, God!

Smoke . . . thick, choking . . .

She stood up, the cigarette falling from her fingers to the floor.

She had the presence of mind to put her foot on it, so that it wouldn't start a fire in the old rug on the floor, but she stared into the thickening smoke in front of her, in strangled horror, seeing vague figures there . . . an outline . . . a face half-formed, a body, huge . . . vile . . . part of the darkness, the cloud of smoke . . . becoming . . . *no, no.*

She turned, trying to find the door. But the walls had changed. The room she was in no longer looked familiar. There were curtains, now, dirty, gray, hanging in folds around her . . .

She tried to scream, but her throat filled with the smoke, strangling her.

Chapter Fourteen

They were building a playhouse in the corner of the barn. Ellen spent most of her time standing and watching Katy, or doing what Katy ordered.

The table and chairs were boxes they had found in a room in the barn, and Katy was arranging them. Overhead, like horses on a bridge, clattered the footsteps of Dwayne and Joey as they ran from one end of the loft to the other. Their voices filtered down, along with bits and pieces of debris, old hay, plain dirt. When it fell into Ellen's hair, she did as Katy did and simply shook it off.

"We need some dishes and things of that sort," Katy was saying. "Do you have little dishes, Ellen?"

"No. Not . . ." Not here, she had started to say. At home there was a box of play dishes, but that, along with all her other toys and dolls, had been left behind.

"Well, then, we'll just have to go back over to my house and get some. Come on, Ellen."

Katy straightened, brushed her hands across the sides of her shorts, and headed toward the open door. She saw that Ellen was still carrying her doll, and stopped.

"Put your baby down, Ellen. You'll have to use both hands to carry things. I'll tell you what we can do, Ellen. We can move all my house things over here and keep this for our playhouse forever, what do you say?"

"All right."

Ellen put her doll down and hurried to follow Katy. She liked having Katy here. It helped her forget about the eyes that followed her, the monsters that hid in the dark places.

They went down the path and through the gate, leaving it open. In the backyard at Katy's house, she stopped in the path in front of Ellen and pointed to a large green collection of evergreen shrubs.

"The Animal Control man put cages out to catch those wildcats."

Ellen shuddered. "In there?"

"Well, I don't know where he put them exactly, but somewhere around here."

She went on walking, and Ellen hurried to catch up.

The path curved through the trees and carefully planted shrubs and came to an end at the edge of the grass. On the patio were table and chairs, similar to the ones at Faye's house, Ellen saw. It was the first time she had been to Katy's house, and she looked around curiously.

"Even though Mama's gone shopping, she won't care if I take these things to our playhouse. She won't even care if I take some big things. I'll tell you what, we can take us a picnic lunch, shall we?"

"I don't know."

"Sure. But come on, first, we'll go up to my bedroom and get my tea set."

They went through a hall and up the front stairs. Katy's room was the second door on the right side of the hall. The house, Ellen noted, was not as big and old as Faye's house.

Katy's room was filled with toys, stuffed animals and more than one tea set. She went down on her knees and gathered things into the only box in which the tiny cups and saucers were already in their slots.

Katy sat back on her heels. "I'll have to go downstairs and get a plastic bag. You be picking the plates and pots and pans out of the toy box, Ellen, uh—" She sniffed the air. "Do you smell smoke, Ellen?"

Ellen looked around. The room was shaded, the blind half drawn. She felt afraid suddenly. Afraid to stay up here alone.

"No," she said.

Katy got up, the smoke forgotten. "I'll go get a big plastic bag to carry these things in. You be getting everything ready, okay?"

Ellen didn't want to stay alone, but she said nothing. She watched Katy exit the room, and for a long minute afterward, she sat staring at the empty rectangle of the door.

She began to smell the smoke.

It touched her nostrils, stinging, burning, and she put her hand to her face. She longed to get up and run . . . run . . . but she couldn't move. The smell of smoke terrified her in deep ways she couldn't understand.

There had been smoke yesterday in the wash house . . .

. . . and there had been smoke . . .

But there was no smoke here, not really. Katy had made her think so just by talking about it. The air around Ellen was clean and clear; there was nothing here to hurt her. The monster was . . . gone. There was no monster in Katy's room. The posters on the wall, of ghouls in a graveyard, were not real monsters. It was only a poster, a picture, a drawing, colored gray and black. The fog that swirled around the tombstones only looked like smoke.

The smoke only looked like fog.

The figures that she dreamed of sometimes never took shape, monsters that were just pieces of things... an arm, a leg, a claw. A snout. A big cat in the bushes, staring out with slanted eyes.

... *slanted eyes* ...

Fear curled up her back and across her shoulders, and she whirled, looking behind her.

No, Ellen, no, it's nothing, she told herself.

She bent over the toy box and began to dig frantically, keeping her eyes away from the door, her thoughts away from nightmares that lay just behind the curtain in her mind.

... things she knew and yet didn't know...

She began a collection of little dishes, of pans and lids and cups, setting them down in a growing pile at her feet. She found knives and forks and spoons. She found a napkin holder with paper napkins, big ones that Katy must have taken from her mother's kitchen.

Somebody appeared suddenly in the doorway, catching the corner of Ellen's eye. She gasped, looking up, wanting to scream, yet not able to. Her throat closed around her fear, like a hand around her throat.

But it was only Katy. Ellen swallowed, relief flooding her like fever.

"Okay," Katy said, her voice busy and casual and so welcome to Ellen's ears. "Here's one for you and one for me. Let's hurry now. And we'll get our picnic lunch and ask your mother if we can eat in our playhouse."

"She's not my mother."

"Well, I meant your stepmother, of course," Katy said, as she scooped things into her plastic bag. "But what are you going to call her? You can't call her by her name. Kids aren't supposed to call grownups by their names. I mean, we call her Faye, but that's because she's so young, Mama said it would be all right. But she's your stepmother. How can you call her Faye?"

"She said we could."

"Oh. All right. I suppose if she said you could."

With their bags full they went out into the hall and down the stairs.

At the bottom, Katy stopped and sniffed the air again. But she said nothing. She led the way on toward the kitchen.

"Mama used to smoke cigarettes," she said. "But Daddy made her quit. He said it wasn't good for her health."

In the kitchen they put the bags down. Katy opened the refrigerator door and looked in.

"There's some cold fried chicken. Do you want some of that? We got it yesterday at Colonel Sanders. We'll take some of that. And cheese. Here."

She handed a chunk of cheese to Ellen, unwrapped. Ellen held it in her hands as if it were melted butter, looking at it, fingers extended.

"Put it on one of the plates, Ellen," Katy said with a sigh of impatience. "That is part of our lunch. I'll take this platter of chicken, too. Mama won't mind. And we'll need some bread."

Katy stretched up over the top of the kitchen counter to a bread box and pulled out a loaf of bread. She looked at it, grunted, shoved it back and pulled out a half loaf of raisin bread instead.

"I like this better," she muttered. "Now, we'll have to make two trips. I know! We'll put it in the little wagon and haul it. The wagon can be our catering cart."

Ellen followed her out the door, where Katy pulled the red wagon up onto the patio. They began to load it with the food.

The day dragged for Beth. She wrote two letters to friends and took them to the mailbox at the end of the driveway. For a couple of minutes she stood looking down the street and into the woods. One car was parked there, and a couple of men were walking around. She could hear the low rumble of their voices; but the car was unmarked, and the men were wearing regular clothes, so they might have not been connected with the police. Still, she felt they were. Detectives, probably, looking for something.

She went back to the house and found that Faye had come down from the nursery and was making lunch.

"Would you mind finding the kids, Beth, and telling them it's time to eat?"

But before Beth could answer, Joey ran across the patio and stuck his head in at the door and yelled, "Is it okay if we eat in the barn? Katy and Ellen brought food from Katy's house. She sent me to tell you."

Faye looked at Beth, half-smiled, and shrugged.

Beth yelled at Joey, "Why did you wait this long to say something, you nerds? Faye is fixing lunch!"

Joey danced, from one foot to the other, undecided. Faye laughed.

"Oh, go on, it's okay."

Joey ran. Faye began putting lunch meats away again.

"Sorry," Beth said, feeling responsible.

"It's all right. I've only made three, and we can probably eat those ourselves. Shall we take them out to the patio?"

Joey and Dwayne came running back, wanting a pitcher of Kool-Aid, and went out again, carrying it carefully.

Beth found that she was hungry. The air in the backyard was cool and shady, patches of sunshine lying on the grass like spilled gold, moving and changing as the sun lowered.

In the afternoon she spent over an hour sitting on the floor of the nursery, doing some hand work for Faye as she ran the machine. Another baby, a little brother or sister. At first she hadn't felt anything, but now, surrounded by the room in which it would live, she began to wonder about it, to feel a tingle like a thrill.

"Do you think I could hold it?" Beth asked.

"The baby?"

"Yes."

"I expect I'll ask you to babysit sometimes. Would you like that?"

"Oh, yes." Beth looked up, smiling at her stepmother. "I would."

"That would be nice," Faye said. "Which would you rather have, a boy or a girl?"

"A boy. No, maybe not. Baby girls can be dressed so pretty."

The afternoon passed faster than the morning, and the first thing Beth knew, Faye was shutting off the sewing machine. The baby quilt she had been working on hung over the edge of the table, three-fourths quilted. It was a pattern of animals, round, soft-faced, perky-eared.

Nothing at all like the cat that had been in the living room.

"It's three o'clock," Faye said. "Let's stop. I'm tired of sitting here, aren't you?"

Beth had been sitting on the floor with her knees out, her legs bent, but she wasn't tired. It had been the best afternoon since . . . before her mother died.

"It's time to send Katy and Dwayne home," Faye said.

Twice during the afternoon Faye had gone to the window at the end of the north hall and listened for their voices. They had continued to play in the barn, voices rising, loud, excited, Katy's and Dwayne's and Joey's. Ellen's, sometimes, quieter than the others.

"I'll go," Beth offered, and ran down the stairs and through the dark central corridor of the house.

It was cool here, even though the air conditioner wasn't on. The big house was kind of like a cave, she thought, remembering their trip to see the caves when she was only nine. It had been dark and chilly in those tunnels in the earth, and this central, lower hall reminded her of them. Mama and she and Joey and Ellen had gone, but Ellen hadn't liked the caves. Even then she had been the nervous one, the scared one.

But something was making her scared now, too, Beth thought, remembering the flame, remembering the other things, the outlines of something that looked like a face, a body, always just behind Ellen. And the cat. It was just a big, old cat, wasn't it? But it had scared Ellen. So maybe . . . maybe it wasn't just a cat.

She had slowed by the time she reached the brighter, warmer kitchen. Sunshine angled in from the west windows, streaks and patches of patterns made by the trees on the west side of the driveway.

Beth crossed the patio, and jumped down the two feet to the ground, though the wide steps were just to her left. She walked through the grass and into the trees at the rear of the lawn. The voices of the kids were still strong and creative.

She could hear Katy saying, "And you're the aunt, who's coming to visit me and my children. You be from Australia, why don't you?" And upstairs, their footsteps like distant thunder, Joey was yelling something at Dwayne, and Dwayne was answering. They were running nearer in the barn loft, their footsteps louder. Then their faces appeared in the open doors above.

"Hey," Beth called. "Come on down, it's three o'clock."

She went into the shadowed overhang of the barn and found the girls had made a large playhouse at the end. Beth stood with her hands on her hips surveying it. Boxes that were tables, piled with dishes and food, boxes that were chairs and beds.

"Where did you find all the boxes?"

Katy said, "They were stacked in that room. They're old orange crates or something."

"Okay, time to go. It's three."

Katy's face screwed up. "Already?"

"You'd better take that food home, too, Katy, and put it in the fridge. Or at least tell your mom you've had it out here in the barn all afternoon. And if you kids don't clean up the messes, the bread crusts and the chicken bones, you're going to have all kinds of wild animals in here eating it."

"That's okay," Katy said. "Come on, Ellen, help me put this stuff back into the wagon."

Beth turned away. "Clean it up," she yelled one last time over her shoulder.

She walked through the back part of the yard, beneath the tall trees that grew as if carefully selected to remain, like the front yard. She passed by shrubs that were flowering in the deep shade, but mostly there were ferns, long-leafed, dark green. What little grass there was beneath and between the trees had been mowed.

At the rear was a fence like the fence at home, but on the other side was another long, sloping yard, going downhill. Trees shrouded a house below, and all she could see of it was different layers and angles of rooflines.

She walked along the fence, trailing her fingers in its links, all the way to the corner. On her way back to the house, she passed behind the barn. It was quiet now, the voices of the kids gone. She looked in to see if they had cleaned up, and they had. The bread crusts were gone, and the chicken bones.

But when she went back out the door, she saw what had been done with it all. A little pile, like an offering, had been neatly laid at the corner of the barn.

For the stray cats and the raccoons? Beth shrugged. One of the boys, probably. Joey, she knew, was especially sensitive toward the plight of animals. He had watched Walt Disney shows all his life, but she felt his tenderness was just part of him, like the color of his eyes and hair. She loved him for it.

She left the garbage alone and went on to the house. The television was on in the den, that room off the kitchen that had been furnished with sofa and chairs and TV stuff, and she went in to join Joey and Ellen. They were sprawled like limp dolls, resting from a hard day of play.

"Where's Mama?" Dwayne asked, looking around, his feet planted in one spot in the middle of the kitchen floor.

"She went shopping," Katy said. "Help me carry this stuff in, Dwayne!"

"But she said she'd be back by three, and it's after three. Where is she?"

Katy came into the kitchen with her arms loaded. She dumped it all onto the cabinet. "I said she went shopping. Are you going to help me?"

Dwayne went running out, but instead of stopping at the wagon, he went on by. Katy put her hands on her hips and let out a disgusted sigh, then gave it up and finished emptying the wagon. Now the pile had been transferred onto the cabinet, part of a loaf of bread, cookies in various bags, lunch meats in packages that were torn and half open, the hunk of cheese, fly-specked.

Dwayne came back into the kitchen, his eyes wide. He stared at Katy.

"Her car's in the garage. Where is she?"

Katy returned his stare. She turned and looked around the kitchen, as if somewhere there they had missed seeing their mother. With her face serious and wondering, puzzled, beginning to show consternation at the silence in the house she led the way through the hall.

"Mama?" she called, and heard it echoed by her brother.

They went upstairs and into the master bedroom.

Out again, they stood in the hall together, arms touching, voices calling, "Mama!"

They went from room to room, opening doors, looking in. They went back downstairs, outside and all around the house, and back in again where Katy stood looking up the stairs.

"Dwayne, did you smell something when we were upstairs?"

"What?"

She hesitated. "Do you remember when Mama smoked cigarettes?"

"No."

"Well, she did, a long time ago. Last year." She began to climb the stairs. At the top she went straight back down the hall toward the storage room.

"Do you smell that?" she asked. "It's smoke. Mama used to come into the storage room and smoke, when she thought we wouldn't know. Don't you remember we found her cigarettes in the dresser drawer once?"

"She's in there," Katy whispered, "smoking cigarettes."

They stood staring at each other. Dwayne looked as if he would be crying soon, so Katy made up her mind.

"She just didn't hear us call, that's all, Dwayne." She knocked on the door and called loudly, "Mama! We're home!"

They waited. The silence was broken only by their breathing and sounds beyond the house that had no meaning for them at this moment: a car going by, soft vibrations, a bird singing, separated from them by several walls.

Katy tried the door. It opened with difficulty as she shoved, only a fraction of an inch. She paused to look wide-eyed at Dwayne.

"Something's holding the door. It's not locked, but something's holding it."

"Mama?"

"Why would she . . . ?"

Dwayne's eyes found the floor and stared. He pointed. "Katy, what's that?"

They stared at it, the round, dark wet blob of red stuff oozing out from beneath the door.

Katy stepped back from the door abruptly, and it clicked shut, pushing from the other side. She backed, into her brother, pushing him toward the wall behind.

Faye sat at the kitchen table with a cup of coffee. Decaffeinated. She had put cream in it, and sugar; and she knew it was probably her imagination, but it didn't taste like real coffee. Still, she was going to get used to it, whether she liked it or not, for her baby's sake. She didn't want any more chemicals in her body than was necessary while she was pregnant. The baby meant . . . the world. It was life. Her contact with the future. The most horrible thought was that she might lose it.

Last night she had dreamed that she was no longer

pregnant. She was searching everywhere for her baby, but it was gone.

A nightmare. She had awakened to continue the search, this time for Gavin. How she needed him.

All day she had been hoping the phone would ring, that it would be Gavin saying he was coming home. But not even a salesman had called, only Nordene, asking if her kids could spend the day with Joey and Ellen.

As if her thoughts had conjured them, suddenly Katy and Dwayne were on the other side of the kitchen screen, their faces pale and serious. Faye stood up, feeling as if her nightmare had returned. Something was dreadfully wrong, she knew. She was aware of someone behind her and saw Beth from the corner of her eye, and behind her, Joey.

"What is it?" she asked, going to the door.

"Mama," Katy said in a strained voice. "We can't find Mama."

Faye went out onto the patio. "Maybe she hasn't come home yet." At the same time looking at the watch, seeing that it was almost four.

"Her car's in the garage. Something is holding the door upstairs," Katy said. "And—and there's blood under the door."

Faye swallowed, unable to challenge Katy.

She went ahead of them, along the paths, through the gate and into the house next door. There, in the kitchen, she paused.

"Where . . . ?"

Neither Katy nor Dwayne offered to lead the way. Faye saw that Beth had come, too, with Joey a few feet behind. She looked back, wondering about Ellen, and was relieved to see that she was there, too, still out in the yard. She didn't feel good about leaving Ellen alone.

"Upstairs," Katy said. "The storage room."

Faye knew where it was. Once Nordene had taken her there to show her an old tapestry someone had made. It was hanging on the wall in that overpacked room, but one corner was torn off, rendering it worthless now.

Faye went through the halls with the kids trailing, up the stairs and down the narrow hall at the back. The light in the ceiling was dim, and the damp spot at the bottom of the door dark, almost black.

Katy had called it blood, and Faye stared at it, seeing that it had seeped out from under the storage room door. But she couldn't let herself think it was blood.

"It could just be water," she said. "Even water would be dark here, in this pale carpet."

"The door won't open," Katy said in a low, frightened voice. "Something is holding it. Mama wouldn't hold it."

Faye turned the knob, and pushed and found that Katy was right. The door was not locked; it unlatched with a soft click, and it yielded, just a bit, before it was stopped.

Faye glanced back at the kids, all five faces, pale and serious. Beth's face, more tanned than the others, was behind and above Katy's. Ellen was still farther back, as she had been all the way, at least fifteen feet behind Joey.

Faye put her shoulder against the door and pushed, puzzled. Whatever it was holding the door must have fallen from the other side, because there was no way it could have been pushed from someone inside, unless that person was still in there.

The door gave, slowly, edging inward. Two inches, three, four . . .

Something fell suddenly, flopping down in the shadows beyond the door to lie white and stained in the opening.

A hand.

Katy screamed.

The fingertips of the hand were dark-brownish red, and the blood had dripped down into the palm.

Faye recognized the diamond bracelet of the wristwatch that Nordene always wore.

Chapter Fifteen

Faye had wanted to run, to try to escape what was coming next, but she simply turned, outwardly more calm than she had ever thought she could be, and said to Beth, "Take the children downstairs, and call the police."

She waited until they were gone, and then she pushed the door farther open. She had to be sure. She had thought the hand and arm belonged to Nordene, but in her heart there was hope that this was a joke of some kind, another item collected in the room, a mannequin or something of that nature. Something grotesque, certainly, but not real.

She pushed the door wide enough that she could enter, edge sideways and look into the room. The faint smell of smoke touched her nostrils, that strange, acrid, burning scent that was there and was gone, as if it were more thought than substance.

She moved into the room only far enough to look down, and then she had to cover her mouth with her hand as her stomach threatened to revolt.

Nordene lay twisted like a thrown and lifeless piece of putty, her legs apart, her skirt ripped off and stringing to one side, blood-soaked. The blood seemed to be everywhere near the door, and Nordene was half-sitting against the door, her back against it. Not as if she had crawled there, but as if she had been placed there, to end her life there.

Faye stepped back into the hall, and the door closed again, pushed by the dead weight of Nordene's body.

Feeling ill, her mind unable to assimilate this, Faye staggered toward the stairwell. She sat down on the top step and put her head in her hands.

"Are you all right?" The voice came from the hall below.

Faye looked, saw Beth. The white faces of the other children were behind her.

"Yes."

Faye stood up and went downstairs, holding tightly to the banister.

She didn't feel like trying to talk to the children. What could she say? She would only lead them outside, away from this suddenly horrible house of death.

Before she reached the kitchen, she thought of Sam. He would have to know. He had a right to know, now, not later. She stopped at the kitchen phone.

"Katy, where does your daddy work?"

Katy's eyes glanced to the left, and to the right. Her lips moved soundlessly. Faye saw her speechless for the first time, and a deep pity surged into her heart. She hadn't really thought of the children until this moment. They had lost their mother.

Just as Ellen, Beth and Joey had lost theirs.

Katy whispered, "I don't know. I don't know the name. It's . . ." She motioned vaguely with her hands. "His office is downtown . We go there sometimes and take him out to lunch."

"I'll make some calls," Faye said.

She knew it was a brokerage company, and she was sure that Nordene had mentioned the name in her presence. If she looked through the phone book, or the address book by the phone . . . of course, the address book. Her hands shook. She glanced at the children, all five of them standing there just looking at her, waiting. Waiting for her to do something that would make everything right again.

How helpless she felt.

A glance through the address book revealed Sam's place of work in block print angled across the first page. She dialed it quickly and spoke to a secretary. She was glad it was someone other than Sam.

"Just tell him there's been an accident, and his children need him to come home," she told the secretary, then, hearing a pause in which she could almost read the woman's thoughts, and anticipating the question that was bound to come up, she broke the connection.

Within a minute, while she was still standing by the desk, the phone rang again. It was Sam.

"Is this Faye? What's wrong?"

She couldn't tell him the truth. What could she say? Anything would unnerve him now, cause him problems with driving through the afternoon traffic. "Nordene has had an accident, Sam. Just please come on home."

"I'll be there within minutes. Did you call an ambulance? What happened to her?"

"Yes, I called for help. Sorry, I have to go now."

She went to the table and sat down. The children were silent, still watching her. Beth was the only one moving about, and, Faye noticed, she seemed to be looking for something. She went from the outside door to the door into the hall, but she came back and looked out the window over the sink. She turned her head, and her eyes seemed to take in every angle of the kitchen.

Faye felt a sharp pain in her abdomen, and she put her hand against the round bulge of her belly instinctively, a faint groan escaping her before she could stop it.

Beth took a couple of steps nearer. "Are you all right?"

Faye nodded, waiting for the pain to ease away.

She took a deep breath and felt the relief that comes after pain. But a new fear was gathering. *Oh God, don't let me lose my baby.*

She realized she was holding her breath, waiting for the pain to come again, signalling a premature labor. Too many things were happening lately.

But the pain didn't come, and she began to relax.

Beth had gone back to looking for something that wasn't there, and the other four had gathered close, pushed against the table. Katy was clutching Dwayne's arm. Both faces were still and staring, their freckles dark against blanched skin. Where they in shock? Should she call a doctor? But Sam would be here soon.

It occurred to Faye that she should take them all to her house, get them away from this.

There was a knock on the back door. Katy screamed, slapping both hands over her mouth. The others looked stunned, white faces staring at the door.

Faye saw right away, even before she reached the door, that it wasn't the police. The man who stood there had a beard, not a very neat one, and he was dressed in tan work shirt and trousers.

"Hello," he said when she opened the screen. "I'm the Animal Control Officer. The lady of the house called me to trap some wildcats, but if you'll come out here, I'll show you what I got."

Faye followed him, the children filing behind her as if they were attached by invisible strings. They went off the patio and into the driveway where his pickup truck was parked.

A cage, sitting on the ground behind the pickup, had a fluffy white cat in it, a Persian with round, blue eyes looking innocently out through the wires of the cage. The only sign of fear it showed was in its hovering back into the corner of the cage.

The man bent, put his fingers through the wire and caressed the cat. It relaxed visibly.

"You can call this a wildcat if you want to, but I'd say it's a local resident. Do you happen to know whose cat it is?"

"I . . ." This one, indeed, she had seen. But she couldn't remember in which yard. "I think . . ."

"It's Mrs. Skimm's cat," Dwayne cried, his voice almost natural, a touch of pink returning to his cheeks. He pointed down the street. "If she knew you'd trapped her cat she'd really be mad."

This distraction was good for Dwayne, at least, she saw. Even Katy seemed less dazed and in shock. All four of the younger children had gathered to look into the cage, but Beth was still on the patio, her eyes searching the yard. Faye knew suddenly what she was looking for: the killer.

"Well," the man said in his casual, unhurried drawl, "I'll just carry this fellow on down to his mama, then. I don't think the lady will be troubled with wildcats very much. If she is, just tell her to call me again."

"I will," Katy said. "I'll tell her."

Faye saw Katy's chin quiver, once, then grow firm. In her way, she had denied the blood upstairs, the hand that had slipped into view.

The man lifted the cage into the back of the pickup and put up the tailgate. Just as he was driving out, a police car came, its light twirling. The car stopped, leaving room for the pickup to go on by.

The police car eased forward, parked, and two men got out. Faye recognized the same faces she had seen only yesterday, the tall young Texan-type and the older, pudgier one with the sandy hair and the round face.

"Upstairs," Faye told them, conscious of the listening children. "Beth, keep the children down here. I'll take the officers up."

Beth reached out for the children, herding them with her arms extended like wings. "Come on, we'll wait on the patio."

Faye asked, "Would it be all right for Beth to take the little ones over to my house?"

The two men looked at each other. The shorter one nodded. "You live just next door, don't you?"

"Yes."

"Sure, that'll be fine."

"Beth . . ." Faye said, and Beth nodded and began herding them toward the gate between the two houses.

And suddenly Katy began to scream.

"No! No! *I want to stay with my mama. I want my mama!* Mama, mama," she sobbed, covering her face with her hands.

Beth caught Katy close in her arms, her own face twisted and on the verge of bursting into tears. Dwayne had begun to cry and was reaching out for Katy, his hands groping.

"Come on," Beth was saying. "It'll be all right. Everything will be all right. Just come with me for a while, then your daddy will be home."

They went with her, through the gate, toward the other house.

Faye watched them, tears blurring them into blobs of color, of reds, blues, greens, and she wondered if anything would ever be all right for Katy and Dwayne again.

For the next several minutes Faye spent her time between the hall upstairs and the patio. The time seemed endless. More police came, and a van with photographic equipment. The detectives began trickling in, coming, leaving. The ambulance came, with a doctor. Police cars parked in her own driveway, too, and she was relieved. The children were safer with the police near.

In the midst of it all Sam arrived, his freckles standing out as if they had been added recently to his face, dropped like melted wax. Faye stood on the patio, seeing the sun go down. She was cold, so cold, yet she wasn't sure if it was the evening air, or this second murder, so close to home.

The third close to Gavin's children.

Had the killer followed the children?

"Sam," she said, when he came down from upstairs, "Sam, why don't you go over to my house? The children are there, with Beth."

He nodded, but she doubted that he registered her words in his tortured mind. He looked as if he might collapse. "Later," he said. "Thanks, Faye."

She left, glad to get away, anxious to be with the kids, to make sure they were safe. How easy it was to have one's mind go blank, to scarcely realize what had happened. To understand that if Nordene had been so brutally killed, then there had to be a killer. A madman.

Suddenly she was running. The children had been alone . . . how long? The police were in the yards, in the neighborhood, but not in the house with them. The sun had not gone down yet, the waning light of it still streaked through the trees in slivers. But the shadows everywhere looked deeper and darker and more ominous. Hiding something. All of them.

She was vastly relieved to hear the television going. But then she remembered that it had been going when they left the house. There were no other sounds, no young voices.

She rushed into the house and to the TV room. And then she almost fainted in her relief. All the kids were on the sofa, all five of them. But their eyes met her at the door, anxious glances.

She sat down in the closest chair. The room was growing dark, with no light except that coming from the television and less from the uncurtained window. She turned on a table lamp beside the chair.

"You daddy is home, Katy and Dwayne—"

They both got up.

"No, wait," she said. "He'll be over to get you."

Dwayne began suddenly to cry. "I want to see Mama," he said. "I want to go home and see my mama."

Faye pulled him to her and held him on her lap. He buried his face in her shoulder and neck and wept hard, and all she could do was hold him and weep in silence with him.

The night was long and cold and nearly sleepless for Faye. She heard the grandfather clock in the lower hall strike one, three and four. She had left her bedroom door open so that she could feel more in touch with Beth, Ellen and Joey, for the fear was growing. If a killer could get into the storage room of Nordene's house and then leave while her body was leaning against the inside of the door, while the windows were locked and unbroken, couldn't he also be . . . anywhere?

She wasn't capable of coherent thought. Her mind jumped from one death to another and back to the children. She kept remembering Ellen's fears, and the cat that had seemed to follow her into the house.

There were other things that she should know, should realize, she felt, but what? *What?*

Sam . . . Katy and Dwayne. She had felt so sorry for them. Sam had come for the children before bedtime, and they had gone away. His parents lived a few miles away, and they were going there, he said.

At least the children had grandparents, Faye was thinking, and their dad would be with them every night.

She got up at four-thirty and walked down the hall. For the fifth time that night she was checking on the children.

Joey was sleeping. Alone in his room.

She only stood at Beth's closed door, listening. The silence beyond worried her, but she told herself of course it would be silent there. They were both asleep.

Only partly comforted, she went back down the hall toward her own room.

Beth heard the footsteps in the hall, soft, light, slow. Part of her knew it was Faye, but there was the other constant dread, the feeling that whatever it was that had killed the laundress, and Nordene and . . . Mama, too, was here, seeing them, waiting, for some reason that she didn't understand, before it killed all of them.

Ellen slept on the far side of the bed, rolled into a knot, like a little animal in hibernation, as Mama used to say. Or like an animal with a vulnerable underside that it was trying to protect.

Beth sat against her pillows, struggling not to fall asleep. But in the quiet hours of pre-dawn, exhaustion overcame her fears, her need to keep a constant watch.

The next she knew the room was light, and Faye was standing in the doorway. Beth jerked up, heart pounding.

"I just wanted to make sure you're all right."

She withdrew, and Beth got up. Ellen uncurled, sat

up and rubbed her eyes.

In an effort to be nonchalant, Beth said, "You can use the bathroom first, Ellen. I'll make up the beds, while you and Joey dress. Don't forget to comb your hair. It's a mess. You had the sheet wrapped around your head all night, like a turban."

Beth followed them downstairs, hurrying after they left and she was alone in the vast second story of the house. She hurried with her own preparations, combing her hair without looking in the mirror, thinking of all the empty rooms behind all the closed doors in the other halls. She hadn't seen half of the house, she felt. How did she know what was there?

But then she remembered, the police had searched it all. Even the closets, they had said, just the day before yesterday.

Was it only that long ago since the other woman had been killed?

She went downstairs and tried to keep busy helping Faye clean up the kitchen after breakfast, but there wasn't much to do.

Joey came in and said, "They're still over there, at Dwayne's house. The police."

Beth said, "You stay away from there, Joey."

"I wasn't over there; I only looked through the fence."

"Well, don't even do that. Go in the T.V. room and watch with Ellen."

At midmorning they came, and Beth knew she had been waiting for them, knowing that sooner or later they would start asking her questions again. Her mind had been closed against it, against knowing that in some way all three deaths were connected. Her own mother's, and these other two.

The killer had followed them. Whoever it was, *whatever* . . .

Faye let the two detectives into the house. "Beth," she said, "these gentlemen would like to talk to you."

Faye led them all into a front room, furnished like a living room except for the desks and the books. The walls seemed covered in bookcases that reached from the floor to the ceiling. It was another room that Beth had not been in before.

Faye withdrew, closing the double doors again.

The men looked at Beth, their eyes friendly. Friendlier than she felt toward them. One of the men had a little pointed beard and a mustache, both of which were black with white streaks at each side. His hair was black without any gray obvious. He turned on a light by the chair in which he sat. His eyes were dark brown.

The other man looked more all-American, with lighter eyes.

"Beth, we have to ask you some questions about your mother's death again, if you don't mind. Now that you've been away from that bad time in your life for a few weeks, is there anything else you remember that you didn't tell the detectives there?"

"No, sir," she added the "sir," sensing the abruptness of her answer without it. "I've tried not to think about it at all."

"That's understandable."

The hour of questions dragged on and on. The men were gentle and tried to make her feel at ease, but there was nothing she could tell them. It was like the first time, as if they felt she knew something she didn't realize she knew.

She didn't tell them that at first she had thought maybe her sister, Ellen, had killed their mother. There was the blood all over her . . . showing that she had been there.

She didn't want them questioning Ellen.

Now she knew Ellen was not guilty, not in that way. She hadn't killed these other ladies, certainly. But . . . there was a connection. She was beginning to know that, in the dark part of her soul, but she didn't know what it was.

When the detectives left, she saw them stop on the patio to talk a short while with Faye, and though she stood inside the kitchen door, she could hear most of what they were saying.

". . . the murders are similar to the one in California . . . death by shock and loss of blood, and in one case by heart attack, by fear, you might say, and possibly in these other cases, too. We'll know more when the medical examiner is finished."

"Was there rape?" Faye asked.

"Rape? Let's call it more a sexual mutilation."

Beth drew back. The voices drifted away, coming, going. She wanted to hear, and yet she couldn't bear to hear it.

The men were leaving now, and their last words hung in Beth's mind, clearly.

"If the children remember anything, let us know, no matter how insignificant it might seem."

Beth went to the door of the T.V. room and looked in. Ellen lay on the floor, her head resting on her hands, clasped beneath her cheek. She was looking at the moving figures on the screen, but Beth had a feeling she wasn't seeing them.

Among the shadows of the room, there was another shadow, an aura beyond Ellen, a filmy, smoky darkness that outlined her bright hair.

Chapter Sixteen

Beth knew suddenly what she had to do. She had to take Ellen and Joey and leave, try to escape whatever this was that had followed them.

She backed out of the TV room and returned to the patio. Faye was still standing there, looking at her feet. Beth watched her from near the door, feeling a sudden sense of closeness.

Would Faye be the next one killed?

No, not if she took the kids and left. Maybe not then. The killer was choosing women, not children, and Faye was in danger. Beth could feel it, as she looked at her, as if that same dark aura was surrounding Faye.

"Faye," she said softly, hoping not to startle her

Faye turned.

"Are you all right?"

"Yes, are you?"

Beth nodded. "I think I'll go up to my room for a while, if it's all right."

"Yes, I think it would be." Faye looked up at the second floor windows. "I think . . . I hope, our house is safe."

That wasn't what Beth had meant, but she didn't speak her feelings. She had only wanted to let Faye know where she would be, so that Faye wouldn't come looking for her and find out what she was going to do.

Beth went through into the silent front of the house and up the stairs, her footsteps lost in the carpets. The halls branched away from the upstairs mezzanine, silent, cool, shadowed, spotted with furniture occasionally. Places where something could hide, waiting.

Beth went toward the bedrooms without looking around.

She began to pack, to choose what clothing they would have to have and to poke it into one bag. They couldn't go around carrying suitcases, because if they did, they would be spotted immediately. She first thought of simply taking nothing, because even one suitcase would be conspicuous.

But they had to have a change of clothes.

One change each, she decided.

The suitcase sat on the bed, open, obvious. Even here, and even though the suitcase was one of the smaller ones, it was too conspicuous. It would mark them as runaways immediately.

She dumped its contents on the bed, closed it and put it back on the shelf in the closet. There was a canvas shoulder bag she had carried on the airplane, sitting deflated on the shelf. After staring at it awhile, she took it down and looked inside. There was a cardboard in the bottom, the rest of it would stretch and carry more than it looked.

It would have to do. She would have to choose their clothes carefully.

She stuffed it as full as it would go, at the last minute putting in a pair of pajamas each. When it was packed, she tucked it into the corner of the closet where it would be hidden in case Faye looked in there sometime during the day, which was a chance in many, because Faye would not look unless she searched the house again.

Beth stood thinking of Faye, feeling a bond she

hadn't known existed. She didn't want to leave her, yet leaving her might save her life. It might save all their lives.

They were going to be running from something that was a total mystery to them. Ellen had called it a monster, right from the start, and something in Beth's mind stirred; but its stirring caused her too much discomfort. She twisted with the pain it caused, unable to open her mind and receive it. But she knew; there was something she should see, as clearly as a shifting of light and as easily missed.

But whatever it was, she couldn't bear to think of it.

She could only start running and pulling her little brother and sister with her.

And hoping, praying, that Faye, left behind, would be safe.

She began next to search for money. She went into Joey's room and looked in the dresser drawers. He had been getting an allowance, and if he had spent any of it, she didn't know when. Every time they went out to eat, Faye paid for it. And after eating they always went to the park. Or into stores where he just walked along with the rest of them.

But she couldn't find his money.

Ellen's had been put into a piggy bank that someone had left in her room. It was on the chest, and it rattled when she shook it.

Beth sat down on the bed, removed the plug from the bottom and began tediously to shake out the coins and dollar bills. Four dollars, five . . .

She felt suddenly that something was behind her, staring at the back of her head.

She turned swiftly, and a shadow moved at the window, something in the tree outside the window. The limb trembled and grew still.

Beth got up and went to the window, opened the

bottom sash, unlatched the screen and leaned out, looking down. There were little patches of leaves left over from winter at the base of the tree, beneath shrubs that were planted around the tree. The shrubs were green and thick, some kind of cedar or juniper. Thick enough to hide whatever it was that had been on the limb. Trying to reach the window? Trying to reach her?

She backed away, closed and locked the screen and window again. Deep in that dark part of her mind, she knew that if it had wanted to reach her, it would have. Through locked screens and windows, even through locked doors. Whatever it was . . . was different from anything they had ever seen before.

She scooped up the coins and dollar bills from the bed and left what remained in the piggy bank.

In her own room she put the money into the coin purse of her small shoulder bag. Besides that, she had twenty-three dollars of her own. It wouldn't buy bus tickets anywhere, but it would buy food until she could figure out what to do.

She started downstairs, pausing on the way to see if Faye had come up to the nursery.

She opened the nursery door and for a moment lost herself in the cheerful brightness of the room. There was a bassinet that Faye had put a long, lace cover on. The colors in it were both pink and blue, as well as white, splashed and streaked on, like candy canes. A satin ruffle that was all white had been sewn around the hood. Against the far wall was a crib, white with little bears and pigs and kittens and puppies, as well as some other baby animals. But, the room was a mess. The center had the sewing machine, the rocking chair, boxes of things not yet unpacked.

Beth wished that Faye had been here, that they could work here together, in peace, the way they had yesterday afternoon.

She closed the door with a deep hurt growing in her chest.

She would never be part of this.

The baby would never know her, and she would never know him.

She could almost see him in the bassinet, kicking his plump legs, cooing, smiling when she looked in on him.

But she would never open this door again.

She turned away, closing the door softly.

Should she call Gavin? Faye wondered. She longed to feel that it would be the thing to do. God knew she needed him. They all needed him.

She stood on the patio, her arms folded across her stomach, her palm clasped against her side where she could see the healthy kicking of the baby, a gentle movement of herself beneath her palm.

Two murders now in two days, one on each side of her house.

She could see the top of a van in the driveway of Nordene's and Sam's house, and the murmur of voices reached her occasionally. She thought of Sam and the kids—she thought of little else, it seemed. How were they? Would they ever be able to achieve a semblance of family life again? Any peace or happiness? Any escape from the loneliness of being without Nordene?

A sudden and terrible rage filled her. An emotion new and frightening in its impotency. What right had . . . whoever he was, to kill someone he couldn't have known? Nordene didn't know the kind of man who would do that sort of thing.

With the other death, the killing of Rhoda Shelly, there was the thought that it was someone Rhoda knew, a person or persons who followed her.

But with Nordene, that was not the case.

And, the detectives had told her, it was quite obvious that the same killer had committed both murders, and—the really strange and ominous part—that it was the same person who had killed Blythe, so far away. The *modus operandi* was the same. That is, the mutilation of the lower part of the body, a sexual mutilation, and then death by other causes. Fear, mainly. Shock. Loss of blood, except the death occurred faster than that. And, except in the case of Rhoda, both had been indoors, where it was physically impossible for the killer to get out without showing some sign of his exit.

She heard a sound behind her and turned to see that all three kids had come onto the patio. Joey was sitting on the edge, his feet hanging off. He seemed to be looking at something there. But then she saw that he was only keeping himself occupied. He leaned over, stretched out on the cool brick and began to crawl on his belly. Faye smiled faintly. Being a little boy.

"Let's get out of here," Faye said suddenly. "I'll get my purse and lock the door. We'll go shopping. We'll eat—somewhere. Bonanza? Do any of you have a big appetite? Their cobblers are good.

Ellen followed Faye into the house and out again. Holding the screen door, while Faye locked the kitchen door with a key, she watched every movement.

She felt safer near Faye. Faye was a grownup, and even though the others had been grownups, too, she still felt safer near Faye than away from her.

Beth made her feel safer, too.

But Joey . . . Joey wasn't much bigger than she.

She was afraid to be the last one on the way to the car, but she didn't want Beth or Joey to be last either. She looked over her shoulder at the dark walls of the house, at the shrubbery that grew all along it, at the short cedar trees and the others that Faye had said were spruce and pine. There were hiding places everywhere. There were more hiding places here than there had been at home. At first it was like she had left the monsters at home, as if they hadn't been able to fly, too. But now they were here, all around, hiding from her most of the time, just letting her see bits and pieces of them: an eye, glittering in the darkness of the green bush; a movement in the dark recesses of the halls, or behind the furniture.

They were there; it was there.

One monster, she knew. Somehow she knew. But it could change shape and look like something familiar. A cat. Even a man.

She hurried and got into the car, slamming the door and holding the handle until Faye pushed and locked all the buttons up front.

Ellen settled back into the plush silence of her corner and watched the movements of the trees as they went by, and then the houses as they came nearer to the streets and closer together. She took a long breath and looked at Joey in the back seat with her. He was playing with something.

She leaned over and looked. It was a small puzzle that he had bought while they still lived at the motel, back home. He had played with it on the plane.

"Can I see it?" she asked.

"No," he said, and Ellen leaned back, more relaxed, more at ease.

Things weren't so different after all. Maybe. Joey sounded just like he always had, and Ellen found comfort in it.

They didn't go home until after dark. They drove north up into the mountains, and to a small lake called Lake Fort Smith, and Ellen waded in the edge of the cold water with Joey. Beth took off her shoes and dangled her toes in for a little bit, but Ellen didn't expect anything else. Beth had gotten so she acted like a grownup. She kept staring out over the hills, that faraway look in her eyes that made Ellen feel so lost and lonely.

On the way home they stopped at Bonanza and ate, and Ellen found she was hungry. She had two helpings of cobbler and ice cream, one of apple and the other peach.

Both she and Joey went to sleep in the car, and the next thing she knew, Beth was shaking her awake.

The yard lights were on, but their large, bright spots were swallowed by all the trees. Ellen stumbled on half-asleep legs into the house with Beth, awake now, seeing again the monsters in the dark. For a while this afternoon, in the bright sunshine at the lake, she had almost forgotten.

Faye unlocked the door, and they went in; but in that last moment before Faye crossed the threshold, she looked toward the house next door, and Ellen looked, too.

It was dark. There was no light tonight in the upstairs window, nor anywhere, except for the yard lights. Yard lights like these that shone on leaves and trees and were swallowed by the dark shrubs, and the vines that covered the fence.

They went into the house, and Faye locked the door behind them, then pushed the bolt. She left on the kitchen light when they went upstairs.

Ellen took her bath after begging Beth to stay with her.

Beth sat on the vanity stool, one leg crossed over the other, her foot tapping anxiously. Something was wrong with her, Ellen was beginning to realize. Something different. But she couldn't ask. She didn't feel much like talking anymore. She thought the questions, but never asked them.

She had to stay alone in the bed while Beth went to take her own bath.

She lay tense and afraid, the blanket pulled up to her chin even though it was too warm. Beth had closed the window tonight, and the breeze was cut off; but Ellen had begged for the window to be closed. Beth had not argued.

Ellen was sleeping in Beth's bed again, and she thought of Joey in the room next door, alone. Suddenly she knew she was afraid for him to be there alone.

She got out of bed and went into the hall. It was long and shadowed, and empty except for the china cabinet that held the little glass figurines and the twin chairs on each side. Her footsteps were lost in the carpet, but still she tiptoes, careful not to draw attention to herself.

Joey's door was open, his light out.

She stood by his bed. "Joey? Joey?"

She heard his breathing and knew how soundly he slept. When he slept. She would have to shake him hard to wake him up. The shadows in his room had no eyes in them, nor movements of a deeper darkness. She looked hard at the shadows before she finally drew away. But she closed his door, to help keep his room safe.

When she got back to Beth's room, Beth was there, standing with her eyes looking scared, her lips parted. When she saw Ellen she smiled, just a little, and Ellen knew Beth was glad to see her.

Then she saw that Beth was dressed in a pair of jeans and a pullover shirt.

"Where are you going?" she asked, impulsively.

"Shhh."

Beth hurriedly closed the door. Whispering, she said,

"Get dressed, Ellen. We're leaving. While you're dressing I'll go get Joey."

"Leaving! But—"

"Shhh. Just get dressed. Hurry." Beth shoved underpants into Ellen's hands. A pair of socks fell to the floor, and Ellen picked them up.

Beth was gone suddenly, the door closed. Ellen stood where she was, wondering. Now she knew why Beth had been acting so nervous and so strange. She had been waiting for Faye to go to bed, for the night to come. Leaving? Ellen didn't want to leave. Where would they go? But she began to get dressed, pulling on the socks, the panties.

In order to get her other clothes, she would have to go back into her own room, and she didn't want to. She was afraid to go there.

I can't go . . . I can't . . .

The monster might be there, waiting for her.

Then she saw that a pair of jeans and a shirt had been laid out on a chair for her, and she pulled them on, snapped the jeans and zipped them. The sound was loud in the stillness of the house. She heard a muffled groan, and recognized it as Joey's voice, grumbling to be left alone, the way he did when someone woke him from a sound sleep.

She was dressed and waiting when Beth and Joey came back into the bedroom.

Joey was dressed, his eyes still glazed. He stood at Ellen's side in silence as Beth fixed the bed to look as if someone were sleeping there, pulling the blanket up over pillows. Finished, she looked around, then she slung straps over each shoulder, one of them her small purse and the other the bag she had carried on the airplane.

"Daddy's going to be mad," Joey said, his face screwing up as if he was going to cry.

"Shhh," Beth cautioned.

"Where are we going? There's no place we can go," Joey whined, expressing Ellen's thoughts and feelings.

Beth came near and put her face down close to theirs. "We have to get away. We have to get the killer away from here . . . we have to run away from it."

"But . . . where'll we go?"

"Be quiet, Joey. Just don't say anything. Don't worry. I'll take care of us. I'll think of something."

Beth opened the door and looked out, then she shut off the bedroom light. For a long hesitation they stood in the bedroom door, and then she stepped out into the hall and motioned them to follow. She closed the bedroom door behind them, softly, so that the click of the latch was no louder than Joey's sigh.

They were running away, but no matter where they went, the monster would go with them.

Ellen knew that, feeling its invisible eyes watching, watching.

What do you want? What do you want?
Why are you killing our mothers?

They went down the hall, Beth holding Joey's hand, pulling him along. Ellen came closely behind them, her hand touching the overstuffed bag that swung from Beth's shoulder, the only emotional support she could find. Beth's free hand reached back for her, and Ellen clutched it gratefully. She hurried to keep up, to try to escape from the deep shadows the pale light didn't chase away.

Faye's bedroom door was open, and the room beyond dark. Ellen longed to go see if Faye was all right, but Beth was pulling her down the stairs.

Joey stumbled but didn't fall. He was making small sounds in his throat, and Ellen realized he was crying. He was scared, and he was crying. Ellen wanted to draw Beth's attention to Joey; but they had reached the lower hall now, and Beth was at the front door.

She dropped Ellen's and Joey's hands in order to unlock the door.

Why was she using the front door? They never used the front door.

It was open, and Beth reached back silently and got Ellen by the arm and pushed her out onto the small front porch with the four white pillars going up to the porch roof at the second floor. Light from the street barely reached the porch, and Ellen stood in darkness, only her feet revealed in light. Now she knew why her sister had chosen the front door. The other doors had lights. The back was lighted by the yard light at the back of the patio, and the door beneath the overhang, where they had gotten out of the car the first day, had a light, too, beneath the roof. The patio doors were lighted by the yard light in the back. Only the front of the house and the side away from Katy's house were dark.

Beth was drawing Joey out of the hall and had her arms around him, her head lowered close to his. Ellen could still hear the soft, choking sound of the sobs, but added to that was Beth's murmurs.

She raised her head as Joey's sounds ceased and pulled the big, heavy door shut. She tried the knob again and grunted softly in satisfaction.

It was locked, but it didn't matter whether it was locked or not, didn't she know that now? The monster came from nowhere, he came . . . it came . . . from . . .

Ellen shook her head, to rid it of the feeling that made her want to scream. She didn't dare make a noise, to lead the monster to them. She looked into the darkness, at bulky black things beneath the trees.

Beth gave her a push, and Ellen went down the steps.

She took their hands again and led them out into the yard, where she stopped. Ellen could see her face, a pale, ghostly oval in the shadows beneath the trees.

Beth was thinking, looking toward the street, and then toward the house next door, Katy's house.

She turned abruptly, leading them back through the darkness on the other side of the house, toward the backyard. Ellen knew why. If they went out into the street and turned left, they would have to pass the place where the laundry lady was killed.

And if they went right, they would pass the house where Katy and Dwayne lived, and where their mother was killed.

Why are you killing our mothers? What do you want?

What have I done?

What do you want me to do?

Ellen had a sudden thought that made her tremble: Beth was beginning to act like their mother.

Oh no, oh no. Not Beth.

She stumbled over something on the ground and almost fell. The windows on this side of the house were black glass set in the brick wall. It seemed a long way around the house.

They came to the backyard, and Ellen could see the yard light through the trees. There was a light on at the back door, too, and two more lights on each side of the patio sliding doors. But the path Beth chose was dark, leading through the trees near the fence, where Ellen had never walked before.

"Where are we going?"

It was a whisper, and Ellen knew it came from Joey, though it seemed to be disembodied in the dark night. A whisper, maybe, from the monster. Teasing them.

They reached the back fence and stopped. Ellen could see the lights of houses, and the lights of town in the valley down over the hill, through the trees.

Beth said, not whispering, "We have to climb over. Joey..."

He held back. "No."

"All right. I'll go."

There were rustling sounds, and Ellen felt something heavy dropped onto her feet. The strap of the bag was thrust suddenly into her hand.

"Hold this, Ellen. I'll climb over. Stay right here, against the fence, both of you."

The fence made soft metallic sounds in the darkness, and Ellen's eyes adjusted to outlines and movements and saw Beth's form as she dropped over the fence. Her pale face looked toward them.

"Hand me the bags."

She was keeping her voice low, her hands, pale as her face, ghostly, flitting like pale birds in the dark, reached toward them. Ellen lifted the bag with the clothes, straining under the weight. Beside her Joey was handing over the smaller shoulder bag.

"Now," Beth said, "one at a time. Joey?"

"What if there are dogs in that yard?"

Beth didn't answer. Joey climbed over, and then Ellen followed, her toes slipping from the narrow links in the wire twice, almost causing her to fall. Beth grabbed her arms and steadied her, then held onto her as she finished climbing over.

She stepped down into the crunch of last winter's leaves.

They stood in the corner of the strange yard as Beth adjusted the straps over her shoulder again. Ellen wanted to offer to carry one of the bags, but her voice failed her.

Then Beth was walking away, down the hill, keeping close to the fence of this strange yard. Ellen could hear Joey's feet, stumbling, crunching in the leaves. *Don't make so much noise.* A dog began to bark suddenly to their left, and another took it up across the fence in the next yard. Ellen could hear them running. Beth stopped, and Ellen ran into her. The dog loped up on the left, a white blur in the shadows, and stopped, no more than ten feet away. On their right the larger dog came to the fence and leaped against it, then backed away, growling.

Beth's hand reached back and clutched Ellen's arm, and they began to run. The white dog followed them, all the way to the street.

It stopped and stayed, in its own yard, its yipping voice going on and on. The big dog in the other yard was silent. Ellen realized now he had dropped back a long ways up the fence. Maybe his backyard was enclosed, so that he couldn't come any farther.

They stood, again, on pavement now. Street lights were ahead and behind, and they would have to walk under them. Ellen could see that Beth was considering that as she looked in both directions.

Beth began to walk, going on downhill where the street curved, and the lights were swallowed by the trees. Ellen followed behind Joey. He looked so little there behind Beth, a short shadow trailing in the wake of the tall one.

Ellen's legs grew tired, and she knew that Joey was tired, too. He kept falling behind, and Ellen had to push him forward. Beth walked ahead of them, looking back occasionally as if to see that they were still there.

They came to a street with shops, closed now. Cars drifted along the street, slowly, some of them with radios blaring into the night and voices of the occupants drifting, laughter broken in passing. Beth led them into alleys and along darker streets.

Ellen looked behind and saw a face watching from a doorway.

It was round, and the eyes were oddly tight-lidded and slanted in the face. Ellen stared at it, but it was gone, leaving its image in her eyes, ragged edges bleeding into shadows, into mist and fog and smoke that swirled and obliterated the features.

It was there, it was following.

Chapter Seventeen

Faye slept as if she had been drugged. When she woke the room was bright, a touch of sunshine turning the curtain to gold, bringing out the colors of the draperies. She sat up, alarmed. What time was it?

Nine-thirty.

Good Lord. The children must have gotten up hours ago. What had they done about breakfast? So far they hadn't made themselves at home here to the point of going to the pantry or the refrigerator for food.

She hurriedly dressed and went downstairs, aware even as she went of the intense silence in the house, as if she were alone in all these rooms, within these thick, old brick walls.

When she got to the kitchen she stood perplexed, seeing the back door was closed and bolted. They had not gone out the kitchen door. The television was quiet. There was no sound at all in the house.

She opened the door, letting in a rush of warm air. It felt good to her, made her realize that she had been chilled by the closed coldness of the house. It had never required air conditioning. The height and breadth kept the interior comfortable, even on the hottest days.

There was no sign of the children.

She stood on the patio looking around.

The silence extended to next door. Today there

seemed to be no activity there, either. It was as if the death of Nordene had ended all life except the birds in the trees and the sounds of traffic from down the hill.

Faye hurried back into the house, leaving the kitchen door open. She retraced her steps upstairs and went down the hall to the rooms of the children.

She opened Joey's door first and saw the lump in the bed. She stood on the threshold, vastly relieved. He was still asleep.

But as she stood there, she realized it was not Joey in the bed.

She crossed the room quickly and threw back the blanket, exposing the pillow.

It was the same in Beth's room.

Both beds had been made to look as if the children were there. It was a deliberate deception, revealing more clearly than anything else that they were gone.

She checked the closet and saw the suitcases were still there. Clothing hung where she had helped hang it. If the beds hadn't been fixed to look as if the children were sleeping, Faye would have thought they had been taken away, without preparation.

They couldn't have taken much with them. Where had they gone?

She hurried downstairs and took the phone off the hook to call the police, then remembered the police were probably next door. She rushed out of the house and along the path and through the gate.

At first Nordene and Sam's house appeared alone, silent, without human presence. Then, as she progressed along the path, she saw the back of a dark sedan. Farther on, she saw a police car, drawn up behind the sedan. A man in uniform was walking between the house and car.

He looked familiar. He was one of the many she had met in the past few days, but she couldn't remember his name.

He saw her and stopped. Then came across the lawn to meet her.

"I'm Faye Pendergast," she said, motioning toward her yard. "I live next door—"

"I remember." He nodded.

"My children—my stepchildren—are gone. They left sometime during the night. I went into their rooms this morning and found they had fixed their beds to look as if they were sleeping, should I look in on them, which I usually do. But—" Tears came to her eyes. "They're strangers here. They don't know the area very well, and they have no relatives, and very little money. Please find them."

Another man had approached while she was talking, another vaguely familiar face. She recognized him as one of the detectives who had come to talk to Beth, but she couldn't remember his name.

"That would be Beth, Ellen and Joey," he said, more a statement than a question, but Faye nodded, feeling into her pocket for a tissue. She had none. The man put his hand gently on her back.

"Why don't you go back home and try to relax. You might find us some photos if you have any. We'll get on it right away. Someone will probably be over later to talk to you."

He walked with her to the gate, talking, reassuring her.

"We know them pretty well. They can't get far; don't you worry."

But she did worry. How could she not?

Sitting alone in the house, she knew the time had come to call Gavin. She wanted to call him, to send word for him to come home. And yet . . .

First, she had to try herself to find the children.

She locked the house, checking doors, finding that

they had gone out the front door. Only the automatic lock was activated; the indoor bolt was open.

She went out to her car and backed out of the garage. The police hadn't told her to stay home, to wait. It was physically impossible to just sit there, wondering where they were. She knew the area well, most of it anyway. Only the old town, with the bars and the dark alleys, was out of her experience. Outside of that realm, which took in a large part of old Fort Smith, she knew the territory, from the river to the boundaries of Camp Chaffee, to the mountains on the north.

The hills on the north.

She had a sudden, overwhelming intuition they had headed that way. And if they reached them, they could disappear forever.

Ellen sought the sunshine. She had grown chilled in the long night, where, when finally Beth had allowed them to stop, they had slept in a cold alley, huddled between a metal barrel that stank of oil and the concrete of a corner building. They had been hidden from the street lights by the barrels and the walls of the buildings, but other things had been in the alley, too, things that made noises in the litter and brushed along the wall. Until she slept, a deep sleep that Beth had pulled her out of at the palest dawn.

Houses were closed and quiet at that time of day. They were in the valley downtown, going toward the green hills beyond town, where layers of hills beyond looked blue with the distance.

The sunshine was welcome, warming Ellen's thin, rough arms, the goosebumps still all along the outer part, below the short sleeve of her blouse. She noticed Joey's arms, the thick, blond hair sticking out. He was cold, too, but she hadn't heard him say a word since they had climbed over the fence last night. He hurried along at Beth's heels, looking down where he was going, half running. Beth was walking so fast. She kept turning her head, this way and that, keeping to the sidewalks where there were sidewalks and then to the edge of the street when the sidewalks stopped.

They were still in town; but the houses were small and shabby, and the stores looked out of place in lots that must have been vacant not long ago. Sometimes they came to a strip of stores that were old, flaking doors leading out onto cracked sidewalks.

People began to appear along the way, to look at them, to stop and stare. There were more black faces here than white, and Ellen felt conspicuous.

When Beth clutched Joey's hand and began to run, Ellen followed. They went into an alley between two of the old stores and stopped, and Ellen saw why they had run.

A police car was going by, slowly. The officer driving was looking around, everywhere, but his head was turned away as he passed the alley.

Instead of going back to that street, Beth led them out the back and into another street.

"I'm hungry," Joey said.

Ellen's stomach felt pressed to her backbone, no longer hollow, just permanently empty.

Beth grunted an answer to Joey.

The sun rose overhead, and cars moved along the street. Pedestrians joined them, black mixed with white, and they were no longer so outstanding on the street.

They were leaving town, at last. Beth began to lead them through the edges of pastures and finally across a short bridge over a sparkling little stream of water. Beth stopped, then led the way down the bank and beneath the bridge.

The day had grown hot, and the shade was cool and welcome. Water ran over a gravel bed, making funny little sounds that were like live things, chickens, ducks . . .

"Stay here," Beth said. "I saw a convenience store across the creek. I'll go there and get us something."

Joey lay down, his head on the bag that held their clothes. Ellen glanced at him and saw that his eyes had closed. He was sleeping.

But she couldn't sleep.

The sounds here were like lullabyes, singing *sleep, little baby, sleep,* and though she longed to close her eyes and let it carry her away, as it had carried Joey, she had to stay awake.

She had to watch, upstream, down.

Always, she would have to watch.

Faye didn't give up searching until nearly midnight. She had driven on nearly every street in town, it seemed, and especially those leading out of town. Occasionally she stopped and asked if they had been seen, but whoever she asked had simply looked at her and shaken their heads. Then, came questions, curiosity aroused. Or advice. "Let them go, lady, if they don't want to stay home," one man had said. She couldn't believe anyone would say something like that. He had blue, washed-out eyes, and a three day beard. An alcoholic on a street corner. His pocket bulged with a bottle of cheap wine. She could smell his breath halfway across the sidewalk.

She had driven through a storm of rain and lightning, her worry making her nearly frantic. Were they out in this storm? Were they wet and cold and lost?

She was not especially glad to go home, though her body yearned for rest. The house seemed too big now, and too dark. But at least there was no police car in her driveway, nor even in the driveway of the house next door.

The house next door.

Only two days ago she had thought of it as Nordene's house. Ever since she was a teenager it had been Nordene's house. Just as she had heard Ellen call it Katy's house.

She had checked in at police stations twice during the day, and was assured the police were looking for the children. The first call she made when she reached the kitchen was to the police station, but the answer was no different. Sorry. The children had not been found. They had been seen a few times, it was reported, but no longer were in the area. Could they have somehow gotten a ride out? Certainly not on a bus. No tickets had been sold to three children. The same at the airport. No tickets to three children. But a lot of big trucks passed through, going in all directions. Who knew but that they had been given a ride? But they were checking.

Faye hung up the phone, hearing the intense silence in the house. At the front, muffled by doors and walls, she heard the faint, deep chimes of the grandfather clock. Twelve, midnight. Three hours short of the Witching Hour.

She had been driving since around ten this morning. No wonder her hands shook, she told herself as she put a cup of water into the microwave to heat. While she waited, she opened a package of sweet rolls and leaned against the edge of the counter eating. Not a very good diet, she reminded herself. The baby was quiet within her after an active day, as if she had exhausted it, too.

For the baby's sake she poured a glass of milk and drank it with a cheese sandwich. Then she went upstairs, carrying her cup of decaf., leaving the kitchen light on, unable to bear the thought of darkness.

The house was so silent. It seemed, oddly, to roar with silence.

Even the rain and the distant thunder were gone, deadened by the walls.

Her footsteps on the stairs were soundless.

Her steps along the hall toward her room were soundless.

The hall of the children's bedroom looked as black as a dungeon, and she turned back and went to the light switch and turned the hall light on. Better now, she thought, and retraced her steps to her bedroom.

She closed the door and sat on the side of the bed looking at the curtains blowing into the room, brought by a spritely south breeze.

She couldn't call Gavin's office tonight. But as soon as the office opened tomorrow morning, she would place the call.

Come home, Gavin. We need you.

Joey stumbled over the rocks as they climbed a hill, falling once and skinning the heel of his hand. He moaned and tried to see this new injury to his skin, but the darkness was coming down too thick now, brought by the tall trees that grew everywhere it seemed, and by the clouds that were thickening again in the west. Ahead of him, going doggedly on, Beth led the way. Ellen was between him and Beth, a silent figure. Sometimes she murmured a few words that brought chills over Joey's shoulders and made him look behind, and it was always the same. "It's following us." A soft whimper in the darkness, unnerving.

Lightning had begun flashing now in the dark sky, and the figures ahead of Joey melted into blurs of ghostly whiteness. He wanted to cry out, but didn't dare to make more noise, because what if Ellen was right, and it—whatever it was—was following them?

Beth stopped, and pulled them into a place that had a smooth, damp floor, and in a flash of lightning Joey saw the low overhang of a small cliff. They sat together beneath the bluff, Ellen in the middle. Joey pushed against the warmth of her body. He could hear the sounds of cars and trucks somewhere, just around the hill maybe, but here they were alone.

"I'm hungry," he murmured, his voice low. He'd been speaking in a half-whisper, when he spoke at all, since they had left home. How long ago was it now since they had left? It seemed longer than two days and two nights. And now another night. "I want to go home."

Beth whispered, her voice sounding very close, which seemed odd in the blackness that surrounded them, "It's a long way home, Joey."

"I mean Faye's home. I want to go back."

Ellen began to weep, a soft sound in the night that seemed to fit with the slow drip of water from the rock edge of the bluff. Rain was beginning to fall again, too, but the drops from the bluff were louder, larger, plopping onto the slippery ground at their feet.

"We can't go back, Joey," Beth said.

"Then where are we going?"

"I don't know."

Joey's voice lifted. "Can we go to the cabin? On the lake?"

"I don't know. No. They'd look for us there."

"Why are we running away, Beth?"

"Because . . . because . . ." Her voice became a whisper. "We have to get away from the—"

Ellen sobbed, "But it's following, I can hear it in the leaves . . . out there . . . Hear it?"

Joey strained to hear, but there was nothing except

256

the rain that was coming heavier and heavier. A jagged line of lightning raced through the clouds above the trees, and a ghostly light filled the area beneath the bluff. Joey could see nothing but the dark trunks of the trees that covered the hillside below the bluff. He leaned harder against Ellen. The light was gone as suddenly as it had come, and the darkness was so intense Joey felt smothered by it. The dripping water sounded louder, louder, as if it were being magnified by the dark.

There was another sound suddenly, close by. His heart speeded, his throat swelled with the sudden lurch of terror. What was it? The monsters that Ellen saw? But then he realized it was Beth, doing something with the zipper on the bag she carried. He heard the crunch of paper. Then her hand was fumbling in the darkness toward him. He felt it touch his arm as she reached across Ellen.

"Here Joey. This is all you can have. In the morning we'll go over to the highway and find a store."

He found himself in possession of a small piece of sandwich. It was hardly two bites. She had saved one from their last meal, an almost fun thing by the side of a creek where they had made and eaten bread and cheese sandwiches. He thought of the sunshine with nostalgia, as if he would never see sunshine again. It had shone on the water like flashes of diamonds, and the water had made funny little sounds, like children laughing far away, as it rolled over the little rocks in the stream bed.

He was also tired, and sleepy, and he wanted to go home, to Faye, where he belonged.

Beth held them as well as her arms could reach, staring over their heads into the darkness of the trees. The rain had nearly stopped, the lightning now distant flashes on the other side of the mountain. Its lights turned the under clouds pink and revealed deep layers of dark stormy gray through the tops of the trees, but it was only like a memory of light gone now, leaving a well of blackness beneath.

The dark should have been a comfort, but it wasn't. Beth felt as if the eyes were out there, watching, waiting for her to sleep, too. Seeing her while she couldn't see it. Every drip of water into the leaves of the forest was like footsteps from whatever it was that stalked them.

She craved sleep like the winos back on the streets and alleys craved wine. It raked at her eyelids and made her eyes burn. Her brain felt heavy with the need for sleep. That night in the alley, for those few hours they had rested, her sleep had been too light to do much good. And last night they had found a barn in a pasture, with hay, and had taken shelter from the storm. Then during the day the storm had continued, off and on, showering, almost clearing, showering again. Slowing them down. And now—again—she dared not sleep.

What was she going to do? Where was she going to take them?

Could they stay forever in these mountains, living perhaps in this cave? Where would they get their food?

No, they couldn't stay here.

If they went on to another town, maybe she could find work . . .

But, didn't a person have to have a Social Security number or something of that sort? Where would she get it? And didn't a person have to be sixteen to work? Would anyone believe she was sixteen? She was five-one, now; but she only weighed ninety pounds, and she was flat. Her nipples were just beginning to puff out, with little bags of flesh around them. They were tender and sore, but invisible under her shirts. She'd never pass for sixteen.

She put her head down on Ellen's and let the tears flow. She wanted to go home, too, to Faye, to her dad. But how could they? Maybe if they just kept running, as far and as fast as they could, they'd be safe. And so would Faye and all the others.

Ellen was wrong. The—*thing* had not followed them. The night was quiet except for the dripping water.

She slept without realizing she had even gone to sleep.

Suddenly someone was moving at her side, and she jerked up to see they were surrounded by daylight. There were even streaks of sunlight in spots through the heavy growth of trees.

But something was wrong.

At her side Ellen sat stiffly alert, staring downhill. Beth was aware of Joey on Ellen's other side, still sleeping, his head lolled now almost into Ellen's lap.

"What is it?" Beth whispered, squinting through sleep-laden eyes, seeing nothing but the trunks of trees, the brown leaves of last winter and the slope of the hill.

Ellen said nothing. Her body against Beth's side was stiff.

Then Beth saw the merest touch of movement, behind and to one side of a thick tree trunk. Someone was standing there, hidden from her by the tree. Someone wearing a long skirt of dull colors, of brown, or faded black, with small splashes of red. Beth leaned, and the figure came into view.

She felt a sharp sense of relief. A little girl. No older than Ellen.

Had they inadvertently come close to someone's house?

Someone was making a strange, deep-throated noise, a moan, a cry that threatened to erupt at any moment. Beth found it was coming from Ellen. She could feel the trembling starting in Ellen's body, the coldness of the arm that was pressed between them.

But it's only a little girl, Beth wanted to say, to reassure Ellen, as she started to rise. She was going forward to speak to the girl when suddenly there was movement at the tree. The girl was gone, and in her place stood the large yellow cat, its slanted eyes glaring at her, its fangs edging down from its lip in a snarl.

Behind her, Ellen screamed, a choked sound of pure terror.

Beth turned, for one instant facing away from the cat at the tree, to look at Ellen, and now Joey, who had sat up beside her, his eyes wide and reflecting the terror in Ellen's cry. And when she looked back the cat was gone, too.

Beth stood there, staring around, seeing the tall, still trunks of the trees, hearing the birds singing in the leaves overhead, catching the yellow touches of sunlight that occasionally penetrated the heavy forest.

They were gone, both the girl and the cat.

Beth felt confused, tortured with frustration and bewilderment.

But she knew now that Ellen had been right all along. It had followed them.

Ellen's scream had awakened Joey, and all he had seen was the flash of something as it disappeared behind the tree. Then it was gone. He sat without moving, and beside him Ellen seemed to collapse. She was quiet again, her head hanging forward. He pushed against her, his shoulder holding her up. Beth was standing a few feet away, out from underneath the bluff.

She turned, and he saw her face looked white and

shrunken, as if she were pinching it in somehow, tightening her eyes and her mouth until they were just puckers of flesh.

Without saying a word, she leaned down and picked up the bags and slung the straps over her shoulders.

"Come on, let's go," she said, and turned toward the sound of traffic around the hill.

"Are we going home?" Joey asked eagerly, rushing out from beneath the bluff. "Back to Faye's house?"

"Come on, hurry," Beth said, going on ahead, picking her way between the trees and around boulders.

Ellen passed him, stumbling as he tried to run over the rocky, slanting ground.

The sound of traffic grew louder, though still there was nothing to see. A truck groaned as it pulled up the hill, shifting down, carrying a heavy load of something.

Joey began finally to see flashes of movement; but Beth paused, and then instead of going on over to the highway, she took a parallel to it, keeping it just barely in sight.

They walked in the edge of the forest, and sunlight warmed Joey's chilled body. He ran half the time to keep up with Beth, stumbling when he failed to see the rocks hidden in the tall grass, too breathless to ask Beth to slow down. Ellen was still between them, following in Beth's path.

His stomach was beginning to hurt with hunger. The sun was overhead, and it seemed they had been walking for hours. He was ready to drop and to stay behind in the grass, like an antelope in the wild, when suddenly, and at last, Beth stopped. They stood closely behind, Ellen, then Joey, and now he saw why they had stopped.

There was a store ahead, a wall of deep yellow, and out in the front were gas pumps. Trees between them and the store kept them hidden. Beth seemed to be looking for something before she went on. Police cars?

If a policeman came along they would be rescued, and Joey watched the traffic along the highway, hoping, hoping. Would the police be looking for them, three missing kids?

Beth turned and bent her head toward them, whispering, her hands on their shoulders, pushing them down. "You stay here. I'll go get something to eat and drink."

No, no, he couldn't let her go without him. Somehow, he had to let the police know where they were. Beth would be mad at him, but they had to get back to Faye.

"I've got to go to the bathroom, Beth," he whispered, his voice growing louder, into a half-cry, half-whine.

"Go in the bushes, just like you've been doing all the time."

"But I haven't—" He hadn't gone at all, all this morning, all this day. Hadn't she known that?

But already she was turning away, leaving them behind. Ellen had sat down and was taking off one of her shoes. He could see the misery on her face as she rubbed the bottom of her foot and turned it so that she could see the broken blisters.

He went down on his knees beside her, his throat filled with the need to cry. He watched Beth as she approached the store, and went out of sight around the corner. There were no police cars. Dejected, he shoved his hands down into his pockets, and his fingers touched the warm metal of two coins.

In sudden, sharp hope he pulled out the coins and looked at them. One quarter, one dime. He had forgotten he had them. Beth would be mad if she knew he had money that he hadn't given to her, but now a plan was forming in his mind.

He put the money back, casting a glance to see if Ellen had seen it, but she was still massaging her feet. He watched her put her shoes back on and tie the laces. A hole was forming in one toe of the leather. If they had to walk any farther, Ellen's toes would be through the shoe.

The sunshine was warm on their heads, the tall grass sealing them in from the people who passed in their cars not fifty yards away.

Beth came back, suddenly it seemed, to sit down with them in the grass. In the few minutes that Joey had been watching the traffic, she had come from the store with a paper bag of things to eat and drink.

There were three more sandwiches and three bottles of pop. She had also brought a package of potato chips.

Joey ate fast, trying all the time to think of a good excuse to go alone to the store.

"I wanted a candy bar," he said.

"We have to save our money, Joey."

He ate. Driven by his hunger, the emptiness of his stomach, and his need to hurry and get to the store, alone, on some pretext. He decided as he downed the last of his pop to try the bathroom thing again.

"I got to go to the bathroom, Beth. Not in the bushes, please. I need to go number two. Let me go to the bathroom in the store. Please."

Beth shrugged. "I guess it'd be all right. But don't you talk to anyone, and if someone stops you and asks you anything be careful what you say, Joey, do you hear?"

"I won't say a word to anybody in the store, I promise."

He had to hurry before she changed her mind. He burst out of the patch of weeds and into the edge of the forest where the grass didn't grow, his shoes striking bits of fire from the rocks as he ran.

When he came to the edge of the paved area he slowed. He had to be sure not to draw attention to himself. That much, at least, he had to obey Beth.

In the store he looked for a telephone, but the only phone he saw was behind the counter. The man at the counter was waiting on some people who were buying things, and no one looked at Joey. He went down one aisle and up another, enjoying for a moment the sense of being in an accustomed environment, of having people around him again, of things on the shelves to buy, good things to eat and drink. He looked at the candy with longing and passed on by.

Was there no public phone?

A glance through the window then revealed it to him. On the corner of the building, with a telephone book hanging by a small chain. He had passed right by it on his hurry into the store.

He went out, hoping the store manager didn't notice that he was leaving without buying anything.

He pressed against the front wall of the convenience store, hoping that Beth couldn't see him, and hurriedly leafed through the book. Was Faye's name here? Her name was the same as his, but even though there were Pendergasts in the book, none of them had a name of Gavin or Faye, or even the initials.

But there was something else he could do, he suddenly realized. He could call the operator and place a collect call to his stepmother. He didn't know her number, but the operator would. And it wouldn't cost him more money than he had.

He put his quarter into the slot on the face of the telephone, and dialed O.

Chapter Eighteen

Faye picked up the phone on its first ring, but the voice she heard was not the one she had been expecting. She had received one call back from Gavin and was waiting for another to tell her what time he would be arriving at the airport. But the voice on the phone had a professional regularity to it that she knew instantly was the voice of an operator somewhere not too distant.

"Is this Faye Pendergast?"

"Yes."

"Will you accept a collect call from Joey Pendergast?"

Oh my God yes.

"Yes, yes," she said, relief making her feel weak, as if she hadn't rested in all the long hours since the children had gone.

Then she was hearing his childish voice, sounding as though he was crying now. "Faye, Faye . . ."

"Yes, Joey, it's Faye."

"Come and get us, Faye. Will you come and get us?"

"Oh yes, of course, Joey. Where are you?"

"I don't know. At a store on the highway."

"What highway? Where?"

"I don't know."

His voice faded away. She could almost see him

looking around, searching for something, a marker, a name.

"Look for a highway sign, Joey. The name of the store. Ask the owner the name of the store. Are you in town?"

"No. In the mountains. In the country. It's just a yellow store. It says Spe-Dee Mart on the sign."

"Ask the owner where you are."

"I can't. The phone is outside. If I hang up I'll lose you."

He was crying now, openly. She felt tense with helplessness. She gripped the phone with both hands, trying to think. If he hung up the phone . . .

"Joey," she said. "Give me the number on the telephone where you are. I'll get the operator to call you back. Then, don't hang up the phone, just let it dangle, and go into the store and ask the owner what highway you're on. Get the location the best you can. If someone hangs up the phone while you're gone, I'll call you back, so you stay right there. Where is Beth? Where's Ellen? Send one of them to ask . . ." She felt the helplessness returning. For a moment she had felt in control, but that was gone.

"They're—they're not here," Joey said. "They're waiting—in the trees—in the grass at the edge of the trees. Beth doesn't know I'm calling you. She'll be mad at me. But I want to come home, Faye, please."

"I'll come and get you. Just do as I said. Let the phone dangle and go into the store, but first . . . Joey? Are you there?" Oh Lord, why had she reversed her instructions to him? "Joey?" But it seemed she could hear him sniffling, trying to control his sobs.

"Y-yes?"

"Give me the phone number."

He told her the number, and she searched frantically for a pen. She found one, and then fumbled it so it rolled out of her grasp. She had to bend down and retrieve it from the floor.

"All right now, Joey," she said, feeling calmer, more in control, "Go into the store and let me know the location. I'll be there as soon as I can get there."

Joey hung up the phone slowly. He had done just as Faye had told him. He had left the phone off the hook and gone into the store and asked what highway they were on, and how far it was to Fort Smith, and then he had run back and relayed the message to Faye. No one had come along and replaced the phone after all.

And now he felt as limp as an old rag, as Ellen's old doll, and he sat down on the bench beneath the telephone. Faye had said for him to wait right there, at the store. She said it would be at least an hour before she could get there, because they had gone a long way.

He didn't know how far it was, but it had felt a long way. Beth would be mad. And he dreaded facing her.

He watched the traffic go by, most if it whizzing on as if the store didn't exist. Occasionally a car or a truck pulled in, parked by the gas pumps, or came on to park at the store. He watched a pickup with a big black dog in the bed. The dog's tongue was lolling, and it was a happy look on the dog's face. He raced from one side of the pickup bed to the other as his owner got out of the truck and came toward the store. The man was long and thin, with tight jeans and a western shirt that fit his broad shoulders without a wrinkle. He had fair hair that looked as if it had been colored purposely, and maybe curled, too. When he passed by, going into the store he noticed Joey watching him, and he said, "Hi there, guy."

He was gone then, and Joey felt a strange yearning. Maybe he would grow up to be like that, and have a dog to ride in the back of his pickup truck.

He felt in his pockets and rubbed the quarter and dime together. Was it enough to buy a candy bar? He didn't think so. Anyway, Beth would be mad enough at him the way it was. He didn't dare make it worse by having her find him sitting at his leisure eating a candy bar.

He looked across the road and saw they were high on a hill. Beyond the tops of the trees, he could see distant hills, big, round, green-shrouded but blue and purple with distance. Somewhere between this big hill, this mountain, and that, there was a valley, with houses, towns and probably a river.

He turned his head and looked for Beth. How long would it be before she came to see about him?

Maybe he should go after her, shorten the time of worry.

But Faye had told him to stay at the store.

He leaned his head back against the cement blocks of the store and watched the corner.

Suddenly Beth was there, her thin face looking pinched, yet, as if she had her cheeks sucked in. Her eyes were darting, searching the parking lot, looking worriedly at the cars leaving, at the pickup truck with the dog in the back as it pulled out, as if she was afraid that he was in there somewhere, too. Ellen was right behind her, being pulled along, her hand in Beth's.

She wouldn't leave Ellen behind.

Then she saw Joey, and she stopped and blinked at him.

He stuck with his spot on the bench, though he moved over to make room for them. There was more relief in her eyes than fury, though he saw that coming on, too.

"Joey! Why are you sitting there?"

"Faye's coming, Beth," he said quickly.

She stood still, staring down at him, her mouth in a round pucker, her eyes looking exceptionally large.

"I called her," he said. "To come and get us. Are you mad, Beth?"

She closed her eyes tightly, whether to shut off tears or to try to get her anger under control, he didn't know. He watched her breathlessly, sorry that he'd had to betray her, disobey her. But couldn't she see that they needed Faye? And their daddy? They couldn't live in the mountains without someone to take care of them.

"Are you mad, Beth?"

She opened her eyes, and he saw no signs of anger. She sat down on the bench beside him, leaned back and sighed.

"Joey, don't you know that by going back with Faye we may be putting her in danger?"

"What danger?" he cried.

"Like those other women. Like Dwayne's mother, and the laundress, and like our own mother, Joey."

He didn't understand. But a feeling went through him that was like a jolt of electricity. It was like the time he'd stuck his finger in the socket of the extension cord, and it was like having a comb raked down the nerves of his back. It made tears start involuntarily in his eyes and spill onto his cheeks. His whole body began to tremble, his hands shaking so hard that Beth took both of them in her own to still them.

"It's okay, Joey," she murmured. "It's okay. Someday it will end, and there won't be any more killings, and we'll all be safe. Somehow, I'll figure it out, and I'll . . . destroy it. *Somehow.*" By the time she finished the sentence her teeth were clinched, and her hands squeezed his painfully.

She held his hands for a while longer, then she smiled and said, "Hey, I know, since we're going home, and we won't need to be so stingy with our money, why don't we all have a candy bar? You two go in and buy what you want, and bring me something really good."

Ellen stood up, brightening, dimples showing up in her cheeks. Joey was cheered just looking at her. He stood beside Ellen, waiting for Beth to unzip the bag and bring out the money. She gave them each a dollar bill.

They ran together, into the store, fighting for who was going to get through the door first, the way they used to. And Beth was going to make everything okay.

Beth stared at the distant hills. The image of the girl in the woods was before her eyes again. There had been something strange about the girl, something entirely apart from the sudden and unexpected disappearance in which the cat had appeared. As if the girl had changed into a cat. Or was the cat a companion of the girl's?

Either way, Beth now felt that neither of them was real. Somehow, they were symbols of something else, as if their presence was trying to tell them something.

She frowned intensely at the distant hills, trying to uncover that meaning, and feeling only frustrated by it.

It was the same cat that had frightened Ellen before, she was sure. But why was the little girl showing up now?

Where did they come from? Both of them? *Where did they come from?*

Ellen and Joey came back, and Beth was unable to think. They were talkative and happy now, and they had brought a whole bag of candy rather than three bars.

Beth sat up, her own sense of pleasure and well-being derived from the sweet treat. The child in her was still alive, unburdened now by the responsibility of taking

care of her brother and sister. Faye was coming.
They were going home.

It was midafternoon when Faye drove into the parking lot of the convenience store. She got out of her car, leaving the door swinging open, and rushed to gather the three into her arms.

Three urchins, she thought, overjoyed to see them. Three unwashed kids, who looked as if they had slept on the dirtiest ground they could find, these three long nights since they had left home.

They responded warmly to her greeting, all of them rushing to hug her at once. She could hardly reach around them, but she tried. She felt Joey's head pressed against the rounding swell of her upper abdomen, and beneath him the baby stirred, as if it were being smothered by so much love and pressure.

She kissed the three streaked faces. Beth looked thinner, not older, but somehow shrunken and younger, more vulnerable. Ellen's face was smeared with chocolate, as well as dried mud. There were spots of chocolate on her chin, at the corner of her mouth, and on one cheek. When they got into the car, Faye handed her a Wet One, and Ellen began washing her face.

Don't scold, Faye reminded herself, once again feeling the rush of anger mixed with fear that she had felt occasionally ever since Joey's call came. Why? She had wanted to scream at them. But she knew why, of course. They were afraid. Having Nordene murdered in the same way their mother was, terrified them. They knew only to run.

And maybe they were right.

Wasn't that what she and Gavin were going to do when his plane landed tonight?

"Your dad's coming in early tonight, kids. We'll pick him up about eight o'clock. We aren't even going back to the house after he joins us."

She turned the car and eased it up to the edge of the highway. An eighteen-wheeler was roaring over the rise at the top of the hill and coming toward them faster than it should have been. Couldn't the driver read the speed limit signs, she wondered angrily. Behind him came a string of cars, and she waited for them to pass before she pulled out onto the highway and headed south toward Fort Smith.

"I've packed enough clothes for us all to stay several days up at the cabin on Beaver Lake. What do you think of that?"

She listened to their happy cries of agreement. Joey leaned against the back of her seat, his chin almost on her shoulder.

"Can we get fireworks again?"

Beth, so sedate in the front passenger seat, said, "Fourth of July is over, Joey. You don't buy fireworks after it's over."

Joey sat back. "Maybe we left some."

"We can go swimming," Ellen said.

"And walk the trails."

"And watch the boats."

Faye added, "We'll rent a boat! And we'll explore all the hollows and arms of the lake."

"Maybe we can even go fishing!" Joey cried, his enthusiasm growing.

Faye drove southwest, toward the setting sun. Red rays shot upward, through a layer of pink and orange clouds, like fireworks frozen in time, for their pleasure. She felt better now, she realized, than she had in a long time. Gavin was coming home. Everything was going to be all right.

Even Beth, so still and solemn at her side, was

beginning to add an enthusiastic word now and then, helping them to plan all the fun things to do in the coming week on the lake.

It was going to be a good week.

It had to be.

She willed the tide to turn, the winds to change, blowing away death and misfortune.

Everything was going to go right from now on.

The plane was an hour late. The sun had long ago set, and clouds had formed. A chilly drizzle began to fall, making time outdoors impossible.

They had gone home just long enough for the kids to bathe and dress in clean clothes, then they had gone out for dinner. Their eagerness for Gavin to arrive and join them dragging the time to a crawl.

Ellen had gotten her doll again, and was using it for a pillow in the corner of the back seat.

Faye had planned so carefully, after talking on the phone at last with Gavin, that immediately after picking him up at the airport they would go north to the lake and the cabin. And there they would spend at least a week, maybe more, if he could borrow vacation time from his job. But now there was nothing to do but wait. The children were asleep, Ellen and Joey, in the back seat of the car, and Beth in the front, her head leaned against the door. They were exhausted. She hadn't asked them how much sleep they had gotten while they were away, but she guessed it wasn't much.

She had parked where she could see the incoming planes. She would leave the children in the car just long enough to meet Gavin.

In the distant gray-black sky, she saw the flashing lights of an incoming plane. It had to be Gavin's, please Lord, she said to herself as she reached over and touched Beth's shoulder.

"Beth," she said in a low voice, hoping she wouldn't wake the sleeping children in the back seat. "Beth?"

With a gasp of fear, Beth jerked up. Faye could feel the tension in her shoulder and arm before the moment of reality came and the relaxation. Beth turned her face toward Faye. Lights spaced through the parking area illuminated the interior of the car just enough to make faces recognizable, and Faye saw the relief on Beth's face, the washing away of the terrible fear that had brought her out of sleep.

Faye whispered, "I'm sorry, Beth. I had to wake you."

Beth rubbed her eyes. "It's okay. Is Daddy here?"

"No, but there's a plane arriving. I'm going to see if it's his. I need to leave you here with the younger children. But I wanted to wake you first."

"Okay. That's okay. Do you want me to get into the back seat now?"

"It's not necessary until we get back, but you can if you want to. Just be sure to keep all doors locked while I'm gone."

"I will."

Faye got out and hurried through the light drizzle, her head down. It felt more like a winter rain, cold and misty. Every year, as long as she could remember, the summer would be cooled down with a three-day cold spell, where the temperature would drop into the sixties and the rain would fall cold and steady and shocking. Mists would rise from the warm waters, the hollows and ravines, and shroud the trees like autumn. This was starting out to be one of those times.

She was glad that she had brought sweaters for all of them, but her own was packed away in the trunk. Later, she would get it out, she thought as she ran into the terminal.

Running was awkward now, she suddenly realized, slowing. The baby was getting to be a heavy little booger. She held her belly with her hands, then became aware of what she was doing. She looked around to see if anyone was watching her; but the people going in and out of the terminal were absorbed with their own affairs, and no one gave her more than a casual glance.

She hadn't realized just how terribly much she had missed and needed Gavin until she saw him coming toward her, firm, shoulders broad in his brown suit, his tie crooked as if he had loosened it and forgotten, his dark hair slightly tousled, as if he had combed it with his fingers, just as she had done hers.

She rushed into his arms, trying to hold back the sudden hysteria she felt coming on. If she laughed with her joy at seeing him, she would cry, she knew. She would be laughing and crying at the same time, unable to control either, if she let herself go at all. She couldn't even speak. She could only hold him so tightly around the neck, with her face buried in his shoulder, that she knew people were probably staring at her now, their own affairs forgotten for a moment.

She felt him trying to move her away so that he could look into her face, and she released her hold on him.

"Are you all right?" he asked, concern making him look older than his years suddenly. She nodded.

Taking his free hand, she turned and walked toward the doors, still not daring to speak. The knot was in her throat, in her chest, and the baby felt heavy in her body. Walking was more difficult now. She had to lean back slightly to keep her balance. She had a sudden urge to laugh wildly, and bit her lower lip. That urge was replaced just as abruptly by tears that came unbidden to her eyes. She blinked rapidly. He didn't need to see her cry, he had problems enough.

"What's this with the weather?" he asked when they

reached the outdoors. "Where are the kids?"

"They're asleep. Do you suppose we should postpone our drive to the lake, Gavin? Until tomorrow at least?"

"Do you want to?"

"Not really. I—so many terrible things have been happening near our house that I just don't feel like going back there yet."

"Then we'll go on. It's only eleven o'clock. We can be at the cabin in an hour and a half. If you feel up to the drive."

The trembling in her legs, she thought, must be from exhaustion. She hadn't slept much either in the days and nights since the children had run away. But she couldn't face going back to the big, silent house just yet. Even with Gavin and the children. To the place where horrible murders had taken place on each side, so near.

"I wish you had called me earlier," Gavin said as they reached the car. "You didn't need to be alone after Nordene was killed. Why didn't you call, Faye?"

"I knew you'd be home soon."

There was no reason to burden him, not then, she thought to herself. It was only when the children had run away that he'd had to be called in from Alaska.

Beth got out of the front seat and kissed Gavin, then climbed into the back, carefully and gently moving sleeping Joey over so that she could sit against the door.

Faye got in and moved over to the passenger side, then asked, "Do you want me to drive, Gavin? Are you tired?"

He leaned over and kissed her on the cheek. For a moment his large hand held hers, his palm warm and comforting on the cold thinness of her own hand. She wished childishly that she could become tiny and snuggle into the safety and warmth of that palm, and

276

then she smiled at the absurdity of that thought. Gavin returned the smile, thinking it was for him. She gave him a quick kiss on his full, warm lips.

"Not as tired as you," he said. "I took a nap on the flight. There wasn't anything else to do, and you know me, I can sleep with no problem."

"Yes, I know," she said tenderly.

He turned the switch and the car started. "Lie back," he said. "Rest. We'll be at the cabin before you know it."

She lay back, feeling the car move out of the parking lot and into the lanes of traffic. Lights flashed against her closed eyelids, and the noise of traffic surrounded her. The car moved forward, stopped, went forward again. She didn't open her eyes to see where they were. By the starts and stops, she could see the signal lights, the street signs; by the turns, she knew the road.

When they reached the interstate and speed picked up, she drifted away into sleep. But she woke again abruptly, a terrible dread shoving her out of restful sleep, as if in the darkness of sleep she had seen something, known of something, too terrible to face.

She turned in the seat. Beyond the window was darkness. Light from the dash cast a pale, pink glow over Gavin's face.

There was no sound at all beyond the smooth motor of the car and the swish of the windshield wipers.

Faye closed her eyes again, determined to sleep, though the feeling of dread had dropped over her like a shroud.

The rise into the Boston Mountains brought the car into the fog. Gavin had known how heavily the fog could hang over the mountains, but to find it here in July seemed preposterous. Fortunately, there wasn't much traffic. In the past mile he had met only three automobiles, two of them large trucks, the other a local pickup. The kind of traffic that would go on through the dangerous mountain roads, fog or no fog.

Gavin slowed the car even more. He was now driving only twenty miles an hour, and the fog washed against the hood of the car like sheets hanging from the sky. He glanced over and saw that Faye was sleeping soundly.

Good. He hoped he could drive on out of the fog before she woke. He knew from having driven these mountains before that the fog lay heaviest on the highest elevations, and once over the mountain range the valleys held only pockets here and there, mostly near the small streams of water.

He began to feel isolated, alone with the silence. He wanted to turn and look into the back seat, to reassure himself that the kids were there, sleeping. All he heard was the soft sounds of the motor, of tires on pavement. He reached to turn on the radio, then drew his hand back. He needed total concentration for this job.

He slowed the car even more. He was driving through a white, thick wall, in which his lights dispersed uselessly. With his foot on the brake, he stopped the car completely. He hadn't met one vehicle in the last mile. The rest of the world had sense enough to park and let the fog have the mountain top to itself. This was a dangerous road at the best of times, a bit too curvy, and taken too fast by most drivers. Popular stickers on the rear of cars and pickups read *I live dangerously. I drive Highway 71.* He thought about pulling off to the side of the road and parking until sunrise, when maybe the fog would lift. But he didn't know where the side of the road was. A few more feet to the right might put him off the road bed entirely and down the side of the mountain.

He rolled the window down and tried to see out, to

find the line at the left of his lane, but the seat belt held him back. He unfastened it, and leaned his head out the window. The rain had lessened to a heavy mist, but it felt unusually cold for this time of year.

He pulled the car to the left. No line.

He eased it back to the right, an inch at a time, and the line appeared, barely visible, at the left of his front tire, catching the light in a spot no larger than the tire itself. It was the middle line, two yellow stripes warning motorists to stay on their own sides.

With the line in sight, his head leaned out the window, he pushed the car forward, determined to go on, to leave this suffocating fog behind.

It swept forward and swallowed the car. They might have been high in the sky, drifting aimlessly in the thickest part of a cloud, had it not been for the solid pavement and the brief twin lines visible just in front of the left tire, below the left headlight.

He heard stirrings in the back seat and thought of the cold mist blowing into the car through his open window. He turned up the heater, a movement that drew his eyes away from the road for no more than five seconds.

When he looked back again there was something on the road, not three feet in front of his lights. Its eyes glowed yellow and savage, glaring through the fog. It seemed huge, leaping out of the black night into the headlights of his car.

He jerked the wheel frantically to the right, and felt the front of the car drop sharply downward. Then it was rolling, turning onto its right side and then its top; but his door had flung open, and when he reached to grasp something, the steering wheel, anything, nothing was there.

Chapter Nineteen

The cold wind had awakened Beth, and she sat up. She saw the thick white surrounding the car, like moist cotton.

She saw her father leaning inward and reaching toward the heater controls.

And she saw the sudden and startling appearance of the big cat directly in the path of the car, in front of the left headlight . . . and a child.

The car jerked then, and the roll began. Her seat belt held her, but in the darkness of the back seat, it seemed like she was in one of those horrible barrels at an amusement park that just kept rolling and rolling on and on though you were screaming to get out of it, though you wanted it to stop, stop.

She noticed the silence. There was no sound at all except the crunching of metal and the breaking of glass as the car kept going over and over. No one cried out.

At last the car stopped rolling. It was lying on its right side, the top slanted, more up than down, as if the right wheels had stopped on the ground.

She could feel the warm body beneath her stirring now, and the whimpers starting. Ellen. Joey. One of them said, "Beth?" But she didn't know who it was.

She began struggling to loosen her seat belt. It was holding her across the lower belly, cutting into her.

One touch of the button, and the seat belt was gone, freeing her. She held on to the back of the front seat to keep from rolling heavily onto her brother and sister. Her fingers probed into the darkness at her side to lower her window. The lights of the car were still on, shining into the cottony world at nothing. The heater whooshed, soft, steady warm air.

The kids were beginning to cry, to call for Faye, for Daddy, for Beth and for each other. Thank God they sounded all right. But where were Dad and Faye?

She didn't have the energy to spare to call them yet. She had to get out of the car.

The window went down in a smooth, whispering movement, and Beth grasped the edges of the frame and pulled herself up and out. Her feet touched the ground. Across the top of the car she could see the limbs of tall trees, their trunks probably holding the car from going on down the mountainside.

With her feet braced against the fender she reached in, finding the flailing hands of one of the children.

"Undo your belts," she ordered. "Take my hands."

The crying lessened. She could hear their movements, their breathing, the small whimpers of fear. She felt their hands reaching for her, and she had a sudden vision of hundreds of hands reaching up from some terrible pit of doom.

She pulled one of them out and found it was Joey. She let him down to the ground.

"Stand there. Don't move, Joey."

He had stopped whimpering. She had a bare glimpse of his face as he went by, a round shadow, a small form; but the white fog blurred his features, and the darkness held him the moment he was out of her grasp. She reached in for Ellen.

"Don't move," she ordered firmly. "Stand with Joey, Ellen. Hold on to each other."

She was apart from them and needed to hear their voices to be assured they were there at all, that she had not dropped them into a bottomless darkness.

"Ellen? Joey?"

"What?"

The voice was a thin sound in the dark, fog-shrouded night. Again, she wasn't sure who had spoken.

"Are you together?" she asked, the odd calm she had felt gathering into a threatening storm of panic. "Are you there?" Her voice was almost a scream, loud, deadened by the fog. The car lights kept burning into the fog, opening a spot of light no larger than her hands.

They both answered, close in the night. And then Joey asked, "Where's Faye, Beth? Where's Daddy?"

Beth swallowed. "I—I'll find them now. You stay right where you are."

She climbed back into the rear of the car and reached forward over the seat. There was no one at all in the driver's seat. No one. Her hands reached through empty air and found the steering wheel. There was barely room for her body over the top of the seat. Above, the roof of the front had been caved in, and her hands groping, found glass.

The windshield had shattered, bits of it falling onto the seat. Cold mist came in at the door. Their dad had fallen out of the car. She could almost see him lying on the hillside, somewhere between the car and the road above. He would be all right, she told herself. He had gotten out of the car. Maybe when it first began to roll he had jumped out.

But there was something wrong with that thought, she knew, a sick feeling, a familiar sick, scared feeling starting in the middle of her body.

She reached to the right to search for Faye.

Her hand first touched Faye's hair, and tears of relief

came to her eyes. With searching hands she found Faye, slumped in her seat belt, her head hanging sideways, the top of the car pressing against the top of her head. There was something warm and sticky on the side of Faye's face.

Beth drew back her hand.

"Faye?" she asked once, tentatively, too terrified to hope.

There was no answer.

"Oh, my God," she said, and drew back, reaching for the window frame and freedom. "I'm coming out," she warned the kids, as she let herself down to the ground.

She heard, as she paused, the stirring of feet in damp leaves, and she reached to find them. Her hands touched a head, a shoulder. She felt for their hands and found them. Neither was saying a word now, no sound, no cry, no whimper.

"Faye's hurt," she said. "Dad is somewhere on the hillside. His door is open, torn off, I think. He must not have had his seat belt on. But he's probably all right—somewhere—maybe. We have to get help. Hold each other. Don't let go. I'll hold one hand. Just one."

She clutched one small hand tightly, feeling the soft bones crush together. She released her grasp on the hand and slid it to the wrist instead and faced uphill. The darkness seemed more total than any she had ever seen in her life. A complete black, a smothering, damp black. She looked over her shoulder. The lights of the car were tiny glows, already eaten by the fog that seemed to have turned from white to black.

"Joey?"

He answered, somewhere in the distant darkness, and she knew it was Ellen's wrist she was holding.

"Ellen, hold on to Joey's wrist the way I'm holding yours. We're going to climb the hill and find the highway..."

The hill was littered with traps of vegetation, of vines that clutched and limbs of trees and brush the car had knocked down, but which now were beginning to rise again, pushed by plants beneath, or by their own flexible growth. Beth fought by them, going on upward, not knowing where her next footstep would take her. She had a goal: the top of the hill, the solid roadbed, the pavement.

The little girl . . . was there another wrecked car? Had someone else gone into the road to look for help?

No.

No. The face was familiar.

Familiar.

Where had she seen that face before? Those strange clothes, dark, old, more like rags than clothes. And the hair, black, long, straight. And the face . . . the face . . . the Oriental face.

That was it!

It was the same little girl who had appeared to them in the woods. The girl with the cat.

Beth stopped, cold fear drenching her. A fear of a different kind. The fear that was so primal, so old . . . as old as the little girl.

"Are we there?" a small voice behind her asked.

She had to go on. Even though her next step might take her face to face with that strange, unreal presence. A thought more terrifying than a step into a bottomless pit.

"Yes," she answered, her voice a croak. "We're almost there."

She began to climb again.

Something slapped her sharply in the face, and she drew back, her free hand going to her face in a gesture of helplessness. She reached out tentatively and found the bent and torn limb of a small tree that had struck her. She pushed it aside and held it as she passed by, climbing on, on. She stumbled over something on the ground, and her first thought, as she fell forward, her hand going out to catch her fall, was that she had found the body of her daddy.

But it was a log, a tree fallen so long ago that its bark crumbled under her hand. She righted herself and stepped over it, telling Ellen and Joey to watch, to be prepared to climb.

His body.

That was what she had thought, she now remembered. His body.

Suddenly there was nothing to trip her. She was standing upright, facing into the oblivion of the fog. She stooped and touched the ground. Gravel. And the edge of the pavement. A couple of silent tears of thankfulness slid down her cheeks.

"The road," she told the kids, keeping her voice low, aware that the little Oriental girl was somewhere here, in that strange world of her existence, that being that was so terrifying to Beth.

At first she had thought the girl might be a helpless victim, someone who somehow needed help, but she had stood in the road and caused the wreck of the car. She was an enemy, too.

They had to keep going, trying to find help. There was no sound in the night except the almost silent whispering of the mist. She put her hand up to her hair and found it was wet. Her arms were cold, the mist soaking the sleeves of her sweater. She hadn't thought of it until now.

"We're going down the road," she informed Ellen and Joey. "Hold on to each other. We have to find a house."

It seemed hours since they had left the car, far, far down on the hillside, but it might only have been minutes. And the distance was distorted, too, Beth thought, by the darkness, the awful wandering in the blackness of the unlighted fog.

But there were houses along this road, she remembered. Clusters of houses in some places. Small towns. Places where people could buy crafts and food. Souvenirs. Places where people could eat.

She pulled Ellen behind her, staying on the edge of the pavement, hoping that she wouldn't suddenly find herself confronted by a huge truck whose lights she hadn't been able to see, or whose motor she hadn't heard. But the traffic seemed to have stopped completely.

They were the only ones on the road tonight, wandering forever in the unlighted world.

"Look!" Joey cried.

Beth felt the pull on her arm as the children stopped, rooting themselves to the pavement.

"Look," Joey said again. "Lights. Somebody's light."

Beth searched the darkness for the light Joey had seen. He had imagined it, she thought with a sinking heart. He was only seeing lights in his mind.

But she was being pulled to her right, and she stared in that direction, her eyes watering with the effort. Then she saw it, higher than she had been looking. A round spot of light, almost lost in the dark. Thick fog swirled around it.

Joey and Ellen were pulling her in the direction of the light. She heard Joey grunt as he fell and, a step later, took her into the same ditch. Ellen scrambled up, and they were climbing the bank on the other side. Joey's sounds of digging his way up the steep inner side of the ditch like the sounds of an animal on *World of Nature*.

A few minutes later they were standing on grass, recently mown, and the glow of the tall yard light was directly overhead. The house had to be somewhere near. It was only a matter of going forward until they found a wall.

The owner of the house was still up, Beth saw when she reached a porch. The light glowed now, a rectangle of welcome.

They stumbled onto the porch, their footsteps loud and clattering, almost deafening, after the long silence below.

Beth pounded on the door.

The light was beautiful. She had never known how good light was, or how welcome a strange face.

The face was puzzled as it peered out, the light of the warm room behind it. Beth could see the crinkled eyes peering, peering, looking from one child to the other, changing expression, losing some of the fear at having a knock on the door in the middle of the night.

"Mister," Beth said, "we need help. Our car has been wrecked, and our dad and stepmother have been hurt. Could you call someone to help us?"

Another face appeared beyond the shoulder of the man. It was a lady, sympathetic, hiding whatever surprise she felt.

"My Lord," she said. "Come on in here. You're drenched."

Beth pulled her sister and brother into the warmth of the house.

Faye woke crying. It was as if she had been weeping in her sleep, and at first she didn't know why. She felt the tears on her cheeks and felt someone gently touch her cheeks with a tissue. She opened her eyes and saw her sister Janet's face bent above her.

"Janet?" she murmured, perplexed. Where was she? *Where was she?*

She turned her head, saw a rose-colored wall, a wide window with venetian blinds. What strange room was this? Then she saw, high on the wall across from the foot of the bed on which she lay, a television hanging, its blank face staring down at her.

A hospital?

She looked again at the face of her sister. Janet's eyes were damp, her smile trembling. A nurse moved into view and Janet stepped aside.

The nurse picked up her wrist. "How are you feeling, Mrs. Pendergast?"

They had been driving north, into the mountains. They were going to the lake cabin for a week. Everything was going to be all right.

"Where's Gavin?"

And then had come the blackness, the feeling of having been thrown into space where there was no light. Of rolling over and over and over, unable to stop. The belts had cut into her stomach, and across her chest . . . they had hurt her baby!

She felt her stomach, but the baby was not gone. As if in response to her touch she felt a feeble movement, like the first movement of its life, its existence within her. A feeble fluttering.

"My baby?"

"Your baby will be all right," the nurse said firmly. "If you lie still."

"The—children? Gavin?" Hysteria, the threat of it, made her voice suddenly shrill. *"Gavin?"*

The nurse said, "We want you to rest, Mrs. Pendergast, so you won't lose your baby. The doctor will be in to see you shortly. It's very important that you lie still. Don't exert yourself in any way."

"I want to know where my husband is." Faye reached for Janet's hand and pulled her near. "I remember a car wreck, Janet. Please, tell me they're all right."

The nurse moved aside, making way for Janet. With Faye's hand clasped between hers, Janet bent nearer to Faye. The tears coursed freshly down her cheeks, and her mouth trembled as she tried to talk.

She cleared her throat.

Faye said flatly, "They're dead."

Janet shook her head. "The children are fine. Not even a scratch, Faye. They climbed out of the back seat of the car and walked a half mile in the thick fog to a house for help. But Gavin—evidently he had unfastened his seat belt for some reason. His door came open, and he fell out of the car as it rolled. He was killed. I'm so sorry, Faye."

Faye stared around at the cold, strange room. She wanted to get up and start running, to run away from this news. To deny it however she could.

A low moan had started in her throat, and her body was gripped suddenly in a spasm of trembles, like a mild convulsion. The nurse had stepped in again and was rubbing her wrists, and saying anxiously, "Mrs. Pendergast, Mrs. Pendergast?"

Janet cried, "Oh God, what was I to do? She asked. She had to know sometime."

"Yes," the nurse said. "It's—it can't be helped. Mrs. Pendergast, can you please—please—try to relax. We don't want you to lose your baby."

Faye heard the words, *lose your baby.* "Oh no, oh no." She turned her head sideways and back on the pillow. Someone put a damp cloth over her forehead and tried to hold it there as she tossed her head back and forth on the damp pillow. She couldn't lose her baby, too. Not this, all she had left of Gavin.

She forced herself to relent, to try to accept, and at last to relax. She felt her infant respond with a stronger movement.

There was a male voice suddenly in the room, asking how she was, and she opened her eyes to see her own gynecologist looking down at her. How had he found her?

But Janet had known her doctor's name. She recalled the conversation they'd had about doctors: "You're surely not going to old Doctor Regis, are you, Faye? He might have been our family doctor, but Lord, honey, that was a century ago. Why don't you get a gynecologist like ummm—well, I thought I'd remember his name, but I've forgotten." And Faye had answered, laughing, "You must think I'm terribly naive, Janet. Actually, his name is David Keatson, and he's been my doctor ever since I needed a gynecologist. I still go to Doc Regis when I've got a sore throat, though."

"The ambulance brought you back here, Faye," the doctor was saying. "Since you were from Fort Smith this hospital was the nearest one, the most practical one. Your stepdaughter requested that you be brought back rather than sent on to a nearer hospital at Fayetteville. It wasn't much farther, and you'll be fine. But listen to me carefully. You have to stay in bed, for at least two, maybe three weeks. You're bleeding lightly, nothing really serious, we hope. But we have to keep you still. We're giving you all the medication we dare to. You have to make an effort to relax on your own. I'm sorry about this. Really sorry, Faye. I know how hard it's going to be for you. Just stay still for the sake of the baby. Try to empty your mind."

Faye looked up at him, saw his thin, long face, his concerned eyes. She saw his lips move and heard part of his words. *You're bleeding . . . you have to make an effort to relax . . .*

"How long have I been here?" she asked. She had a feeling now of being distantly removed from that night of darkness. Perhaps days. The sunshine at the window was bright on the venetian blinds, though they were turned so the room was shadowed. "How... long...?"

"Not long," he said. "You were brought in night before last."

She drew a deep breath. "Then—Gavin's funeral...?"

He shook his head. "I'm sorry, Faye. I know this is extremely hard on you. But for no reason are you to get out of bed. I don't even want you sitting on the side of the bed for at least a week. We have to watch you very closely and try to stop that bleeding. That has to come first." He caressed her hand. "Tell me you understand that?"

Her eyes were closed. The tears stung her eyelids and squeezed out from beneath them. Someone wiped her cheeks again with the tissue. "I understand," she whispered.

"Fine." He released her hand, tucked it in beneath the blanket. "We're going to let you rest now. Your sister will be here for a while, but don't talk more than you have to, all right?"

"All right."

She heard footsteps leaving the room and the silence that was left behind when the door was softly closed. She didn't open her eyes to see if Janet had stayed with her, or if she, too, had stepped out into the hall.

Where were the children?

What was going to happen to them while she was in the hospital?

"Janet?"

"Yes, dear."

"Gavin's funeral..."

"I'll take care of the plans, Faye. He'd want you to follow your doctor's orders."

291

"Yes, I know. But—the cemetery that our folks are in, Janet. Get a double lot there, in a nice location under a tree. Have both our names put on the stone."

"Faye," Janet protested. "I wish you wouldn't think about it."

"I can't help but think of it. That's my husband, Janet."

"I know that, sweetheart. But—"

"The hillside cemetery, Janet, promise me. A double plot, a double stone."

"Yes, I promise."

"When is the funeral?"

"It hasn't been arranged. I'll do that this afternoon."

"Day after tomorrow, then, Janet." Then, a fear surfacing, she asked, "Are they sure he's dead, Janet?"

Janet sounded shocked when she answered. "Of course they're sure, Faye."

"I just always have this fear—when someone dies. Even when our pets died. Are they sure? Don't bury—until—"

"Please sleep."

"What about the children, Janet? Are they here?"

"Yes, they're in the waiting room. But I don't think they should come in yet. Why don't you sleep; promise me you'll try, and I'll go take them to lunch?"

Faye nodded. "Go on. They must be very tired."

Janet stood by Faye's bed for a few more minutes. Faye had turned her face toward the window, but her eyes were closed. One of the nurses had come in silently and nodded at Janet, and Janet knew she was dismissed. She drew a long, soft sigh as she left the room.

She felt so damned sorry for Faye. But what could she do? She had left her own child and husband in order to come here, and that meant she couldn't stay long. A week, perhaps, before she needed desperately to go back home. Her baby was spending his days with his paternal grandmother, and that was great up to a point. But Grandma had a way of spoiling him that Janet didn't like very well, and she had to get back. Also, she was dreadfully homesick.

She went down a long hall and into a waiting room. The three kids sat together watching the door, their faces turned toward her. The younger girl, Ellen, had a comic book open on her lap, and the boy was sideways in his chair, one leg drawn up, as if he had problems trying to sit still.

He needed to be out playing somewhere, running, jumping, working off his energy.

The three faces tugged at her heart. Three orphans, now. They looked so vulnerable, so helpless. So young.

What on earth was she going to do about them? Faye would not be able to take care of them now.

Turn them over to the state? Let them go to foster homes? Send them away to a private school?

Had their father left enough insurance to put them in a private school?

The best solution would probably be to turn them over to the state; but she had to talk to Faye about it first, and she didn't want to worry her with it for at least a week.

She had to think of something, and fast. She couldn't keep dragging them around with her, from house to hospital. It was tiresome for them, she knew, to sit here and wait, wait.

"Is she better?" Beth asked, her voice expressing the anxiety that showed on all three faces.

"Yes, she is. She's awake now."

"Does she know that Daddy is—is dead?"

Janet nodded. "Let's go have lunch now, shall we?"

They rose, gathered up the things they had brought with them, the box of colored pencils and crayons, the coloring books, the comics, things she had bought for them to help pass the long hours.

When they reached the hall, she spoke her thoughts aloud, without realizing she had. "And after lunch we have to go to the funeral home and make the final arrangements. We have to choose the plot, and the stone, too. And then—" she realized she was speaking aloud and bit her lower lip, finishing the sentence in her mind. *And then we have to decide what to do with you children.*

Chapter Twenty

On the morning before the funeral they were allowed to go into Faye's room to see her. Only for a minute, a nurse had said. Beth had been wanting to see Faye, to be sure in her own heart that Faye was all right. That all the grownups had not been lying to them for some reason of their own. Several times she had gone down the hall to stand outside Faye's door, to hear the muffled sounds of low voices inside, Janet's and someone else's that might be Faye's. But she hadn't dared stay long, to leave Ellen and Joey alone in the waiting room.

Faye looked pale and thin, her face small, her head supported by a big, thick, unyielding hospital pillow. Not like the soft, down pillows at home.

Beth asked, before she thought to arrange any sequence of words, "Shall I bring you a pillow from home?"

A smile of surprise barely touched Faye's lips, like a glimpse of a butterfly. "Why, that would be nice, Beth, thanks."

Ellen and Joey stood in bashful silence, shoulder to shoulder, staring at Faye. She reached for them, and Janet pushed them nearer to Faye so she could take their hands for a moment.

"I'll be out of here soon," she said. "Meantime, are

you staying at home?"

They nodded.

"Are you being good? But of course I know you are."

It was time to go, to let Faye rest.

Beth led the way out of the room, unshed tears making her throat ache. Faye was all they had left. *Lord please, don't let her die, too.*

They went back to the waiting room.

Janet sat with them for a while, leafing through a magazine from the stack on the table, occasionally looking up at people who came in or got up and went out.

Then, after looking at her watch, she got up again, and said, "I'll be back in a few minutes, kids."

Beth sat still, watching the door again, waiting for Janet to return, for the door to open and emit anyone. Time went so slowly.

Once more she got up and went down the hall to linger outside the door, and this time it was partly open and she could hear the voices clearly.

A man was talking.

"I think your sister's right, Faye. The children should be turned over to someone else now. You owe it to yourself to worry as little as possible."

"If they were given to the state, don't you think I'd worry?" Faye cried.

"But they are no longer your responsibility, Faye," Janet said. "You're simply not able to take care of them—"

Beth turned and ran, her sneakers silent on the floor of the hall. She didn't want to hear any more.

It was as if she had suddenly stepped out of summer into a cold, bleak winter. Why was it that she hadn't thought of the future at all? She knew her daddy was dead. She had been to the funeral home and seen his body lying so still and cold in the gray casket. And today, this afternoon, they were going to the cemetery to bury him. So why hadn't she thought about the future? She had just supposed they were going to live with Faye, in her house, she guessed. As soon as Faye went home, they would go home, too.

Was that what she had thought? Yes, that was what she had thought.

She slowed and went on down the hall looking at her feet. But outside the waiting room she stopped and stood in the shadowed corner, unable to face the sunny room and the faces of her little sister and brother.

Oh God, if only she were old enough to take care of them.

Did being turned over to the state mean they would be separated?

That she might never seen Ellen or Joey again?

Who would be there to protect Ellen from the . . . monsters . . . that followed her, that killed and mutilated?

They could run away again, but this time they had even less money. She had been spending it, bit by bit, letting Joey and Ellen go down to the snack bar and buy things: candy, pop, nuts. Things that helped pass the time. They got so tired just sitting and waiting.

So most of their money was gone.

And they had tried running away, and it hadn't worked.

The monsters—Ellen's monsters—had followed.

A thought came to Beth, a shocking thought that pulled the curtain in her mind again, more tightly it seemed, as if she couldn't face it. For a swift second she had known what the monsters were and where they came from. And in knowing that, she had known also how to fight them, how, even, to win.

But the thought, the knowledge, was gone. And she was left feeling blinded.

She had nothing left of the one shocking flash of enlightenment, that brief slip of knowledge, of wisdom.

"I can't, I can't," Faye wept. She couldn't send the children away.

"Rest now," Janet said. "I'm taking care of them now. Just rest. I don't want to upset you, Faye. I'm sorry I brought it up. I thought you might be able to talk about it now."

"Is—are you going to the funeral now?"

"Yes. It's starting at two o'clock."

"You'll be back? Afterward?"

Left alone, except for the nurse who had been hired to stay with her during the day, Faye tried to turn her mind away from this latest worry. To do as she had been ordered and relax, not worry, just let go. Give her baby a chance to live, to grow, to become fast again in her womb. To eliminate the danger of miscarriage. It might be viable, her doctor had said, but for the baby's sake it needed to stay where it was, to finish maturing.

She had to lie still.

And now they were saying she had to stay in the hospital for three weeks, and then when she went home she might have to keep a nurse with her for at least another week.

She didn't need the extra worry of the children, her doctor had said, siding with Janet. But in no way was she going to turn them over to the state.

But to let them go . . . after all, they weren't really hers . . . if she knew they would be well taken care of . . . if she knew . . . if she could be sure.

She watched the clock. One-thirty, and then two. Two-thirty. Her heart felt the drop of the clods of dirt upon the top of the casket, and it screamed in its pain, a silent cry of death. She would never see his beloved face again.

Gavin was gone.

She closed her eyes.

As if something had died within herself, she gave up. She wouldn't try to hold them. Three young children . . .

The subject was not brought up again for two days, then Janet said, "Faye, I must get back home and see how my own two guys are getting along."

Faye reached for Janet's hand and squeezed it. "I'm so sorry, Janet. I've been selfish, keeping you here. Of course, go on home."

"You're going to be well."

"Yes, I'm going to be okay. The baby is stronger. I can feel it. Go on home, and thanks, Janet, for spending so much time with me, for doing all the things you've done."

"I'm taking the children with me, Faye. If you'll give permission. I've located a private school in Little Rock, a small place that will give them individual care. Rob has been looking into it for me. Later, when you're up and around, you can decide if you want to—make other arrangements. Okay?"

"A private school?"

It was better than a foster home. At least, in her mind it was. She visualized small classrooms, a homey atmosphere.

"Have you seen this place, Janet?"

"No, but Rob has. And they'll be close enough we can look in on them now and then. And the price isn't exorbitant. You'll be able to handle it easily, I'm sure."

"Maybe it would be better." Better than letting them

stay at home, even with a housekeeper. At home so near the place of the murders and the weird and unexplainable happenings.

"They've been all right, haven't they, Janet?" She kept asking, not ready to try to explain to Janet her fears. Janet wouldn't have understood. So far as Faye knew, Janet wasn't even aware of most of the things that had happened. Of course she knew of the deaths. Anyone who read newspapers knew of them. And she knew of the proximity. But that was all.

What else was there to know?

Faye wasn't sure.

"When are you leaving?" she asked Janet.

"This evening. I'll be back on the weekend."

"Thanks for everything, Janet."

She was alone, completely alone, it seemed. Janet brought the children in one more time, and Faye held their hands and kissed their cheeks, and told them she would see them soon. And all the while she had to keep almost unbearable control to keep from breaking down into hysterical tears.

She knew in her heart they were going away forever. She would never see them again. They had a right to be settled somewhere safe and secure, as safe and secure as possible. Maybe their next home would provide that security.

"You understand why we must do this, don't you?" Janet asked as she hurried around, supervising the packing. "You understand that Faye must stay in the hospital, maybe for as long as a month, and after she's out she simply must have rest."

Beth saw that Joey and Ellen were looking at Janet with wide, dread-filled eyes. They didn't understand.

Joey asked, "Is Faye sick? Is she going to die?"

"Not if she is left alone. She has to be undisturbed."

"Why can't we stay here?" Joey asked. "Beth can take care of us."

Janet drew a long breath. "Beth is only twelve years old, Joey. She may seem—uh—capable, but she's too young. And getting a housekeeper to live here with you, someone who is qualified, is impossible at this point. It takes more time than we have. Really, Joey, you'll like the school. You'll like it just fine."

"We understand," Beth said, and directed a *shut up now* look at Joey.

He saw her looking at him and caught the message. With his head bent low he emptied his drawer of socks and underwear. There wasn't a lot. All his clothes went into one large suitcase that Janet had found somewhere in the house.

"Ellen," Janet said, "go into your room and check to see if we got everything, please." She glanced at her watch. "We do have to hurry. I'm sorry kids. But I told Mrs. Sanders that we'd have you at the school before eight o'clock. That doesn't give us much time."

Beth saw Ellen hesitate. She was afraid to go into the room alone. But then she was going, obediently, across the hall and toward the open door.

"I'll go with her," Beth said quickly.

Ellen had stopped in the middle of the hall, and Beth took her hand in a brief gesture.

"I'll do it, Ellen," she said. "You don't have to go in there. You wait here."

The room was small and dark, smaller and darker than Beth remembered. She turned on the light. The curtains were drawn over the window, and the bedspread was pulled neatly and smoothly over the bed. It looked empty. Nothing of Ellen's was there, out in sight. Beth crossed the room to the dresser and opened the drawers one by one. Janet had been here, gathering Ellen's clothing, while Beth packed her own and Ellen helped Joey. She had emptied the drawers. There was nothing... no lost sock... no missed panty... but... there was something else... something that should not have been there. Beth sniffed the air. The room seemed dim, as if filled with smoke. And it was in the air now, in this corner, a strange, strong, sweetish, suffocating smell, invisible in the air.

It lingered here in Ellen's room.

And she remembered having smelled this same exotic scent of—not tobacco but something else, before. In the wash house, and again in the upstairs hall in the house next door.

And in her own home, in the living room, where her mother lay dead.

She hurried out of the room, turned out the light and shut the door.

The air in the hall was fresh, as if a window had been left open at the front of the house.

Janet was carrying suitcases into the hall and lumping them into a pile. She glanced at Beth. "Is everything okay?"

Beth nodded.

"Did I get it all? Out of Ellen's room?"

"Yes." Had Janet not smelled the smoke? Was it there only for Ellen and now for her? What was it? She sensed it was no more real, nor more actual than the girl in the woods had been.

"Are we ready then?" Janet asked, looking around as if she thought she had overlooked something obvious. She picked up two suitcases. "Take what you can. I can come back after the rest."

These suitcases were large and heavy, one for each of them, with two small ones. Beth gave the old zippered bag to Ellen and placed the long strap over her shoulder.

She gave Joey the other small suitcase after he'd struggled and failed to lift the heavy one.

Beth followed behind them down the stairs, her arms feeling stretched by the weight of the bag. When she reached the end of the hall she looked back. The light had been turned out, and although a shaded daylight came in at the window at the end of the hall, the distance between, with the dark, old wallpaper, seemed to lie in a twilight world.

She was not sorry to leave the house; she had never felt at home here. She was only sorry to be leaving Faye.

They rode for three hours along the interstate, the tires blip-blipping over the seams on the concrete, rivers and lakes and cedar trees that were the shape of perfect Christmas trees slipping along on the roadside. In the back seat of the car, Ellen and Joey were silent. Occasionally Janet tried to make conversation, but Beth only felt awkward and shy, as if she'd never learned any conversational skills. Finally Janet turned on the radio. They listened to news, and to music, and a disc jockey who liked to make jokes.

No one laughed.

Janet drove the car off the interstate and onto the streets of the city, stopping at a McDonald's. "Is this all right?"

She seemed to expect happy shouts, and she turned to look at the faces in the back seat.

"Don't you like McDonald's? My little two-year-old boy thinks there's no greater place in the world to eat. He likes the Happy Meal, or whatever it is. Do you?"

Beth said. "Yes, they like it."

Joey had sat forward, but his face showed more bewilderment and fear than excitement.

"Will I get to stay with Beth and Ellen?" he asked, and Beth saw it was a question that had been on his mind since he first heard the phrase Private School.

"Oh yes, of course." Janet reached back and patted his head. The only gesture of concern that Beth had seen her make toward the little boy. "It's only a very small school. It will be just like living at home."

Janet felt her first grip of guilt as she led the children into the building for their dinner. She had thought McDonald's would be a treat, something the younger ones, especially, would delight in. But during all the preparations, she had not looked at this change in their lives from their perspective. Faye had not wanted them to go. Maybe she should have made more of an effort to locate a housekeeper to stay with them.

But no. She felt in her heart, for some reason she couldn't really define, that Faye would be much better off without them.

As soon as they had finished eating, none of them able to eat the food that was ordered, Janet drove through the streets to Mrs. Sanders' Private School. She would have preferred to go home first, to see her husband and her son, but that would have been awkward for the children, she knew. It was better to settle them in and let them begin their adjustment.

She found the school was a large house on a tree-shaded street. Although it was near a factory district, the school itself looked like a comfortable home. The only indications that it was anything else was the fence. Wrought iron, it surrounded the yard, front and back. Only the driveway was free from the enclosure. The other homes along the street were not fenced at the front.

The woman who opened the door for them was middle-aged, slender, dark-haired. She was dressed in a cotton blouse and matching skirt that emphasized her small waist. She smiled, but there was something hard and professional about her eyes.

"I'm Mrs. Sanders," she said, opening one half of the double doors so they could enter the foyer. "I've been expecting you. Our bedtime here is eight o'clock, so the other children have already gone upstairs." She directed her gaze at each of the three kids in turn, as if this last statement was made exclusively for them.

The foyer was large, with double stairways at the rear, one going up to one wing, and the other to the opposite wing, although the hall that connected them was visible from the foyer.

There was a desk and a couple of chairs. The officelike atmosphere extended to the paintings on the wall, obviously chosen only to cover bare places. Janet found herself thinking, home atmosphere? The school had probably advertised itself as such, and Rob had taken the school's word for it.

But, what could they do?

They both had jobs. They had home and family. They didn't have time to search farther than this.

One advantage, she told herself, was the location. At least it was close enough that she could run over and see the children if need be.

When she left the school, it was with a sense of relief, of a burden lifted. She drove toward her own house with eagerness, hoping that Rob had taken the baby home, and they would be waiting for her.

*   *   *

Beth hadn't felt so much like crying in her life. Even when she had stood at the side of her daddy's grave, she hadn't felt as abandoned as now.

They had been given a room together, she and Ellen, and she stood in the middle of it looking at the walls with the two framed prints, at the twin beds, one against one wall, one against the opposite. Along the wall at the foot of the beds were twin chests, scarred, ugly, matching nothing.

But it wasn't the size of the room, or its furnishings that made her feel so hollow inside, so afraid, so lost. It was something else . . .

The feeling of coldness. Of regimentation.

A lack of happy sound, though she knew there were other children present, and it was only eight-thirty.

And it was the separation of boys from girls.

The room Mrs. Sanders had given her and Ellen was in one wing, and Joey, looking so little and so alone, had been taken into the other wing. Mrs. Sanders would not even let Beth go along to his room.

In her heart she could see him yet, going down the long, narrow hall, looking over his shoulder toward her.

And then, to make her feeling of having lost him more confirmed, a door had been closed at this end of the hall, double doors much like the entry doors at the foyer.

"Do you like this room?" Ellen asked in a small voice.

"It's okay," Beth said, hoping that Ellen would not see her cry.

The door opened suddenly, and Mrs. Sanders looked in, her eyes roaming from wall to wall as if checking on something. She gave the girls a brief smile.

"Lights out, dears, at nine o'clock sharp. If they aren't turned out in the rooms, they will be turned out at the main switch downstairs. That's to ensure that you get proper rest. It's much easier to sleep in the dark."

"Ma'am," Beth said quickly, before she could withdraw. "We're used to a nightlight. Can't we have a nightlight? My little sister—sometimes—has nightmares."

"Oh really?" Mrs. Sanders' dark eyes opened a little wider. She stared unblinking at Beth, then at Ellen. "No one told me of this."

Beth didn't know what to say. Would Mrs. Sanders put them out now? Were nightmares unacceptable? She longed suddenly to be free in the hills again. It was not as bad in the small cave as it was here. She hoped Mrs. Sanders would say they would have to leave. That she couldn't have anyone here who disturbed the night with cries of terror.

But she was saying, "There's a certain amount of light at the window, from the yard lights and street lights, and I think it will be better if you get used to that. Maybe these nightmares will end. I understand you've lost both your mother and father. Under the circumstances bad dreams are to be expected."

She came into the room briskly and pulled the blind. "You'll be undressing in front of the open window, if you don't watch out. After you're ready for bed, you can let the blind up. You remember where the bathroom is, don't you? There are two for this wing, but even so you'll probably have to stand in line in the morning. Everyone rises at seven. Breakfast is at eight. Now," she said as she stood again in the door, "if you should need anyone during the night just come into the hall and press this button. Come, both of you, and see where it is."

They went into the hall to see her pointing at a button enclosed behind a small glass door. The words *for emergency only,* were printed in red above it.

"As you can see, it's only for emergencies of the most serious kind. Such as fire. It's connected to the rooms of Mr. Bower, our maintenance man, and general—um—caretaker. Well, girls, good night. We'll see you at breakfast. Sleep well. I'm sure you'll enjoy our school as soon as you get acquainted with the other children who are staying here for the summer."

Beth was going back into the small, unfamiliar room when the voice spoke again.

"Remember, lights out promptly at nine. Be in bed."

"Yes, ma'am."

There was no clock in the room, and Beth felt an anxiety to hurry, hurry, before lights out.

"Will you go to the bathroom with me, Beth?" Ellen asked.

"Yes."

The bathrooms were across the hall from each other, and both were dark, small dungeons they had to go into in order to find the light switches.

"You go to that one," Beth whispered, "and I'll go to the one across the hall."

"No. Don't leave me."

So Beth waited while Ellen brushed her teeth, went to the bathroom and washed up. They were only halfway back to their rooms when the lights blinked, then went out.

Then suddenly total blackness in the hall was like being back on the mountain in the fog, and Beth felt Ellen's hand groping for her.

How would they find their room in the dark?

The lights came back on suddenly, and blinked again, and Beth knew it was a warning. With Ellen's hand tight in hers, she ran for the open door of their room.

The lights went out again, and in the darkness Beth

raised the blind on the window. A tall yard light in the backyard threw streaks of light through the evergreen trees that clustered near the window. Behind her, she could hear Ellen breathing, small gasps of nervousness.

"It's all right, Ellen," she said. "It's going to be okay here. We won't have to stay long."

But as she got into her bed, she wondered if they would ever be leaving. The window had bars, just as if they were in jail. They were decorative wrought iron bars, but they were there, nevertheless. Making sure that no one tried to go out a window during the night.

Beth lay awake, listening to Ellen's even breathing as she fell asleep.

Then she turned her face into her pillow and let the tears come.

She slept, realizing that she slept only on waking. The room was only less light than it was when she had gone to bed, the streaks of light from the yard mere stripes in the darkness, illuminating nothing. The chests across the room were at first sight the monsters of Ellen's fears, the monsters that were in some way real.

Something had awakened her, and she lay still trying to pinpoint the disturbance to her sleep. But there was nothing, nothing visible in the dark room. She could hear Ellen breathing, but the breathing was different now. Instead of deep, long breaths, Ellen was taking short, gasping breaths, in which there was a delay, before she gasped again.

Beth sat up and looked through the darkness at Ellen's bed.

It was pushed against the wall, yet as Beth stared toward it she began to see a scene beyond the bed, a barely visible movement of a lighted room in the distance, in which something swirled, cutting off a clear conception, a clear vision.

It was like the fog on the mountain top.

Or smoke, thick, moving upward from a dimly burning light. A lamp, with a feeble flame.

Beth stared into it, straining to see, to understand.

Then Ellen drew a long breath and turned in her bed, the sheets rustling, and the strange, dim, faraway light beyond the bed was gone.

Chapter Twenty-One

Faye walked through the house slowly. She had come home in a taxi, without a nurse, after only two weeks in the hospital. Her youth and her natural good health had brought her through miraculously, her doctor said, as well as the good health of the baby. They were both fine now, no problems. No physical problems. The emotional pain, the trauma, were something she would have to handle without chemical assistance. No tranquilizers. No anxiety medicine, not even a glass of wine.

Faye had never had a dependence on chemicals anyway.

She was prepared to face her losses, and adjust to them.

She let herself in at the side door beneath the *porte-co-chere*. Although it was only mid-morning, the house was in a state of twilight, as if the sun had gone down and darkness threatened.

She had never seen the house in this light before. She had never known it was so big, so dark, so quiet.

She walked through the lower halls, going into rooms she hadn't opened in ages, then she climbed the stairs.

Only the nursery was a bright and cheerful room, she felt, as she paused to sit in it.

But she knew, suddenly and definitely, that she could not live here.

When she had made arrangements to buy the house from her brother and sister, it had been with Gavin at her side. Without him, the house was too large.

And now it was too filled with something—dreadful.

It seemed to echo the sounds of the children, although they had lived here only a short time. Everywhere she looked in the halls, in their rooms, she felt the absence of Beth, of Joey and Ellen.

She went back downstairs and into the library, where she sat at the desk and picked up the telephone book.

Now that she had made up her mind, she would waste no more time than she had to. She didn't know what she was going to do beyond selling this house and buying another. A smaller house. One story. Built of native stone, perhaps, ranch style, on a smaller lot.

A safe place to rear her child.

She leaned back in the chair. She hadn't felt weak while she was in the hospital. Her strolls along the hall had been restless ones. She'd been eager to get out of there, to come home. Two weeks in the hospital had been two weeks too long. She couldn't have stood three. But coming home was not easy either.

It would have been easier to come home if Gavin's children had been here, waiting for her, but also she wondered if the doctor, if Janet and Rob, and other people who had talked to her about it were not right after all, and she should let the children go. Maybe she should go ahead and let the state take custody of them. Maybe in that way they would find homes.

No, children that age were considered unadoptable.

Perhaps Joey . . .

But no, that would be wrong, to separate them at their ages now.

She looked at the clock. Her sister would be at work, but it was almost noon, time for a break anyway. Where was her number? She rummaged through her personal book, found Janet's home number, but not her work number.

She gave it up and sat back. Her brother was too far away to bother reaching, and he wouldn't want the house anyway. That had been established when she purchased his share. She was almost positive that Janet didn't want it either, but she felt obligated to at least offer it to her.

She needed to talk to Janet. To get the number of the school where the children were. She needed to know how they were.

She went to look in her purse, to check the tiny brown leather book of addresses and phone numbers she kept there, and she found, written in tiny numbers above the home phone, the number where Janet worked.

She returned to the phone and dialed, and after being put on hold once and transferred twice, she reached Janet.

"Hey, babe," Janet cried. "Great to hear your voice. Are you home?"

"Yes, finally."

Janet had visited the hospital only last weekend, she, her husband Rob, and their son, Lanny. But Lanny had not been permitted to come into the wing where she was, so Rob had only stuck his head in to say hello and had gone again to babysit. Janet had stayed only a short time, too, and now it seemed as if they hadn't seen each other in ages.

"I'm selling out, Janet," Faye said, after a couple of minutes of positive banter, of how work was, and Janet's family. "Do you want to buy the house?"

"Oh . . . why? I mean, why are you selling? You were

so sure you wanted to raise your kids there. I know things have changed, Faye, and right now you're terribly lonesome for Gavin, but you're still going to have your child. And the nursery looks great. All the work you've done on it."

"I know. But this is something that won't pass, Janet, I'm sure. It's not only being alone here—and it's such a big house. It's the other things that have happened. My neighbor, murdered, right next door. That house is empty now, too, and a 'for sale' sign is out front. And the laundress murdered in the woods across the road. And the kids—Beth, Ellen and Joey—it's so lonesome here without them. How are they, Janet?"

Janet hesitated just an instant too long. Faye felt the dread she'd been trying to suppress come to the surface like boiling oil on a stagnant pond. She felt restless suddenly. She had a need to go after them, wherever they were, bring them home . . . but . . . there was the other . . . the strange happenings that seemed to be drawn to them in some unexplainable way. The series of horrible deaths that occurred near them.

"They're fine," Janet said cheerfully. "Just fine."

"I want the number of the school, Janet. Do you realize I don't even know the name of the school?"

Janet said, "Faye, let them go. They're not your responsibility."

"Whose responsibility are they if not mine?"

"Legally you are not responsible. Let the state take over. Faye, haven't you noticed that those murders always take place *near them?*"

To hear Janet put into words exactly what she had been thinking all along infuriated her. "What are you trying to say, Janet?" Faye asked in her iciest voice, "That they are the murderers?"

"Well—it's been considered possible, hasn't it?"

"Look, and I want you to listen to this very carefully,

Janet. That kind of killing is not possible for any child—"

"Children, Faye, children," Janet interrupted, her voice as stinging as Faye's. "More than one, Faye. Three of them. Be reasonable."

"I am responsible, damnit!" Faye's attempt at coldness dissolved into fury and frustration. "The police were here! They do not suspect those children! I know they are innocent!"

"And how do you know? How can you be positive?"

Faye was thankful Janet couldn't see the tears that erupted from her eyes, hot, furious, helpless tears. Her hand shook holding the phone. "Are you crazy? I was with them! Understand? I don't know why you people are so fast to accuse innocent children of such heinous crimes—"

"Faye," Janet said gently, "Get hold of yourself."

"I am hold of myself!" Faye shouted, then collapsed into a tearful laughter. She felt like strangling Janet, if only she could reach her; but they had disagreed many times in their lives, and it always ended like this.

"You okay, babe?" Janet asked.

"Okay." Faye calmed herself. She was an adult now; she needed to act like one, she reminded herself. The time was gone when she could respond to her older sister with a screaming fit. "All right now, Janet, listen to me. The children were with me, and we were at the park, when the laundress was killed. And Beth was with me, and the younger children playing with Nordene's children, in my barn, when Nordene was killed. Also, Nordene was in a room from which no one could get out. The window was locked, and her body was lodged against the door. I know my kids had nothing to do with either of those murders, *nor with their mother's!*"

There was a slight pause, then Janet said, "Do you

realize you called them your kids?"

"Uh—no. But—"

"Faye, they're not yours. Maybe they didn't directly kill those women, but they are in some way connected. I feel it, Faye. I felt it when I was with them. They're—weird, those kids. They're so quiet, so . . . so . . ."

"Janet! They've been through terrible experiences. What do you expect of them? Their dad was just buried; their mother was buried just weeks ago. What do you expect?"

"I know. I'm sorry. But it's more than that. There's something there, Faye, and it's dangerous. Please, please don't take them to live with you again. Please. At least give it time. Let your baby be born first. Sell that old house if you want to. I wondered at the beginning what you wanted with it. Get yourself one like mine. Enjoy your child. *But leave those children where they are.*"

Leave those children where they are.

All else Janet said to Faye was lost under the power of those words, and as the afternoon and night wore on, they repeated themselves in Faye's mind. After she had hung up the phone, she remembered that Janet had not given her the name of the school nor the phone number. She thought about calling her back, demanding the information. But she didn't.

Leave those children where they are.

She slept, and she dreamed of Ellen standing in a burning building where fire and smoke swirled around her, licking up from her feet in long, consuming sheets of flame from which Ellen's small face pleaded for help. She woke, trembling with fear.

The house was dark and still. Somewhere far away she could hear the call of an owl, that deep-throated scream that always chilled her.

She sat up and turned on the light. Almost three o'clock.

She got out of bed and went out into the silent, empty hall, and around the banister to the hall that went back to the children's rooms. She stood for a few minutes looking in that direction. She had a strong, eerie feeling that Ellen had returned to her room.

The hall was narrow and dark, even with the overhead light on. Shadows hung heavily in the corners, in the junctions of wall, ceiling and floor. Her footsteps were soft whispers as she went toward the closed door of Ellen's room.

She opened the door.

The odor was strong, as if someone had left a cigar—something—smoldering there. Smoke. Fire. Death.

Faye pushed the door back and turned on the light. Strange, this smell of smoke, this acrid, sweetish smell, not quite of tobacco, but of something else. She remembered the first time she had smelled it, the first night the children had been in this house. And she recalled that she went into the hall and found Ellen there, walking in her sleep. The odor of smoke had surrounded her. And yet it had not come from her. Ellen had smoked nothing, as kids sometimes do. She was sure of that.

Then what was the source of this odor?

With eerie chills going up and down the backs of her arms, Faye crossed the room and opened the window. A faint night breeze blew the curtains into the room, waving them in the air like scarves waved from invisible hands.

Beth woke, blinking into the darkness, trying to grasp reality and the thing that had awakened her. At first there was nothing, then a faint moan came from Ellen's bed.

Beth turned, her skin going cold. The distant, reddish light was there again, on the other side of Ellen's bed, pale and far away, yet outlining the bed and even the lump that was Ellen's body. Ellen stirred, moving, and her moans rose in volume to cries that sounded strangled. And in the pale, moving, reddish background a tiny light appeared, a dewdrop light, a candle flame or a tiny flame from a lamp. It flickered brightly just above Ellen's bed.

Ellen was screaming suddenly, not just cries, but words, part of them distinguishable. "No—no! No please, help me . . . no—NO!"

Beth tried to get out of her bed, but her blanket curled around her, like an arm in the darkness, and held her. She fell onto the floor, and the floor trembled with her fall. She rolled, trying to extricate herself from the blanket. When she was finally free, she stood up and stumbled in shock.

A figure was forming in the reddish, smoky light beyond Ellen's bed, a huge figure made up of a body and a great unformed lump at the top that could be a head . . . the outlines indistinct . . . but arms at the sides, reaching toward Ellen.

Ellen was no longer asleep, Beth saw. She had risen from the bed, and still screaming was backing off the bed, her face turned toward the figure in the . . . *the fire that glowed dully where the wall of the room should have been.*

The tiny streaks of light coming from outside, from the real world of trees, yard lights and street lights, illuminated the profile of Ellen's face and body as she backed across the room toward Beth.

Then suddenly there were footsteps in the hall, the door was thrown open, and light streamed in through the open doorway. A flashlight's beam jumped about the room and settled on Ellen's face.

The scene beyond the bed, the huge, forming figure, the dull fire glow, was gone.

Ellen collapsed to the floor, weeping.

The caretaker came on into the room, shining his light down on Ellen. Behind him were the other girls of the dorm, eight faces peering into the room.

"What's wrong?" he asked, then pointed his light into Beth's face. "Take care of her until I can get some of these goddamned lights turned on. What the hell . . . having the main switch off. I've got a mind to quit and go someplace else to work. Here." He thrust the flashlight into the hands of one of the girls as he pushed through. "I'll find my own way. Keep the light. Hang on there, little girl, someone will be here in a few minutes."

He went away cursing out loud, his words a comfort to Beth's ears. He was going for help. For help.

But who could help Ellen?

What was it that was after Ellen? For now Beth was sure that's what was happening. Somehow, all the killings had something to do with this—this thing that had begun forming. Was this the monster Ellen had seen the night their mother was murdered? Had it finished materializing and murdered their mother— instead of Ellen?

Beth held Ellen, felt the trembling of her small body, her hands that clung so hard they hurt. She sat on the floor with Ellen, rocking her as if she were a baby and Beth the mother. The other girls, the girls whose names Beth had learned were Christine, Heather, Jessica, Teri—there were others whose names she had forgotten—had gathered closer, their voices birdlike murmurs of sympathy.

"What's wrong with her?" a girl with red braids and

freckles asked. Beth looked up. Tracy? Yes. She was the only girl who was near Ellen's age. The others were older, ranging in age from ten to fourteen.

"I've heard her having nightmares before," one of the other girls said. "I heard her crying last night."

"Yes," Beth admitted.

Every night since they had been here something had happened. But tonight—tonight was the worst. She held Ellen desperately, her mind trying to find something to understand. There was nothing, she felt, in her brain but burning confusion—and the images left over of the strange glow, the flickering flame and the forming body.

The little girl, the Oriental girl, and the huge cat were tied in, too, somehow. But her brain refused to assimilate it, to understand.

The lights came on suddenly, their brilliance blinding. Beth blinked, closed her eyes briefly and opened them again. The light was less blinding.

There were footsteps in the hall again, the heavy steps of the man, and lighter, quicker, harsh steps. Beth recognized the footsteps of Mrs. Sanders. Forceful. Impatient.

The girls who had hovered around Beth and Ellen moved back, to stand in the small room, making it seem smaller than ever. As the steps drew nearer, the girls began edging toward the door. Three of them managed to get out into the hall before Mrs. Sanders, followed by Mr. Joiner, came into the room.

Mrs. Sanders took Ellen by the hand and lifted her, leading her back to the bed. She looked around the room as if she expected to see something that wasn't there.

"I understand your nightmares are getting quite severe, Ellen," she said.

Ellen looked at Beth. For a moment it seemed she

might speak, deny that it had been a nightmare, but then she merely nodded. Mrs. Sanders patted her back awkwardly, as if she wasn't used to patting children's backs. Her eyes kept darting around the room.

"Has anyone been smoking here?" she asked abruptly.

Beth shook her head. "No."

Mrs. Sanders' fixed look on Beth had clearly doubted. Then she went toward the door.

"Tomorrow we will make other arrangements. For tonight, go back to bed, all of you. Lights will be turned out again—"

Beth hastily followed her, grabbed her by the arm. "Please, Mrs. Sanders, don't turn out the lights. Please. Ellen—Ellen's nightmares aren't so bad if there's a light. Please!"

It formed in the darkness; it came from the depths of hell, where there was fire and brimstone, just like the Bible said.

If the lights were left on, it would not come.

What of the day the laundress was killed? It was not dark then.

"Please, Mrs. Sanders, please."

The dark ... the dark ... take away the dark, please.

"Oh, all right. Since it's so late anyway. In another one and a half hours it will be daylight. Go to your rooms, girls. Go back to bed. Keep your lights out. You may leave one small light on, Beth, for the rest of this night, and tomorrow we will make other arrangements."

Other arrangements?

Through the rest of the night Beth stared at the ceiling and wondered what kind of arrangements Mrs.

Sanders was talking about. Ellen slept again, miraculously, it seemed to Beth, or as if she had been drugged. As if there were something in her brain that opiated her, making her sleep afterward.

Beth had barely gone back to sleep when Deloris, the girl whose responsibility it was to wake the dorm, came by, knocked on the door and turned on the ceiling light.

"Up. Time to get up," she announced in a loud, firm voice.

Beth got up, and with Ellen half asleep beside her, went to stand in the small line that had formed at the bathrooms.

By the time her turn came, she was awake again. She went alone into a bathroom, brushed her teeth, washed her face and hands, and went to the toilet. She went out, and the girl named Teri took her place in the bathroom. She went back to the room to dress. As she was pulling on the anklets which were part of the school uniform, Ellen came in. Beth waited until Ellen was dressed. She stood by the door watching Ellen, seeing her arms like reeds, so thin. She was looking smaller and skinnier; instead of growing she seemed to be shrinking.

Beth had a sudden and terrible premonition: *Ellen was going to die.*

Something had to be done. But what?

She had to call Faye. Only Faye would help them.

"Ellen," she said gently, "do you remember your—your dream last night? Your nightmare?"

Ellen looked up as if surprised, her eyes widened, fear growing there. "I—I didn't have a nightmare. It wasn't a dream."

"I know. I just called it that. I saw it, Ellen."

"You saw . . . ?"

"Something. A man? It looked like a big, big man. I've seen it before, Ellen; I've just never told you about it. Who is it, Ellen? What is it?"

Ellen stared at her. She moistened her lips with the tip of her tongue.

"I don't know," she whispered. "I don't know!" And then—"I can't remember."

There was another knock on the door, and a voice. "Breakfast."

They went out into the hall. There would be no more time together now until evening. The day was regimented. They stood in line to go to breakfast where they sat at a long table with the girls. They were in the same room with Joey and the fifteen other boys who were here for the summer, but they barely had time to speak to him before the meal was over and they went to their separate classrooms.

The first break was a recess in which they had supervised play in the fenced backyard. Their second break was at noon, and afternoon was the quiet time, as it was called. A sort of study hall in which they were to spend two hours reading.

After that, an hour of television was allowed, then dinner, then another hour of study and bedtime.

Beth looked into the day ahead wondering how and when she would get a chance to contact Faye.

Before she could request an appointment with Mrs. Sanders, one of the secretaries came to her and said, "Mrs. Sanders would like to see you in her office, Beth. And Ellen. Will you come with me, please?"

Beth and Ellen followed the secretary down the hall. She was a young woman who Beth had seen only a few times before, young, dark-haired, pretty, a stranger in all ways. Her expression said she was doing a job, but she had little contact with the girls and boys of this private school, kids who were sent here for a hundred different reasons, none of which interested her very much.

She opened the office door and stood aside, favoring Ellen with a quick smile as the girls entered.

The door closed behind them.

Mrs. Sanders sat behind a large desk, in front of windows that looked out into the branches of a Colorado blue spruce tree. Beth saw the bright feathers of a cardinal as it disappeared into the thick blue-green of the needles. But it seemed a world removed from the browns and beiges of this somber office.

For a few minutes Mrs. Sanders talked of the school, its history, its faultless reputation. Her father had founded the school, and she had taken over when he retired. When he was able, he still visited. They hadn't met him yet, but they would. and how did they like living here?

Politely Ellen nodded, and Beth said, "Mrs. Sanders?" Trying to get permission to ask her question. But Mrs. Sanders seemed not to hear her.

"Usually we try to let sisters, or brothers, share the same room, especially when they are close, and one is somewhat younger than the other. In your case we felt Ellen should be with you, Beth. But now that you have been here a few days, and nights, it has come to my attention that perhaps Ellen would be better off sharing with another girl."

"Oh no, please," Beth cried. "She can't, Mrs. Sanders."

Mrs. Sanders held up her hand, a flesh-and-blood stop sign. "The next step after that, Beth, if the disturbances in the night do not stop, is to take Ellen to a psychiatrist. We do have a counselor, and she will talk to Ellen this morning." She sat forward, and as if she had touched a button invisible to Beth, an adjoining door opened and a sweet-faced, smiling lady looked in, settling her eyes on Ellen.

"Would you come with me now, Ellen? I'm Mrs. Raleigh, and I'm here to help you."

Beth rose, too, but she stood still and watched Ellen go toward the lady in the doorway.

When Ellen reached the threshold, she looked over her shoulder at Beth, a look of frozen terror.

Beth hoped that the counselor would get nothing out of Ellen. Whatever she might have to tell, and that was probably only the same confused story about monsters, she couldn't tell it to this lady. Or to anyone else here at Mrs. Sanders' school. Did Ellen know that? They would send her to an asylum if she did.

Beth had to get in touch with Faye. They needed Faye. Maybe she could help them. With her, that look of fear would leave Ellen's face, and she would smile again.

"Mrs. Sanders," Beth said when the door closed behind Ellen. "Could I please make a phone call?"

"A call? Where? To whom?"

"My stepmother. Faye Pendergast. In Fort Smith. I could reverse the charges."

Mrs. Sanders waved her hand. "I'm not concerned about the charges. When a student wants to call home she, or he, is usually allowed the freedom of the phone. Each student is allowed a certain number of calls. But I understood when you children came here that there was no one for you to contact. I'm sorry."

"But . . . my stepmother. Faye."

Mrs. Sanders rose and came briskly around from behind the desk and toward the door.

"I'm sorry. There are no numbers left here that you are to be permitted to call. And that is a prerequisite, Beth. Certain numbers are left for each student to use. And there are none for you."

Mrs. Sanders touched Beth's shoulder in a gentle pat, and Beth saw pity on the face that looked down at her. But Beth froze beneath that pity. Sympathy would not help them.

"You'll be staying in your present room, Beth. Alone for the time being. Go now, return to your class."

"Mrs. Sanders, please," Beth pleaded. "I know Faye would want me to call her."

"I'm sorry, Beth. You've only been here a few weeks. Why don't we give it more time?"

Mrs. Sanders accompanied Beth to the classroom and stood at the door until she was seated, as if she knew, she suspected, that Beth would disobey and go in search of a telephone on her own, or even worse, go out the front door.

Beth stared down at her open book, the words blurred streaks on the page, and thought to herself, it's like being in jail. Bars on the windows, locks on the gates, fences that can't be climbed.

What would happen to Ellen now?

They had to be in their rooms by eight o'clock, after which they had one hour to prepare for bed, to read awhile quietly, a book of their choosing.

Reading was stressed in this school. There was only one hour of television allowed each day other than the video lessons in the classrooms. The hours of learning were long. But the library was well stocked with story books, mysteries, romances and adventures.

When Beth was permitted to go into the library after dinner, she chose to read again one of her favorite books, *Call of the Wild,* by Jack London. There was a quality in it that called to her this lonely night. She sympathized with the dog, that lonely creature under the dominance of man. Sometimes she felt the animals—the dogs, cats, cows in the field—had more feeling and more heart than mankind. And as she curled on her bed dressed in pajamas and robe she lost herself in the white and frozen north, and in the heart of the dog. Her own pain mingled with his, and she forgot where she was.

Sometimes she lifted her head and wondered, why did Faye not want to hear from them?

But there was no answer, and she lowered her face to read again.

The lights went out suddenly.

Had they blinked? That warning blink? She hadn't noticed.

After waiting a few minutes for the lights to come back on, she knew that nine o'clock had come. She closed the book and laid it on the bedside table.

As she crept beneath the summer blanket, she wondered how Ellen was. Would she sleep? Would she be all right tonight?

Joey was doing okay. She had seen him on the playground running with a couple of boys his own age. And later, she had seen him involved in a ball game. Yes, Joey was okay.

Joey would always be okay.

But Ellen . . .

It was Ellen who had found the magic lamp.

Magic lamp!

She sat upright in bed, staring at the opposite wall where tiny flecks of light came through the trees beyond the window and made firefly splashes on the wall.

That thing that Ellen had called her Aladdin's Lamp!

Oh God, oh dear God.

What had happened to it? Ellen had rubbed it, and her hands had burned, and she had screamed. Beth remembered picking it up and finding it cold, but Ellen's palms were hot and red.

And from that moment on the terrible things had

started happening.
She had to find that lamp.

"Hey, Ellen," Teri whispered in the sudden dark of the room. "Don't go to bed."

In the darkness, Teri's hand clutched Ellen's arm and kept her from going to her own bed. They had been sitting on Teri's bed playing some of the games that Teri had with her. Not completing any one, but trying one, then the other, with Teri talking a mile a minute and almost making Ellen forget that she was in a strange room, and she didn't have her doll anymore.

She wanted to cuddle it close in her arms, and bury her face in it, and comfort herself. But it had been in the car wreck, and she didn't know where it was anymore. The doll was lost. She hoped it would be at Faye's house, and that she would find it when Faye was well and they could go home again.

Teri was tugging on her arm, her voice dropped to whispers.

"Can you keep a secret, Ellen?"

"Yes."

"Then come with me."

Ellen allowed herself to be led blindly through the darkness. She heard a door squeak, a small sound like a mouse would make.

"Oh, be quiet, you damned door," Teri whispered. "Come in here, Ellen."

Ellen sensed they were in the closet. Clothes brushed against her face and her shoulder before Teri drew her to the floor. She sat down, and the door squeaked again as Teri pulled it closed.

There were rustling sounds of something soft being zipped open and something taken out. Then suddenly there was a flame flickering, and Ellen jumped back, fear rising like vomit in her throat.

But then she saw it was a tiny flame on a cigarette lighter. Something real. Not the . . . other thing.

"What are you doing? she whispered urgently, staring at the partly illuminated face over the flame of the lighter.

Teri's eyes glowed in the dark with mischief. She leaned closer to Ellen.

"Promise you keep this secret? Cross your heart and hope to die?"

Ellen nodded, stunned into agreeing to almost anything.

"Then do it," Teri demanded. "Cross your heart."

Ellen drew a cross over her heart with her finger.

"Say it."

"Cross my heart and hope to die."

"All right. Now, I'm going to share with you." She dug again into the little zippered case.

"Share what?" Ellen demanded in a whisper of horror. What terrible rule was Teri asking her to break? What awful sin were they going to commit? Ellen was both fascinated and repelled.

"This," Teri said triumphantly, and held up a battered cigarette. "You can share it with me. It's the only one I've got left, but I'm glad you're here to share it with me."

"You *smoke?*"

"Sure. Don't you?"

Ellen shook her head.

"Didn't you *ever?*"

Ellen started to shake her head, then she remembered the unopened package of cigarettes she and Joey had found one day in the lot of the convenience store behind their house. They had hid in the shrubbery and smoked until their mother found them.

"Well, once," she admitted. "But our mama caught us."

"Oh, horrors. What did she do?" Teri held up the bent and mashed white tube in the air as she waited to hear Ellen's story.

"She didn't do anything. She just took them away and told us never to smoke. She said it was dangerous to smoke. That it would give us bad diseases, and things like that."

Teri wrinkled her nose. "Maybe some people, but my mother and dad both smoke, and they don't have diseases. Besides, your mother isn't here."

A faint frown touched Ellen's forehead, a ripple of pain in her heart. It seemed so long ago since her mother had died.

Teri lighted the cigarette, puffing hard. Smoke lifted from the tip, curled upward like an exotic snake in a foreign land, writhing, dancing. Ellen watched it, fascinated, almost hypnotized. She could hear faintly a strange music, a tinkling sound, as from a snake charmer.

"Hey, what's wrong?" Teri asked, and held the cigarette toward Ellen. "Here, your turn."

Ellen drew back, held in the cold throes of terror forming, seeing the background change.

Instead of clothes forming a background behind Teri, smoke swirled, everywhere, thickening, turning to a dull, reddish glow, as flames from another world, another time, licked through an invisible room. The little girl who sat with her legs crossed on the floor in front of her was now surrounded by the smoke, by the glow of the fire, but she seemed not to know it.

"What's wrong?" Teri asked, a voice almost lost, thin and distant, it too in another world, another time. Fear was beginning to be etched on her face as she stared at

Ellen. "What's wrong? Hey, why are you acting so weird?"

Didn't she know a figure was forming behind her? The outlines of a huge body, a man, his hairless head becoming visible against the glow of the fire.

Teri turned, looking behind her, and then she began making noises in her throat, smothered screams that would not be heard beyond this world that had opened and was sucking them in.

Ellen heard another scream. She was on her feet, fighting a gray and dingy curtain that hung over the entrance to the glowing room, trying to get away from the huge, naked man who was reaching forward now . . .

Beth heard the scream, at first seeming to be in her own mind, an extension of her own feeling. The lamp had been magic after all, in a terrible way. She had to get out of this prison and go there, back home, and find it and—

Footsteps pounded in the hall, and the scream vibrated as it came nearer. It was real. It was hideous, terrified, human or animal, she could not tell.

She crawled on her hands and knees to the foot of the bed and then was herself running, jerking the bedroom door open and going out into the dark hall.

The footsteps had stopped, but all along the hall, doors were opening and voices were rising, calling out to one another, half-drowned beneath the continuing scream.

Then Beth saw a glow, rising . . . the fire again, that silent, unreal fire that she had seen behind Ellen . . .

And now she saw the girl, outlined against it.

The girl in the woods. The girl in the fog.

Suddenly the girl was rushing toward her, carrying

behind her the glow of the terrible fire, and Beth saw in the almost non-existent light that it was Ellen.

Ellen was reaching for her, and Beth grabbed her, shook her, held her; and the screams died to sobs, and words, half-formed.

"Fire—Beth—help—her—the monster—Beth—"

And Beth saw then, beyond the shadowy bodies of the other girls as they ran toward the double, locked doors at the end of the hall, that the glow of the fire was real.

Chapter Twenty-Two

Faye rose at dawn, got a drink of water from the bathroom and went back to bed. She had not rested at all. The whole night seemed to be spent in turning over, trying to find a comfortable position. And now she was exhausted.

She closed her eyes again, and the next time she opened them, she found she had gone back to sleep, and it was now late. She sat up and looked at the clock.

Not as late as she had thought. Nine, a bit after.

She reached for the remote control device and turned the television on to the weather channel. For a couple of minutes she listened to world weather, sitting in her bed, her knees drawn up, her arms resting on her knees. She longed for a cup of coffee; but she had switched to decaf, and she felt what she really wanted was a jolt of caffeine. But of course that was out of the question. She dared not subject her baby to any drug, even one so mild as caffeine.

Bored with the weather, yet not ready to leave her bed, Faye swtiched channels again. Phil Donahue on one, game shows on others. An old *I Love Lucy* show on yet another. A black and white movie on another, on two more, in fact. And the news.

She switched it back to the news, something telling her to *listen*.

". . . in the dorm of a private school. The two little girls were alone in the room. The fire started in the closet; Teri Rodenale died, and the other child, Ellen Pendergast, escaped without physical injury. On the foreign front . . ."

Faye switched off the television and sat stunned. Then she got quickly out of bed, went to her desk phone and called the local station.

"Where," she asked, when she got a connection, "was that school fire? I mean, what is the name of the school?"

She listened as the information was looked up and given to her. She hung up and dialed Information and asked for the number of the school. But after it was written down she sat tapping her pen against the paper.

Then, moving quickly, she dropped the pen and went to the closet. She pulled out a maternity dress and threw it across the bed. Comfortable shoes, pantyhose. She went into the bathroom and hurriedly prepared herself for the day.

Then, minutes later, she left the house and backed her car out of the garage.

Halfway to Little Rock, she left the interstate long enough to stop at Stucky's for a sandwich and a cup of coffee. She wasn't hungry; but she knew she was running on nerves, and she needed to reserve her strength for what lay ahead.

It didn't matter what anyone else thought was best for her, she was going after those children. Whatever it was that followed them, that plagued them, she would fight it at their sides.

She drove into the wide driveway at the school to see that two marked police cars were there, and another that Faye suspected was the car of a detective. She felt frozen as she walked up the steps to the front door. The gate had been left open, but she didn't fail to see the padlock that would close it at night.

The front hall was wide and polished, lighted by wall lamps. Combined with the smell of polish, books and old wood, was the pervasive stink of smoke and of something else, perhaps the chemicals used to put out the fire, or of something more horrible. Standing around in silence were a few older girls, ages perhaps fourteen or fifteen. Their faces were as still and emotionless as if they had been carved from alabaster, but in their eyes were vestiges of shock.

A woman came forward to meet Faye. There was no smile on her face.

"I'm Mrs. Pendergast," Faye said. "I've come to see my children."

The woman stared at her, as if to question her identity, then she turned toward a closed door and knocked. She opened it, disappeared inside and then returned almost immediately.

"Go on in. Mrs. Sanders will see you." She turned toward the girls and made a herding motion with her hands. "Let's go to the study hall, girls."

Faye stepped across the threshold of the brown and beige office. Other than the woman behind the desk, there was one man, wearing a brown suit, standing at the end of the desk, his hands in his pockets. He was of indeterminate age, but there was no question of his interest in her. He watched her with steady eyes, as if trying to find whatever answer he sought somewhere within her.

Faye went to the desk. "I'm the stepmother of the Pendergast children. I want to know if they're all right."

"Do you have identification, Ma'am?" the man said, holding out his hand.

Faye took her driver's license from her purse and gave it to him. The photo on it was only a few months old. He looked at it, then at her, nodded and gave it back. "Mrs. Faye Pendergast," he said, in confirmation.

"Won't you sit down, Mrs. Pendergast?" Mrs. Sanders said. "They're as well as can be expected. There was no physical injury to Ellen, I'm glad to say. But the other child has died."

Mrs. Sanders' chin began to shake, and she stopped talking.

The man said, "I'm Detective Coleman, Mrs. Pendergast. I understand that your daughter, Ellen, has been involved recently in other deaths. Could you tell me about them?"

"Involved? It was a fire, the newscaster said. Ellen is not—would not—she couldn't have started that fire. There has *never* been another incident of that kind to my knowledge."

Both people seemed to squirm. Their movements were sudden and instinctive, a need, perhaps, Faye thought, to be removed from the circumstances, whatever they were. Other deaths? Involved? What were they talking about? Not . . . !

A terrible fury threatened to consume Faye. Her voice quivered. The fear of the unknown hovered beneath her anger. "You're not trying to tell me that you suspect that little girl, Ellen, of being responsible for the other girl's death! Hasn't enough happened to her? It is true her mother was murdered. And her father died in a car crash, but Ellen's involvement was only her proximity. She certainly was not responsible."

"What of the other deaths, Mrs. Pendergast?"

"The other deaths!"

"Of course we know Ellen was not responsible, but—"

"But nothing! You solve them, Detective—! You solve them, and then you tell us! Don't accuse a seven-year-old child of being involved. Whatever tenuous meaning there is behind that!"

It seemed a long time that he simply stared at her, into her eyes, still searching for something he hoped to find.

He said at last, "No, of course we aren't accusing Ellen of anything. She was found in the hall, running, screaming. The other child had been smoking in the closet. It wasn't the first time she'd smoked cigarettes in there. But whatever happened to her defies understanding, Mrs. Pendergast. But perhaps you know that. We were going to contact you, ask you some questions. I'm glad you came. And your kids will be glad to see you."

Faye backed up and found a chair. She sat down, weakness overcoming her.

Mrs. Sanders said, "Beth has been asking to talk to you. Demanding, in fact. I didn't know what to do. Your sister said you were not well and were not to be bothered with problems at this time."

"I'm perfectly well," Faye snapped. Her anger switched to Janet. Why couldn't she mind her own business? But immediately she felt guilty for being mad at Janet. She had only done what she thought was best for her. Janet could hardly be expected to put children she scarcely knew above the welfare of her own relatives, or what she thought was that welfare.

"May I see Beth now?" Faye asked. "And I want to take the three children home with me this afternoon."

Mrs. Sanders looked pointedly at the detective. He shrugged.

"I see no reason why you can't. Just so we know where to find you when we need to." He removed his hands from his pockets, took a cigarette from an inner pocket on his coat, looked at it, then started to stuff it back into the rumpled package.

Mrs. Sanders said, surprising Faye, "You may smoke if you want to, Detective Coleman."

"Oh no, thanks. I'm trying to quit." He looked at it longingly.

"Mrs. Pendergast," Mrs. Sanders said. "Before you see the children, I would like you to talk with our counselor." She rose from behind her desk and went toward a side door. She looked back at Faye expectantly.

Faye got up and followed her.

Mrs. Sanders said, "You might be interested in this, Detective, if you want to come along."

"Yes, thanks." His eyebrows had raised slightly, and Faye could see he was as puzzled as she.

They crossed a short inner hall from which opened a bathroom on one side and looked into the dim recesses of a storage area on the other. Shelves on the walls held files. Faye suspected that every child who had been in this school from its foundation date of 1935 still had a file stashed here.

They went through another door and into a smaller office. It was equipped with a desk and several chairs. The woman who rose from the desk was perhaps ten years older than Mrs. Sanders. A gentle, motherly type with pleasant eyes and soft hair that had been tinted a pale blond-gray.

"Our school counselor, Mrs. Raleigh. Mrs. Pendergast, Ellen's stepmother, Mrs. Raleigh. And Detective Coleman."

They sat down. Faye looked at her watch. It had been almost four hours since she left Fort Smith. She was anxious to get the children and leave. Too anxious, perhaps, as if she had a deep, subconscious feeling that in the end they would not let the children go.

What were her legal rights? Why hadn't she talked to an attorney about this? But yesterday she had been facing the future without them, she remembered, passively willing to let others say what she should and should not do.

Mrs. Raleigh said, "I talked with Ellen yesterday for quite a while. She had been having nightmares, and she had shown unusual fear in her daily life. She seemed afraid of her own shadow, you could say. She hadn't been making friends. She was a quiet student, and not a very good one. We know she's capable of more. Her tests put her in the above average group."

She paused, looking from one face to the other. She had their attention. Faye had stopped looking at her watch and was now listening.

The counselor continued, "At first she wouldn't talk. I asked her what was terrifying her, and she simply looked at me. But when I asked her about her mother, and her mother's death, she told me—and I want you to understand she fully believes this—that it was a monster, or monsters. Then, in further conversation, she said it changes form, it has followed her, it goes everywhere she goes and it kills people. It killed her little friend's mother, she said. And today, in hysterics, she cried that 'the monster' killed her roommate."

Mrs. Sanders supplied, "We suggest, Mrs. Pendergast, that you have Ellen evaluated by a psychiatrist, as soon as you can get an appointment."

Detective Coleman folded his arms across his chest. There was a slight smirk on his face. He started to speak, then changed his mind, and the smirk became a frown.

Mrs. Sanders said, "There was no one in the room with the girls when the fire and the death happened, that we can determine. The outside doors were locked as always, that is, the doors leading into the girls' dormitory, and the windows are secured. The police are working on that, of course. And of course there are keys . . . but . . ."

Faye's voice sounded unnatural to her own ears when she asked, "How exactly did the child die? Smoke inhalation?"

"Oh, no," Mrs. Sanders said quickly, too soon. "That is, we don't know."

The detective cleared his voice and said, "The body has been taken to the medical examiner. The results are not in."

"There was blood," Mrs. Sanders said, putting one hand to her face in a wiping motion. She ended it with a deep sigh.

Faye stood up. "Is there any reason I can't see my children now? I'd like to get started home." She had to get them away from here as fast as possible.

The counselor said, "You will see that Ellen is taken to a doctor?"

"Yes."

Mrs. Sanders nodded. "Call Marietta and have her bring Beth. Tell her to get their things together, then she can bring Ellen and Joey to the waiting room out front. Beth wants to talk to you in private, Mrs. Pendergast. If you'd just wait here, she'll be along soon."

Mrs. Raleigh was giving instructions into the telephone. The others stood up, and Faye remained standing. In private? The counselor stayed, she saw, and the door was left open when Mrs. Sanders took the detective back through the short corridor. Faye could hear their voices, growing fainter as they passed beyond walls. Then a door closed, and there was silence.

Mrs. Raleigh smiled at her. "You've had a long drive today," she said with a tone of small talk. "Do you plan to drive back today?"

"Yes."

"Umm. I see. I thought you might spend the night here. You do have a sister living here?"

"Yes, I do."

"Ummm." Mrs. Raleigh eyed her, a distant smile on her face, questions in her eyes.

Faye hoped she wouldn't ask them. She didn't know the answers either. She knew only that she wanted the kids with her, and they would fight . . . whatever it was they had to fight.

"Mrs. Pendergast," the counselor finally said, softly, "Do you believe in the supernatural?"

"Supernatural? Like ghosts and things of that nature? Of course not."

"I think you should prepare to believe," she said very softly, as if she were whispering terrible secrets. "I didn't want to say anything in front of them, but there is something truly horrible attached, somehow, to that child. She told me of fire, and smoke, so thick you couldn't see, and of figures—or a figure—forming in it and becoming real. A huge figure. She believes it, and after seeing Teri, the little girl who was killed, I believe, too. If you hadn't come today, the children would have been sent away. Ellen to a psychiatric hospital, probably, and the other two to foster homes. I asked you in front of the detective and Mrs. Sanders to take Ellen to a doctor, but that was only a formality. You need more than a doctor, Mrs. Pendergast. If you're a religious person, you might try a priest. Someone who believes in demons. And if I were you, even if you aren't a religious person, I would seriously consider a priest who believes in demons. Because that's what you've got here. And it's somehow part of that little girl. Ellen."

Faye stared at the counselor, but before she could begin to formulate her thoughts on this startling information, the door opened. She had only a glimpse of the two at the door, before Beth flew at her with her arms out.

Faye hugged Beth, her hand on the back of Beth's head. She felt the thin body trembling, and the wetness of Beth's tears dampening her shoulder.

"Oh Faye. I'm so glad you're here. I've been trying and trying to get in touch with you. They wouldn't let me call you, Faye."

Faye looked down into Beth's face, her anger rising again. "Why on earth not?" But then she knew. Janet had told them, no doubt, that she wasn't to be bothered with their problems.

"Well, I'm here now. And I'm taking you home."

A light came on in Beth's face. "Are you? Are you really?"

"Yes. For always."

"I've got to talk to you, Faye," Beth cried urgently. "It's very important. I've got to talk to you, tell you something. I don't want anyone to hear."

Mrs. Raleigh gave Faye her smile, back again, covering whatever she was thinking. "I'll step out for a few minutes."

As soon as the door closed behind her Beth cried out with that awful urgency that held her features in their tight expression, "Faye, I know what it is. The cat, the little girl, the—the thing that kills. Faye, it's the *lamp,* that thing that Ellen bought at the garage sale last spring. Before Mama died."

"What? Slow down, Beth. Here, do you want to sit down?"

"No, no. Faye, we've got to go back. We've got to go home, to my old home, to Mama's house, where she was killed. It's there, somewhere. We left it there. I haven't seen it since the day Ellen bought it—"

"Beth, please. Start at the beginning and explain it

to me."

Beth looked at her feet, licked her lips and swallowed. Then, in control, she told slowly and carefully of the small instrument that Ellen had bought at the garage sale.

"She called it her Aladdin's Lamp. We all laughed at her for spending her allowance on it. She took it up to her bedroom, and Joey and I went with her. She began to rub it, calling for the genie, and then she screamed. It was hot, she said. And it had burned her hands, I could see that. But when I felt it I couldn't feel anything."

"What happened to it?"

"I don't know. It's still in her room, I guess. We have to go back and get it, Faye. We have to, don't you see? We've got to get rid of it, destroy it."

Faye tried to put it all together, all that she had seen, all the counselor had said, and now this. Incredible. *Impossible.*

"Please, Faye, please." Beth held her hands so tightly they began to hurt. "Oh God, Faye, please don't say no. You're the only one who will help us, I know. If you don't, it may kill us all. It will, it will kill Ellen, I know."

It was Beth's desperation that made up her mind. The rest of it seemed too preposterous to even be able to consider, even remotely. It was as if she were standing on the edge of a terrible knowledge, and her human brain just could not see it. She felt her limitations. What a child believed, was true, but as an adult, taught not to believe these things, she had to stand apart from it. She wanted to ask, "What on earth, in heaven or hell, did a little metal pot have to do with all this?"

"An evil genie," Beth said, and Faye realized she had spoken her question aloud. "Ellen brought forth a genie! Just like she believed she would!"

"Then . . ." she felt foolish asking this question.

"Why has it not killed you, me, Joey, and even Ellen herself?"

Beth's voice was scarcely audible. "I don't know. But it will, if we don't get rid of its—its beginning, its source."

"And you think that will destroy it?"

"It has to."

Beth looked into Faye's eyes, and the terror Faye saw there seemed as endless as space.

"It has to," Beth whispered.

There was a tap on the door, and the door opened a second later. Mrs. Sanders looked in.

"The children are in the waiting room. Their things will be brought down and put into your car, Mrs. Pendergast."

"Thank you."

With Beth's hand in hers, Faye followed Mrs. Sanders across the main hall and into the waiting room. Joey and Ellen stood in the middle of the room as if they were two lost lambs, and Faye dropped Beth's hands and opened her arms. Joey ran to her immediately, but Ellen stood staring as if she didn't believe Faye was really there.

"Ellen," Faye said gently. "I've come to take you home."

Ellen rushed toward her, wrapping her arms so tightly around both Faye and Joey that Joey began to squirm.

Faye gave Ellen a kiss on the forehead. "It's all right. It's going to be all right, Ellen."

If only she could make those words, that promise, come true, she thought as she drove back toward Fort Smith.

They stopped in a small town at a McDonald's for

Happy Meals. The moment Joey had seen the sign he started calling for a stop, and to Faye's delight Ellen had joined him. This simple thing seemed to take her out of her depression, at least for a while.

"Are we going . . . ?" Beth asked, looking at Faye beseechingly.

Faye knew what she meant. "Yes, as soon as we get home and make the arrangements, as soon as we can get a flight out."

"Where are we going?" Joey asked.

"Eat," Beth said. "We have to hurry."

"Why?"

Beth looked at Faye again for help, and Faye said, "We're going back to your old home, Joey, in California."

"Why?"

"We have to get something."

They were surrounded by booths, tables, people. But none of them were paying attention. Feeling that in some way the presence of all the kids and parents might help Ellen to feel less threatened, Faye said, "Ellen, do you remember the lamp you bought at the garage sale?"

She looked up, eyes widened. "My Aladdin's Lamp?"

"Yes. Where is it?"

"I don't know." Her eyes darted left, in thought, then she frowned. "I don't know. There. Somewhere. It burned my hands, and I put it in the corner of my room."

"Well, we're going back to get it."

Ellen drew a long breath. "Okay."

Joey looked from one face to the other and evidently decided it wasn't worth pursuing. He finished eating his cheeseburger.

Faye looked out the window at the green symmetry of the cedar trees that were scattered over the slope of the low hill as if they had been planted. A bright red cardinal sat on the very tip of one of the nearest trees, and although she couldn't hear its song, she could see that it was singing, its beak opening, closing, its head tipping back. A moment later its mate flew near.

She felt a rush of longing for Gavin. For the first time she wondered if his death was in some way tied in with the others.

Would any of them survive even to get to California, to look for the thing that Beth was so certain was the source of the horror?

But what choice did they have but to go and try to find it, and . . . let the next step take care of itself? They were pursued, this she fully believed now, even if she couldn't accept, in her conscious mind, the convictions either of Mrs. Raleigh or Beth. She didn't understand what was happening, what had happened. She was only filled with terror of what might happen now.

"Where's my doll?" Ellen asked suddenly.

Faye was brought back from her black thoughts with a jolt. "Why . . . it's at home. The police took it from the car, along with the luggage, and brought it home when I got out of the hospital. I washed it for you. I was going to give it to you the first chance I got, but I forgot to bring it this morning. I'm sorry, Ellen."

"Can we go get it? Before we leave?"

"Yes, of course. We have to go back to the house to get the key to the California house."

Beth said, "Hurry up, Joey."

Joey stuffed the last of his French fries into his mouth and stood at the end of the bench on one knee. "I got to go to the bathroom."

"Okay, go on," Beth said. She looked down the hall toward the bathrooms. A few people were walking along, coming, going.

He had to go alone, Faye realized, though she would

have liked to keep all three of the children in sight, within reach. Her own need for bathroom facilities was increasing, it seemed, with each day. She got up.

"We'll go down the hall with you, Joey. All of us need to go wash our hands."

She didn't want to transfer her fear to them. Joey seemed almost normal, just slightly less boisterous than the other boys his age in the restaurant, and she wanted him to stay as happy as he could. As long as possible. She didn't know what they were facing, but she was terribly afraid that none of them would escape unharmed.

Was her baby destined never to live at all?

Chapter Twenty-Three

The sun had gone down when they reached the large brick house on the hill above Fort Smith. Where once Faye had loved the turn into the driveway and the tall trees that filled the long front grounds between house and street, she now felt an eerieness racing coldly along her spine, as if she were being warned: *don't go into that house.*

She said brightly, her voice forcing something she didn't feel, "I've put this old barn up for sale, kids. We're going to buy us a house that's all on one floor. We'll get one with four bedrooms, one for each of us, that has bunches of sliding doors out onto a long deck. Other than that all we need is a big family room and kitchen. Maybe a utility room. More decks or terraces. We'll have cedar and pine trees in the yard, instead of so many oak. We'll have lots of windows."

"What about the baby's room?" Beth asked.

Faye was startled by the question. Not for one instant had she counted the baby.

She drew the car in under the *porte-co-chere,* and the kids began piling out. By the time she had her house key out and was unlocking the door, they were crowded behind her, waiting.

Joey ran back and started to drag his small suitcase out of the car.

"Leave it," Beth ordered, then looked at Faye for confirmation. "Do we bring our clothes in?"

Faye opened the door and turned on the hall light. The end of the hall seemed lost in darkness, and she wished in sick longing that Gavin was here to go ahead of them with his strength and his fearlessness. But she must not let the children know how anxious she was to hurry and get out of this house. She was developing an urge to run and keep running.

"Yes, let's bring it all in. We need to repack, to take only enough to last a couple of days. Only what we can carry with us on the plane."

She helped them get the bags into the house. And then she went to the telephone in the kitchen and called the airport. The agent told her there was a taxi plane out to Dallas in three hours. But they would have a wait of four more hours in Dallas before they could get a flight on to Los Angeles.

She heard a soft sound behind her, a murmuring moan. For a short time, while she was talking on the phone to the agent at the airport, she had forgotten the fear that was stalking her, and it came back as she realized she was still in the big, silent house. She turned but saw Ellen, her face lowered to the scruffy, battered old rag doll. There was on her face a look of love and tenderness, a soft smile.

She had only been crooning to the doll.

Beth came rushing in from the inner hall, with Joey behind her. Each of them was carrying a small suitcase, and Beth had her old canvas bag slung over her shoulder.

"We've packed," she said, and opened a suitcase. "Is this all right? Is this enough?"

There was animation on their faces, Faye saw with relief. Ellen was absorbed in her doll, comforted beyond belief by it. Beth was so involved in getting ready to go she had forgotten to be afraid. And Joey . . . Joey seemed to have the miraculous ability to live in the moment.

Three hours later they were in a small taxi plane and lifting off for Dallas. The night sky showed stars of incredible brilliance over the huge, flat plain. Ellen sat beside Faye, and Joey was with Beth in the seat behind.

It seemed they had hardly gotten into the air before the lights of Dallas were below them, and the plane was circling and getting ready to land.

Faye had never been so glad to feel land under her feet again. The queasiness she had experienced in the body of the small plane had kept her mind occupied, but it was not a pleasant experience.

In the Dallas airport they had to stay where they would not be separated from Joey, and the four hour wait was another period of misery for Faye. The kids curled up on a padded bench and slept, Ellen with her doll clasped tightly in her arms.

Looking at her, Faye wondered at the weeks the child had to be without the emotional security of the doll. Well, they were together now.

Faye leaned her head back and almost went to sleep, but not daring to let herself go, to take a chance on missing their flight.

Time slipped by, minute by minute, and then the voice was calling out their scheduled flight number. Faye roused the kids. They got up, sleepy-eyed and wordless, and followed her.

She slept on the plane, her seat back, a soft pillow under her head. Ellen sat beside her, and Beth and Joey were across the aisle. It was a time of quiet suspension, of dreamlessness and timelessness.

A few hours later they stepped out into the murky,

smoggy sunlight of Los Angeles in the early morning. A line of cabs was parked at the curb, and Faye sank gratefully into the corner of the seat, the kids crowded in beside her. The driver asked if one of them would like to sit up front, but they each shook their heads.

The taxi stopped at the entrance to a weedy, overgrown driveway, and Faye stood on cracked pavement, through which the weeds grew, and looked at the closed and abandoned house. She hadn't formed a picture in her mind of what this house, this former home of Beth, Ellen and Joey, looked like, but she felt surprise now, at the rundown condition, the overgrown yard, the peeling paint.

It was a cottage style, of the twenties or thirties, with a deep front porch, and a second floor with slanted roofline, the dormers on all four sides. There was only one tall tree, and that in the backyard, but the front yard seemed filled with overgrown shrubbery. The area around the house, up and down the street in both directions, and on the streets adjacent, had gone commercial. She could see something like a warehouse beyond the yard boundary on one side, and the signs and activities behind of a convenience store.

The children stood beside and slightly behind her as the taxi drew away and left them alone with the house. They were silent. When she glanced back at them she saw three solemn faces staring at the house.

Faye removed the key from her purse. "Well, are we ready?"

Beth moved forward, going along the cracked pavement of the old driveway, toward the small, detached garage. Faye followed. The key, Beth had told her earlier, when they had taken it from among Gavin's papers, was for the back door. She didn't know if the front door even had a key. They had never used it; they had never unlocked it from the outside. They had opened it only to company, to guests.

They followed a path up a narrow walk to the rear screened porch. The screen had been knocked out of the lower part of the screen door, and Joey said adamantly, "Who's been tearing up our house?"

No one answered him. Beth pulled the door open, and they crossed the boards of the back porch.

Faye inserted the key into the lock.

Joey had gone along the porch, peering into the windows. "They didn't break any windows, did they?" he said, and still no one answered him. "But they broke the screen."

The lock turned reluctantly, requiring Faye to use both hands and put all her strength behind it.

The door opened, and Faye replaced the key in her purse. Without entering the house, she put one hand against the door and pushed it inward. It swung about six inches and stopped.

A musty odor boiled out, the smell of a house closed for a long, long time, unaccountably, since it had only been three months since Blythe had been killed. Perhaps it was the smell of death, of blood not cleaned out of the walls and floors. Of memory seared into the wood. Of the unknown still lingering, this its original lair.

The house was dim, what sunlight there was, what air and freshness, left beyond the blinded windows. Faye did not move to lift the blinds as she entered the kitchen.

She saw cabinets at one end, and a table and chairs beside double windows at the other. The floor was covered in linoleum, and there were streaks of darkness by the inner door, a rustiness that Faye looked at and recoiled from. But she had to go on, to reach that upstairs bedroom where Ellen had left her Aladdin's Lamp.

Faye felt herself frowning. Suddenly she wondered what she was doing here. Of what possible harm could a toy be? But before she could turn and leave this house of death, Beth had entered and walked past her. She stopped by the door.

"It's this way," she said in a lowered voice. "We have to go through here."

Joey hung back on the porch.

"I don't want to go in there," he said.

Beth looked at him. She hesitated. Then said, "Okay. Is it okay if he stays out there, Faye?"

"I don't see why not."

Beth said, "But Ellen . . . do you want to stay with Joey, Ellen? Just tell me where you left it."

Ellen was shaking her head. Then she handed her doll to Joey. "Will you keep my doll, Joey?"

"I don't want it."

"Please, Joey."

"Well, okay. I'll put it on the porch. And you can get it when you come out. I'm going out to the garage to see if my old bike is still there. Want to go with me, Ellen?"

Ellen shook her head. Her eyes were on the inner door, her head lifted as if she were listening for something above. The stance, the appearance of the child, so removed in some way suddenly, sent a cold rush of terror into Faye's heart. Suddenly here they were, and she had become the most fearful of all. It was something she did not want Beth and Ellen to know. She tried to smile, but gave it up.

"Shall we go in now?" she asked.

Beth nodded, but Ellen seemed unaware that she had spoken. She was moving toward the door almost like a sleepwalker.

Ellen entered the dim hallway. She could see the big

arch of the doorway into the living room; but someone had hung a blanket over it, and the living room was hidden. She could see the newel post at the bottom of the stairs, and she could see the dark spots on the rugs.

She stared at the dark spots.

They were no longer red; they were dirty brown.

Her mother's blood grown old.

She moved forward into the shadowed house, her hand trailing along the wall. Being here seemed strange. Everything looked familiar, and now she remembered it, but it was a forgotten familiarity, as if her mind hadn't remembered it until now. Images flashed through her mind, like a playback on the VCR when it was fast-forwarded.

She and Joey running down the hallway, happy, trying to keep the other behind, shoving each other, stumbling, running, racing for the door to the kitchen where the smell of waffles came sweet and happy. Their mother had made waffles for this special day. What was it? Her birthday? Joey's birthday? Beth's? Then their mother's head came looking at them around the door, trying to look mean. Stop that running in the house. Stop fighting. Stop shoving each other. It was a special day just for love, their mother said.

Ellen went on, another few steps toward the foot of the stairs. She knew that Beth and Faye had entered the hallway, too, now. She could hear their low voices behind her, but their words meant nothing. Ellen listened now only to the voices within her.

"Ellen, what's wrong, dear?" her mother had asked, meeting her in the doorway, the arched doorway. "Ellen, Ellen," she had said, as if she were talking to someone far away. "What are you carrying, Ellen?" Not until then did Ellen realize she held something in her hands.

She had reached the newel post, the bottom step of

the stairway that clung to the wall. She looked at the dark blanket hanging across the archway of the door and the dark brown spots that streaked across the rug. On the stairs were more spots, and one of them, on the second step up, was the footstep of a little person. The toes, the heel, dark brown. Made with her bare foot and her mother's blood.

Someone was touching her on the back, and she jerked away, terror bitter like medicine in her throat. Then she saw it was Beth.

"Show me where it is, Ellen," Beth said.

What are you going to do with it? But her voice was silent. The words spoken only in her head. She climbed the stairs, her legs thin and weak. She had to hold to the banister to keep from falling back down the stairs.

The upper hall in this house was short. It opened only into four bedrooms. The door at the front was closed. Her mother's room. The next door was hers. She stood looking at the knob until Beth reached past her and pushed the door open.

The room had shrunk, and faded, and darkened. The blind on the window shut out the light.

Beth flicked the switch at the entrance, but the light didn't come on.

"I forgot," Beth said. "The electricity is off."

Faye walked past them and went to the window. "Can't we raise the blind for a few minutes?" And the blind went up, letting in light that didn't touch the shadows in the corners.

"Where did you put it, Ellen?" Beth said, and Ellen looked toward the corner that was hidden behind the opened closet door. Beth followed the direction of the gaze and shut the closet door. In the corner was one old teddy bear and a doll with a rumpled dress that once had been fancy. They were leaning against each other, a dark, sooty dust crusted on their heads.

Beth bent and moved them, but the Aladdin's Lamp wasn't there.

Beth asked her again, but she only stared into the corner. She had taken it off the bed, moved it carefully over to the corner and put it on the floor. She was afraid of it now. It had burned her hands.

The night was dark. She had gotten out of bed sometime, somehow, she had no memory of when or why, and she had gone downstairs, very slowly, carefully putting one foot, then the other, on the next step down, and the next. She hadn't been holding the banister because her hands were full. She reached the foot of the stairs, and the archway of the living room and light, and her mother rose from the sofa where she was reading and came toward her. She talked, spoke soft words, at first, then she took the thing from her hands and put it on the piano. Aladdin's Lamp.

Beth began looking around the room, under the bed, in the closet. Faye stood in the middle of the room, turning, then she, too, began to look. It was like they were playing the game I-Spy, find the thimble. They were silent figures in a video, the sound muted.

She rose again from her bed, not long after her mother left the room, and she went downstairs again. there was the smell of smoke, an odor that stung her nostrils and burned her eyes. She stood in the archway of the living room and saw her mother standing there, looking at something in the smoke that rose from the hollow stem of Aladdin's Lamp.

A Genie!

It trailed up, twisting as it formed, the head, huge, shaped like an enormous egg, with no hair. Its eyes thin and slitted, with nothing in them. Its body, then, great, bulging. It had great, massive thighs, and there was something between them—a weapon—for killing—

It was wavering above the floor, this genie from her magic lamp, and it was coming to kill her, its slitted eyes pinned on her where she stood in the archway. Its naked body terrifying and bad. It wanted her. It was reaching for her. But the figure of her mother was suddenly between them, and she shoved at Ellen and told her to run; but her mother had pushed too hard, and she fell instead. But the genie turned then, and his hands found her mother.

She fought. Her hands struck his huge body, and the sound was like the soft thuds of a heartbeat. He picked her mother up and began killing her—

The genie was killing her mother, and the blood was flowing; and Ellen rose to her hands and knees and crawled forward, into the blood that dripped down from the limp body of her mother.

Then her mother was lying on the floor, and someone was leading Ellen away. Up the stairs and to her bed. Someone was covering her.

A little girl. Dressed in rags, her black hair stringy. She looked, and the girl was gone.

And then she forgot.

But now she knew where the Aladdin's Lamp was, and she turned silently, while they weren't looking, and went out of the room and down the stairs.

She stopped at the blanket, and her arms and legs were cold with the terror that came from somewhere inside her and rippled warning over her skin. Her breath was shallow and fast, as if she had been running hard for a very long time.

It was her genie. She had brought him forth from his lamp. She had freed him. Only she could put him back into his lamp.

She pushed aside the blanket and entered the dark living room.

She stood, heart pounding, saliva rising into her mouth, and then her mouth turning dry when she swallowed.

The front windows had light beyond the blinds, but only a small part of it came into the room. It took a minute for her eyes to adjust. First of all she saw the dark blotches all over the rug. Her mother's blood. Mama had crawled on her hands and knees, trying to get away. And at last she had fallen, face down, over the spilling of her own body. Ellen saw the dark brown of where she had been.

She lifted her eyes. There was the fireplace, against the wall opposite the archway. And to the left, against the end wall, were the sofa and the lamp table. And nearer, to her immediate left, was the old upright piano.

Aladdin's Lamp sat on the top of the piano, at the far end.

Ellen went to it, and looked up at it. The stem seemed to be more blackened, and there were smoke stains she didn't remember.

She drew a long breath.

She reached for it, held it in her hands and felt the heat begin to rise and grow hotter and hotter.

The genie wanted her; it was her genie. If she let him go, he would kill Beth, and Faye, and sometime, before he was through, he would kill everyone around her, perhaps even Joey. Just as he had managed to kill her daddy.

She had released him to prey upon others around her. He was formed of fire and smoke and all things bad and evil. Of embers and coals from that terrible place she had heard about, hell.

The smoke rose from the bowl; the heat began to sear her hands. But she held to it, even as the smoke turned to flames. The figure began forming, the great, naked, egg-shaped head, the massive shoulders . . . the thighs . . . *the thing that killed* . . .

Ellen dropped the magic lamp and stumbled back. She started to run, and then she remembered. He had followed her, wherever she went, and he had killed. He had let her live, because she was his master, but it was she he needed.

"Go back," she cried, "go back in to the lamp, Genie. go back!"

But he kept rising, larger and larger in the room. Smoke swirled around him so that he seemed merely a part of it, and behind, like a distant forest fire, or a setting sun, the red glow began.

"Go back," Ellen cried once more, but it was too late. She didn't know the magic that would make him go away.

He had come for her.

She had made him; she had revived him from long, long ago when the magic lamp was made, when people made magic lamps. He was hers, and she was his.

That, then was the answer.

She was his master. He had no mind of his own. Only hers.

He needed her to lead him back where he belonged.

She had to go with him.

There was no way out.

She turned and looked toward the door, and saw the curtain, no longer a blue blanket but a dirty, colorless, coarse rag, shredded and torn at the bottom. And standing in front of it was a girl, the girl in the woods, the girl in the corridor at the school. She had raised her hand and was beckoning for Ellen to follow her. She turned and went through the curtain, through the thick and choking smoke, out of the reach of the flames. Ellen followed her. She reached the archway of the room, the door to escape, and stopped.

Then she turned back and faced into the fire and heat and smoke, and the roiling figure that was forming within it.

Beth stood like a stone all at once, alert, eyes rounded, troubled. "Where's Ellen?"

Faye caught the alarm in her voice and almost instantly smelled the smoke. She looked toward the door and saw that it had been closed. The smell of the smoke was growing stronger, and it seemed to Faye in her sudden panic that she could see tendrils of it coming into the room around the door.

"Where's Ellen?" Beth screamed.

Faye rushed toward the door and pulled it open. Smoke, like a wall, almost knocked her back into the room. It obscured the hallway, the top of the stairs.

Fire!

"Beth! Beth, where are you?" Faye shouted. *"Ellen!"*

Beth's hand fumbled for hers, and with it clutched desperately against her, Faye stumbled out into the hallway, her free hand over her nose and mouth. She bent low, hoped Beth would do the same, and felt her way along the hall. The stairs were gone, smothered in the thick, dark smoke that writhed like clouds in an angry storm.

Her toe felt the drop of the top step, and she moved down, trying not to hurry so fast that she would stumble and fall. Somewhere in the thick smoke below she could see a wall of flames. The sound of it reached her, a living sound of a different kind of life, devouring everything in its way.

They had to pass by the flames in order to reach the door, and the lower they got on the stairway, the more intense the heat became.

It tortured and burned, the pain almost unbearable.

Faye could see it only as a red glow, across the hall.

She turned toward the back of the house, led only by memory but Beth was resisting, pulling against her. Faye gave in and turned.

Within the swirling smoke, a figure emerged, small, vague in outline, moving through the flames as if untouched. Faye's burning eyes lost her, then found her again as she paused and looked back.

Ellen.

And yet . . . Ellen's blond hair had turned dark. It hung long and straight down her back, glistening in the light of the fire. Smoke obscured her again, and she moved away.

Beth pulled Faye, following the little girl, blindly. Faye moved with them, nearer to the fire, it seemed, and then against a wall.

They had gone the wrong way! Faye pulled against Beth's resisting figure, no longer able to judge directions. They were trapped in the dense smoke.

Faye realized Beth was fumbling at the wall. The front door. The heat pushed at them as Beth released the lock. Then the door was open, and they were stumbling out onto the front porch, into the blessed light and air.

Behind them the roar of the fire increased.

Flames licked out the doorway, smoke rolled in clouds. Ahead of her, standing safely now in the yard, Faye saw Ellen . . . no, not Ellen. A strange child with long black hair and slanted almond eyes. She saw her clearly, and then she was gone in a swirl of smoke.

Coughing, Faye collapsed against the porch railing, bent over, aware of a sharp pain in her stomach. Then someone grabbed her arm and forced her on, away from the house, into the driveway.

Joey came running around from behind the house, his eyes moons of alarm.

"The house is on fire," he cried, his voice almost swallowed by the roar.

"Where's Ellen?" Beth asked. "Isn't she with you, Joey?"

Across the fence behind the house a crowd had gathered. Cars passing along the street slowed and stopped. Faces stared.

Somewhere in the distance sirens screamed, coming closer.

Faye ran, looking for Ellen, but she was not among the crowd that was gathering at the edges of the yard.

She faced into the flames of the burning house, and it seemed for a moment that she could see Ellen's face, like a painting, or a photograph, still, unsmiling, accepting.

Then it was gone.

Epilogue

David ran down the sidewalk with a great sense of freedom. Christmas vacation had started, and he didn't have to go to school for two weeks. He wished Joey still lived down on the next block so they could play.

He paused and pulled out of his pocket the crumpled Christmas card and letter that Joey had sent him, straightening out the wrinkles so he could read the words again. Cars, passing him on the right, rumpled the page in his hand with the wind they stirred.

> Dear David. Merry Christmas. How are you? I am fine. I and Beth are living in our new house with Faye, our mom. We have a new baby sister. She's two months old now. We named her Mary Ellen. After our sister Ellen. I really miss Ellen. I miss you, too. My bedroom has got glass doors that open out onto the deck at the back of the house. And I like school. I'm sending you my address so you can write to me. Joey.

A truck came roaring along the street behind David, and he turned to get a look at it. An eighteen wheeler, big as a house, thundering like a hundred horses in a western movie it swept by almost within his reach. Wow! Maybe someday he'd drive one of those.

A gust of wind pulled at him as if he were in the center of a hurricane, and the envelope, card and letter were jerked out of his hand and engulfed by the truck.

It passed on by, making the earth tremble where David stood. Behind it came a car, then another. Then came a moment of stillness, and David rushed out into the street to look for his letter. But it was gone, swallowed by the truck in the hurricane of wind generated by its passing.

David got out of the street to avoid the next car and stood staring.

Gone. The letter from Joey, his best friend.

The address was gone. Everything.

Now he didn't know where to write to let Joey know he had gotten the card and Joey's new address.

He stood still for several minutes remembering Joey and the good times they'd had together.

He remembered the fire, too.

It had been the biggest and loudest fire David had ever dreamed of seeing. He had seen the flames rising toward the sky even before he heard the screams of the fire engines, and he had run out of his house to go see about it, with his mama yelling at him to come back. So he'd had to go back and stand on his own porch, while no more than a block away the fire had burned and burned.

Finally, it had died down, and in the night he had looked out of his window and watched the glow of the coals. He had gone to sleep by his window, and the glow was still there, shrinking, like a strange creature from outer space that couldn't bear the atmosphere on earth.

His folks had told him to stay away from the burned lot, but that was almost three months ago. Now, his day suddenly long and lonely, he walked on down the street toward the place where Joey used to live.

He entered the yard slowly, looking at the dark pile of ashes where the house had burned. The fire had burned the grass, too, in jagged black streaks out toward the fences; and it had turned the bark of the tree in the backyard black on one side, and the leaves were shriveled and curled. His dad had said the trees would die now. The garage looked funny standing there all by itself on the burned grass of the empty lot. The shrubs that had clustered in front of the house were all gone, as if they had never been there at all.

He had heard that Joey was here that day of the fire, and Ellen burned up in the house.

Right here, somewhere in these ashes, was all that was left of Ellen.

He felt awful, thinking about it.

Ellen was gone now, and so was Joey because his old house was burned to the ground. In a way it was like both of them had died.

David went closer, wading into the ashes, and suddenly it was as if the heat of the fire was still there soaking into his shoes.

He ran on his toes to get back out of the weird heat, and he kicked something hidden in the ashes. It clattered ahead of him, rolling like a tin can out into the seared ground beyond the ashes.

David stomped his shoes to get rid of the ashes, and then he kicked the can farther away and watched it roll. He saw it was not a can. It had a long, thin spout with a little chain hanging from it.

He reached down to touch it and found it hot.

He spit on his fingers, pulled out his shirt tail and used it to pick up the can.

Holding it by the chain, he watched it swing slowly, rotating round and round at the end of the chain. There were other things on the top of it, little spouts like chimneys.

"Hey, neat!"

He had never seen it before, but it looked like something that might have belonged to Joey.

It was black with smoke and fire; but all he had to do was wait until it cooled, and then he could clean it up.

He carried it home, dangling at the end of its chain.

WILLIAM W. JOHNSTONE IS ZEBRA'S BESTSELLING MASTER OF THE MACABRE!

THE UNINVITED (2258, $3.95)
A creeping, crawling horror had come to the small town of Lapeer Parish, Louisiana. Restless, unstoppable creatures, they descended upon the unsuspecting Southern community in droves, searching for grisly nourishment—in need of human flesh!

THE DEVIL'S CAT (2091, $3.95)
They were everywhere. Thousands and thousands of cats in every shape and size. Watching . . . and waiting. Becancour was ripe with evil. And Sam, Nydia, and Little Sam had to stand alone against the forces of darkness, facing the ultimate predator!

SWEET DREAMS (1553, $3.50)
Only ten-year-old Heather could see the eerie spectral glow that was enveloping the town—the lights of Hell itself! But no one had listened to her terrified screams. And now it was Heather's turn to feed the hungry, devouring spirit with her very soul!

WOLFSBANE (2019, $3.50)
For years Ducros Parish has been free of the evil, seductive scent of wolfsbane. But now tiny yellow buds are once again dotting the bayou. And when the wolfsbane blossoms in the springtime, an ancient, unspeakable horror will be back in full flower!

THE NURSERY (2072, $3.95)
Sixty-six unborn fetuses, they had been taken from their human mothers by force. Through their veins flowed the blood of evil; in their hearts sounded Satan's song. Now they would live forever under the rule of darkness . . . and terror!

Available wherever paperbacks are sold, or order direct from the Publisher. Send cover price plus 50¢ per copy for mailing and handling to Zebra Books, Dept. 2255, 475 Park Avenue South, New York, N.Y. 10016. Residents of New York, New Jersey and Pennsylvania must include sales tax. DO NOT SEND CASH.

THE ULTIMATE IN SPINE-TINGLING TERROR FROM ZEBRA BOOKS!

TOY CEMETERY (2228, $3.95)
by William W. Johnstone
A young man is the inheritor of a magnificent doll collection. But an ancient, unspeakable evil lurks behind the vacant eyes and painted-on smiles of his deadly toys!

SMOKE (2255, $3.95)
by Ruby Jean Jensen
Seven-year-old Ellen was sure it was Aladdin's lamp that she had found at the local garage sale. And no power on earth would be able to stop the hideous terror unleashed when she rubbed the magic lamp to make the genie appear!

WITCH CHILD (2230, $3.95)
by Elizabeth Lloyd
The gruesome spectacle of Goody Glover's witch trial and hanging haunted the dreams of young Rachel Gray. But the dawn brought Rachel no relief when the terrified girl discovered that her innocent soul had been taken over by the malevolent sorceress' vengeful spirit!

HORROR MANSION (2210, $3.95)
by J.N. Williamson
It was a deadly roller coaster ride through a carnival of terror when a group of unsuspecting souls crossed the threshold into the old Minnifield place. For all those who entered its grisly chamber of horrors would never again be allowed to leave—not even in death!

NIGHT WHISPER (2092, $3.95)
by Patricia Wallace
Twenty-six years have passed since Paige Brown lost her parents in the bizarre Tranquility Murders. Now Paige has returned to her home town to discover that the bloody nightmare is far from over . . . it has only just begun!

SLEEP TIGHT (2121, $3.95)
by Matthew J. Costello
A rash of mysterious disappearances terrorized the citizens of Harley, New York. But the worst was yet to come. For the Tall Man had entered young Noah's dreams—to steal the little boy's soul and feed on his innocence!

Available wherever paperbacks are sold, or order direct from the Publisher. Send cover price plus 50¢ per copy for mailing and handling to Zebra Books, Dept. 2255, 475 Park Avenue South, New York, N.Y. 10016. Residents of New York, New Jersey and Pennsylvania must include sales tax. DO NOT SEND CASH.